In Heaven, Among the Angels,
A Demon Awaits Justice

The head of the angel's weapon collided with the once-beautiful face at the same moment that the tips of several swords punctured her scaly skin. An explosion of blood and flesh spattered the cushions, the rugs, and the tent wall as the demon's head disintegrated.

The muscles in her arms kept working for a heartbeat longer.

The blades sank deeply into flesh. The two life-forces that were there, one inside the other, grew faint, then vanished.

The unborn child was lost to him, slain by its own mother.

But Demons
Aren't Known For Patience

THOMAS M. REID

The Empyrean Odyssey

Book I
The Gossamer Plain

Book II
The Fractured Sky
November 2008

Book III
The Crystal Mountain
Mid 2009

Also by Thomas M. Reid

The Scions of Arrabar Trilogy

Book I
The Sapphire Crescent

Book II
The Ruby Guardian

Book III
The Emerald Scepter

R.A. Salvatore's
War of the Spider Queen

Book II
Insurrection

THE GOSSAMER PLAIN

THE EMPYREAN ODYSSEY
BOOK I

THOMAS M. REID

THE EMPYREAN ODYSSEY, BOOK I
THE GOSSAMER PLAIN

Cover art by Jeff Nentrup
First Printing: May 2007

9 8 7 6 5 4 3 2 1

ISBN: 978-0-7869-4024-0
620-95553740-001-EN

U.S., CANADA,
ASIA, PACIFIC, & LATIN AMERICA
Wizards of the Coast, Inc.
P.O. Box 707
Renton, WA 98057-0707
+1-800-324-6496

EUROPEAN HEADQUARTERS
Hasbro UK Ltd
Caswell Way
Newport, Gwent NP9 0YH
GREAT BRITAIN
Save this address for your records.

Visit our web site at www.wizards.com

DEDICATION

For Gina,
who always helps me keep my head on straight
about the nature of Good and Evil.

PROLOGUE

Tauran knelt upon a protrusion of rock and surveyed the shimmering pool far below. The distant surface of the water rippled and gleamed, disturbed to a golden foam by a roaring, tumbling waterfall. The astral deva's perch jutted from the top of the cliff alongside the lip from which the cascade plunged. Spray from the churning torrent peppered him with a fine, cool mist and made the rocks beneath his bare feet slick.

It was a long drop.

Behind the angel, the surging headwaters of the river spilled out of a cleft in the side of a towering pinnacle of rock. It was the tallest, most delicately thin peak among a high, sharp ridge of jutting stone that formed a deep basin surrounding the pool on three sides. On the distant bank, opposite where Tauran rested, the water spilled over a lower lip of the ridge, vanishing from sight to other basins even farther below. From the astral deva's vantage, it was as though the pool lay within the confines of a great crater, like the belly of a steep-sided volcano. He knew the far slopes of that circular ridge fell away just as sharply, where they eventually vanished into a sea of white, fluffy clouds.

The powerful effusion of water, coupled with the slenderness and loftiness of its host peak, liberated more power and beauty than any mere spring. The gushing flow of the cataract bursting from the crevice owed its vigorous current to primal and potent magic. Those headwaters held the might of gods, the puissance of deities, within them. In many ways, the essence of divinity itself spouted from that peak.

It was the Lifespring.

The Lifespring derived its amber hue from both its own inner glow and the warm rays of the late afternoon sun illuminating its surface. Even from his lofty perch, Tauran could smell the sweetness of that glow wafting upward. It filled him with energy and confidence, infused him with the glory of Tyr, his beloved and benevolent lord. The urgency the angel felt to bathe in it made his skin prickle in anticipation, but he waited, watching.

Other creatures swam in the water. Tauran could see them despite the glint of the sun reflecting in his eyes. They were angels, like himself, though not all were astral devas. He observed a handful of emerald-skinned planetars frolicking in the pool. Even a pair of solars, silvery gold and larger than the others, had come to relax and soak up the glory of their deity. They remained near the far shore, gathered together for conversation and games. A few swam or drifted toward the center, content to enjoy the spiritual invigoration of the Lifespring in their own way. But none of them approached the cascade.

Nodding in satisfaction, Tauran stood. He unfurled his feathery white wings only slightly, gave a measured appraisal of the distance, and leaped off the outcropping. He straightened his body and pointed his fingers and toes. The wind rustled the feathers of his wings for a moment, then he caught the breeze and lifted in a gentle arc, rising above the churning waters that fell directly beneath the cataract.

The air currents held the angel aloft for a heartbeat. He floated at the apex of the arc, and it seemed to the deva that he hovered there, perfectly balanced between the pull of the world below and the buoyant updrafts of the breezes. In that moment, at that instant of equilibrium, Tauran felt unbridled joy, harmony, contentment. He felt the embodiment of all that was the House of the Triad.

Then the angel's forward momentum carried him through the apex of his arc, and he slid downward, toward the pool. Tauran had to resist the urge to unfurl his wings fully, had to fight to avoid catching the updrafts once more and gliding through the air. That would have been easy for him. But he wanted the greater challenge.

The deva stayed rigid, his body an arrow, his wings the fletching. He nosed downward, increasing speed, plummeting toward the water. The winds whistled past his ears and his long amber hair blew. He accelerated, truly falling, and shifted his wings by fractions, making subtle corrections in his descent.

The exhilaration of the drop mingled with a hint of fear. Tauran had made the dive before, of course. Many times, in fact. But there was always risk, no matter how experienced he felt. One wrong shift, one overcompensation and he might lose control, might crash against the surface of the water rather than knifing through it with barely a ripple. With that uncontrolled fall would come pain, injury. Even with healing magic at his fingertips, the angel dreaded such wounds. He remained vigilant, wary, concentrating.

Tauran's skills proved equal to the task. The deva held his form and kept his angle accurate. Just before he penetrated the surface of the pool, he drew a great breath. Then he was under, gliding into the depths of the water.

The angel felt a surge of raw energy. It permeated every nerve and pore. His body drank it greedily, crackling with life and exuberance. It was exhilarating, overwhelming him, driving him to burst forth again, yet he wanted to loll within it forever, bathe in its cleanness, its holiness, for all eternity.

The surface light faded as Tauran sliced deeper into the depths, but he had no fear of striking the bottom, which he knew lay much farther beneath him. As his momentum ebbed, Tauran arched his back, angling himself upward. He began to swim then, pulling himself with powerful strokes of his arms and kicks of his legs, back toward the surface.

At last, his head burst forth. He lunged out of the pool and drew in a great gulp of sweet air. He soared up, freeing himself from the water, and spread his wings. Two, three, then four powerful beats of those wings carried him aloft, dripping, into the air above the pool. The angel stretched his arms and legs, rejoicing in how good it felt to be alive, to be in such proximity to unbridled vitality. He hovered a moment, a few feet above the surface, and closed his eyes, soaking in the life-giving force of the pool.

It wasn't just physical, that energy. All of Tauran's cares, all his troubles, seemed to have been washed away in the plunge. He felt more alive, more confident, more capable. He felt spiritually bolstered, close to his god. He was ready to accept any challenge. He felt unstoppable.

"Why do you do that?"

The voice startled Tauran, though he recognized it as Micus, his friend. He had believed himself alone. The other bathers had been at the far edge, away from the place where he had dived.

Tauran blinked and looked at his friend, another deva with wings spread wide, hovering nearby. "I didn't hear you approach," he told Micus.

The other angel smiled when he said, "You seemed preoccupied. I hated to disturb you, but we are summoned."

Indeed, Tauran could hear the faint clarion call of dozens of trumpets. He could see then that the others who had been relaxing in the golden waters were departing, moving away from the water and down the mountain. He and Micus flew together toward that same shore.

"Feeling refreshed?" Micus asked as they neared the rocks at the edge of the pool.

"Yes," Tauran answered and gathered his loose-fitting pants, belt, and massive mace. "I know some might term it a weakness, a vanity, but I like to reward myself with a dip after accomplishing something of import. It's not an end unto itself, but it makes the trials and tribulations less heavy." He finished dressing and the pair launched themselves into the air once more, following the others.

"No harm in that," Micus said. "Blessed Tyr would not have made this place if he hadn't intended for us to take advantage of it. But you didn't answer my question."

"I thought you wanted to know why I dive into the water."

"I do," Micus said. "But not the water part. Why do you start from way up there," he asked, pointing at the outcropping just before it disappeared from view, "and let yourself fall like that? Why not just glide to the surface like the rest of us and settle in gently?"

"Ah," Tauran replied as the pair plunged into the clouds. "It helps remind me."

"Remind you? Of what?"

Tauran could not see his friend in the mist of the clouds, but he could hear the other deva's voice clearly enough. "That the easiest path is not always set before me. That I must be ready to accept the harder road, and stay wary of distraction or lapse of attention." The angels broke through the clouds and saw the lower slopes of the great mountain from which they had descended. Three lesser mountains ringed the larger, each the home of one of the Triad—Tyr, Torm, and Ilmater. Atop the nearest peak, the gleaming white walls of Tyr's Court reflected the sunlight.

"Diving from up there keeps me alert," Tauran continued. "I know that even one mistake will be very painful or disastrous. Out there," he said as he swept his hand around, "one mistake might cost someone his life. Even mine. Complacency has no place in our duties. I dive to help me remember that."

Micus turned and gave his friend an appraising look. "That's very insightful. Perhaps you can teach me how to do it."

"I will," Tauran answered. "When we return."

The two angels neared a great pinnacle of rock jutting from the mountainside where a host of others like themselves had gathered. The various devas, planetars, and solars hovered in orderly ranks, all facing a dais at the top of the pinnacle. A great arch pierced the stone directly below the dais, like the mouth of a tunnel. Instead of blue sky shining from its far side, though, a curtain of pearlescent light veiled the arch.

Tauran and Micus took their places among the other devas as a great silvery solar settled upon the dais. As she furled her wings, the gleaming being's golden eyes surveyed the gathering critically for a moment, as though assessing the attendants' worth. After a moment, she spoke.

"Today, we fight another battle in the war to free the oppressed. Though we seek the destruction of all that is evil and depraved, we strive by equal measure to offer redemption to those worth redeeming, to save those who can be saved. Our goal, our duty, is not merely to provide salvation to all who wish it, but to rescue those who cannot fight, or even speak, for themselves."

A murmur of approval ran through the assemblage. The solar waited until the noise abated, then continued. "Blessed

Tyr has bid us embrace this duty, so that one day, all the multiverse might glow with the shining warmth of equality and acceptance." The solar paused, then delivered her next words punctuated for emphasis. "Today, we once again take the fight to our enemies, and thwart their foul schemes before they have a chance to grow to tainted fruition!"

The gathered crowd roared with eager acceptance. Tauran and Micus cheered along with the rest. After his glorious swim, the deva felt ready for anything. He thrilled at the prospect of fulfilling his duty, shivered in delight at the chance to bring Tyr's glory to one who had never known it before.

"You know your tasks. You've prepared. Go and bring Tyr's light to the multiverse!" the solar commanded.

Another roar rose up from the host. The planetars sounded their horns, a cry of battle that reverberated through the skies, echoing from the mountaintops. To Tauran, the sun seemed to blaze just a bit brighter, the sky seemed to turn a sharper hue of azure, and the air smelled faintly sweeter. The atmosphere was electric with expectation and impending triumph.

The angels began to sing as they sorted themselves into bands. A hymn of Tyr's glory, extolled in perfect harmony, accompanied the horns. Micus gave Tauran a hearty pat on the back and a handshake before he moved away to gather with his own group. Tauran lifted his voice in song, joining with the chorus, as he bid his friend farewell with a wave and went to join his own band.

His was a small force comprised of Keenon, the solar leader, and four planetars. He was the lone deva, assigned to the group for a special purpose. He grasped his mace and steadied himself, waiting for the command.

Other units swarmed around the arch in anticipation. In orderly succession, they passed through the veil, disappearing in a wink. When it was time for his own unit to surge into the portal, the angel drew a deep breath, remembered his admonitions of staying wary, and followed his team.

The landscape twisted and changed. Light bent and warped around Tauran, deepening into a purple gloom. The crisp, clean air vanished, replaced by the charnel scents of a battlefield. Lightning crackled and thunder pealed in a sodden sky that sent a cascade of fetid rain down upon all beneath it. The deva settled upon slick, clutching mud and surveyed the scene.

The angel and his cohorts stood within a low river valley, along the rim of a great bowl surrounded by the silhouettes of low hills. Two armies collided within the middle of that valley, slipping and slogging through the torrential rain and mud to slaughter one another as best they could. One force, badly outnumbered, found itself surrounded on three sides by its enemy and pressed hard against a churning, frothing river.

"There!" Keenon shouted to be heard above the din of war and weather. "Near the river!" He pointed, and very quickly, he and the four planetars took flight, racing in that direction.

Tauran took to the air along with his companions, but his mission was different. They went to save the brave-hearted defenders who desperately called for the angels' aid. The deva sought a different life-force, one that wouldn't be eager to welcome him. Knowing he would not be well received, he cloaked himself in innate invisibility.

Swooping over the plain toward the center of the engagement, Tauran soared above snarling clusters of savage beasts, orcs and ogres—and worse things from the Abyss—that surrounded tiny defiant pockets of men and women in mismatched armor. The mercenaries—and they were mercenaries, hired to fight for some petty lord—stood back to back in tight circles, clinging to their final moments in desperate hope that someone or something might save them.

The deva felt remorse course through him, saddened that he could not spare the time or energy to save them all. But they prayed to different gods, and ineffectually called on other celestial beings for salvation. Their lives were not his to assist. He had a different goal.

He quickly found what he sought. At the far end of the battlefield, near one edge of the great bowl-shaped valley, flapping pennants atop a pavilion tent marked the location of his quarry. Numerous campfires, sputtering feebly in the rain, surrounded the tent, and brutish creatures huddled near those fires, cursing their ill luck at both the weather and their guard duty. They wished to be out among the others, gleefully fighting and killing.

Tauran drifted unnoticed past them, the soft whisper of his wings drowned out by the concussive clash of combatants in the distance, as well as the rumble of thunder overhead. He settled upon the ground near the entrance to the tent and studied the two guards flanking the opening.

Each creature appeared as a hulking, upright toad, equally as tall as Tauran himself and easily surpassing his own bulk. The slick skin covering their bloated bodies was green and bumpy, but unlike a normal toad, rows of jagged teeth lined their mouths. They both wielded massive axes, which they held cradled in their arms. The pair exuded a nauseous stench that nearly made the deva gag, but he stood still for a moment to adjust to the smell before he approached them.

Gripping his mace, Tauran stepped as lightly as he could, hoping to catch the creatures off balance for an initial strike. Though he moved with deftness and grace, one of the two must have sensed something was amiss, for it jerked upright and hefted its axe. A low, menacing growl issued from deep within its voluminous body.

"I smell the stench of a celestial!" He snarled, taking one step forward and drawing his axe back as though to strike. Tauran saw that the demon's beady eyes shifted back and forth, and he was reasonably certain the demon could not sense where he was, but his moment of subterfuge had come and gone. Not waiting for the creature before him to determine his location, the deva channeled divine energy, summoning the holy power of his kind and pouring it into his weapon. He swung his mace with both hands, smashing it against the demon's shoulder with a brilliant flash.

The beast snarled in rage and pain and staggered backward as Tauran spun and struck the other in the same manner. The second demon howled and stumbled against the side of the tent, but Tauran could not close in and finish him with a blow to the head, for the first one had recovered enough to take a swipe at him.

"Your time is over, fiend," Tauran said, once more calling on his innate divinity to aid him in the fight.

He blurted out a word of power, a word of divine force, a holy word. He spoke it clearly, and there was no mistaking that the two guards heard its utterance. Simultaneously, they shrieked and dropped their weapons. One clutched at his eyes, while the other wrapped his arms around his head and cowered.

Tauran drew his mace back, ready to crush the skull of the first demon as he writhed before him. Just as he brought the weapon down in a great, sweeping arc, though, the fiend vanished. His weapon thudded hard against the sodden ground, spraying muddy water everywhere. The deva growled in exasperation, but his frustration was short-lived, for a cloying miasma enveloped him, as though a greasy darkness had descended upon him.

The angel's stomach roiled and he doubled over in agony.

All his limbs ached and lost their strength. He thought he would retch. Tauran stumbled away from the remaining demon and gasped for breath. The clinging, sickly blanket of darkness moved with him, filling his nostrils with horrific odors. He spat, trying and failing to expunge the awful, sour taste.

Slowly, the cloaking darkness evaporated, leaving the deva standing in the rain once more. His stomach still churned, but he could breathe again.

Tauran turned toward the tent and saw the demon flailing about blindly with his axe. The beast stopped and listened, cocking his head to one side for a moment, then swung the huge blade once more. The massive axe whistled through the air, seeking flesh to cleave.

The angel left his feet and soared above the demon. He ascended sharply and swung the mace with all his might, once more drawing upon the holy power of Tyr to aid him. The crushing blow landed true, right against the back of the demon's head, and he heard the satisfying sound of crunching bone as the thing's skull collapsed.

With a sickening plop, the demonic toad sprawled forward into the mud and quivered. The beast's axe slid to one side, no longer needed.

Tauran spun away from the creature and approached the opening of the tent. Not knowing what other defenders might be lurking within, he nudged the flap sideways with the head of his mace, expecting an assault at any moment. When no attack was forthcoming, the deva stepped inside and drew the flap shut behind himself.

The dimness of the tent did not hinder the angel. His acute vision allowed him to easily discern the interior. He gave a quick glance in the direction of a table with maps spread upon it, but the figure before him, languishing upon numerous rugs and cushions, interested him most.

He stepped nearer.

"No closer," the figure said. "Your stench is awful enough from this distance." It was the voice of a woman, though she sounded husky, tired. A cough followed by several wheezing gasps confirmed what he already knew.

She was wounded, dying.

Tauran paused to let her show herself fully. A human torso and head rose up into a sitting position, her six arms pushing her upright. Where her legs should have been, twenty feet of reptilian flesh writhed in discomfort. The massive, coiled body might have been capable of crushing him, had she been hale and hearty, but Tauran saw an arrow protruding from her chest directly beneath one bare breast. It penetrated her from front to back, and though very little blood leaked from the wound, he knew the missile was killing her.

It was also holding her there, preventing her from traveling back to the plane from whence she had come. She could seek no solace, no rescue among her own kind in the Abyss.

"You're dying," Tauran said, taking another step toward the fiend. "I can help you," he said. "I can ease your suffering."

"Stay back!" the demon snarled, and she hoisted swords in several of her hands. The blades shook, would not stay on guard.

Tauran looked at her face, saw the pain glazing her eyes. She might have been beautiful, had she been fully human. Even half-human in shape, she was attractive. But her dark hair hung in bedraggled clumps from her head, and her skin was sallow and glistened with the sweat of sickness. She swallowed hard, then groaned and collapsed back upon her pillows.

"Gloat and get it over with," she mumbled, closing her eyes. "I don't have much time left."

Tauran shook his head, though he knew she did not see. "I am not interested in dancing on your grave. I cannot even claim the honor of having fired the arrow that leeches your life away."

"Then what do you want?" she asked, her eyes still closed, her voice growing more hoarse by the moment. "Whatever it is, I won't give it to you."

"It's not yours to give," Tauran replied, "but if you do not fight me, I will ease your final moments before claiming it."

The demon opened one eye and looked at him. "No," she said simply. "I would never bargain with your kind." She coughed, tried to catch her breath, coughed again. Blood dribbled from her lip. When she regained her breath, she said, "That you would try to bargain tells me it is very special to you. You have piqued my curiosity. Tell me what you want. Perhaps I will make an exception and give it to you, just this once."

Tauran breathed in and out slowly. He was obligated to give her the chance, though he knew that revealing his desire would most likely enrage her, making his task that much harder. But he was obligated.

"The child growing in your womb," he said.

Both of the demon's eyes flew open then, and she shrieked in realization. "No!" she screamed, and the coils of her body twitched to life, writhing and whipping around the tent.

Tauran had to leap into the air to avoid being struck.

"Never!" the demon cried.

She rose up, her blades out, as though ready to fight him to the last. He braced himself for the duel, but then he saw the cunning gleam in her eye.

Just as she began to reverse the blades and drive them into her own body, to slice the burgeoning life out of herself to deny it to the angel, he reacted. With explosive force, he flung the mace forward, channeling every bit of strength, both natural and preternatural, that he could muster.

The weapon sailed across the space between them. Tauran watched it tumble through the air as though it moved in slow motion. The blades of the demon's long swords descended, and the mace moved closer.

The head of the angel's weapon collided with the once-beautiful face at the same moment that the tips of several swords punctured her scaly skin. An explosion of blood and flesh spattered the cushions, the rugs, and the tent wall as the demon's head disintegrated.

The muscles in her arms kept working for a heartbeat longer.

The blades sank deeply into flesh. The two life-forces that were there, one inside the other, grew faint, then vanished. The unborn child was lost to him, slain by its own mother.

Tauran hung his head in sorrow for a long moment, reminding himself that the easy path was not always the one set before him.

He turned, grief and disappointment hanging heavy around him, and departed, returning to the House of the Triad to report that he had failed.

CHAPTER ONE

Thin, wispy clouds scurried across the night sky, passing in front of gibbous Selûne and deepening the gloom upon the land below. Aliisza glanced up, careful as she shifted on her perch upon an outcropping of stone. The alu-fiend didn't want to dislodge loose rubble beneath her feet. Though invisible, she feared clattering stones would reveal her position to anyone below and thus spoil the ambush. The notion of ruining her little trap annoyed the half-demon for an instant, but she dismissed the thought in the time it took to reassure herself that she had made no sound.

She could still make out the pale, glowing near-orb, though the high clouds diffused its light and encircled it with a strange halo. At any other time, she might have taken a moment to marvel at the strange sight. The alu strayed to the surface of Toril only rarely and had few opportunities to gaze upon such useless but intriguing wonders. That night, however, she could not long keep her attention away from the impending clash in the narrow valley below. Fingering the hilt of her sword in anticipation, she turned to stare downward once more.

To all but fiendish eyes, the approaching Sundabarian patrol had vanished. Moonlight no longer glimmered off a bared blade or polished helm, but Aliisza had no trouble locating the darker shadows gliding silently through the murk of night. The mounted figures moved in single file along the path in the center of the valley. They rode without caution, never hesitating as they approached the defile where Aliisza and her invisible tanarukk soldiers waited.

The half-fiend put a magical whistle to her lips and blew it as hard as she could. The shrill tone that emanated from the device echoed all through the defile, piercing the otherwise still and quiet night. Almost immediately, an answering roar went up all around Aliisza. The tanarukks responded to the signal with fierce delight, screaming in battle lust or cheering in joy at the impending fight. She could hear the clatter of weapons and the clack of dislodged stones as her minions raced forward, charging at the patrol.

The soldiers milled in confusion and panic. Some, perhaps the veterans, attempted to dismount and fan out, preparing to receive the onslaught that they could not see. Others wheeled their horses back and forth, disrupting the line of their comrades already on foot. Their lack of discipline and experience disintegrated the defense before it ever had a chance to properly form up.

The half-fiend stood still and watched for a moment. When her minions were finished, there would be no evidence left of the patrol. Aliisza's task was to sow mystery and doubt; it was too soon to alert the populace of the danger that lurked on the periphery of the valley. A foe they couldn't see or counterattack was far more insidious than an open siege. The people of Sundabar had to be left wondering. Their Ruling Master, Helm Dwarf-friend, had to appear ineffectual. It was all part of Kaanyr Vhok's grand plan.

At the bottom of the defile, the first of the tanarukks reached the patrol. They slammed into the half-formed defensive circle of men and horses, popping into sight as they swung battle-axes and jabbed with spears. The two groups became a swirling mass of howling, screaming confusion. Human and horse fell before the onslaught of the horde. It would be over all too soon. The patrol never stood a chance.

The half-demon sneered at the scouts' foolishness. Green, the alu surmised. Hardly worthy sport.

Disappointed but feeling assured that her charges knew what to do, Aliisza departed, leaving the horde of savage tanarukks to complete the ambush and subsequent vanishing act by themselves. Mauling an inexperienced band of scouts might satisfy the fiendish orcs' brutish yet simple bloodlust, but it had hardly been worthy entertainment for the half-demon herself. And she had other places to be, other things to do.

Still under the cover of invisibility, Aliisza soared into the sky and winged her way toward the community of Sundabar. As she flew, she mused over all the preparation, all the effort that Kaanyr had put into his latest plans to conquer the city.

In some ways, it had long ago become a fool's errand to the alu, but she knew her lover would never stop trying to unseat the current ruler, Helm Dwarf-friend. Vhok had tried many different paths to victory. Through the years, he had thrown countless troops against the city's walls, even managed to get inside once or twice. Always, though, he had been driven back, for the folk of Sundabar were hearty and wary, and they had the aid of the wretched dwarves who lived in the great halls beneath the city.

Aliisza knew Kaanyr's hatred of Helm Dwarf-friend burned strong within him, a seed of resentment planted long ago from some slight or insult the ex-mercenary had delivered against the cambion. Kaanyr had never spoken in detail of the event, though she knew that it had somehow caused him to lose face in the eyes of his mother. That had been years before, when Dwarf-friend had still led the Bloodaxe mercenaries, and Kaanyr's mother Mulvassyss the Sceptered, a marilith demon of considerable power, stood prominent among the fiends of Hellgate Keep. Whatever had happened between half-fiend and mercenary, the cambion had repeatedly vowed revenge in the intervening years. Aliisza held no doubts that her lover would spend the rest of his days strategizing Dwarf-friend's downfall.

At least he's finally wised up, Aliisza mused as she drew nearer the object of her lover's desire. He's finally trying cunning and deception instead of brute force.

The alu was pleased with Kaanyr's latest plan, particularly because she had her own prominent role to play in the scheme, one which she was all too happy to fulfill. Kaanyr had been clever indeed, the alu admitted with glee, even if his scheme had tried her patience. Tendays of plotting, of establishing her cover before she ever set foot inside the city walls, had often driven her to distraction.

In the beginning, it was all maneuvering and surveying, noting the strength of defenses and routes of patrols. Aliisza had grown quite bored with it all. During those first tendays, her thoughts often drifted back to the time she had spent pursuing Pharaun Mizzrym of the mysterious and treacherous drow, during Kaanyr's aborted siege of Menzoberranzan. That had been a far more exciting pastime for her than endless scouting. She even complained about the lack of action to Kaanyr, not just for herself but on behalf of her restless troops. She could sense that they were growing impatient, too.

"Hardly the sort of banal recreation you promised the hordes after the fiasco at Menzoberranzan," Aliisza had complained to Kaanyr one day between forays to the surface.

"Patience, my petulant love," Kaanyr had replied absently, never looking up as he studiously pored over a tabletop full of maps. "These matters take time and planning."

Unsatisfied with the cambion's distracted explanation—and more than a little put off by her lover's apparent disinterest in her—Aliisza longed to liven things up a bit.

Then she learned what her own role would be in the coming attack when her lover and commander told her he had a separate assignment for her to carry out. Aliisza almost pouted, but after he explained the plan in detail, she had jumped at the offer.

She was to be the cancer that ate at the city from within, created the doubt and weakened the resoluteness of its people. She was to be the seed that flowered into full-blown distrust. She was to be the source of Helm Dwarf-friend's downfall, and Kaanyr would have his city.

But it was only the beginning. Kaanyr had much grander military ambitions. Laying siege to the fortress-city of Sundabar with his fiendish hordes was only the first step in his larger scheme of conquest over all of the Silver Marches.

The alu arrived at the perimeter of the city, and she glanced down at the icy moat below her as she soared over the walls and darted down toward the roof of the Master's Hall. The prominent government building within Sundabar, the Master's Hall housed every city office and also served as Dwarf-friend's abode. It was a fine place for her to land unseen and transform into the winsome girl Helm Dwarf-friend was so enamored of, but she remained cautious.

The alu circled the building a couple of times, still invisible, just to be certain there was no trouble. Aliisza peered in every direction, along every balcony and walkway, letting her fiendish vision penetrate the darker shadows. She even utilized Pharaun's ring to try to spot the telltale signs of cloaking magic. A patrol of the city's watch, the Stone Shields, approached from the distance along one street, but she saw no one else. She settled silently to the stone roof. After shifting form, she dispelled her invisibility and slipped through a tower door into the interior of the hall.

Aliisza's disguise was that of a sprightly young human girl with green eyes, lovely auburn curls hanging to her shoulders, a tiny little upturned nose, and dimples in her rosy cheeks. It was Helm Dwarf-friend's vision of heaven. Secretly rooting out that most private of desires while watching him from a distance had been a simple matter for the half-fiend, but the manipulations afterward had been a bit more tricky.

Adopting the name of Ansa, the alu had taken every additional precaution to disguise her true character. She had employed her wizardly magic to mask her thoughts and her aura, preventing others from detecting her treacherous intentions and demonic nature. Then she had insinuated herself among the Master's Hall staff. Dwarf-friend's seneschal, an intoxicatingly handsome man named Zasian Menz, was her first obstacle.

The tall man with long dark hair and a flowing mustache scrutinized her severely and inundated her with questions concerning her skills and her past. Aliisza had expected some resistance to her efforts, knowing full well how careful the seneschal must be. But the man truly unnerved her, and that was a feeling she had rarely experienced. At one point, the alu was certain Zasian knew her true identity and was merely toying with her before exposing her to the house guards. Finally, he had relented and turned her over to one of his senior matrons.

Ginella, the burly and severe woman in charge of the staff, took an instant dislike to Ansa and beat her regularly, even when she was doing a good job. It was all Aliisza could do not to strike the hateful woman down where she stood. The menial tasks Ginella had given to her had been the worst sort of labor, always filthy and backbreaking jobs, but Aliisza made sure she carried them out well. She would not risk getting cast out before she could get near her quarry.

The alu had discovered that it was harder to get close to the master than she had imagined. Dwarf-friend was often locked away in meetings or out in the city on business when Aliisza was working. Ginella brooked no loitering of any kind, and she had forbidden Aliisza to go anywhere within the hall beyond the reach of her chores. Most of Aliisza's duties had kept her in the lowest levels of the place, under the watchful eye of Ginella and other matrons. It was almost as if they sensed her desire to get close to Dwarf-friend and were determined to put a stop to any moon-eyed girl cavorting with the most important man in the city.

At last, Aliisza had gotten her chance. It had been laundry day, and she had been ordered to gather linens from a particular wing of the hall. On her way back, she had made a point of passing through a great hall where Dwarf-friend was discussing city matters with a pair of his advisors. As luck would have it, the girl tripped and spilled her bundled wash over the side of a banister—right onto the Ruling Master's head. Ginella had witnessed the gaffe, but before she could drag the girl back to the wash room for a sound beating, Dwarf-friend had spotted her and ordered her brought before him.

Aliisza had feigned a severe case of blushing embarrassment and had moved as reluctantly as she could, but Dwarf-friend was smitten with Ansa the moment he got a good look at her. From then on, it was almost too easy. After discovering that the girl could read and write, he had insisted to Zasian, over Ginella's protestations, that she be reassigned to him to assist him as a scribe. Aliisza had received plenty of scowls from

Ginella in the days since, but the elder woman had left her alone, for which the alu was thankful. She had no desire to stir up suspicion by being forced to get rid of the matron.

It wasn't long afterward that everyone in the hall knew that Ansa shared Helm Dwarf-friend's bed. Whenever they were alone, Helm frequently exclaimed that he could not believe his good fortune at having such a lovely creature stumble into his life, and Aliisza had heard him quietly thank Tymora on more than one occasion during their trysts.

Aliisza's thoughts returned to the present as she descended the stairs from the tower and entered a great hall in the wing housing Dwarf-friend's private chambers. It was late, and only a few lanterns burned, turned low to save oil. The hall, which soared three stories high and was ringed by balconies at each level, lay shrouded in shadows. A great table rested in the middle of the chamber, surrounded by high-backed wooden chairs as uncomfortable as they were imposing. Aliisza crossed the hall and crept down the passage toward the master's abode.

A figure up ahead caught her attention, coming from Dwarf-friend's office. It was Zasian Menz.

Aliisza froze, wondering if she could duck out of the way before the man spotted her. She was in no mood to feign intimidation at that moment. She had been clever enough to adapt a reasonably modest nightshirt as part of her disguise for the evening, but appearing in such outside of the bedroom was the slightest bit improper to the Sundabarians, and she had little doubt Zasian would raise an eyebrow and scold her for it.

Before Aliisza could melt into the shadows unnoticed and let the seneschal pass, he faltered a step, and she knew he had seen her. She stepped to the side as though to let him by, keeping her eyes lowered deferentially. Even though she shared Helm's bed, she still worked for Zasian on the master's behalf.

Zasian strode before the girl and stopped. "Look at me, child," he said, lifting Aliisza's chin with one finger.

Aliisza let him tilt her head, but she kept her eyes cast down a moment longer before meeting his gaze. A genuine shiver ran through her. Under different circumstances, the alu wouldn't mind wrapping her arms and legs around that tall, muscular body and stealing a kiss. She struggled to look fearful rather than hungry.

"You know you shouldn't be out here," the seneschal began, "especially not dressed as you are. I know how fond Master Helm is of you, and I am willing to look the other way, but only so long as you do not disrupt the smooth operations of my hall. The last thing I need is more tongues wagging about Master Helm's half-naked whore traipsing through the common rooms. I've already had five visitors to my office this tenday, complaining about the impropriety of it all. You put me in a very difficult position, child."

"Yes, Seneschal," Aliisza answered, doing her best to sound chastened. "I will be more careful." Secretly, she was thrilled. The seeds were being planted. Folk were starting to frown upon the master's indiscretion, to question his actions. It would grow.

The alu blinked and realized that Zasian had said something else, but she had not been paying attention. She searched her memory to draw out his words, and realized she couldn't remember them. In fact, she had the oddest feeling that she had been standing there, listening to him, for quite some time, but the time had simply . . . vanished.

"I said, get yourself out of sight," Zasian instructed, pointing down the hall toward the master's rooms. "And don't let me catch you out like this again."

Aliisza stared at the man, a bit unnerved over the puzzling sensation, but she dismissed it. I'm just tired, she decided. To the seneschal, she replied, "Yes, my lord," then turned and almost ran to the door of her lover's chambers. By the time she was inside the master's rooms, she had forgotten about the gap in time.

❖ ❖ ❖ ❖ ❖ ❖ ❖ ❖ ❖

Kaanyr Vhok stood in the middle of an ancient dwarven thoroughfare, deep beneath the streets of Sundabar. The low ceiling hung only inches above the cambion's head, giving him the unnerving urge to duck. A series of stone double doors flanked the wide passage in pairs as far as the half-demon's eyes could observe. Each set of portals bore runes inscribed into its surfaces, holy texts and clan names in honor of the dead buried behind it. Vhok ignored the crypts and made his way toward the end of the hall, to a final set of doors that stood at the top of a short stairway. The dust he stirred as he walked reassured the half-fiend that he was the only one who had tread that route in many years.

At the top of the steps, Vhok stopped and perused the inscription. The ancient words marked the chamber as a shrine dedicated to Moradin, god of the dwarves. Smirking, Vhok was relieved to see that the craftsmen who had constructed the shrine had not seen fit to place arcane runes upon the surface of the doors, protective sigils that would have barred him entry. Satisfied that no fell magic would harm him, he pushed on the stone. The twin doors swung ponderously open, as silent as the day they were first hung. Cool bluish light spilled into the thoroughfare from within.

The cambion stepped inside and shut the doors behind him. The chamber was hexagonal in shape, not very far across from one side to another, but quite tall. A series of thick square columns stood around the periphery of the chamber, one at each of the eight corners. A set of torches rested in brackets mounted on each of the columns, casting the chamber in a surreal azure glow. Vhok knew of such illumination. The torches would burn forever, their flames preserved with magic.

The spaces between each pair of columns formed private alcoves. Within seven of the niches, a large stone sarcophagus lay parallel to the wall behind. Atop each sarcophagus rose a statue of a dwarf hero, clergy members who had died in service to Moradin. Each of the seven was unique in stature, dress, and appearance. Inscriptions carved into the sarcophagi identified the dwarves laid to rest within, but Vhok ignored the names. He knew those interred were only so much dust by that time.

A whisper of wind and a faint flash of ruddy light upon the walls were the only clues that another had appeared within the shrine.

Vhok turned, knowing who stood halfway across the room. Zasian Menz, a young, handsome fellow with long black hair and a flaring moustache, grinned at Vhok. He dressed himself in finery, black leather pants and shirt with a black and gold tunic over both. He gestured in the air around himself. The remnants of a crimson-tinged magical doorway snapped out of existence behind him, leaving the shrine bathed in bluish light once more.

"You found it," the man said as he peered around the chamber and twitched his nose in apparent distaste.

"You choose an odd place to meet, Zasian," Vhok replied, letting the swirls of afterimage fade from his vision until he could see through the darkness again. "You did not tell me that we would be trespassing upon Moradin's holy ground."

"Do you care?" Zasian asked, strolling around the perimeter of the room as he gazed at the effigies of the fallen dwarves. "I did not take you for a pious being."

The cambion almost smiled at his counterpart's joke. "Only insofar as I must be wary of divine retribution. The doors or the interior of this place might have been warded."

"Yes, but they weren't," Zasian answered. "We dispelled such nuisances long before inviting you here."

Vhok waved his hand in dismissal. It was not a conversation worth pursuing, in his mind. "How is she?" he asked.

"She is well, and still has Dwarf-friend firmly in her charms," Zasian confirmed. "I performed the enchantment earlier tonight, in fact. All is set."

Vhok nodded thoughtfully. "And she does not remember it?" he asked. "She has forgotten everything?"

"Everything of significance," he replied. "She seemed a bit disoriented, as you might expect, but that will pass from her mind quickly enough. She will have far too many other things to think about."

Vhok nodded once more and tapped his finger upon his lips, lost in thoughts of his alu lover. Aliisza was in a very delicate position, and any complication could mean her life. Though the cambion would be disappointed to lose the beautiful creature as his consort, he was far more concerned with the implications of her failure to complete her mission. Should her true purpose be exposed, should she fall before she completed her tasks, the rest of the plan would almost surely fail, and he would not be able to orchestrate Helm Dwarf-friend's downfall. That, above all else, was paramount.

"You are certain this will work?" asked the half-fiend.

Zasian shrugged. "As with any plan of this complexity, there is always the chance of unforeseen complications. I cannot say that I am certain, and I give you no guarantees.

But I know what Tyr's lackeys are about. They are becoming proactive, seeking to turn any opportunity to their advantage. They will seize any excuse at all to stake a claim in her future. If we have laid the groundwork subtly enough, they will take the bait. Now we can only let it play out and see what transpires."

"Are you certain of her condition?" Vhok asked. An odd feeling of remorse passed through him for a moment, but he brushed it aside.

"I checked again this evening, before traveling here to meet with you. Your own divinations are accurate."

"The deception is necessary," Vhok said, as much to himself as to the priest. "There is no other way to reach the garden and the Lifespring. She cannot know yet the part she plays."

Zasian shrugged again. "As you said yourself, it is but a single piece of the puzzle. An important piece, to say the least, but only one."

Vhok nodded once more, then drew himself out of his worries. There were more immediate things to deal with. "Very well, let's conclude this business. Lead the way."

Zasian nodded and moved to the sarcophagus directly opposite the doors through which Vhok had entered. Moving behind the massive stone coffin, the man made a motion with his hand.

Vhok felt a deep, low rumble reverberate through the room. He watched as a portion of the wall behind the sarcophagus shifted and slid from view, revealing a passage just beyond. An orange glow spilled from the chamber, the light of several ordinary torches. Zasian gestured to Vhok and to the passage.

"After you," he offered.

The cambion stepped past his counterpart and entered the hallway.

Two paces later, Vhok found himself in a very different sort of temple, one far more sinister in appearance. In shape and structure, the chamber was identical to the one he and Zasian had vacated. Unlike the austere simplicity of the previous room, the second chamber felt menacing. The square stone columns were replaced by twisted, sinuous pillars, and the stone itself was ruddy in color. Instead of a series of sarcophagi, each niche housed a dais topped by a high throne. Each chair faced the center of the room, where a forbidding altar of black marble shot through with green veins and carved in the shape of a jutting fist rested.

Figures dressed in a manner similar to Zasian occupied each seat except one. As Vhok surveyed the men and women arrayed before him, haughty and self-assured gazes returned his own. Some of those gazes roamed over his noble, almost elven features, noting the silver hair contrasting his olive complexion, undoubtedly finding him handsome. Certainly many a female, human or otherwise, had fallen under his sway after being charmed by that exotic countenance. Other eyes lingered on Burnblood, the elven long sword resting on his right hip, or Scepter Malevolus, the steel rod engraved with black runes that dangled from his belt on the left side. The potently magical scepter marked Vhok as ruler of the Scourged Legion. He had taken that title after he had slain his mother, the marilith Mulvassyss, and pried it from her dead fingers. No doubt some among the Banites in the secret chamber pondered the cambion's prowess with it, perhaps assessing his worth to stand among them.

The cambion was hardly intimidated, though he could imagine how a mere human might be cowed into submission before an audience of seven priests of Bane. The power radiating from the group was palpable, and Vhok knew enough to appreciate and respect the minions of the Black Hand.

Zasian manipulated the door through which he and Vhok had entered, shutting it silently. Then he moved to the empty throne and seated himself upon it, joining his companions. Once he was settled, the leader, whom Vhok knew as Dreadlord Holt Burukhan, held his hand up, as though commanding silence, though no one had spoken. The high priest uttered a soft prayer to his dark god, then gestured around the chamber. When he finished, he gazed at Vhok.

"The chamber is warded," Burukhan said, his voice dispassionate. "No one has followed you to this sacred but secret place. We may speak freely."

Kaanyr Vhok wanted to snort in derision, but he managed with some effort to keep the noise to himself. He knew enough about spies to understand that no secret meeting chamber was foolproof, and anyone who thought otherwise was asking for trouble. Even hidden away in a room concealed behind the tombs of the dead, far below the world of daylight, someone might figure out where they were and employ magical means to listen and watch.

From where he stood near the entry, Vhok surreptitiously cast a spell of his own. He kept the gestures concealed and muttered softly to himself so that the gathered Banites would not notice his work. When he was finished, he strolled to the altar, confident that he would be aware of someone listening or watching the proceedings magically.

"Let us beseech the Black Lord to grant us wisdom and strength," the dreadlord began, turning his gaze from one priest to the next. "Let us ask him for the might to bring all our enemies low and the cleverness to rule our ever-growing dominion in his name." He bowed his head and closed his eyes, and the other priests joined him.

Vhok wanted to grimace, but the cambion kept his face bland as he looked around at the praying clerics. Each one seemed to smile in fervent delight at the prospect of wreaking havoc in the name of their god. The zealousness of Bane's followers never ceased to annoy Vhok, but he knew he had to keep such disgruntlement to himself. If he had any hope at all of ruling Sundabar, he would need their help. The city was too well defended, too difficult to overthrow by force. He had tried and failed too often to continue down that foolish path, so he needed a new plan, with allies on the inside. It was a shame that the only ones with any true potential to assist him in his endeavors were such mindless fanatics. Vhok found almost all of them exasperating.

Only Zasian seemed to think for himself, to exhibit any cleverness at all. Vhok liked him. The man was confident but not arrogant. He knew the dangers of pride, and sought in all things to find accord among his own kind—so unusual among Banites, for whom competition and strife seemed to ruin as many machinations as brought fruition and success. Zasian actually had potential as a long-term ally. Vhok doubted he would be able to tolerate the other priests at all, if not for Zasian.

Burukhan finished his prayer and began eyeing the other Banites. His gaze was both critical and expectant, as though he sought to confirm the eagerness in their faces, ensuring that they reveled in their god's power as much as he did, but hunting for some sign that their piety might be lacking. Their rapturous smiles and glittering visages seemed to satisfy the dreadlord.

"Step into the center of the chamber, hellspawn," Holt Burukhan demanded, gesturing toward the altar. "Step forward so that we may hear your words clearly and judge their worth plainly."

Vhok eyed the dreadlord with distaste, but he did as the high priest bade and moved nearer the altar. For long moments, no one spoke, and the cambion began to grow agitated under the assemblage's scrutiny.

"Zasian has told us of your offer," Holt said at last. "You wish an alliance."

It was more a statement than a question, but the silence following the high priest's words dragged.

Vhok nodded at last and said, "There is much we could gain, working together."

"Indeed," one of the Banites, a woman, replied. "We well understand what *you* might gain, seating yourself upon the throne of Sundabar, but how does that serve *our* interests? Share with us, if you will, what benefit you see for us in this proposed alliance."

Vhok glanced at Zasian, taken aback slightly. The cambion presumed that the other man had already won the assembled clergy over, and that the meeting was just a formality. It seemed the alliance was not as sealed as he had thought.

"You get to see Helm Dwarf-friend deposed, and your church becomes the sole divine power in the entire valley," the half-fiend replied. "All your adversaries—the servants of Helm, Torm, and Tyr—are cast out of the city, their temples destroyed. Your companions, the Zhentarim, establish a monopoly on commerce within the walls. Quite a lucrative bargain, if you ask me."

"Such a utopia is within our grasp without your aid, fiend," another cleric said, his voice gruff.

"Why should we trust you?" Holt Burukhan asked. "You and your brutish Scourged Legion have attacked our city repeatedly in the past. We know that the devilish horde you call an army sits now on the periphery, waiting for the right moment to strike. Will you bring them down upon us once more, after you hold the seat of power?"

They're demonic—not devilish, you simpleton, Vhok thought.

"If you had the means to drive out the Tyrrans and Helmites, you would have already done so," the cambion answered. "My Scourged Legion will be needed to tear down the walls of those temples and quell any rebellion within the ranks of the city's army and guardsmen. Once that is complete, I will send them to conquer more territory in my—in *our*—name, and they will do as I command. All I ask in return for this is that you let me unseat Helm Dwarf-friend before all the citizens of Sundabar, to humiliate him and drive him out of the city, branded a failure. I know you want to see the mercenary gone from Sundabar as badly as I do." Well, not as badly, but maybe close, he silently added.

"And how will you ruin Helm Dwarf-friend?" Holt asked. "What assurances can you give us that you will turn the populace against him?"

"A fine question," Vhok replied. "The answer to which I will keep to myself. But suffice to say I will have a means when the time comes. You risk nothing in accepting that answer, for I ask you to do nothing until I return. By that time, my preparations will be complete, and I will share my secret with you."

And Helm Dwarf-friend, Vhok said to himself, I will witness your fall from grace. I will be the instrument of your utter and unending misery. Mark my words.

For a moment, the cambion reveled in the image of the human mercenary exposed as a fraud and a traitor to his own city. The half-fiend daydreamed the scene playing out, the folk of Sundabar gathered in the square, bearing witness to Dwarf-friend's downfall and Vhok's triumph.

A triumph that would not come to pass without the Banites' aid.

"Very well," Holt said, just a hint uncertainly. "We shall concede this secrecy to you for the moment. But we will not seal this alliance, at least not yet. Though you have made a compelling case showing the mutual benefit of our cooperation, you have not assuaged my concerns over the outcome should you—we—fail. If we cannot unseat Helm Dwarf-friend from the Master's Hall, you and your army simply return to your infernal pit beneath the ground, little the worse for wear. But we"—he gestured around the chamber—"we are drawn out, exposed, and our power crushed between the city and temples. That does not sit well with me. You must bring proof that you can lead the populace, control them. Only then will we lend you our aid."

The chamber was quiet for some moments longer. Vhok again resisted the urge to grimace, though for a different reason. Dreadlord Holt Burukhan was a fanatic, but the half-fiend grudgingly acknowledged that he was not a complete fool. All the risk lay in the Banites' lap, and the priests knew it.

No matter, Vhok thought. Once I have the power of the Lifespring, convincing them of the plan's worth will be the simplest of things. They will feel foolish for ever doubting me. I will have this city. And Bane be damned.

The meeting was over. The gathered assemblage rose to their feet and began to slip out one by one, each by magical means of one sort or another. Vhok watched the priests as they vanished, leaving behind nothing more than a sparkle of magic or a zephyr of breeze to mark their passing. In moments, only he and Zasian remained behind.

"He is a fool," Vhok said at last, sighing loudly. "A fool's fool."

The remark drew a raised eyebrow from Zasian. "Perhaps, but such comments are dangerous. He or his spies might be listening to us at this very moment."

"It's all right," Vhok said. "I warded the room before we began tonight."

Zasian nodded. "Wise," he replied. "As did I. Burukhan rarely gives proper consideration to such precautions, I fear."

"Exactly," the cambion said. "A fool. And don't think I don't know you feel the same way about him, Zasian. I see the wisdom in your eyes—wisdom that flinches whenever that bag of winds speaks. For all his dedication and charisma, Dreadlord Holt Burukhan is not best suited to lead your church, Banite. You are far more able than he to command the hordes who worship your Black Hand." Vhok knew he spoke that last bit with more sarcasm than was probably wise, but he couldn't refrain from letting his true feelings trickle out.

Zasian seemed to ignore the jibe. "It is not so uncommon for a man to serve as the power behind a throne," he said. "Sometimes the masses need a face—a 'bag of winds' who can work them into a fervor on his behalf—more than they need a wizened contemplator. I accomplish far more behind the scenes, away from the scrutiny he receives. Burukhan can be the king. I prefer the role of kingmaker."

Vhok smirked. "If you say so. I could not be so content in such a role." Then his eyes narrowed. "When we have the city, is it your intention to continue to work behind the scenes?" he asked.

Zasian smiled, a charming grin that gave the ladies unsteady knees. "Almost assuredly," he purred. "Though I'm sure that when Kaanyr Vhok sits in the Master's Hall of Sundabar, High Priest Zasian Menz of the Temple of Bane will be busy with his own pursuits. I'm sure we'll reach some sort of agreement of coexistence. You do not have any interest in spiritual matters, and I have little interest in the day-to-day affairs of secular rulership. What's good for you and your city will undoubtedly be good for me and my temple."

"Indeed," Vhok said. Silently, he added, Though I might

prefer the incompetent blowhard at the head of the temple. Less dangerous most of the time.

The cambion dismissed future confrontations from his mind and changed the subject. "Are you prepared to leave tonight?" he asked Menz, though he knew the answer already. Both had been planning their impending journey for a long time.

"Yes," Zasian answered. "And what of your preparations? Will we have access to the portal by this evening?"

"Yes," Vhok replied. "Lysalis and the others are working now. It shouldn't be much longer."

Zasian nodded and said, "I will meet you at the forges then, when it is time."

"And our guide will be waiting on the other side?" Vhok asked.

"I have made the offerings and sent the messages. The price has been paid, and the guide should be waiting for us on the far side of the portal."

"Then I will see you tonight," Vhok said. He watched as Zasian nodded curtly once, summoned a magical doorway of reddish light, stepped through, and vanished.

CHAPTER TWO

The Everfire filled the massive chamber with an orange glow. The channel of simmering, molten rock illuminated every surface, its light even shining faintly upon the ceiling. From his vantage point high atop one of the great ruined Forge Towers, Vhok could survey the entirety of the massive room. He could feel waves of heat radiating upward, even several hundred feet away. The oppressive warmth did not bother the cambion, and the smell of scorched stone reminded him of familiar places in the Abyss.

The tower upon which the Sceptered One and his bevy of fey'ri sorcerers had gathered stood opposite its twin. The upper reaches of the counterpart had long ago shattered in some cataclysm, and the great stone bridge that once connected them simply hung in space, a jagged protrusion going nowhere. Together, the identical towers might have appeared as dual sentries, watching over the dwarves as they worked their forges in the sweltering heat.

Kaanyr Vhok had failed to conquer Sundabar because it was actually two cities, one on the surface and one below. The dwarves occupied the lower levels, far down in the depths. They had arrived many centuries before the humans and had learned to harness the potency of the Everfire for their forge work.

During the heyday of their activity, the dwarves had constructed side channels intersecting the natural lava course—great troughs that ran perpendicular to the large crevasse. At those smaller fiery canals, the dwarves performed most of their labors, heating and tempering the steel they forged into weapons and armor and the precious metals they crafted into beautiful things.

To protect themselves from the searing heat of the Everfire, the dwarves placed powerful dweomers upon the magma channels. They trapped most of the heat within protective barriers of invisible force. Using arcane tricks they allowed only small amounts of the liquid fire to flow into the side channels, and magical irrigation gates controlled the flow. In that way, they harnessed the power of what otherwise would have been a most destructive force.

Vhok knew that even after so many years, the protective magic remained in place, cordoning off the flow, keeping it from overrunning the forging chamber. Though the dwarves performed only a fraction of their work within the Everfire's tempering heat, they still came occasionally to create their most beautiful—and most magical—works.

And, because they still valued the primordial lava flow, the dwarves fiercely protected it from enemies. The Vigilant, a small but elite force of dwarves, sworn defenders of the Everfire, stood always ready to drive back subterranean invaders.

The Vigilant posed a serious problem to the cambion. They could rush at a moment's notice to aid the citizens above should an attack occur. Their combined might had proven sufficient to hold back the tide of the Scourged Legion's tanarukks on more than one occasion. Even with the cambion's subtle plan taking shape, the Vigilant might prove a thorn in his side. Vhok hated them and wanted to crush them—indeed, all the dwarves of Sundabar's labyrinthine underlevels—once and for all. But the dwarves were a hardy folk and not easily destroyed. So Vhok intended to use one of the oldest tricks of warfare. He would turn the dwarves' own strength against them. When the time was right, he would scorch them to oblivion with their own Everfire.

But for the moment, the cambion merely needed to distract them, get them away from the molten rock.

"You are certain you can bring down those barriers?" Vhok asked the fey'ri sorceress standing beside him.

The other creature nodded. A lithe female, Lysalis had the delicate but angular features of an elf, and the blazing red eyes and prominent fangs of a fiend. She dressed in gaudy splendor, an affectation she had adapted in the heady days immediately following their escape from the utter destruction of Hellgate Keep. Though the cambion found Lysalis's choice of clothing a bit too flashy for his tastes, he otherwise thought her charming and sultry. He had bedded her a time or two, though it was never anything more than a moment's diversion, much in the same way he knew Aliisza pursued other dalliances on occasion. Lysalis would never be anything more than a useful minion to him.

A perfectly capable minion, though, he thought.

"It will take all of our talents melded together," Lysalis was saying, "and it will not be quick, but I believe we can channel sufficient power into the dweomers to disrupt them and stir the Everfire to life."

Vhok was pleased. He looked past Lysalis's shoulder to the handful of other fey'ri gathered there. They were the most competent, the most powerful among all who served in Vhok's Scourged Legion. He would need every last scrap of their talents.

"Excellent," he said. "Have them begin. We shall return in a while to see how they fare."

Lysalis nodded and turned to the fey'ri. She gathered the handful of them together and issued instructions. Soon, the sorcerers were deeply involved in their preparations. None paid the slightest heed to Vhok.

The cambion peered over the edge of the tower once again. Far below, glowing ruddy in the light of the eternal furnace of the Everfire, he could see a handful of dwarves moving around. Whether they were patrols of Vigilant or craftsmen immersed in their work, he could not tell. It did not matter. Soon, he imagined, they would all be scrambling to escape the expanding inferno. The image made him smile.

Once Lysalis was satisfied that her compatriots had preparations well in hand, she and Kaanyr Vhok took their leave and began to make their way down a wide spiral staircase leading deep into the tower. When they were well out of both earshot and view, the half-fiend stopped.

"We must pay Nahaunglaroth another visit," he said. "It is time to offer more enticement."

Lysalis smirked, her elf's eyebrows arching in bemusement, but she said nothing. She passed her hands before herself and muttered an incantation. Instantly, the pair was whisked far from the dwarven stronghold.

Vhok took a steadying breath as he found himself standing upon a stone balcony exposed to the crisp night air of the mountains. He had expected the change, but it still unsettled him. Lysalis stood right beside him, and her own gasp confirmed to the cambion that the sudden shift in location and temperature startled her, too.

Behind the pair, the glow of torches cast orange light in a corona around them, throwing their shadows upon the balustrade of the balcony. Beyond that railing, the blackness of night cloaked the world like a velvet cape. The gibbous moon was low on the horizon, and filmy clouds crossed it like gauzy ribbons.

A hoarse growl chorused with a clank of metal, and Vhok turned in time to spy a pair of unusual creatures snarling and pointing. They were of a similar height as he, though more muscular and stocky, and their features were brutish and ferocious, with exposed canines and thick, prominent noses. Vhok would have considered them hobgoblins but for a few bizarre features. They both sported wide, leathery wings that fanned out to either side as they advanced. Their skin was pale blue, rather than the usual tan or yellowish of hobgoblins. Vhok knew of them, the Blood of Morueme, sired in the mating of a blue dragon and a hobgoblin slave.

The two draconic guards, dressed in heavy chain shirts and brandishing blackened battle-axes, loped forward, twirling their razorlike weapons overhead.

"You trespass!" one of them snarled.

Vhok fought the urge to yank Burnblood, his ancient elven long sword, free of its scabbard on his hip. Beside him, he noted that Lysalis clenched her fists, as though she, too, were resisting the urge to blast the two oafs with fell magic. Taking a calming breath, Vhok kept his hands out, showing that he remained unarmed, and said, "We have come to see Master Nahaunglaroth, and we bear him gifts of gold and jewels."

At the mention of their lord—and quite possibly their father—the two half-dragons slowed their advance. The one who had spoken cocked his head to one side and asked, "Where is this treasure? I see no chests or sacks of coins and gems. I think you're lying."

Vhok rolled his eyes ever so slightly but smiled and replied, "There is too much to carry—it would be too heavy.

We bring it magically and will present it once we have an audience with Master Nahaunglaroth."

The draconic hobgoblin considered the cambion's words for a moment, perhaps trying to puzzle out how much he should trust the half-fiend.

After a lengthy pause, the guard nodded and said, "You wait here. I will find out if the masters will see you." The half-dragon spun on his heel and marched through a doorway into the interior of the building, leaving the other guard to watch the two interlopers. The second draconic hobgoblin stood mutely, eyeing the pair with undisguised suspicion.

Vhok gave the brutish creature a deprecating smile and turned to stroll toward the edge of the balcony, intent on enjoying the view while he was forced to wait.

Lysalis had brought the two of them to Doomspire, a great castle perched on the side of Dragondoom Mountain, in the far eastern end of the Nether range. It was not the first time the cambion and his sorceress had visited the mountain fortress. Vhok had begun negotiating with the dragon lords some time before, hoping to forge better relations with the Morueme clan. It had been a slow process. The history between the wyrms of Dragondoom and the fiends of Hellgate Keep had been unpleasant.

"You leave all your weapons out here, and you can come inside," the guard said upon returning.

The routine was familiar to Vhok and Lysalis, who had been made to disarm each time they had come to visit. The cambion thought that Nahaunglaroth was being paranoid, considering all the wondrous gifts he had brought the great dragon in the past, but he wasn't about to strain the fragile peace he had managed to establish with the clan over something as trivial as a sword.

After leaving their blades and other gear in a pile on the

balcony, the two half-fiends followed their escort into the interior of the castle, leaving the other guard to stand watch over their belongings. The route through the passages of the castle was long and circuitous, descending several flights of stone stairs and winding down through numerous corridors into the deeper levels. Vhok paid little attention to their journey. The fortress was a crude thing in his estimation, built by the earliest hobgoblin thralls serving the great dragons of Clan Morueme. Despite the considerable magic and dragon ingenuity that had subsequently been spent to improve the castle's defenses, it still bore the unmistakable coarseness of its original makers.

Vhok noted that the stones forming the walls were rough and uneven, and in many cases, walls leaned or slanted at inexact angles. Doorways were not of consistent heights, and hallways often ended with no destination. The whole place had a foul odor, something akin to a mixture of bad meat and an overabundance of stable dung. Vhok often wondered just how close to collapse the place might be were it not for the dragons' will.

As they walked, the trio passed numerous other half-dragon, half-hobgoblin denizens. They also spied a handful of pure-blood hobgoblins, all of them female and appearing sullen and craven in the extreme. Some hurried to one unseen destination or another, but a few simply lurked in doorways or large open halls. Some loitered with young draconic offspring at their feet. The entire place reminded Vhok of a rundown festhall in a city slum.

At last, the décor shifted to something more opulent. The path their escort followed widened into a broad hallway that angled downward and changed from worked block walls to natural stone, shaped smooth and carved with imagery of great winged wyrms inciting terror across the land.

Vhok leaned close to Lysalis and whispered, "Next time we come for a visit, bring us directly here. That festhall overhead is anything but festive."

"So long as you can convince all of them not to behead us on sight," the sorceress replied, nodding toward the ranks of guards who flanked the hall every ten paces or so. "I rather value mine."

Vhok smirked but did not reply, for their guard had led them to a great chamber filled with a vast assortment of gleaming artwork. The half-dragon guard gestured into the room, then spun on his heel and vanished the way he had arrived.

Though he had visited the room before, the cambion was still taken aback by the sheer beauty—and volume—of treasures on display. It was on par with some of the greatest private museums or vaults in all of Faerûn, he supposed. Tapestries woven of the finest silks hung on every wall, stands displaying magnificent weapons, shields, and suits of armor lined the perimeter, and glass cases revealed ancient coins, fragments of fine dishes and service sets, crowns, tiaras, jewelry, and much more.

"I see that you still marvel at my collection of fine antiques," boomed a voice from overhead.

Vhok and Lysalis simultaneously jerked their gazes up to peer at its source. A massive serpentine body reclined upon a large gallery that circled the chamber. His brilliant blue scales glittered in the light of the various lanterns placed throughout the room. A large, horned head rested upon a thick neck, with reptilian eyes studying the two visitors intently.

Vhok bowed in deference and said, "You are looking fit as always, Nahaunglaroth."

"And you are as wretched a flatterer as ever, cambion," the dragon replied, uncoiling himself and slithering over the side of the gallery's edge. As his body descended to the floor where Vhok and Lysalis stood, the sorceress took an involuntary step back. Vhok did not flinch, though he felt a moment of dread wash through him. Nahaunglaroth was a dragon, after all.

The scaled body began to shift then, shrinking and melding until it was no longer serpentine. When the transformation was complete, no evidence remained that a dragon had ever been in the room. Only a man, dressed lavishly in navy breeches and silk shirt, with a lighter blue silken doublet, stood in the company of the visitors. His eyes, however, still possessed that intense, reptilian gaze.

"So, you've come to bring me more trinkets?" the man said, striding forward. "Whatever other unworthy qualities you may have, fiend, you at least know the way to a wyrm's heart. What have you to show me?"

Vhok had to smother a chuckle. Nahaunglaroth was, like all of his draconic kin, too greedy for his own good. Even with all of his finery on display, the creature wanted more, always more. For that, the cambion was thankful.

"Lysalis—if you please?" Vhok said, and the sorceress obliged him by beginning an incantation. Nahaunglaroth tensed for a moment, but when the fey'ri produced a tiny chest in the palm of her hand, set it down, and stepped back, the dragon could not resist the urge to peer down at it eagerly.

The chest expanded in size until it was as large as an overstuffed chair. It was a remarkable piece of furniture on its own, crafted of hand-rubbed duskwood with platinum fittings. Knowing that the dragon would be suspicious, Vhok opened the latch, then slowly lifted the lid.

The three of them gazed upon a trove of ancient elven and dwarven items. Vhok had brought his host numerous weapons, tomes, fabrics, and gem-encrusted valuables, all scoured from the lost places in and beneath the High Forest.

The contents of the chest represented years of the cambion's life, both before and after the fall of Hellgate Keep.

It was no pittance he was parting with.

Nahaunglaroth knelt before the chest, his eyes gleaming in excitement. He almost cooed as he lifted first one item, then another from the container. Vhok knew he didn't need to explain the value—financial or historical—to the dragon.

If anyone understands the true value of a priceless artifact, it's a dragon, the cambion thought.

"Quite impressive," Nahaunglaroth said, standing again. Vhok could see him working to hide his eagerness. "And appreciated as much for your generosity as for its value. It must have taken you a while to gather such trinkets."

Trinkets? Vhok thought. A bit more dismissive than is warranted. Aloud, he replied, "Worth only a pittance compared to what I may gain should we be able, at last, to reach some sort of arrangement."

"Ah, yes," Nahaunglaroth said, strolling about his museum and casually examining the many items on display. "The alliance you have spoken of. Remind me again what it is you seek?" he asked, his back to the pair of half-fiends.

Vhok let one corner of his mouth turn up in a smirk, but he didn't let the disdain creep into his voice as he said, "Of course. It seems to me that neither of us is going to succeed nearly as well in our relative pursuits so long as we remain at odds with one another. The simplicity of establishing a peaceable coexistence seems so natural. This would be especially true should I ascend to the master's seat in Sundabar, as you already know I desire."

"The problem with that," the dragon said, still not turning around, "is that you fiends rut like there's no tomorrow, and before we know it, you're spread all over the place. My mountain would be overrun with your brutish Scourged Legion in no time."

Lysalis let out a low growl, but Vhok cut her off with a sharp gesture.

Nahaunglaroth turned around then, looking at both of his visitors with a knowing smile. "Touched a nerve, did I?" he asked.

"As long as we're all being civil," Vhok said, "my problem with the bargain is that you greedy dragons can never get enough of what glitters. I don't mind so much, giving some of mine to you—after all, I have much greater political ambitions—but your demand for more would never stop. I'd bring you a bar of gold, you'd ask me why it wasn't two."

Nahaunglaroth glared at Vhok for a moment, and the cambion was almost certain that he had crossed the line, that whatever tenuous foothold he held on establishing a neutrality pact had just crumbled beneath him. He silently cursed himself for being so forward.

But then the dragon began to laugh. At first, it was a snicker, but it grew louder, deeper, and soon, the human in front of Vhok was outright guffawing, bent over and slapping his knee. Vhok couldn't help but grin a bit in response to the comical scene. When the transformed wyrm managed to regain his breath and stand upright, Vhok could see that tears of mirth streamed down his host's cheeks.

"I've never heard a dragon's greed described quite so aptly," Nahaunglaroth said at last. "I will give you credit, cambion— you don't lack for bravado or wit. Not too many folk choose to show their true disposition while standing before a dragon. Now, I've got a surprise for you." The creature put his fingers to his lips and gave a shrill whistle. "There are things these human bodies are much better for," he said, smiling, as they waited. "Never could do that until I learned how to shift shapes. Whistling is so . . . interesting." He began to twitter a tune then, some common drinking house song that Vhok recognized but couldn't recall the words to.

The cambion just smiled and nodded, surprised at what might amuse a dragon. *Is he being cagey, or eccentric?* Vhok wondered.

After a moment, another half-dragon entered the room. It was similar in appearance to the guard that had escorted Vhok and Lysalis to the chamber, but it was slighter of build and seemed to hold a more intelligent gleam in its eyes. It carried a small silver coffer to Nahaunglaroth, then turned and left.

The dragon turned and passed the coffer to Vhok. "You brought me gifts, now I return the favor. Think of it as sealing the pact." At Vhok's surprised gaze, the creature nodded. "Yes, I'm willing to talk terms. I've had some time to think about your offer since your last visit, and honestly, the idea has merit. My father lost touch with the outside world, and my brother and I want to extend our reach farther, and gain influence and favors. So we are willing to enter into agreement with you, provided we can address a few concerns.

"In particular, we want to start acquiring a supply of magically enchanted weapons and armor for our Blood. You *do* intend to rekindle the forges of the Everfire once you seize control, don't you?"

Vhok nodded absently and said, "Undoubtedly." He opened the box and found an odd item resting inside. It was an alabaster carving of a vine-covered archway, perhaps the size of his fist. The cambion removed it from its case and held it up, examining it. He could sense latent magic radiating from within.

"My diviners knew you were coming tonight, and they also told me you are about to embark on a great journey," Nahaunglaroth said, standing beside the half-fiend while

Lysalis crowded next to him on the other side. "Perhaps this small token will aid you," the dragon added.

Vhok, slightly concerned that his plans were known to others, nodded his thanks. Let's hope my enemies don't glean as much about me, he thought.

"Here," Nahaunglaroth said, taking the carved arch from Vhok, "let me show you how this works."

◆ ◆ ◆ ◆ ◆ ◆ ◆ ◆

Myshik Morueme paused and sniffed the dead air around him, gauging his path as much by intuition as by any mental map. The blue-scaled hobgoblin chose a direction and proceeded, drawing on his half-draconic heritage to feel his way. His heavy boots thunked rhythmically as he walked. He held his massive war axe cradled in the palms of his clawed hands. He knew that, should he confront any dwarves with it, the anger in their eyes would delight him.

The passage was worked stone, precisely carved out of the bedrock of mountains by dwarf tools wielded by dwarf hands. The quality of the architecture interested him not the slightest bit, except insofar as it helped guide him. For two days, Myshik had ascended out of the Underdark, passing through countless tunnels, ruined gates, and hallways that marked the outer boundaries of Old Delzoun. Steered by his knowledge of the ancient dwarven territory, he made steady progress toward its heart. Soon, he would reach the outskirts of an area he knew to be inhabited. There, he hoped to finally reap the rewards of his search.

Myshik paused at an intersection of two great hallways, breathing in the stones. He knew he was close. His instinct nudged him to his right, so he turned that way. The passage approached a grand staircase that ascended toward a pair of massive stone doors, easily three times the half-dragon's height. The portal had been closed for centuries, judging from the scattering of debris that littered the landing. Myshik stopped before them, frowning. He could not see a way to open them.

Then he spied a side passage, a crude tunnel that someone—or something—had bored through the rock to one side of the twin doors. He stepped toward it, gripping his axe a bit more tightly.

The tunnel digger had been in a hurry. The work was rough, crude. It was also considerably smaller than the surrounding tunnels. Certainly no dwarf handiwork, Myshik decided. The potential for ambush somewhere within its depths was not lost on the half-hobgoblin. Shrugging, he entered the passage anyway. It was the only route past the massive doors, and it was the direction he must go if he wished to find his quarry.

Thinking of his goal made the half-dragon smile. Treasure was precious. It let the clan live. Treasure reaped through battle was always more precious. He hoped that dwarves guarded great hordes of the stuff.

Myshik pushed through the cramped tunnel, keeping his leathery wings tucked close to his body. The passage did not travel far, only through the thick wall that supported the doorway. He wondered for a moment why the digger hadn't chipped through the doors themselves, but dismissed the thought as he emerged on the other side. He entered what must have been a grand chamber, a massive hall so large that his darkness-attuned eyes could not make out any features within the limits of his vision.

He stood quite still for a moment, listening. All seemed perfectly quiet. Though he knew it would be risky, Myshik decided to illuminate the place so he could get a better look.

Reaching into a protected pocket, the half-hobgoblin produced an oblong bundle. Slowly unwrapping the cloth, he exposed a prism-shaped white crystal twice as thick as his clawed thumb and as long as his hand. As he folded back each layer of the covering, the intense glow of magical light grew stronger, until at last, blinking from its harsh glare, he held it openly in his palm.

Myshik held the stone aloft and slightly behind his head, using its brilliant glow to study his surroundings.

An abandoned stronghold.

The place where Myshik stood must have once served as a welcoming entryway marking the periphery of a dwarven settlement, though judging from its construction, the dwarves had been cautious hosts. The roof of the chamber soared high overhead, but directly before him stood formidable defenses. With his back to the stone doors, the half-hobgoblin faced a large wall that rose perhaps halfway to the ceiling. The top of the wall bristled with crenellations, and Myshik could see that its entire surface was pierced by arrow slits.

Another large portal bisected the wall, though solid doors did not seal that ingress. Instead, a great iron portcullis defended it. The immense metal grate hung almost all the way to the floor. Had it settled all the way down, the pointed iron protrusions lining its underside would have bored nicely into circular depressions in the stone. But a pair of large wooden braces erected beneath the huge portcullis held it aloft, preventing it from descending completely.

The braces had been crafted from immense rough-cut timbers lashed together with stout rope like gigantic saw-horses. The timbers' girths were easily as big as Myshik's chest, and the rope was as thick as his wrist. The half-dragon wondered how those who had constructed them had managed to drag such large timbers all the way down from the surface. They looked stout enough, but the thought of several tons' worth of iron bars crashing atop him unsettled him. He might decide to seek another route, perhaps by scaling the wall itself.

Of more immediate concern was the gaping chasm that separated him from the formidable wall. Fully thirty feet across, the yawning crevasse extended the width of the chamber and proceeded into the side walls. Indentations and markings lay upon the stone floor on his side of the chasm, as well as the remains of what looked like immense hinges on the far side. They suggested that a large drawbridge had spanned it at some time. Myshik suspected that the bridge had come to rest at the bottom.

The half-dragon approached the edge and peered over, shining his light down and searching for the bottom. The void descended beyond the limits of his illumination.

Myshik strolled to his left, following the edge of the cleft toward one wall. His gaze roamed over the place, seeking some safe means of crossing the chasm, but he spotted nothing. He repeated the process to his right. He found no spikes or ropes, nothing to suggest a safe means of traversing. He sighed.

Only one way, he decided.

The half-dragon backed up a number of steps and turned to face the chasm. Taking a few deep breaths, he mentally urged himself forward. Myshik took off at a sprint and dashed directly toward the gap, refusing to look down and instead eyeing the opposite side. When he reached the edge, he leaped up and forward. Under normal circumstances, no hobgoblin could have cleared such a wide barrier. But Myshik unfurled his leathery blue wings and fervently flapped them as he glided over the yawning chasm. True to his intentions, he never looked down.

Though the vestigial appendages inherited from his draconic father did not enable Myshik to truly fly, they were sufficient in size to allow him to glide a fair distance, and with their aid, he was able to navigate the boundary, landing in a trot on the far side.

Heaving one deep sigh of relief, Myshik settled easily into stride and approached the massive portcullis. He examined the braces to reassure himself that they were secure. He grasped one of the braces with both hands and shook it, testing. It groaned and seemed to shift ever so slightly, and the portcullis did, too. A smattering of dust sifted down from above, but the braces held.

Myshik gave the tremendous gate one last wary look, then darted beneath the huge bars and passed beyond the portal into the prodigious space beyond.

On the other side of the gate, Myshik's light proved inadequate to illuminate the entire chamber. The half-dragon could barely discern the far reaches, but his crystal was bright enough for him to see that the structure of the cavern ascended in grand scale. The dwarves had adapted their architecture to suit the shape of the chamber, which was not even or smooth, but sloped upward, like the side of a miniature mountain filled with ridges and draws. The space had been tiered, like a great rippled ziggurat, rising up to prominences at the far end. All of it was stout stone, crafted for stability. The dwarves had given little care to decoration; instead, the place exuded practicality.

From his study of old maps of the region, Myshik suspected he knew where he trod. He had reached an outpost, a peripheral bastion of defense against the dark things that tended to ascend from the Underdark. Beyond the upper limits of the chamber, the corridors and halls beneath Sundabar waited.

Without warning, Myshik felt a presence in his mind. It was powerful, familiar. It was Father.

Myshik, the great blue wyrm Roraurim's voice said, penetrating his offspring's skull. *Myshik, answer me.*

"I am here, Father," the half-dragon responded. "How may I serve you?"

I see you, the dragon's voice said. *You are near the city of Sundabar.*

"Yes," Myshik answered. "Below it, actually."

Good, Roraurim said. *I have a job for you. My brother, your uncle, has entered into a pact with the fiends disgorged from Hellgate Keep. You must find their leader, a cambion demon named Kaanyr Vhok. Go to him, and offer yourself in service to him.*

"I don't understand, Father," Myshik said. "Do we not hate the creatures that invade our mountains? Why would Uncle Nahaunglaroth do such a thing?"

Yours is not to understand—only to obey.

"Yes, Father. Of course," Myshik bowed his head in subservience. "Command me."

Go and do as I have said. You will accompany this cambion on a journey. Aid him, defend him from his enemies. When you have his confidence, this is what you are to do. . . .

When Myshik's father, the great Roraurim, finished, Myshik smiled and said, "Yes, Father. It will be as you say."

I have faith in you, my son. And the voice was gone.

Fearing that his light might betray his presence, Myshik wrapped the crystal again and tucked it into a pocket. After spending a moment adjusting to the darkness, the half-dragon advanced, picking his way toward the first of a series of sloping pathways leading higher into the stronghold.

They were the first steps of a new journey, a new quest.

CHAPTER THREE

Aliisza lay very still and listened to Helm Dwarf-friend snoring softly next to her. The man's breathing was slow and steady, a familiar sound. She knew he was truly asleep. She rose up on her elbow and peered at the Master of Sundabar in the dim light of the lone lamp burning on the table nearby. The ex-mercenary's face was lined with age and the weight of responsibility, even in sleep. His hair and beard, still thick and worn in braids like the northmen, had as much gray as red in it. His frame still bulged, but as much paunch as muscle was evident. He was no longer the young man the people of Sundabar had embraced so many years before, the stout warrior and battle captain of the Bloodaxe mercenary company who had saved the city from destruction first, and corruption afterward. Time and care had stolen his vibrant youth from him.

It would not be difficult to turn the people away from a man who looked as tired and infirm as Helm Dwarf-friend. They would need only a little nudge and a more capable alternative to see the truth. An alternative who looked young and handsome, like Dwarf-friend had twenty years or more ago. Someone like Kaanyr Vhok.

Careful not to disturb the sleeping master, Aliisza rose from the bed. She took up her nightdress from the floor, where Helm had carelessly tossed it aside. She did not don it immediately, but instead moved toward the mirror above the washbasin to gaze at the reflection of the innocent girl who would betray a city. The impish face that stared back at her smiled in satisfaction, with a hint of smoldering lust.

I'll hand that to him, the alu thought. He's got an excellent eye for beauty. Aliisza turned herself back and forth, appraising her shape and curves, her head cocked to one side. Hells, I'd bed Ansa, too, she thought with a grin. She giggled, softly so that she wouldn't wake the man.

Aliisza wriggled herself into the nightdress and moved to the door leading into the master's study. She pulled it open, being careful not to make noise, and slipped outside.

The study was a mess, as usual, and it was ostensibly Ansa's job to straighten it. But Aliisza conveniently avoided the task as much as possible. She wanted to perpetuate the image of an overwhelmed, disorganized leader, but she also detested such menial chores. Despite the chaos in the room, she had a very good idea where everything was, and she had taken advantage of the master's long days attending to the duties of office to sift and sort through it all, gleaning as best she could how the man tried to run the city.

She had even begun, very slowly, to make changes to some of his official documents. Requisitions, records of accounting, even specifications for equipping and deploying the watch received adjustments. Always subtle, the changes effectively weakened the city in some small way, or created confusion in some warehouse or barracks. Slowly, inconspicuously, Aliisza was undermining Dwarf-friend's rule, making it appear that he was beginning to lose his ability to do so effectively.

The alu moved to a pile of military supply requisitions

and sat down to examine them. Outwardly, she claimed to Dwarf-friend to be sorting and filing the stack, but in truth, she poured over it for details on Sundabar's martial might. Already she had found ways in which she could shortchange both the Shieldsar, Sundabar's army, and the Stone Shields, the city watch. It would be a long, tedious process, but within a few months, the half-fiend would have substantially weakened both forces. More importantly, she would make Helm Dwarf-friend look the fool. Watch commanders were already sending curt notes from time to time, complaining to the master that needed provisions were in short supply and not being replenished when expected. Aliisza was intercepting the messages, though, and Helm never saw them.

The alu sat down lazily, thinking to spend some time at her subversive task, but a premonition, a familiar tingling sense of danger, washed over Aliisza and froze her in place. She recognized the subtle, almost subconscious augury. Such signals coursed through her from time to time, warning her of impending peril. Her intuition was an inherited gift from her demonic mother, and she knew better than to ignore it. Right then, she felt as though she were being watched.

She scanned the room, looking for some sign that her premonition was warranted. The alu's gaze penetrated every corner, every shadow within the ill-lit study. She sought any potential hiding place, but the furniture was sparse and functional rather than posh, and there was no place for someone to conceal himself.

What is it? the alu wondered, shivering. What am I not seeing? Remembrance made her breath catch. Pharaun's ring!

Without looking down, Aliisza brought her hands together and felt for the trinket. The strange signet ring encircled the fourth finger of her right hand. She knew it granted her a preternatural ability to recognize magical emanations, but in the couple of months since she had claimed it from the drow wizard Pharaun Mizzrym's remains, she had not grown accustomed to drawing on its power. Brushing aside the self-chastisement of not thinking of it sooner, the half-demon summoned the wizardry of the ring and focused her attention all around the chamber, seeking the telltale signs of dweomers.

Magical emanations of various hues and strengths exploded in her vision from numerous points. A set of bound scrolls on a bookcase glimmered with arcane radiance. A cane leaning in a corner burst into light. And the shield that hung over the mantle radiated power, too. But the source right in front of her caught Aliisza's attention.

A single figure standing near the hearth erupted into a dazzling display of glowing radiance. Myriad magical colors shimmered around it, outlining the form and revealing it as a human-sized male. He stood very still, tucked half behind the fireplace, seemingly watching her. He had taken great pains to keep from being spotted or heard, drawing on magical invisibility and uncanny silence to remain undetected. He bore numerous defensive enchantments as well as powerful weapons. He was clearly ready for a fight.

Aliisza became aware of all this in the blink of an eye.

Aliisza hesitated. Her instinct told her to draw weapons and attack the trespasser, take him by surprise before he could react, but she also knew Ansa would never do that. She was loath to ruin her carefully planned deception.

Then, in the time it took the alu to wonder whether it was the master or herself being hunted, another wave of subliminal warning washed over her. A hint of light and motion caught her eye, coming from her right. A figure materialized, stepping through a magical doorway in the center of the room. Multicolored emanations swarmed around him as well, a visual cacophony of magical protections revealed by Pharaun's signet ring. He immediately waved a wand at her.

Instantly, Aliisza's surroundings grew unearthly silent. She could not even hear the rush of blood in her ears as her heart pounded.

Me, Aliisza understood in that dreadful instant, knowing most of her spells had just been rendered useless. *They've come for me. But how? I was careful. So very careful.*

And yet someone had ferreted her out. The deception was ruined. Kaanyr's plan to disgrace Helm Dwarf-friend was lost. Rage coursed through her, made her want to flense someone. The fool with the wand would do nicely.

As Aliisza turned toward the wizard, the door to the outer hall burst open and a third figure entered. It was a woman, heavily armored and radiating powerful magic. She gestured at the disguised alu.

The half-fiend swore, recognizing the divine motions. *Time to go,* Aliisza decided, feeling concern replace her rage. *They aren't playing games.* She began to summon innate magical energy, intending to create an extradimensional portal through which to flee.

She was not quick enough.

A flash of emerald arced across the alu's vision as a glowing green ray shot from her adversary's fingers. She twisted around in an attempt to dodge the shimmering energy, but it struck her on the shoulder. Instantly, a glowing field of similar color coalesced all about her. She was surprised to discover that she felt no pain. The beam had not directly harmed her.

In the next breath, Aliisza had her magical doorway created. Without waiting to see what sort of vile magic had ensnared her, she stepped through.

And bounced back.

The doorway would not permit her passage. To the alu, it felt as if she were trying to move into a stone wall. She could sense the magic of it, feel the innate control she had over the portal, even detect the location beyond, where she had anchored the other end of the extradimensional pathway. But she was barred from using it.

Cursing to herself in her soundless state, Aliisza understood the nature of the green magic that clung to her.

They've anchored me, she thought as a brief wave of panic washed through her. She forced the abhorrent emotion down. Better cut my way out of here the old-fashioned way, she decided.

The alu shifted into her true form.

The silly wisp of a girl dressed only in a nightshirt vanished. The half-fiend, dressed in sinewy black leather armor and with unfurling black leathery wings, replaced her. Aliisza drew herself up to her full height, giving a disdainful stare at the three adversaries arrayed around her, and jerked free the magical elven blade she wore at her side.

The transition had just the effect the alu wanted. All three of the intruders paused, staring at the fiendish creature before them.

Aliisza took advantage of their startled hesitation and lunged at the wizard with the wand. She felt the blade slip through arcane protection, its own magic overwhelming the cloaking armor surrounding the man. The keen tip of the sword pierced the wizard in the abdomen and doubled him over in a single deadly stroke. The half-fiend yanked the blade free and spun to face her other two opponents, heedless of the man as he crumpled to the floor.

Only then did she spot the fourth figure.

Zasian Menz filled the doorway, his arms folded across his chest and a pompous smile on his face.

"You," Aliisza snarled, seething, but no sound issued from her, the silence as mocking as the seneschal's gleeful stare. She wanted to run him through with her blade, to wrap her fingers around his neck and choke the life from him.

Zasian stepped into the room and made a gesture. The alu saw his mouth move as he pointed, directing the two remaining assailants confronting her. The man's intentions were clear enough, even if his words were lost to Aliisza's deafened ears. Surround her, do not let her escape. She was the quarry he was after.

To her left, the figure by the fireplace unfurled a weighted net. To her right, the priestess sidestepped, making room for the seneschal to join the fray.

Knowing she was out-muscled and lacking any spells, Aliisza backed away, looking for freedom. She glanced at the window, closed against the cold of night, and wondered if she could bull her way through it. Though Dwarf-friend's quarters were on the fourth floor of the Master's Hall, her wings would negotiate the fall and speed the alu to safety. But she would first have to break through the stout wooden shutters.

Aliisza must have taken a faltering step in that direction, for immediately, her foes rushed to try to encircle her. She dared not engage one of them and put her back to the other two, but she also couldn't stand there and let them pick her apart with magic. She eyed the distance and wondered how much it would hurt to hurtle herself though the wooden panel.

The floor lurched beneath Aliisza's feet. The room tottered and shook, and the alu stumbled, off balance. Piles of parchment, precariously stacked on many surfaces, slid to the floor, scattering everywhere. Books fell from the bookcases. The lamps swayed, and a candle fell to the floor, spilling wax and setting fire to some of the scraps of parchment strewn nearby.

It took Aliisza a moment to realize what was happening. Then her mind wrapped around it. Earthquake!

The trio of assailants shifted and stumbled, caught as much by surprise as the alu. The priestess grabbed at the table to steady herself, while Zasian staggered backward and grasped the doorframe with both hands.

That distraction was all she needed. Fighting the swaying world, Aliisza darted forward, intent on launching herself through the window. The shifting of the floor and the scattering of scrolls and parchment made it difficult for her to build speed, but she closed the distance. When she was several steps away, she began to tuck, anticipating the trajectory she would use to hurtle herself through the shutters and escape into the night.

The rogue by the fireplace, deft on his feet, recovered quickly. In a blinding swirl of motion, he sent the net spinning, fanning out into a large circle. Aliisza sprinted and jumped, lifting herself off the ground. She tucked herself into a ball, desperate to evade the trap and break through.

She was a step too slow.

The net settled around her body, the weights attached to its edges pulling it tight. She thrashed and fought its confining embrace even as the rogue pulled on a trailing rope, yanking the net taut.

Unable to complete her leap to freedom, Aliisza jerked to a sudden stop and tumbled to the stone floor. She landed hard, absorbing most of the impact on one shoulder. She felt jarring, burning pain shoot through the joint and felt one of her wings crack as it bent at an angle beneath her weight. The pain nauseated her, and spots swam in her vision.

Fighting panic, Aliisza rolled to a sitting position to face her oncoming attackers. The ground seemed to have ceased pitching, and the trio was closing the distance with her. She fumbled to bring her magical blade to bear, trying to pull it free of the confining net, but the tangle of hemp strands made her efforts fruitless.

Aliisza gave up and frantically fumbled a hand toward one of her pouches. She knew a spell she could cast without speaking, one that would permit her to transform into a puddle of liquid. If she could summon the magic to do so, she reasoned, she might be able to slip away by oozing through the gap between the shutters. But she needed a pinch of gelatin to conjure the transformation. She slipped her hand inside the pouch and began fumbling for the packet of powder.

Her seemingly endless streak of bad luck continued.

The priestess, a lackey of Torm judging from the markings upon her breastplate, loomed over the half-fiend. She hit Aliisza hard on one shoulder with her mace. The blow hurt, knocking her back and sending the contents of her pouch tumbling onto the floor beneath the writing table in the center of the room. The crushing strike sent spidery pain all through the alu's body, unnatural holy burning that caused Aliisza to cry out, though no sound could escape her lips.

The alu tried to roll backward, to swing her feet over her head to end in a crouch, but the netting hindered her. In frustration, she kicked out at the priestess, but the woman sidestepped and smacked her mace against the half-fiend's ankle, sending another jolt of agonizing pain through her body.

As Aliisza crumpled in injury and exhaustion, the hateful priestess stood proudly over her, brandishing the blessed weapon. Something inside the alu, a deep-rooted survival instinct that she could feel but not understand, overcame her. She named it cowardice, an unwelcome trait undoubtedly inherited from her human father. She loathed herself for succumbing to it, even as she raised her arms in defeat.

The priestess never stopped smiling as she swung the heavy weapon down, slamming it into Aliisza's forehead.

All the world melted away in a torrent of pain and blackness.

❖ ❖ ❖ ❖ ❖ ❖ ❖ ❖

"Remember, no unnecessary risks," Vhok instructed his lieutenant. "The legion will grow restless, but keep them out of sight." He gazed at the city of Sundabar in the distance, illuminated by watch fires along the walls.

Rorgak nodded. "They will question why," he said, giving Vhok an expectant glance.

"Theirs is not to question," the cambion snapped. "Explain to those who do that it had better not get back to me. The wait will be worth it."

A chill wind blew across the low hillock where he, his lieutenant, and Lysalis stood. Around the three of them, the half-frozen grasses of the Rauvin Valley rustled. The ice that coated the scrub crackled in the wind, reminding Vhok of dissonant bells. He shivered, finding the arctic breezes unpleasant on his hot skin.

"Make sure you maintain the illusion that I am still here," the cambion warned. "The tent and guards remain in place. I have set the wards to permit you to enter. The cloaking magic will keep prying eyes and ears from learning that you are actually alone when you 'receive' new orders from me."

The red-scaled, hulking tanarukk nodded again. "I will visit you daily," he said. Then, after a lingering silence, he asked, "What of Aliisza? What should I tell her if she returns?"

She won't, Vhok thought. Not if we're lucky. Out loud, he

said, "Tell her the truth. Explain to her that I have undertaken a separate, secret mission to retrieve powerful magic to aid us in the impending conquest. She will discover it in due time herself, regardless. She has access to the tent."

"You don't think she's going to return," the tanarukk lieutenant said, as much a question as a statement.

Vhok shrugged, not wishing to give away what he already knew. "As always, she plots her own course, whatever instructions I give her. She . . . intrigues me that way," he said, more to himself than to his subordinate. It was a good lie, because it was still the truth.

Rorgak knew better than to respond to such a comment. Instead, the lieutenant asked, "How long will you be away?"

Vhok considered his answer before he lied again. "A day or two, maybe three."

Any longer, the cambion thought, and Rorgak might decide it was time to start commanding and do something impetuous. Vhok knew full well that the burly officer relished the chance to control the seething, war-crazed legion. He harbored no doubts that his lieutenant had designs of taking over for him some day—with or without Kaanyr Vhok's blessings.

Far in the future, Vhok silently insisted. I am not done with them yet.

"Good travels, then," Rorgak replied, saluting.

The cambion returned the gesture and looked at Lysalis. She mentally commanded the magic that whisked the two of them deep under the surface.

Rorgak's competence was already gone from the cambion's thoughts when he and his sorceress appeared upon the spiral steps within the abandoned Forge Tower. He could feel that the heat was more oppressive than the last time he had visited.

The fey'ri magic must be going well, he thought.

Vhok ascended the staircase and stepped into view of his minions, still hard at work magically disrupting the Everfire. He saw evidence of a recent battle atop the tower. One of the fey'ri sorcerers lay unmoving, his skin blackened, and several others showed signs of injuries. A pair of the demonic elves perched on the edge of the roof, wands in their hands, gazing down into the depths of the chamber below.

Lysalis surveyed the situation, examining the dead and wounded fey'ri and studying the floor far below. She turned to Vhok and caught his eye, then gave a jerk of her head to indicate that he should see what was transpiring. The cambion strolled to the edge and peered over the side.

The Everfire roared and bucked, sloshing scalding hot liquid rock. It swelled and spilled over the sides of its channel, sliding across the vast floor and cooling in uneven mounds. Dwarves had scattered throughout the cavern, furiously working to stop the onslaught of fiery destruction. Their efforts were hampered by the churning lava, the magical attacks from the sorcerers on the tower, and a horde of tanarukks that pressed the attack directly.

Some of the dwarves had formed a shield wall. They defended a second, smaller group from attack, fighting to keep the swarming tanarukks away from their charges while the smaller collection worked magic. The wizards, clerics, and sorcerers struggled to repel the mass of fiendish orcs. At the same time, they flung destructive magic at the sorcerers atop the tower.

Even as Vhok watched, a sizzling nugget of fire soared upward from the cluster of arcane spellcasters. He recognized the fireball well before it reached him. The cambion chuckled as the blast of searing fire erupted all around him. The burst singed the heated air, but he and his sorcerers remained unscathed.

The diversion seemed well in hand, so the cambion looked at Lysalis. "It's time to go," he said. He pointed to an overhang of natural rock jutting from the cavern wall near the sloshing, churning Everfire. "Whisk us over there, please," he instructed the sorceress.

Lysalis gave Vhok a slightly chagrined look and shrugged. "You've had me whisking you here and there all evening," she said. "I can't perform that particular trick again for a while. At least not until I rest and recuperate."

Vhok frowned, eyeing the vast space between the base of the tower and the promontory he sought. "Then I guess we'll get there the old-fashioned way," he said, pulling his long sword, Burnblood, free of its scabbard. "We'll drop down on the far side and work our way around those sluice channels, which will give us some cover from the fight. Over the side it is, then."

The fey'ri nodded, chanted a few lines of sorcery, and moved to join him on the far side of the tower. Together, they stepped off the edge and began to plummet toward the bottom. Near the halfway mark of the fall, Vhok invoked an innate ability and immediately slowed his descent, creating a magical disk of force beneath himself and levitating upon it in the air. Beside him, Lysalis also slowed, though her reduced speed hinted at a gentle drifting, as though she were light as a feather.

Two different tricks, similar outcome, Vhok chuckled. "Race you down," he called, allowing his disk to accelerate its descent. He dropped below his sorcerous minion and reached the rough-hewn floor of the great cavern a few heartbeats before she did.

As soon as Lysalis joined the commander of the Scourged Legion, they crept around to survey the battlefield. The dwarves were hard pressed on two sides. It wasn't quite a flanking maneuver, but it served its purpose well enough, pinning the stout folk and keeping them away from the Everfire. It appeared the cambion and his fey'ri sorceress could reach the wall unhindered and unnoticed, as long as they stayed on the far side of the sluice channels, which were overflowing with lava.

Kaanyr Vhok nodded to himself in satisfaction and began to trot across open ground, angling toward the nearest channel. Lysalis fell in close behind him. If the pair could reach the barrier unseen, then they could follow its length to the Everfire itself without engaging the enemy. Though he would enjoy beheading a dwarf or two, Vhok felt a greater sense of urgency to reach that point of rock and begin his journey.

As the pair of half-fiends made their way toward their destination, a small group of dwarves appeared from a side tunnel nearby. They noticed the pair of demonic visitors and immediately charged across the gap toward them. Vhok sighed in exasperation. So much for staying out of sight, he thought. He went into a defensive crouch, counting enemies. There were nearly a dozen.

A billowing cloud of steam erupted across the cambion's field of vision as Lysalis generated a magical effect aimed at the dwarves. Vhok could feel the tingle of extreme cold, though he did not experience the damaging effects of it. As the cloud of steam dissipated in the scorching air, Vhok could see that more than half the dwarves had fallen. A thin rime, all crystalline white, coated them, and though the ice was melting quickly, it had done its job.

The remaining four dwarves rushed on, and Vhok could see more entering from the same side cavern nearby.

We don't have time for this, the cambion thought in mild irritation as he slashed at the first dwarf opponent. As much fun as this is, if the main battle group notices us, we'll never get through.

The blade he wielded, an ancient elven weapon crafted during the height of Aryvandaar, carved through the dwarf's shield and gashed deeply into his neck and shoulder. With a grunt of pain, the stout one stumbled away, his place taken by another. Vhok swung again, but his new foe was more wary and stepped back. They began their dance, Vhok and his fey'ri companion, working side by side to keep the heavily armored dwarf soldiers at bay.

A rapid series of glowing darts shot from Lysalis's fingertips, pummeling her closest opponent directly in the face. The dwarf screamed and dropped to one knee, clutching his face with his gauntleted hands. Vhok took the opportunity to slip his sword between the segmented plates of his armor, silencing him. Even as the dwarf toppled, the cambion spun to parry the slashing attack of another dwarf with an oversized battle hammer.

As Vhok dropped his last enemy, Lysalis grunted in pain. The cambion turned to see her reel from a dwarf who had slammed her with his spiked shield. Her face was ashen and her expression spoke of agonizing pain. She slumped down next to the cambion, gasping for breath.

"Blessed!" she managed to blurt out, her eyes growing wide with horror. "Beware its power!"

Vhok was no longer watching the fey'ri, though. Upon hearing her warning, he turned his full attention upon the dwarf with the deadly shield.

❖ ❖ ❖ ❖ ❖ ❖ ❖ ❖

As Myshik worked his way through the abandoned stronghold, a faint sound reached the half-dragon's ears. The ringing clang of battle softly resonated, the iron tones of clashing steel reverberating from somewhere ahead.

Puzzled, Myshik made his way higher through the stronghold, climbing the tiers one by one. When he was perhaps two-thirds of the way to the top, the stone beneath his feet rumbled and bucked, nearly knocking him to the ground. The half-hobgoblin stumbled and fell against the wall, which cracked threateningly along its base. Echoing reverberations thundered through the cavern, accompanied by the sounds of cracking and falling stone.

The earth sounds angry, he thought, concerned. Who makes it so?

Regaining his balance, Myshik resumed his pace, working toward a bridge in the distance. When he arrived at the causeway, the half-dragon gazed doubtfully at it and peered down into the chasm it crossed. As before, near the entry gate, a great crease divided the chamber, both above and below. The dwarves had utilized the obstruction to their advantage in preparing their defense. The chasm divided the topmost tier from the rest of the stronghold, a natural barrier impossible to cross in force.

Myshik took a few tentative steps onto the causeway, testing its integrity. It seemed stable enough, so he began to cross. As he neared the apex of the curved slab of rock, he felt another vibration and started to run. He had almost reached the far side when another deafening rumble rocked the stronghold. The force of the earthquake pitched the half-dragon forward, dropping him to his knees. A great booming crack jarred him and everything around him. Overhead, molten rock burst from the crevasse and spilled down, forming a magmafall that tumbled, hissing and smoking, into the chasm below. It struck the causeway mere feet behind the half-hobgoblin, scorching the air all around him and blasting him with terrible heat. The bridge groaned and trembled beneath the onslaught of the fiery stone cascading down atop it.

Myshik scrambled forward, away from the great heat, staggering off the causeway and away from the edge of the chasm. The bridge shuddered and groaned behind him, then it shattered and tumbled away, falling into the great crevasse below along with the stream of lava.

Myshik stared wide-eyed at the remains of the bridge jutting out into space, where he had been standing only moments previous. Even where he sat, the heat was oppressive, and he feared that spattering gobs of viscous liquid stone would strike him if he remained. Scrambling to his feet once more, the half-dragon put distance between himself and the deadly magmafall.

More rumbling earthquakes shook the environment as Myshik hurried ever upward. More than once, he was forced to evade falling debris or to leap cracks that formed suddenly across his path. He warily eyed the ceiling, wondering how much longer the cavern could remain intact under the onslaught of the seismic assault.

At last, Myshik reached the peak of the stronghold. He found a great winding staircase leading upward into the stone ceiling. Above, he thought he could hear the ring of steel on steel, the telltale sounds of furious battle. He hesitated for a moment, questioning the stability of the path and what he might encounter at the top. When yet another reverberation made him stumble and sent a large wall tumbling down to spill debris in his direction, the half-dragon began running up the steps two at a time.

The staircase twisted up and up. The sounds of fighting grew louder, more distinct. Myshik gripped his battle-axe firmly, expecting to hoist it at any moment. The stone around him continued to grumble and groan, and the steps beneath his feet shuddered and bounced.

At last the stairway ended, rising up from the depths into

another great chamber. A columned cupola had once stood over the opening of the stairway, which lay in the midst of a subterranean plaza. The stonework of the cupola had tumbled down around the opening, though whether the destruction had happened moments or centuries before, the half-dragon was not certain.

Ancient buildings lined three sides of the plaza. The fourth faced what Myshik suspected must be the source of the magma which had nearly sent him plummeting to his death. A great river of it flowed on the far side of the chamber. The lava churned and sloshed, spilling over the sides of its natural channel, oozing across the floor.

Between Myshik and the expanding lake of lava, a great battle raged between a paltry force of dwarves and a swarming, snarling horde of orcs. Myshik blinked, for he had never seen orcs like them before. Unlike the filthy creatures Clan Morueme routinely battled on the surface, along the slopes of the Nether Mountains overhead, the creatures attacking the dwarves were diabolical in nature, more fiendish in their aspect.

Myshik decided they must be part of the army that served Kaanyr Vhok, the cambion his father had spoken of. He had found the object of his quest at last. With a grin, Myshik hefted high his war axe, stolen from a dwarven tomb long centuries before, and charged into the fray with an eager cry. Several dwarves turned to face the charging half-dragon.

Dread filled their eyes.

CHAPTER FOUR

Vhok stepped over the fallen Lysalis, straddling her, thrusting and feinting with his blade. The dwarf gave the cambion's ancient elven sword a wary eye and parried each stroke and thrust with both shield and axe. Vhok's quickness gave him pause, even though the cambion had to remain in place to defend his injured companion.

The dwarf shifted tactics, circling around Vhok more rapidly, using his parries to knock Burnblood to the side. Vhok realized what his foe's intentions were. He was trying to force the cambion off balance by making him spin in place while mindful of stepping on Lysalis. The dwarf had no interest in getting in close and engaging his foe. He merely wanted to tire the half-fiend and force him into a deadly error.

Time to end this, Vhok decided after another parry from the dwarf whipped his sword arm out to one side.

The cambion feigned a stagger, as though he had over-balanced and tripped on the fey'ri's writhing form. When the dwarf saw the stumble, he charged forward, ready to deliver a killing blow with his axe.

Vhok freed his scepter from his belt with his other hand. With a mighty swing, he smashed the magical rod hard against the shield. There was a roaring burst of sound, and Vhok felt the satisfying crack of a sundered shield beneath his blow.

The dwarf staggered back and fell on his rump. Vhok maneuvered to avoid stumbling over Lysalis. By the time he stepped free of the fey'ri sorceress, the dwarf was up on one knee. Vhok expected him to flee, but at that moment, his eyes flickered toward something behind the cambion. Vhok risked a glance back. What he saw made him groan in exasperation.

A full dozen or so additional dwarves poured from the same tunnel that had disgorged the initial group. They trotted toward the demonic lord, their armor and weapons clanking rhythmically.

Damn them and their stubborn ways! And damn me for thinking how clever it would be to lure them all in here! I should be careful what I wish for.

Vhok growled to himself and turned his gaze to the dwarf with the sundered shield. The stout fellow seemed to have recovered his wits. He held a second hand axe in place of the ruined shield and came at the cambion again. Vhok let his foe make one sweeping slash. Without the hindrance of standing over Lysalis, he could maneuver much more easily. He sidestepped the attack and counterthrust with his blade in a single fluid motion. The strike penetrated the dwarf's armor right at the armpit, slipping through the gap in the metal plates. The dwarf grunted as Vhok shoved the blade deeper, a sound that turned into a wet gurgle as the half-demon punctured a lung. Before the humanoid dropped to the floor, Vhok had yanked his blade free and turned.

The dozen oncoming dwarves were still thirty paces away. Though they moved tirelessly, their short legs and heavy armor prevented them from gaining much speed. Vhok decided he could outrun them, even with the burden of his compatriot, noting that he was near the lava sluice. He could feel the heat radiating from where molten rock had overflowed the channel. It hissed and steamed as it cooled in great, gooey piles on either side. Acrid smoke wafted past him from the sizzling, bubbling liquid stone.

The cambion bent down and scooped up Lysalis, who was panting and gasping, her skin turning a sickly gray color. Slinging the petite fey'ri over his shoulder, he began to trot toward the promontory of rock.

"Zasian will heal you," he said to the sorceress as he loped along. If he ever gets here, the cambion added silently. We could use his help right now.

"Hurry!" Lysalis gasped. "It burns!"

The dwarves, seeing Vhok's intention to flee, picked up their pace, too. Despite their difficulties in moving quickly, Vhok could see that they were going to cut him off from his destination. Lysalis slowed Vhok too much to outrun them. He slowed as he realized it was fruitless to continue. He eased her off his shoulders and let her settle at his feet once more.

Blast and damn, he seethed. He began to consider that he might have to leave her in order to save himself.

Cursed Vigilant! he silently oathed. Their name suits them only too well.

The dwarves fanned out and formed two semicircular lines as they moved to surround the pair. The first rank presented their shields. They were too few in number to form a proper shield wall, but they created a practical barrier. Vhok might have been able to force his way between them, but at great cost. Behind the shields, a second line cocked heavy crossbows. The stout folk intended to keep their targets pinned down, unable to escape, while they remained at a distance from their enemies and the heat, then wear the intruders down with missile fire.

Desperately, Vhok muttered the chant of one of the hand-ful of spells he knew. He felt a large magical disk of force wink into existence in front of him, even though he couldn't see it. As the magical shield materialized, the dwarves fired their first volley. Though most of the missiles struck the magical barrier and bounced harmlessly away, one of the projectiles grazed his shoulder, creasing his skin and causing a thin line of blood to well there. He clamped his mouth shut to stifle an angry outburst, not wanting to give his enemies the satisfaction of knowing they'd bloodied him.

As the dwarves reloaded, Vhok swore again and peered around. Behind him stood the churning, overflowing lava sluice. He could feel the great heat emanating from it, a nice deterrent against the dwarves coming any closer. But there was no way he could get through the molten muck and up to the top of the sluice wall, especially while carrying the wounded sorceress. Though the heat didn't trouble him, it would be nigh impossible to clamber through something the consistency of thick porridge. Even with the benefit of his magical shield, the dwarves would fill him with crossbow bolts before he ever slipped away, if the stuff didn't harden around his legs and trap him there.

Unless . . .

The cambion squatted down and fished around in Lysalis's pouches, seeking the wand he had seen her use earlier. He yanked it from a bag on her hip and gripped her face with his other hand. She was fading rapidly.

"The trigger word!" he said, making her focus her eyes on him. "What is the command word for this?" He held the wand in her field of vision to aid her understanding.

" 'Glacious,' " Lysalis mumbled, her eyes glazing over.

Vhok stood and aimed the wand, not at the dwarves but at the lava near his feet. He spoke the word the fey'ri had given him. A ray of frosty crystals erupted from the tip, churning into a billowing cloud of hissing vapor as it struck the molten rock. The steam surrounded the cambion and obscured his vision. He felt comfortable warmth envelop him, but cries of protest and pain emanated from several dwarves as the super-heated vapor reached them.

Before him, the magic yielded the desired effect. The lava cooled and hardened to black stone. Safely hidden within the shroud of steam, the cambion took one tentative step upon the blackened stone and found that although it was spongy, it held his weight.

Excellent, the half-fiend thought. Not waiting to see how long his cover would last, Vhok bent low, grabbed Lysalis, and hoisted her on his shoulders. He took several steps onto the hardened lava, and when he felt it beginning to give way beneath him, he discharged another blast of frosty magic from the wand. Clouds of steam billowed up all around him, emitting harsh seething sounds.

He progressed forward and upward. Each time the hot stone became too soft, he chilled it with the magic of the wand to keep going. Each blast also served to hide him from the furious dwarves, who continued to fire at him. The magical barrier he had erected served him well, and the missiles did not reach him.

Eventually, Vhok could no longer proceed. The ascent was too steep to negotiate without the use of his hands, which held both the wand and the groaning, thrashing bundle on his back. Frowning, Vhok blasted the lava several times in succession, following a line all the way to the top of the ever-increasing slope. The resultant cloud of steam billowed so thickly that for a moment, the cambion could hardly see his hand in front of his face.

He tucked the wand away and pulled out his scepter. With

several powerful swings, he gouged indentations into the surface of the hardened rock. Each strike created a deep boom that echoed around him, drawing more missile fire.

Lysalis cried out and jerked, nearly toppling the two of them backward before Vhok managed to regain his balance. He suspected she had been struck by one of the bolts, but he dared not stop to see if she was still alive. Again he considered leaving her and making good his own escape, but he loathed abandoning her—or rather, abandoning the treasure trove of magic she carried.

Determined to continue on, Vhok chopped a column of indentations into the face of the stone, staggering them slightly. When they were as high as he could reach, he tucked the scepter away and began using them like a ladder, pulling himself up by both feet and one hand, one step at a time.

At last, he reached the top of the sluice wall. He eyed the glowing, roiling barrier of fiery magma as it churned through the channel, spilling over the sides. The steam was dissipating by then, and Vhok could see that the sluice was only five feet wide. With one mighty thrust of his legs, he leaped across to the opposite side. Not pausing, he pushed himself forward again, using his momentum to increase the distance of his second jump.

Well clear of the majority of the oozing magma spilling down that side, the cambion drew on his innate fiendish power of levitation and slowed his fall. He wobbled to a stop and worked to keep his balance, no small feat with the burden on his shoulders raising his center of gravity. He stabilized himself and gently descended to the floor, leaving the great stone channel behind him as a barrier between himself and his pursuers.

The mists Vhok had created to hide his escape were much thinner on that side, and even as he strode forward to breach them, they dissipated, giving him a good view of the terrain. Vhok could see the promontory of rock directly in front of him. He had a clear shot to that place across an open plaza. More importantly, Vhok spied Zasian there. The priest had reached their departure point and waited for him.

But his clever escape had managed to put the cambion more directly in the midst of the large battle. And the massive cloud of vapor Vhok had created also attracted unwanted attention. A number of dwarves broke off from the primary fight with the tanarukks and moved to investigate the disturbance. As he emerged from the cloak of steam, Vhok discovered dwarves directly interposed between him and his destination. Seeing the half-fiend, the dwarves gave a collective shout and advanced at a rapid trot, raising their weapons.

Not again, the cambion groaned to himself. In desperation, he pulled the arctic wand free and aimed it at the oncoming dwarves, hoping to blast his way through them. But when he uttered the trigger word, nothing happened. He had exhausted its magical power. Vhok threw the worthless stick away, snarling. He doubted he had the strength to bull his way through another pack of dwarves.

At that moment, a figure charged from the ruins of a cupola along one side of the plaza. The figure raced across the open ground, heading straight toward the dwarves. As the creature waded into the midst of them, swinging a huge war axe, Vhok recognized it. It belonged to the Blood of Morueme, the ferocious draconic hobgoblins sired by the Clan Morueme dragons.

The cambion heard a sharp, concussive thump as the half-hobgoblin struck, then saw one of the Vigilant sail several paces through the air before landing with a muted splash in a patch of lava that had spilled over and seeped close. The dwarf screamed in agony and tried to escape, but the conflagration that erupted around him quickly silenced his cries.

At the same time, a massive stone wall appeared in the plaza. The barrier divided the dwarves and sealed a significant number of them away from Vhok and the half-dragon, but it left an open alley to reach the promontory. The rest of the stout folk still advanced.

Vhok looked up, knowing where the stone wall had come from. As he gazed over at Zasian, the priest gestured frantically for the cambion to hurry.

With hope of victory restored, Vhok drew his blade and strode forward to cut his way through the dwarves as best he could with Lysalis draped over his shoulder. The sorceress had become still, and he feared she was already dead. As he fought, Vhok kept an eye on the Morueme half-breed and worked to reach the half-hobgoblin's side, hoping to benefit from his protection. Each time the half-dragon's huge axe connected with a foe, Vhok could hear a loud pounding as the enemy it struck was knocked backward with preternatural force. The half-hobgoblin used the weapon to good effect, aiming his blows to slam his victims into other dwarves, cutting a swath for himself to reach Vhok.

When they at last met, the cambion tilted his head once in acknowledgment of thanks. He eyed the mighty weapon his new companion wielded, and noted that it was dwarven in make.

No wonder they're so angry, Vhok thought with a chuckle.

The half-hobgoblin returned the nod and kept swinging, plowing a gap through angry, howling dwarves. Step by step, they made their way together toward the Everfire and Zasian.

At last, the few remaining dwarves had stomached all they wanted of the fierce cambion and his unusual companion, and they fell back. A few of them fired crossbows at Vhok and the others, but Zasian acted quickly, erecting another wall of stone to block their line of sight. The cambion and the half-hobgoblin crossed the remainder of the plaza unmolested. The two of them scrambled up to the point of rock where Zasian waited.

At last, exhausted, Vhok set Lysalis at Zasian's feet. Breathing heavily, he gestured at the fallen sorceress. "She is badly wounded," he told the priest. "Struck by some holy weapon that seems to be taking her life. Can you revive her?"

Zasian frowned and knelt beside the fey'ri, who had lapsed into unconsciousness. "I will try," he said, "but my healing skills are elementary compared to my other talents."

Vhok turned and looked at the half-hobgoblin. The half-dragon wiped some of the blood off his axe, using a tattered cloak he had torn from a dead dwarf.

"My thanks for your aid in this fight today, Son of Morueme," Vhok said. "What brings you to the Everfire in the midst of my battle with the tempestuous dwarves?" He suspected he already knew the answer, but he wanted to see how the half-dragon would reply.

The creature bowed deeply. "I bid you greetings, Sceptered One. I am Myshik Morueme. I come on behalf of my father, Roraurim, and my uncle, Nahaunglaroth, Lords of Dragon-doom, Masters of the Cerulean Skies, Patriarchs of Clan Morueme. I have been instructed to join with you and offer my services on your impending journey." The half-hobgoblin smiled.

Vhok eyed Myshik critically for a moment. He doubted the dragons' offer was completely magnanimous, pact or no, and he desired no spies in his midst as he began his journey to reach the Lifespring.

"Your father asked you to accompany me? His offer is most generous, but where I travel, you do not wish to follow."

Myshik smirked. "My father instructed me to keep a close eye on you in the event that you would not accept his invitation." The half-dragon paused, as if weighing his next words carefully. "I would do his bidding, but I do not relish a game of chase with you. I know you have little reason to trust me, despite your new alliance with our clan, but I am most curious about the great Kaanyr Vhok, commander of the Scourged Legion. I could be of great assistance on this journey of yours, as I hope I have already proven," he said, hoisting his axe for emphasis. "Please consider permitting me to accompany you. It would be something of an honor."

"There's nothing I can do for her," Zasian said, rising to his feet. "Whatever poisoned her is beyond my ken to assuage."

Vhok looked down at Lysalis, who opened her eyes and stared up at the cambion with trepidation. Then he looked at Myshik again. "You do not even know where I'm going. You're not prepared for this journey, believe me."

"Indeed," the half-dragon replied. "I am at a disadvantage, but I believe I can hold my own if you give me an opportunity."

Vhok sighed and pondered the offer for a moment. With Lysalis near death, he was short a member of his expedition. Very well, he silently decided. He has proven formidable enough to take a chance.

Drawing his sword, Vhok took hold of Lysalis's right hand and sliced it from her arm. The fey'ri screamed in pain and passed out.

The cambion removed a ring from one of her fingers and handed the magical band to Myshik. "Put this on, then," he said, dropping the hand beside the maimed sorceress.

The half-hobgoblin took the ring from Vhok and examined it carefully. A set of four stones—ruby, emerald, sapphire, and garnet—had been inset into the gold band.

"What does it do?" he asked, appraising the ring with a critical eye.

"It keeps you from being turned into a cinder as we cross through the Everfire into the Elemental Plane of Fire," Vhok replied.

Myshik's eyes grew wide for an instant, then he nodded and slipped the ring on his clawed finger. The band immediately adjusted to fit perfectly.

"I am ready," he said.

"So it would seem," Vhok replied, wondering how long the half-dragon would survive. "Let's go." Turning to Zasian, the cambion said, "Lead the way."

The priest nodded and moved to the end of the outcropping, where it hung over the churning river of lava. He stood there a moment, surveying the maelstrom of fiery liquid below and twisting a ring, identical in design to the one Vhok had given to Myshik. He selected a spot and jumped off the perch. Zasian fell into the molten rock and disappeared beneath the surface.

Vhok and Myshik followed.

◆ ◆ ◆ ◆ ◆ ◆ ◆ ◆

Aliisza found herself flowing. Nothing surrounded her but a formless gray void. Up and down held no meaning. She was weightless, drifting. She thought to unfurl her wings, to fly in some direction or other, but strangely, the sensation of having wings was absent. She knew where they should be, knew how to control them, but they seemed to be . . . gone.

The alu tried to remember how she came to be there. Her

head swam. She recalled a struggle; she had been injured. The mace! Aliisza remembered the priestess, and the weapon she wielded. It had come right down on her head. There had been a deafening crack of metal on bone, a blinding flash of light, then . . . nothing.

Is this the Abyss? the half-fiend wondered. Am I dead? No, that cannot be. I have no soul. I cannot exist beyond my body.

A flash of blinding light filled her vision, and Aliisza gasped and flinched. Something else had arrived within the void, and it hovered near her, a presence. It was cold and hot at the same time. She could feel power emanating from it. She squinted against the painful, radiant light and took a peek.

She could barely make out a figure, a creature similar to herself, but unlike anything Aliisza had ever seen before. It looked vaguely like a man, though it seemed much taller than any human the alu had ever laid eyes on. After a moment, the intensity of the glow surrounding it diminished. She could see the rich brown skin of its bare chest, but its legs were hidden beneath loose white leggings, or a kilt of some sort. As she gazed at the thing's face, she found its features nothing short of beautiful. Two great, feathered wings sprouted from its back. It hovered before her, surveying her with the gentlest expression of sympathy and caring. Aliisza was both repulsed and drawn to it.

Without warning, a deep rumble shook the void and a gargantuan shadow fell across the creature and Aliisza. The half-fiend let out a startled gasp and spun in place, trying to detect its source. A great stone wall, made of boulders as big as caverns, burst into view nearby, sliding through the void as if it grew from a ground that didn't exist. It rose up and past them, out of sight, looming over the pair. A second wall joined the first, sliding into place with a reverberation so low Aliisza felt it more than heard it. Then a third, and a forth—four massive stone edifices, surrounding her and her companion. And Aliisza was no longer floating, but lying on her back upon a stone floor that was simply there. She hadn't seen it arrive, like the walls. It just *was*.

The alu stared everywhere. She had the feeling of being inside a massive fortress, solid and forbidding. The walls bore no doors, no windows. No light illuminated the place, as far as she could see, but she could see, and it wasn't just her dark-attuned eyes. The whole place shone with its own inner light, though it wasn't warm and glowing, like the being with her. It was power and force, unyielding strength.

Aliisza looked up. A second figure stood upon a balcony, staring down. Shining plate armor completely encased the warrior, who stood motionless, watching. From the glint of it, Aliisza guessed the armor might be pure mithral. Though she could not see the figure's eyes, she could feel its gaze upon her, and the sensation was more than a little unsettling.

"Remain here," the creature beside her said, then ascended into the air by means of his feathery white wings.

The alu found his motion elegant and watched him with interest as he flew upward to the balcony near the top of the forbidding tower. The creature landed upon the balcony and bowed deeply to the armored figure. The two seemed to engage in a long conversation, and after a time, the celestial being took to the air and descended once more.

As he landed, he curled his wings against himself, a frown upon his face. "Well," he said, almost to himself, "The moment of truth."

"Do you understand the question put before you?" a voice asked, reverberating through the limitless tower.

Aliisza wasn't sure how she knew it was the armored figure, but she knew. It chilled her, made her tremble where she lay upon the floor. It was the voice of a god.

Aliisza turned toward the angelic figure, though it hurt her eyes to look directly upon him. He looked back at her, his face an expression of earnest seriousness. There had been a question?

"You must surrender willingly," the creature said. "I cannot coerce you in any way to abide by the terms. Do you understand this?"

Aliisza tried to shake her head, but could barely move it. She had no strength. "I don't—how can—what terms?" she finally managed to whisper. "Who are you?"

The celestial creature smiled then, and Aliisza found the expression strangely soothing and troubling at the same time. She knew it was genuine, that there was nothing but complete forthrightness in everything he said and did. But there was holy power in that gaze, too, and such divine energy twisted Aliisza's insides, made her cringe in discomfort. They were so opposite, such clashing energy. She could barely abide his presence. She wondered if he felt similar discomfort from her.

"None of those questions require answers at the moment," the creature said, still smiling. "Though I will answer them to the best of my ability once you make a decision. But you must choose first, right now. First, you must understand that, until you agree, there is no compulsion upon you. Once you agree, you will be magically and divinely bound to honor the terms. Know, though, that if you reject my offer, of your own free will, your life is forfeit and the soul of your unborn child will journey to the House of the Triad, to become a petitioner there."

The meaning of the words rushed through Aliisza's weakened body, made her tingle with realization. The knowledge exploded like a thousand candles, all at once, in her mind. She carried a child. The half-fiend knew that the radiant creature standing over her, so powerful and frightening all at the same time, spoke the truth. She *did* carry a baby within her. Though she'd had no inkling of the situation until that very moment, she knew—no, felt—the truth of it in her bones. She was pregnant.

The thought of bearing a child did not thrill the alu, nor did it dismay her. She had often considered propagating with Kaanyr. It was a pragmatic consideration, fostering offspring that might someday aid in Aliisza's conquests of power. But she also knew that a child born of a union of two half-fiends would likely harbor its own ambitions, its own lusts for dominion. It would want to claim its birthright, and the two creatures standing in its way would be Kaanyr and Aliisza. Just as the cambion had slain his own mother years before, in order to claim her control over the Scourged Legion, so, too, would Kaanyr's whelp eventually try to exterminate its parents in a quest for its rightful place at the top of the pack.

So the alu had always held in check her enthusiasm for reproducing. And she never felt any maternal instincts, any secret joys at the thought of having a baby. At least, she hadn't believed she had, until that very moment. But suddenly, with the celestial creature's utterance of one simple phrase, she knew she had to protect her unborn child.

"So?" the creature asked. "What say you?"

"I still do not know the terms you offer," Aliisza answered, frightened of choosing to abide by anything a holy creature would lay before her, but equally as frightened of the alternative.

"We will travel to the House of the Triad together. For the duration of your pregnancy, you will remain a guest of the Triad, in a habitat suitable for your creature comforts. You will not attempt to escape, nor shall you attempt to cause harm to another in any fashion, either through word or deed. You may choose to spend the duration of your visit on any mental exercises that appeal to you; no one will impose any rhetoric, lectures, or moral tests on you unless you wish it.

"Shall you break any of these rules, your life shall immediately be forfeit, and the spirit of your unborn shall immediately transform into a petitioner in the service of the House of the Triad. At the end of your pregnancy, once you have given birth, you will be called before a tribunal of judges to stand trial for your crimes against the many you have wronged throughout your life."

Aliisza's head swam. She could remain alive, so long as she was a good girl. But it seemed too easy, too simple. The alu suspected a catch.

"How do I know you are dealing honestly with me?" she asked.

The creature seemed surprised. "You have my word," he said, "though I'm not sure that it means much to a creature of your nature. However, given the alternative, I don't see how accepting what I offer can prove any worse."

Aliisza wanted to smirk. You'd be surprised, she thought.

There were times when she was certain that creatures suffering under her auspices would have preferred annihilation to the continued torturous existence she forced upon them. But the urge to protect her child from harm, to see it born, was strong. The thought of failing in that maternal duty was a cold knot in her stomach. She didn't understand why she was reacting so protectively for something she might not ordinarily care for, but she could not deny her feelings.

Besides, the alu thought, suppressing a grin. If nothing else, I will have more than half a year to plan my escape and retribution. I can abide by their oppressive rules and regulations for that long, surely.

Aliisza looked at the creature, who stared down at her, waiting for her to decide her fate, and the fate of the creature growing within her womb. "I accept your terms," she said.

"Of your own free will?"

"No one within this chamber coerces me," the alu responded. "No one compels me to say these words, nor do they manipulate me in any fashion. The decision is my own, freely given and without remorse."

Another blinding flash of light slammed Aliisza. She wanted to scream, but couldn't. The forbidding tower vanished, leaving her floating in the gray void once more before her body seemed to explode into a million pieces.

CHAPTER FIVE

The smell of sweet summer grass wafted into Aliisza's nostrils. She could feel a carpet of it beneath her, soft and warm. The scent was pure, almost overwhelming. It made her heady with arousal. The sun shone down upon her, not too hot, but pleasant, like a warm spring day. The glow of it bathed her in tranquility, soothed her every ache. The sound of insects and birds buzzing and chirping in the distance hummed in her ears. She felt life vibrating there, passion and sorrow and fear and death, all swirled together in a magnificent dance of existence.

In the void, she had forgotten how to feel. Her body had ceased to be for a while. In the new place, she felt more alive than she could ever remember. She existed more completely than at any time before. It was too much; she was afraid to open her eyes. Filled with trepidation mixed with yearning curiosity, she dug her fingers into the rich, damp soil to brace herself, and risked a glance.

To say she lay in a meadow would have been a poor excuse of a description, yet she could find no words to capture the raw energy and beauty of it. Every sight and sound, every sensation and color, every scent and movement breathed more life into

Aliisza. The intensity of it was almost painful. The alu stared at a copse of trees nearby. Flowering vines climbed the trunk of a dead tree closer to her, and she could detect their blossoms' fresh scent in the gentle breezes that caressed her skin. In the distance, she heard the faint gurgling of a stream.

As she took in more of her surroundings, Aliisza realized that the meadow seemed isolated, out of place. There was no horizon, no line of hills surrounding the edges, no forest in the distance. There was only brilliant azure sky. The world seemed to end on every side only a few paces in each direction.

The angelic creature stood beside her, and when she at last looked up to gaze at his face, that same radiant beauty shone from him, and it still hurt her eyes. It was raw energy, pure and sweet, like the land itself. She wanted to drink it in, yet it scalded her, left her feeling tainted in some way.

Beyond her guide, hazy in the distance, a great mountain reared up. It seemed close, very close, making the meadow where she lay feel alpine in nature. But it was all wrong. There was no beginning or end to it, no bottom or top. It simply appeared and disappeared, below and above, vanishing in all directions in white, puffy clouds. To the alu, it seemed more like a massive, forbidding cliff wall.

And it moved.

Aliisza sat up. She peered more closely at the mountain, thinking perhaps it was a trick of her imagination. Surely the clouds were drifting past, and the mountain was stationary. But no—as she gazed at it for several moments, she realized it definitely shifted against the closer surroundings of her meadow. The mountain was moving.

"Where are we?" Aliisza asked at last, turning to squint at her escort once more.

The creature squatted next to her. Aliisza flinched at his

proximity and averted her eyes, looking at the mountain as it drifted slowly from her left to her right.

"The House of the Triad," he answered.

The half-fiend jerked her gaze back to the angelic figure in surprise.

"What?" she asked. "This?"

The creature chuckled. "Yes," he said, "though I brought us to this spot because I thought it would not be quite the shock to you as elsewhere. I guess you were expecting something more . . . majestic?" When Aliisza didn't answer, he turned briefly and pointed to the mountain, still slowly sliding across the alu's field of vision, before meeting her gaze again. "Behind me, you can see Celestia, surrounded by three other peaks. Martyrdom serves as Ilmater's home, Trueheart is where Torm resides, and the Court, where we shall journey, serves as Tyr's residence. Perhaps that will be more what you envisioned."

The alu frowned. "Who was the armored one in the stone tower?" she asked.

"Ah, we were within Everwatch, the tower-home of Helm. All who come to the House first visit his domain to determine if they are worthy to continue on."

"And those he finds lacking?" Aliisza asked.

"They do not leave," the angelic figure replied, his mien grim. "But you satisfied his concern with your oath, so it is irrelevant. And to answer your question from before, I am Tauran, a servant of Tyr."

Aliisza stared around, and again at the gargantuan mountain, with a growing feeling of concern. My oath, she thought, thinking fully on what she had acceded to. Easily broken, she decided, amused at Tauran's foolish trust.

For the first time, the alu realized that she existed as she had before, prior to her battle with Zasian's intruders. She stood up and performed a cursory self-examination. All of her possessions were in their proper places. Her elven blade was strapped to her hip and leg, her pouches of magical triggers were tied to her belt, and she could feel all of her innate abilities at her command. She could employ magic to escape, she could draw her blade and run Tauran through, or beguile him with her considerable charm into doing as she wished.

She could do all those things—and yet she couldn't. The thought was there, but she had absolutely no desire. She reached for her sword, but the moment she gave thought to using it to fight her way free, her hand dropped to her side. She frowned, concentrating on moving her arm toward the weapon.

"I told you that once you agreed to the terms, you would be held to them, by magical coercion," Tauran said, his smile appearing a bit sad. "I cannot stop you from thinking the thoughts, nor would I want to. But until such time as you are safely ensconced in your quarters, you do not have the free will to act against the agreement you made."

Aliisza chuckled, but inside she was seething. She suddenly felt a puppet upon strings. She decided to try a different tactic.

"So, you brought me here to keep me all to yourself," the alu purred, moving closer to the angel. She wrapped her arms around his waist and nestled her head against his chest. "What are you going to do to me now?" she asked, giving him a sultry smile and invoking her preternatural charms. She strained very hard not to squint at his brilliance.

Tauran's sad smile turned to a look of pure sorrow as he gently disengaged himself from the half-fiend's embrace.

"Take a moment," he said. "Regain your wits. It is a startling adjustment from what you are used to, I am sure. We can remain here, in this meadow, for a few moments more, until you feel more at ease."

Aliisza stared balefully at her counterpart and withdrew. She practically stomped away from him, scowling, and folded her arms across her chest.

How impertinent! she thought. Suggesting I have lost my wits.

As the fury within her waned, the alu realized she was more dismayed than angry. The discovery that her charms were useless against the creature was unnerving. She was beginning to fret that she hadn't thought through the oath carefully enough.

What have I done? she asked herself in growing dread.

For a moment, she fought vertigo and claustrophobia all at once. The strange sense of not being able to act even while thinking about acting sent tremors of horror through her. She could not imagine feeling more helpless.

The panic did not last long. Aliisza reminded herself of all the various difficulties she had extricated herself from in her long years of life. She would find a way to succeed with Tauran, too. As her confidence returned, she looked at the angel once more, letting her eyes glitter with a suggestive hint of a smile.

"Oath or no, I don't see why we can't enjoy one another's company, hmm?" she said, sauntering toward him. "I promise I won't misbehave, if you promise to punish me when I do," she said, batting her eyes.

"You already promised not to misbehave—earlier, within Everwatch," Tauran replied, unmoved. Then a hint of a smirk grew on his face, too. "But I don't find your company unpleasant. Which is good, as we will likely be spending much time together. Now, are you ready to go?"

Aliisza pouted for a moment, then nodded.

"Then follow me," the celestial creature said, and took to the air.

As Aliisza unfurled her wings, she remembered that she had injured herself when she tried to escape Dwarf-friend's study. Spreading her appendages wide, she moved them experimentally. All traces of injury seemed to have vanished. She leaped into the air, soaring up into the sky, the sun warm on her pale skin. She almost felt happy.

Climbing higher into the sky, Aliisza was shocked to discover the true nature of the meadow. The grass and trees, even the small pond with a trickling brook, rested upon a chunk of rock that floated in the air. Shaped like some bizarre inverted pinnacle, the top of the hovering island had been smoothed flat, while the underside was twisted, jagged, and warped, as though violently torn from some larger place. The water from the stream fell over the side of the earthy edge, tumbling into space. Far below, Aliisza could see clouds, stretching as far as the eye could see.

Other floating islands, some much larger than the meadow where she and Tauran had arrived, drifted in view. All exhibited natural landscapes of varying climates. She spotted structures upon a few, far in the distance. She gazed at them in awe, noting that the earthen tracts didn't move in a coordinated or uniform way. No breezes sent them drifting.

Aliisza stared at the massive mountain, where she knew the gods lived. Suddenly, she understood. It was adrift as well, a mass of stone and earth so large that it dwarfed everything else around it. The clouds near the top parted for a moment, and she could see much more of the four peaks. She noted that Tauran's description of three shorter mounts surrounding a fourth, taller one, had been accurate. The nearest peak sloped severely upward, its surface a mix of rocky outcroppings, stands of stunted trees, and the white of snow pack. The very top seemed to have been sliced away, and the alu thought she could make out a gleam of white there, perhaps something polished, shining brightly in the sun. Then the clouds drifted across it once more, obscuring the view.

Tauran set an easy pace, and Aliisza was able to study her surroundings as they winged their way toward the slopes of the closest mountain.

Below, the alu could see more meadowlike floating islands. She noted that many teemed with life. The alu spotted a small group of insectoid creatures upon one of the islands, hard at work moving a large stone. At first Aliisza thought they were massive ants, but then she noticed that they stood upright and that some of them, the larger ones, employed simple weapons. She glanced at Tauran, raising her eyebrow in question.

"Formians," the angel explained. "Simple-minded creatures, governed by law above all else. They have little independent thinking, acquiescing to a hive mind in all things."

Sounds dreary, Aliisza thought, grimacing.

They moved on, flying higher, slowly approaching the upper flank of the nearest mountain. They ascended into the cloud cover and the alu felt a brief moment of moist chill. Then they broke through and she was stunned by the majesty of the place. As the distance shrank, Aliisza could see that her earlier guess had been correct. The top of the mountain had been leveled or shaped flat in some manner, and a great tiered building of white stone rested upon its crown. The outer facade was all columns and steps, and the sun glinted brightly off the smoothly polished surfaces. The alu could see that creatures came and went from the structure, which was easily the size of a small hamlet.

A pair of creatures took flight and angled straight at the two of them. Similar to Tauran in appearance, bronze-skinned and white-winged, they approached rapidly, bearing large maces. She gave another questioning look at Tauran, growing concerned that they intended to attack.

When the two creatures drew close enough, they pulled up and hovered. One of them eyed Aliisza with obvious distrust, while the other held up a hand, palm facing outward.

"Hail, Tauran. Why are you bringing this fiend to our doorstep?"

Tauran bowed and said, "Hail, Micus. This creature has submitted to me a willingness to abide by the strictures of our realm so that her unborn child may escape harm from her execution. I escort her now to the Court of Temperance for sentencing."

The angel named Micus nodded. "Excellent," he said. "May the blessings of Tyr grace you and your child," he said to Aliisza. Then, before she could answer, he and the other celestial creature turned and shot away, soaring low above the treetops.

Aliisza shivered. *The blessings of Tyr are the last things I expect to receive,* she thought as she watched them depart.

"Shall we continue?" Tauran asked.

The alu turned her attention toward her escort as they flew toward the great columned city ahead. "I fear I have agreed to much more than I bargained for," she said, her voice slightly amused. "You're all being too nice, too patient. There's a catch somewhere."

Tauran cast a meaningful glance over his shoulder at the alu as they neared a plaza cut into the mountain. It rested upon a tier about halfway up the side of the facade.

"When the soul of a being calls to us," the angel said as he alit upon the marble tiles of the plaza, "and requires aid in surviving and blossoming into a beautiful creature, we are overjoyed. It is the wish of all who dwell here that we might assist in raising high a spiritual being, to help it attain all of its glorious potential. There is no 'catch.' "

As soon as the half-fiend landed, the angel led her toward

an archway. She could not see through it, for it was filled by a pearlescent barrier. Two powerfully built humanoids stood guard there, flanking the passageway. They had the heads of dogs, though intelligence gleamed in their eyes. Their skin had a ruddy hue, and Aliisza could see greatswords strapped to their backs. They seemed serene, but ready for action at the slightest provocation. Tauran bowed deeply before the two of them, then stepped through the doorway and vanished.

Aliisza hesitated, standing between the two sentries. She wasn't sure she wanted to go where Tauran led. She glanced at the twin guards and saw both looking at her. There was more than mere intelligence reflected in their eyes. She saw keen wisdom as they appraised her.

Sizing me up for battle? Or questioning the merits of me being here?

"Hurry," one of them said, "before you are mistaken for an intruder and slain." His voice was unnaturally deep and rich. It vibrated the alu to her bones.

Aliisza swallowed and darted after Tauran.

The barrier enveloped her and she found herself within a colonnaded walkway, moving toward an open space filled with sunlight. Tauran was up ahead. She reflected for a moment on his words as she caught up. He and others like him came when called, answered those in need.

"I did that?" she asked aloud as they walked. "I called to you? I don't remember."

"No," the winged being said as they entered the interior courtyard. "You did not."

Aliisza shook her head, puzzled. "But you just said—"

She stopped in mid-sentence, gazing around at the beauty of the cozy space the two of them had just entered. A fountain stood in the center, a gurgling display with a statue of a magnificent winged being, even more angelic and powerful in appearance than Tauran. It was crafted of what must have been gold, and the sun blazed off it, giving it a most dazzling aspect.

All around the fountain, a topiary garden stretched in every direction. A wide assortment of trees loomed over the walkways, and benches stood beneath convenient arbors. Some trees were huge, offering shade. In other places, fruit trees blossomed, the fragrant aroma filling the area. The space was utterly devoid of other creatures.

The angel led Aliisza to one side of the courtyard, following an angled path that passed beneath an apple tree. "A spirit called, but it was not you," Tauran explained as he strolled out of the garden and back to the colonnaded balcony that surrounded the courtyard. He led her through another archway. "Though you might have uttered some outcry of despair in your final moments, it was not a clarion appeal to give yourself over to Tyr's benevolence."

They reached an open chamber with windows set high in the walls and in the ceiling, allowing sunshine to pour in. Everything was of the cleanest white marble, with hanging plants, rugs, and sculptures of gold, silver, and other materials decorating it and giving it life.

It took Aliisza a few moments to realize she was in a suite of rooms—cozy quarters. She saw a pool and a small fountain, a shelf filled with books, and a second doorway leading to more chambers. Beyond, she found a bed and a writing desk, as well as a balcony where sunshine streamed in. Aliisza crossed the floor to the balcony. The view beyond was startling. She could see the greater mountain that rose above the other three, majestic and forbidding as it towered overhead.

Aliisza turned to look at Tauran. He gestured at the limits of the room and said, "Make yourself comfortable. I must consult with others before I can take you before the tribunal. I should not be gone long."

The half-fiend frowned and asked, "But if I did not call, then who did?"

Tauran smiled at the alu again, but she could see that there was sadness in his eyes. "It was your child's cry that I heard. Your unborn offspring summoned me to rescue it."

Aliisza gawked at the angel as he turned and strode out, pulling the door shut behind him.

❖ ❖ ❖ ❖ ❖ ❖ ❖ ❖

At first, Myshik simply sank in the lava. Despite following both Kaanyr Vhok and the mustachioed human into the swirling Everfire, the half-dragon felt genuine fear. He didn't doubt that the ring the cambion had given to him was real. The fey'ri he had cut it from was obviously one of Vhok's consorts and a trusted minion who had expected to follow the half-fiend on the journey. Myshik was not afraid that he was being intentionally led to his fiery death.

No, the half-dragon feared that Vhok simply overestimated the efficacy of the magic in the ring. No dweomer could save them from the scorching conflagration that was the Everfire. The heat was too pure, the flames too infernal.

Still, the half-dragon had jumped.

He could see nothing. Everything was brilliant white, swirling yellow fire. He clenched his eyes shut to block the intensity of the illumination from penetrating, blinding him.

The sinking slowed, and Myshik felt himself being tossed about, as though being thrown by a great giant at play. He wanted to scream, but he feared to open his mouth, lest liquid fire pour down his throat and incinerate him from within.

The churning battered him, pounded him, and he began to try to swim away from its effects. He clawed his way through the lava, pulling hand over hand, stretching toward the surface. He hoped that he moved in the correct direction.

Myshik felt one hand break into open air. He lunged, trying to climb from the soupy fire that surrounded him. His head broke the surface, but he still felt the syrupy magma covering him, drenching him. He foundered, reaching out to nothing, trying to find anything, an outcropping of stone, to hold on to.

A hand grabbed at the half-dragon. Myshik felt fingers close around his own clawed digits, grip him in a handshake. He welcomed that touch, pulled on it, felt it pull back. He scrambled forward, using his other arm to paddle through the lava, and his foot struck something hard—solid ground just below the surface. He stood.

"Hurry up!" the half-dragon heard, and it was Vhok's voice. "Get out of there before it scorches everything off you! Come *on!*"

Myshik felt the hand tug at him, pulling him forward. He followed it, stumbling as clumps of liquid flame sloughed off his body. Much of it clung to him, though, and he could already feel it hardening as it began to cool.

Myshik wiped his face clear and risked opening one eye.

The landscape was fire incarnate.

The trio stood near a pool of molten stone, similar to the Everfire, at the base of a cliff where a firefall tumbled over the side, splashing into the lava like a waterfall. The pool lay in the midst of a small valley, with rolling hills on every side except for a narrow defile, where the magma drained away, tumbling through a series of cataracts and vanishing into lowlands in the distance.

The land resembled the foothills of the Nether mountains,

terrain Myshik was familiar with. Instead of rock, grass, shrubs, and trees, everything was flame. The ground was an endless glowing ember, orange and smoking. Gouts of flame shot up everywhere, in various sizes and colors, from dull red and yellow to brighter blue and even white. In an insane sort of way, they reminded the half-dragon of plants and trees.

A small gathering of herd animals foraged along the far edge of the pool. They looked faintly like deer, standing on four slender, graceful legs and sporting antlers on their heads. But instead of flesh and skin, they were made of embers and fire. A few seemed wary of the trio's presence, stock still and staring, but they otherwise ignored the interlopers.

Everything hissed and smoked, and the horizon shimmered and vanished through waves of unending heat. The sky was nothing but low-hanging, angry red smoke as far as the eye could see. Every breath Myshik drew was hot, and though he knew he wasn't dying, it felt worse than the scorching dry air he was used to in the great desert, Anauroch, near his home. Right then, home seemed impossibly far away.

As quickly as he took it all in, the view around Myshik started to fade. Smoke began to drift past him, growing thicker and thicker. It filled his nose with another, even more acrid scent.

As Myshik pivoted, scanning the horizon on every side, he saw great volumes of thick black smoke blowing toward them, sweeping across the valley like a dust storm in Anauroch. The wind that drove the smoke ahead of it also kicked up flames along the landscape. The fires leaped and danced like a wildfire on an open plain, though the half-dragon did not see what fuel let them burn as they zipped along.

Very quickly, visibility diminished to a few paces, and Myshik found his eyes stinging. He hurried to close the gap between himself and Vhok, but the cambion vanished from sight, and the draconic hobgoblin could barely make out his own hands in front of his face.

"Beware!" Zasian hissed from somewhere nearby. "They're charging!"

"What in the Abyss is char—" the cambion uttered, his words sounding strangely distant.

Something shot past Myshik. One of the grazing creatures he had spotted a moment before bounded into the travelers' midst and was gone again before Myshik could free his axe.

Another darted past the half-hobgoblin, moving close enough that its heat made his skin hot. Then two more came at him, one bounding to his left and another leaping directly over him. Myshik dropped into a crouch, expecting one to attack him at any instant. The soupy mess of liquefied stone that coated him made him stiff and heavy. He tried to wipe it off, but it stuck to him like thick mud.

As several more of the herd animals flew by, Myshik realized the danger lay not in attack, but in sheer numbers. One or two of the creatures became five, six. Then an entire horde of the things raced through the group of travelers, buffeting them as they stormed past. The flames of the beasts singed the half-dragon's exposed skin and left smoking scorch marks everywhere they touched him or his clothing and possessions, despite the magic of his ring.

Vhok began to rise into the air, levitating out of the stampede of fiery creatures. Myshik cursed. Without such a luxury, he was forced to crouch, to make himself as small a target as he could. Even so, he suffered several singeing blows from the creatures.

The thundering, flaming herd of fire-animals began to dwindle, and Myshik thought for a moment that the danger was past. Then he felt a deep, thumping vibration rise up through the ground . . . then another, and another. A last few straggling deerlike things shot past him as the thumps grew more powerful, louder. Myshik strained to peer through the thick, stinging smoke. His grip on his axe was iron-tight.

With the next powerful thump, the smoke dissipated for an instant, and a huge creature loomed into view, right before the half-dragon. Its great bulk was all smoldering coals and crackling flames. Six long serpentine necks snaked out of a bloated round body. Each head atop those necks sported draconian features, with wide, fanged jaws and blazing blue eyes. In addition to the four ponderous legs the creature strode upon, it manipulated two strange tentaclelike appendages, one from each side of its torso. The appendages thrashed around in irritation, capped on the ends with wide flat flanges, like the end of an oar. A horrific sulfurous odor poured off the thing, filling Myshik's nostrils.

"By Maglubiyet's bones!" the half-hobgoblin breathed, stumbling back.

The fiery thing's six heads writhed and roared, and it lunged forward.

CHAPTER
SIX

With only a thought, Kaanyr Vhok levitated, rising into the acrid, smoky air in front of the huge creature of fire. A pair of the thing's six heads spotted the cambion and lunged upward to snap at him. The first attack missed, but the second head managed to nip at Vhok's arm. He felt a surge of heat through his armor and jerked his hand away.

When he was slightly higher than the outstretched necks of the beast, he slowed to a stop and pulled from a pocket another of the wands he had taken from Lysalis. He aimed the wand down at the creature and spoke the trigger word. The magic of the wand made it vibrate in his hand and he saw four glowing darts erupt from its tip. The magical missiles slammed into the nearest head of the behemoth, causing it to flinch. Three of its six heads roared in pain and snapped at him, just out of reach.

Excellent, Vhok thought. Keep coming after me. Let the others get in close.

The injured head roared at him and a wave of noxious fumes wafted over Vhok, making him choke but falling just short of gagging him. The half-fiend had to cover his nose and mouth with one hand. As he cringed from the smell, the beast reared up on its hind legs and stretched two of its necks forward. Eyes blazing a superheated blue, the two heads latched onto Vhok's feet and pulled.

With a yelp, the cambion staggered and pitched forward, losing his balance. He felt himself slipping off his levitating perch as the twin heads tugged him closer. The searing pain of molten fire penetrated Vhok's boots, scorching his flesh. Despite the protection of the ring, the fiery heat broiled his flesh and made him arch his back in agony.

Desperate and enraged, the half-fiend drew Burnblood and slashed at the head on his right. The blade bit deeply into the skull of the fiery creature, nearly slicing it from its neck. A hiss of steam and liquid sprayed from the wound, spattering the cambion. The globules sizzled as they ate through his clothing and scalded his scaly skin. Vhok clenched his teeth in pain but held on to his sword.

The jaws released their grip on Vhok and the entire appendage recoiled. The neck flopped about crazily and the head bounced awkwardly, screaming in anguish. More of the white, superheated blood spewed from the wound. The quivering, thrashing neck grew weaker and the head grew silent. The blue-hot eyes faded to darkness as the appendage crumpled to the ground.

The other head still had a firm grip on Vhok, and it seemed to have a mind of its own, unaffected by the damage to its mate. With another ferocious yank, it pulled Vhok off his levitation platform. The cambion's hip felt nearly dislocated. Vhok cried out and tumbled into space.

In his armor, the cambion was too heavy for the creature to hold aloft. Still clutching him in its mouth, the beast slammed him to the ground head first, striking him hard against the ashy terrain on one shoulder as he landed. The jarring blow knocked the wind from him, and Vhok gasped as spots filled his vision. His knee wrenched as the yanking, thrashing head jerked him across the scorched ground. The cambion rolled to the side, twisting himself in a desperate attempt to keep from being torn apart.

The beast paused and adjusted its grip upon Vhok's leg. The cambion took advantage of the delay and slashed at its neck. His cut was awkward and only glanced off the glowing skin with a shower of sparks. He raised his arm high for another blow. A second head swooped in and bit at the cambion's blade. It grabbed hold of Burnblood and began to wrest the sword from the half-fiend's grip.

Vhok snarled. No, you infernal thing, he thought. You're not taking it!

The half-fiend clung to the weapon with one hand, gritting his teeth as the head tried to yank the sword away. Vhok winced as his arm was whipped back and forth. He felt the two heads tug him taut and lift him from the ground.

"Gods and devils!" he cursed, throwing his head back in anguish. The cambion was certain he would be ripped in two.

Fighting through the pain to refocus his efforts, Vhok remembered the wand, still clutched in his other hand. He aimed it at the head tugging on his leg and activated the magic. The cambion watched with satisfaction and relief as a burst of four blazing darts smacked it in the face. The thing released its grip on both his sword and his foot, and roared at him. As Vhok fell again with a painful *thunk*, the two heads snaked away in retreat.

Vhok rolled into a kneeling position, gasping for breath. His foot and ankle throbbed with searing pain, and he wasn't certain he could stand. He wanted to crawl away from the massive beast, but he knew that Zasian and Myshik still battled it. If he didn't aid them, they would surely be overwhelmed. Their deaths would leave him stranded in the scorched and blazing hell, forced to make his way alone. Such a journey did not appeal to the cambion.

Vhok turned and looked for a target. He saw that several heads lay unmoving upon the ruddy, glowing ground, the blue light of their eyes dimmed. The cambion noted with surprise that he and his companions were wearing down the terrible creature.

Vhok saw the half-dragon step into view from the swirling smoke that obscured so much of the terrain. Myshik had been bloodied. A large gash oozed thick black blood from the back of one shoulder, and another, on his thigh, made him limp. Still, the half-dragon seemed eager to keep up the fight. He held his magical war axe at the ready and grinned once at Vhok before advancing toward the floundering, snarling beast.

Vhok watched as Myshik feinted to one side and got one of the heads swaying that direction. The half-dragon stepped the opposite way and in close, swinging the dwarven weapon. The blade connected and the cambion heard a deep thump. The beast's head and neck snapped up and back, recoiling with violent force from the strike. The whole appendage bounced against the beast's flank before it slid down to the ground and lay still.

Myshik raised the axe in defiant glee and let out a whoop of triumph. Then the draconic hobgoblin limped forward to press the attack home against the great beast's body. The smoke swirled thickly and obscured the half-dragon once more.

The cambion heard Zasian's voice rising from his other side. The man chanted in a clear, forceful voice. Vhok peered that way and caught a glimpse of the priest as the thick, swirling smoke parted briefly. One of the behemoth's serpentine heads still battled the human, but Zasian was deft enough to evade it while finishing his spell. When the magic was complete, the priest stepped closer and made himself an easy target. The creature's head shot forward, ready to bite at its foe. Vhok flinched, worried that his companion had grown foolishly bold, but Zasian calmly slipped to the side of the snapping jaws at the last possible moment. The priest then smacked his hand against the fiery hot neck.

Vhok saw the head shudder from the slight blow and jerk back. It emitted a shrill scream of pain and whipped back and forth, as though trying to dislodge something that stuck to it and hurt badly.

At that moment, Myshik appeared again, chopping merrily into the great bulk of their foe. With both hands, the draconic hobgoblin drove the head of his axe deep into the creature's breast. The strike raked down its embered flesh, cutting open a wound that sprayed white-hot goo. Myshik spun away, flailing at the scalding fluids as they overwhelmed the magic of his ring to burn his face and hands. But the blow he had delivered was the killing one. The giant thing shuddered and collapsed to the ground. For a few moments, a few of its necks twitched and writhed, but the cambion was certain it was dead.

Thank the Abyss, Vhok thought, sagging onto his back, exhausted. Being mangled by a giant six-headed beast of fire was not the way I wanted to start this expedition.

As Myshik nudged one of the necks with the toe of his boot, Zasian squatted beside him. The priest gasped for breath, too.

"Well, that was interesting," Zasian said. "Don't see one of those every day."

Vhok snorted at his companion's levity and took a closer look at his wound. His boot was rent badly, and his olive skin beneath lay gashed and bleeding in several places. The flesh was badly seared, and the cambion suspected that the wounds had been partially cauterized from the heat of the creature, or he would have been bleeding more profusely.

"Heal me," Vhok instructed Zasian.

The priest gave him a single sidelong glance, and Vhok suspected he saw a flash of anger in the human's eyes, but Zasian placed his hands upon his companion's leg and muttered the chant of a healing prayer. Instantly, Vhok felt relief course through his injured limb. The torn flesh knitted together before his eyes. The charred skin regained its normal color and no longer ached.

Vhok then muttered a spell of his own, a simple cantrip capable of repairing objects. His boot began to reform, the tears and gaps closing until no sign of damage remained. The cambion rose to his feet and tested his footing.

"Excellent," he said, nodding. "Good work."

Zasian gave him a fleeting half-smirk and turned next to Myshik, who was still studying the corpse of the great beast.

"Careful," the priest said, tending to the half-dragon's wounds. "It can still bite you, even in death."

"What is it?" Vhok asked, unsure whether he had ever seen anything resembling the thing before, on any plane.

"It looks like a gulguthydra," Zasian replied. "Though I've never seen one made of fire stuff before. They're nasty creatures even under normal circumstances. Let's hope we don't run into any more." As he said this, the priest turned and looked at the cambion with a twinkle in his eye. "Back on Faerûn, they are always hungry, but fortunately, very rare," he said. "If this is any indication, I suspect many other things roam this plain."

Zasian finished his ministrations on Myshik, then the half-dragon ceased kicking at the dead creature and looked at his two companions. He held up his hand. "The rings protect us in this uninhabitable place?" he asked. "And where *is* this uninhabitable place?"

Vhok nodded. "We are somewhere on the Elemental Plane of Fire itself, the birthing place of all that burns. Beyond that, I cannot tell you with much certainty. I have a map, but it would be best to examine it later, when we are in safer environs."

The cambion took a moment to mop at his brow before continuing. "But yes, without the rings, we'd all be crispy ash blowing in the infernal winds by now." In a lower voice, more to himself than anyone, the cambion added, "I feel like I might just dry up and blow away, even with the ring."

"We can't stay here long," Zasian said. "We must find Kurkle, our guide. He promised to meet us here, but he warned me that we had chosen a dangerous spot to arrive. This pool is favored by creatures native to the area, and those that feed upon them."

"No doubt," Myshik replied, giving the dead beast another glance. "I'd hate to run into whatever feeds on *that.*"

"Me, too," Vhok added. "Zasian is right. We need to get moving."

Myshik's look grew grim. "What will we eat? Drink? How will we sustain ourselves?"

"All will be taken care of," Zasian said before the cambion could answer. "Vhok and I have a few tricks up our sleeves. But if you don't want to continue," he added with a slight smirk, "I'm sure the dwarves on the other side of the portal will welcome you back through the Everfire with open arms."

Myshik glared at the human, not appreciating his humor. "I'll stay," he said.

"Good," Vhok said. "You're pretty handy with that axe. We can use you here," he added, gesturing vaguely around.

"You'll get plenty of chances to wield it, I'm sure."

Myshik gave the cambion a measured stare before nodding.

Vhok found the reaction odd, but he dismissed it for later contemplation. He turned to the priest and asked, "Well? Where is this guide?"

"I don't know," the human replied. "But he'll find us when he's ready. Let's follow the stream that drains this pool and see what we discover."

Zasian took the lead and Myshik brought up the rear. The trio ventured away from the molten pool, toward the defile where it splashed out of view. The ground beneath the half-fiend's feet seemed almost spongy, but his boots sank into soft ash rather than damp loam. With each step he took, puffs of gray smoke wafted into the air, drifting on the scorching breeze.

The defile became a canyon. Zasian picked a path among tumble-down rocks that glowed and sparked with inner heat, while the stream of magma flowed like syrup along the bottom of the ravine. Jets of flame shot from fissures in the ground, some as low as knee-high, others towering in gouts that soared as high as the tallest trees of Faerûn. The massive geysers lit the underside of the clouds of smoke in the ruddy sky.

As they progressed, the cambion got the uneasy sense that something was watching them, perhaps following them. Every time he looked back along their trail, however, he saw nothing. Still, he couldn't shake the feeling. The alien landscape served only to heighten his unease, for he doubted his ability to notice aspects out of the ordinary when *everything* was out of the ordinary.

The sensation became overwhelming and Vhok instinctively looked up the side of the canyon. What he saw made him stop dead in his tracks. Zasian had frozen in midstep, too, seeing the same thing. Myshik nearly ran into Vhok from behind before he, too, caught a glance at what they saw.

A creature crouched on a precipice, a fierce hound of black fur and glowing red eyes. Its tongue lolled out of its mouth as it watched the procession.

Vhok fumbled a wand free of a pouch. At almost the same instant, Myshik pulled his dwarven axe from its straps and stepped wide, creating space to swing the weapon. Zasian kept his hands firmly on the staff he carried, though he made no overt sign of aggression.

"What's it doing?" Vhok asked, of no one in particular.

The hellish hound panted, but its eyes seemed preternaturally intelligent, and the beast watched them intently without moving. Then, as the stand-off lingered, the canine rose up on its hind legs and began to shift its shape. Right before the half-fiend's eyes, the dog became a humanoid, a male orcish-looking fellow with rust red hair and unkempt beard, a charcoal gray chain shirt, black pants and boots, and an oversized coal-colored scimitar. Once the transformation was complete, the half-orc stood still, one foot propped upon a glowing rock, his arms crossed on his knee.

Vhok's eyes narrowed in suspicion. "He's been tracking us," he said. "I've sensed him on our trail for a while, now."

Myshik gave the half-fiend an appraising sidelong glance. "You felt that, too?" he asked. "I thought I was the only one."

"Yes, following you," the creature barked as he made his way down from the precipice. "To see if you were the three who will pay me. When you called to me, you did not talk of a drako," he finished, nodding toward Myshik. "I had to be sure."

Vhok sensed the half-dragon bristling at the derogatory appellation, but Myshik held his tongue and waited, deferring to the other two.

"Kurkle," Zasian said, as much a statement as a question. "It seems you've found us."

❖ ❖ ❖ ❖ ❖ ❖ ❖ ❖

For a long time after Tauran departed and the door closed behind him, Aliisza stood in the middle of the room, stunned. The celestial's last words chilled the alu to the core of her being.

It had been her child, her unborn offspring, that the angel had come to save.

How is that possible? Aliisza thought, imagining the thing growing in her belly sending out a plea for survival. The notion scared her. What else is it capable of?

Then resentment and jealousy coursed through her. Why it and not me? she silently demanded. Why does Tyr care more about my unborn whelp than about me?

The answer to her question was so straightforward, so simple, that when it occurred to the alu, fury replaced jealousy. It had *always* been about the child. Aliisza herself was already forsaken to them.

They have no intentions of sparing me, of allowing me to redeem myself. They believe me lost and will do nothing on my behalf once I give birth.

The half-fiend sneered. Of course not, she thought. They played me as well as I might have played them. A wry chuckle escaped her. They pretend to be so holy, but they manipulate and deceive as well as any demon. Very clever, Tauran. Bastard, she added, seething again, silently hurling that anger at the door and the figure she knew receded beyond it. You can all rot in the Abyss.

As her rage diminished to smoldering irritation, she was startled by the idea that she had actually grown attached to the thought that Tyr had some interest in her well-being. When it happened, it was more than simple survival instinct. Tauran had presented a compelling case, to be sure. She could die, or she could submit to their game, play by their rules, and live. It was an easy choice.

But it was not the sum of her desire.

It had been more than a question of life or death. Some sense of worth, some sudden feeling of importance had been dangled in front of her, and she had snatched at it. Why? Realizing, too late, that it had been merely bait, she felt more than anger at being deceived. She was . . . disappointed. She had wanted that sense of importance, had craved that feeling of value. Her anger was replaced by a sense of self-loathing. She felt weak, worthless.

Enough of that, Aliisza chided herself. Figure a way out of this.

She moved to the balcony, stepped beyond the curtained doorway, and peered out. The drop below was significant. The Court had been built to hang over the side of a steep escarpment on that side, where a ravine in the side of the mountain tumbled down to vanish into the clouds below. The horizon stretched away as far as Aliisza could see, all rolling white and blue sky.

So much space.

I could go right now, she thought. I should go. I *must* go.

She remained there, looking at the vista. Despite her dismissal of the inherent beauty in landscapes and natural wonders, the alu found herself feeling a bit breathless, awed by what lay before her. It was distracting her.

Just leave, she told herself. Fly off, now. For reasons that escaped her, Aliisza didn't budge. Damn it! she yelled at herself. Go!

But the harder she tried to make the first move, to take

the initial step to flee, the more rooted to the spot she became. Somehow, the part of her mind that should act on her desires wouldn't cooperate. It was maddening.

Just spread your wings! she told herself. Only that.

Her black leathery wings unfurled behind her. She stretched them out, enjoying the sensation. The wound she had suffered upon hitting the floor of Helm Dwarf-friend's chambers was gone. She felt hale and whole, as though the injury had never occurred.

She wanted to fly, to soar around the flanks of that great mountain. She stepped up upon the railing of the balcony, ready to launch herself into the air, solely to circle overhead.

Aliisza thought she was about to do it, to take wing, but her actions only made her remember that she was trying to escape, and her momentum ended. She stood stock still upon the railing, unmoving once more.

By all the storms of Fury's Heart! the alu swore. What in the Nine Hells did you do to me, Tauran? she silently demanded.

No, another little voice inside Aliisza's head countered, you did it to yourself. You let them bind you, agreed to it. You should be dead. Are you afraid to die?

No, came the answer.

Then don't let them win, she told herself. Take their prize from them.

The thought panicked Aliisza for a moment, but she reined the feeling under control and considered. Could I do it? she thought. Could I kill myself? She didn't remember any part of the oath that prevented her from harming herself. Only others were protected.

It would serve them right, she decided, a faint smile playing across her face. Just when they think they've got what they want, poof! It's gone. The smile faded from her. And I have no love for this baby, she thought, feeling resentment again. I should end you right now, she projected at the thing.

But something kept her from following through. It wasn't Tauran's magical restraint. She didn't feel the same inability to act. It was deeper, more personal. For some reason, whether she loved it or not, she had to protect the offspring growing inside her.

The alu threw her hands up in frustration.

This stupid child is addling my brain, she finally decided. I need time to think.

Knowing she couldn't take wing from the balcony and make her escape, Aliisza instead turned her attention to the chamber where she was a guest. Like the rest of the massive place, everything was constructed of gleaming white marble and highlighted with rich fabrics, precious metals, and vibrant plants. In fact, she realized, it was all very luxurious. The bed was large and soft, and the many pillows piled atop it could easily become a lover's nest. The gently swirling pool was set into the floor and had steps leading down into it. Water from a fountain mounted on the wall above it splashed into the pool.

Maybe she could not escape, she reasoned, but perhaps there were other ways to turn the situation to her advantage.

With a soft sigh of delight, Aliisza began to disrobe, and she shifted form as she did so, becoming a tall and lithe human woman with sapphire blue eyes, bronzed glowing skin, and hair the color of summer wheat.

The classic beauty, she thought, and giggled. The transformed alu dipped a toe into the water and found it to be the precise temperature she desired. She descended the steps and lowered herself into the pool, then reclined against one wall, throwing her arms back to rest on the edges.

For a long while, the half-fiend just closed her eyes and

soaked, letting all her cares and concerns drift away with the steam. She wished she had some scented oils to add to the water, and as suddenly, she could smell and feel their effects. She opened her eyes and saw that the water splashing from the fountain was tinted red like the oils she often procured to pamper herself.

Curious, she imagined the water chilled rather than steamy, and instantly, her skin prickled with goose bumps as the temperature dropped within the pool. Delighted but shivering, Aliisza returned the temperature to a comfortable level and closed her eyes once more.

It wasn't until Tauran spoke some time later that Aliisza realized he was in the room with her. "You look quite comfortable." Somehow, the angel had entered without her hearing him.

Aliisza's eyes flew open to see him standing near the door, observing her with a carefully neutral expression on his face. She saw with a glance that the sun was lower in the sky from the way the shadows slanted sharply across the walls and floor.

Recovering her wits quickly, Aliisza gave her celestial host one of her best come-hither stares and said, "I didn't hear you enter. This bath is so relaxing, I must have dozed off. Maybe you'd like to join me? I need someone to scrub my back."

Tauran gave her that same sad smile and said, "Tempting me won't work, Aliisza. I can revel in the pure delights of fleshy contact as well as any human—or half-fiend—but such experiences pale in comparison to the glory of my duties. Besides, I would know it is not real."

Aliisza swallowed hard at the stinging words, but she kept her face steady and tried one last lure. Rising from the water, she slowly came up the steps and said, with a hint of a pout, "You don't think this"—and she gestured down at the perfect body she had molded for herself—"is real?" She walked slowly and seductively toward the celestial.

Tauran met her stare evenly, without flinching. His eyes didn't even roam down her figure.

"It's nothing but a mask," he said. Then he turned away. "I'll wait outside while you get ready. It's time to go to the Court of Temperance. The tribunal is prepared to render judgment and sentencing."

CHAPTER SEVEN

The half-orc that had been a hellish canine only moments earlier approached the trio and came to a stop a few paces from them. He folded his arms across his chest and studied them, as through appraising them. "You came ill prepared," he stated, a brief smirk crossing his face. "Your magic may protect you now, but it will not help when creatures attack. You will still burn."

"We've found that out already," Vhok replied wryly. "We'll keep it in mind for next time," he added.

"You are Kurkle?" Zasian asked, stepping forward. "Our guide? I am Zasian, the one who contacted you and hired you. You received the first payment, I trust."

The half-orc barked a laugh. "I am," he said. "But I did not know three fools had hired me. You cannot travel this place as you are, unprotected. You must go back to your own plane."

Vhok narrowed his eyes. "We hired you to guide us to the City of Brass. You've been paid, so guide. We'll keep our own counsel, otherwise."

Kurkle let out a low growl, deep in his throat, and his fiery red eyes gleamed in anger. Then he shrugged. "So be it. If the fires consume you, Kurkle will get your treasure."

The foursome set out then, the half-orc guide in the lead. As before, Vhok strode behind Zasian, with Myshik in the rear. As they hiked, the cambion made a point of keeping a watch, hoping to prevent any nasty surprises from sneaking up on them. He found the constant crackle and hiss of the ever-present conflagrations disconcerting. The noises made it difficult to listen for sounds of pursuit, especially since he suspected that most things living there would also blaze and crackle as they moved.

From time to time, Kurkle would drop to all fours and transform into a hound, then go loping off into the hazy distance, running in wide arcs ahead of the other three. He would disappear for some time, while the three visitors continued along the path he had set for them.

At the first occurrence, Vhok grew concerned that their guide was abandoning them, but Zasian shook his head. "I think he's scouting," the priest commented. "His senses are keen. He is renowned for his skills, and his reputation is equally well known. He will not betray us."

Vhok grumbled his acceptance, but he did not like being so dependent on anyone or anything he could not control.

Eventually, Kurkle returned and transformed into his humanoid shape again before resuming the lead. He said nothing, but corrected their course according to landmarks only he seemed aware of. To Vhok, the landscape was an endless stretch of smoldering embers and blowing ash broken only by the incessant jets of fire.

On Kurkle's third such scouting foray, Myshik posed a question. "What is Kurkle?" Vhok assumed that he was speaking to Zasian, since the priest had been the one to arrange for the creature's services.

"Canomorph," the human replied. "The hell hound is his natural form, but some of his kind have learned how to shapeshift into humanoids. He's feral and instinctual, but he will get us there."

After a time, the land flattened, and Vhok turned to look back in the direction they had come. He could barely make out the ridge of flaming, scorched mountains from which they had descended. The peaks were low and smooth, and their flanks were ribboned with streams of molten fire, magma flowing down their sides like water.

The land did not remain flat for very long. Soon enough, Kurkle led them into what Vhok would have considered badlands on Toril: steep-sided hills, plateaus, and pinnacles separated by scree-filled gullies, trenches, and washes. The terrain popped, flamed, and glowed all around them. Noxious gases wafted everywhere, stinging Vhok's eyes and making sight difficult.

As the day's journey wore on, Vhok had to concentrate to keep from grumbling. They seemed to be moving at a slug's pace, and the half-fiend was not accustomed to traveling on foot for such long distances. He sorely missed the creature comforts of riding in his military palanquin, and he grew more and more irritable.

The cambion even suggested that they employ some form of magic to convey themselves, but Kurkle warned against it, claiming it was harder for predators to spot them if they remained low, using the winding defiles to improve their concealment. Even if they had wanted to ignore that precaution, Myshik and Kurkle were both at a disadvantage, for they had no magic to draw upon to aid their passage. Resigned to traveling like a common merchant, Vhok's mood grew more foul as the journey progressed.

To make matters worse, they attracted the attention of bandits. Vhok caught a glimpse of them when the foursome was forced to cross some stretches of open ground. Perhaps half a dozen riders shimmered in the distance, their outlines distorted by the wavering heat of the terrain. Though Kurkle steered his charges away from the threat, the bandits pursued them. They seemed persistent, and Vhok wondered why.

The sojourn became even less pleasant when thick black clouds of smoke roiled over the group. As before, the caustic murk stung eyes and lungs and made for treacherously poor visibility. Kurkle took advantage of the cloaking vapors to change their direction, cutting back and to the right and following a narrow canyon for a long distance. The cambion questioned the wisdom of losing ground, but the canomorph insisted that it was a far better inconvenience than being ambushed by their pursuers.

When the smoke cleared, the expedition seemed to have lost the bandits, and Vhok thought they had seen the last of them. But soon enough, Kurkle reported signs that the enemies were close again, deepening Vhok's gloomy mood. Determined to avoid them if they could, the foursome continued on.

Any time Kurkle feared that they might be discovered, he sent the trio scrambling for cover while he prowled around, sniffing the acrid air, scrambling up the sides of gullies to peer into the distance. Sometimes he disappeared entirely for long stretches of time.

After one of the canomorph's scouting runs, Kurkle came loping back in hound form. "They are close at hand," he said, motioning for a sudden halt. All three travelers knew the routine by then. They went to ground, seeking available cover, as their guide darted off to observe the bandits. They found plenty of places to hide in the gulley they followed. Vhok ducked behind a large outcropping of glowing rock. The superheated stone sizzled and crackled loudly in the cambion's ears as he crouched, waiting for Kurkle to return.

Vhok watched his sweat vaporize in tiny curling puffs of steam as he waited, his mood truly black.

Something large stepped upon the outcropping right above Vhok, and the cambion was aware of it a heartbeat before it knew of him. He jerked back and stared as the creature, which he first thought was a rider upon a basalt black horse, peered in his direction. Vhok realized his mistake immediately. It was not a mounted rider, but a single creature, and he recognized it as a centaur. But unlike the horse-men of Toril, the creature looming over Vhok had skin the color of onyx, its hair, eyes, and hooves seemed to be made of flame, and it exhaled gouts of smoke. The bandit clutched a long spear in one hand, and Vhok could see a bow slung over one shoulder.

Upon spotting the cambion, the fiery centaur reared on its back legs and snarled in glee as it raised its spear high in an overhand grip. The tip of the weapon glowed orange, while the haft seemed to be chiseled of black stone. Vhok deepened his crouch and reached for his long sword, but his foe had both reach and a height advantage. When the spear came jabbing down at the cambion, Vhok darted beneath the outcropping and gave a shrill whistle of warning. The spear slammed into the ground where Vhok had stood, releasing a shower of embers and sparks.

Not waiting to see which side of the outcropping Vhok might pop from, the elemental centaur leaped down into the defile and spun to face him. At that moment, Zasian rose up from his hiding place behind a large boulder and struck the creature across one flank with his morningstar. The centaur was steadying himself to run Vhok through with the spear, but the blow made him start and shift, and the attack was ruined.

Faster than Vhok could think, the centaur kicked out with

his hind legs at Zasian, catching the man hard in the chest. The priest let out a *whoosh* of air and staggered backward, gasping.

The distraction was enough for Vhok to shift his sword to his off hand and pull out the wand he kept handy. When the centaur turned to face him again, Vhok leveled the magical device and let loose. Three of the four glowing missiles slammed into the upper torso of the bandit—and the fourth caught Myshik squarely as he leaped on the centaur's back for an attack. The half-dragon flinched and swung his great dwarven war axe wildly, only grazing his foe's shoulder.

The attack had the desired effect on the molten centaur. The creature reared up, flailing in the air with his human arms, trying too late to evade the attack. The sudden shift tossed Myshik backward, off the bandit. The half-dragon landed hard against the smoking ground and bounced away, losing his grip on his axe.

Kurkle exploded into Vhok's view, rushing the centaur from the side in hound form. The scout leaped up and snapped at the bandit, his jaws clamping onto the creature's throat as he sailed past. Already weakened from Vhok's strike, the bandit could not evade the attack, and Kurkle tore free most of the front of the centaur's neck.

The centaur clutched at its throat and tried to scream, but the only sound coming forth was a sickening gurgle accompanied by gushes of smoky blood that oozed through his fingers. Staggering to one side, listing off balance, the centaur tried to keep his feet beneath himself, but the life was leaving his eyes. The glowing yellow orbs dimmed to a dull orange even as the bandit toppled to the ground. His head bounced hard upon the burning stone and his eyes faded to dim red, then guttered out. His arms flopped aside and he lay still.

The gash in the centaur's throat still spilled blood, and

as the spatters dripped and hit the searing ground below, they crackled and sizzled. The fluids rapidly evaporated in a noisome, foul-smelling cloud of vapor.

Myshik groaned and tried to climb to his feet, but he was wobbly and dazed. Zasian moved to the half-dragon's side and uttered a prayer of healing while Vhok crept to the top of the rise to see if any more bandits had drawn near. He didn't see anything, though with the billowing smoke blowing across his field of vision, he couldn't see very far.

"Outrider," Kurkle muttered, shifting into his half-orc form. "Scouting the bandits' flank and stumbled upon us."

Vhok coughed. "Not such a formidable foe," he commented, eliciting a raised eyebrow from the canomorph. The guide still had black blood on his lips, which he was enthusiastically licking off.

"One, maybe, sure," he said. "But a band of five or ten of them can trample you in a heartbeat. When they come at you from all sides with those spears and hooves, beware."

Vhok thought the image through for a moment and nodded. He would have to consider carefully the tactics they would employ should they come face to face with a larger group of the bandit centaurs.

"Why are they chasing us?" he asked, wondering again at the enemies' persistence. "What makes us so special?"

Kurkle grunted. "Just because," he said. "Good sport. Treasure to trade with the salamanders or the efreet. They know you aren't natives, figure you must have powerful magic to keep you alive. They want it. And good sport," he repeated, seeming to think that was explanation enough.

Vhok sighed. "I suppose," he grumbled.

Zasian had finished tending to Myshik's injuries and his own, and the two of them were gathering themselves. The half-dragon picked up his axe with a chagrined look while the priest spent a moment sorting through some items in his pack. The cambion noticed that Myshik's weapon exhibited numerous smoking scorch marks along the handle.

"Shouldn't have dropped that," he commented wryly.

The half-dragon gave him a scathing look. "It won't happen again," he replied.

Shrugging, Vhok turned away and spoke to Kurkle. "How much longer must we travel through this accursed terrain?"

The canomorph scratched behind one ear. "The rest of this day, and all of tomorrow," he said. "Beyond that is open plain for a while."

Vhok groaned. "All right," he grumbled, "let's get going, then. Tonight, I'm getting a foot massage."

Kurkle raised one eyebrow, obviously confused by the cambion's comment, but shrugged and turned away.

The others fell into line and soon they were trudging silently along, following the meandering defile while Kurkle continued to travel the high ground around them, keeping watch for more dangers.

As they walked, Vhok noticed what at first appeared to be a strange, dark gray snowfall. It didn't take him long to realize that it wasn't snow at all, but ash. As he looked up into the sky, the fluffy black stuff began to fall harder. In no time, it covered the ground in a layer that was ankle deep.

"How long will this last?" he called out to Kurkle as the canomorph trotted by in hound form. As he spoke, Vhok gestured in the air at the falling ash.

Without bothering to transform into a humanoid, Kurkle began to utter a series of barking words. His diction was awkward, tricky to understand, but Vhok made out the message clearly enough. "Could last all day. I've seen it pile to twice an efreeti's height before."

The cambion sighed and continued trudging, watching

with dismay as the three of them left easily discernible foot-prints in the growing cover.

"Just terrific," he said.

Vhok realized it was time to stop. He was miserably hot, tired, and thirsty. He looked at his two companions and they, too, appeared worn out.

"I think it's time we called a halt and rested," he announced. "Between the progress we've made so far and all we had to go through to get through the Everfire, we shouldn't push our-selves much more."

Kurkle frowned. "This is not a good place to rest," he said. "For me, it's all right. But for you, too many things can find you."

Vhok looked at the humanoid with the bright orange hair. "I have the means to protect us from anything that wanders this way," he said. "We stop here for a night's rest." Without waiting for approval from the others, he slipped his hand into a pouch within his pack and pulled out an odd bundle. Unwrapping it, he revealed the gift from Nahaunglaroth, the sculpture of ivory in the form of a vine-covered stone archway.

The cambion held up the archway and blew through its opening. Immediately, a shimmering doorway very similar in appearance to the archway materialized directly in front of Vhok. He looked at both Zasian and Myshik.

"You both may enter," he said. "Inside, you will find a hearty meal and magical servants to tend to your needs. There are guest quarters for each of you. The door at the top of the stairs is my chamber."

Zasian entered without a second glance at the strange doorway. The priest vanished the moment his foot passed through. Myshik took a moment longer to stare at the magical portal, but after stroking his chin for a moment in consideration, he, too, entered the magical doorway.

Vhok turned to Kurkle. "Within this, we three shall be protected from anything that wanders by. You are welcome to take shelter within, too, but the environment is not like here," he said, and gestured around. "I do not know how much you will like it."

The canomorph paced around the doorway, his face an expression of wary disbelief. "Where did they go?" he demanded.

"They are inside," the cambion answered. "It is a magical shelter. Like a room at an inn," he added, before figuring that Kurkle had very little idea what an inn might be.

"No, I will stay here," Kurkle said at last. "I am safe here. I will guard your door for you while you rest."

"That won't be necessary," Vhok replied. "The doorway will vanish from your sight once I enter and close it. But it will reappear again, when we have rested and refreshed ourselves. We will meet you here then. Yes?"

Kurkle looked doubtful, but he nodded. Before Vhok could enter the sanctuary of his magical mansion, the canomorph had changed into his hound form and was loping away, vanishing in the thick, blinding smoke.

Vhok smiled and passed through the shimmering doorway. Behind him, the portal winked from sight.

❖ ❖ ❖ ❖ ❖ ❖ ❖ ❖

Tauran's face was stoic as he led the half-fiend into the private courtyard of her quarters. He strolled toward the portico where the pearlescent archway waited to transport the two of them to the Grand Hall of Temperance. The alu followed him willingly. She remained as he had found her when he returned to her chambers, in the form of a beautiful human woman, though she added a simple dress to her guise. He noted that she had patterned the outfit after the garb common to the Court, white and flowing, with a gold belt and accents on the hem.

She's been paying attention, the astral deva noted. He wasn't sure how that made him feel.

The others had cautioned him to be wary when bringing her to the House. She took the devious cruelty of her succubus mother and the relentless perseverance of her human father and mixed them together to become even more enterprising than either of them. And she was beautiful. Her trickery had no effect on the angel, but he still found her delightful to look at.

Tauran wondered how much she knew of celestial beings. *Does she comprehend our love of life, of all things both spiritual and physical that enhance the joys of existence? Can she possibly know how keenly appealing she is for her human foibles even as she seems so treacherous? If I could teach her to harness that craftiness, to find better ways of employing it, let her see the consequences of her actions, what a delightful creature she could be!*

But she was a half-fiend, dangerous in every way. And they had warned him to be careful.

No one within the Court had questioned his decision to select her. No creature serving Tyr or any of the other revered deities of the House of the Triad would hesitate to seek a way to save the spirit of the unborn being growing inside Aliisza. The tricky part was separating the mother from the child, to break the bonds of corruption that would otherwise influence the scion, even before it left the womb.

The hard part is done, Tauran thought, as the two of them stepped through the magical barrier. Beside him, Aliisza gasped softly when she discovered that they did not appear where they had before, upon the balcony with its guards. The angel had shifted the magic to take the two of them directly to the Great Hall.

They stood upon a pedestal, one of the floating islands of earth and stone that drifted throughout the plane. Directly before them, covering almost the entire surface of the pedestal like a gargantuan soap bubble, was a great orb. The mammoth sphere's surface gleamed in iridescence in the light of the sun, a magical barrier identical to the pearlescent portal through which the two of them had just stepped.

The angel crossed the distance to the orb's surface and gestured for Aliisza to pass through it. She did not come immediately. Instead, she stood rooted to her spot upon an outcropping of rock near the edge of the pedestal, staring at everything around her in impressed awe. The celestial could see wariness in her visage, too.

Far below them, the gleaming white of the Court shone brightly. The pedestal drifted above it, separate from much of the rest of the palace. Other celestial beings drifted all around, some coming near and passing through the orb to tend to their own business within the hall. Few of them gave Aliisza a second look in her new form. The beautiful human guise the alu had adapted blended in far better than her native winged shape. Tauran suspected that she had chosen to remain in that appearance for that very reason.

He waited while she moved slowly to stand next to him, turning her head back and forth, gathering the images. It was not uncommon for a first-time visitor to the Court to appear overwhelmed by the beauty and grace of the place. Even a fiend would be hard pressed to deny feeling at least somewhat influenced by the glory of it.

"Aliisza," Tauran said. The alu turned to look at him and hesitated. Instantly, the angel could feel the tug of his magical binding. She was thinking of escape, or causing harm to someone, or another possibility that went against the terms she had agreed upon. The divine power he had employed on her would never have worked had she not willingly accepted the terms, had she not freely given herself to be bound by them. But that single act of concurrence had made the magic possible and unbreakable. She was bound to follow through with the rules as surely as if she had been wrapped in adamantine chains and dragged to her final destination.

The astral deva felt her tug against the magic, felt her try to resist it. She would not sense it that way, of course. To the alu, she simply couldn't muster the will to make one damning move. She could think on such acts easily enough, but her willpower to follow through had been locked away within the bonds. The harder she fought against it, the harder she tried to force her body to act as she wished, the more pressure Tauran felt on the divine bond.

At last, he felt her struggle wane, and the alu reached out to the strange glowing surface of the orb. As her hand touched it she vanished, whisked beyond it to the inside. Tauran followed.

Aliisza made a slight strangled sound as she took in the Great Hall for the first time. The pair stood in a colonnaded walkway that circled the orb's interior. Beyond the walkway, tier upon tier of benches descended into the lower half of the hemisphere like a grand theater surrounding a central stage. The stage itself was the focal point of the Court. It hovered in the air above the seats, crafted of smooth white stone. Upon it, the tribunal sat in attendance, hearing all petitions brought before it.

Overhead, the top half of the soaring white dome rested upon massive marble columns veined in gold and silver. The underside of the dome bore a complex pattern of gold foil surrounding a fresco of Tyr's benevolent face watching from above. The entirety of the dome glowed with indirect light, filling the place with a happy radiance. Tapestries of vibrant colors all throughout the cavernous chamber depicted the glories of the members of the Triad and their devoted servants. Other astral devas and their charges came and went almost constantly from various points around the periphery of the orb.

Tauran led Aliisza down an aisle toward the stage. The carpeted steps were long and shallow, so it took them two steps across for every step down to make their way to the bottom. Once there, Tauran sat, then motioned for his ward to join him. The alu nodded and sat on the edge of the bench. She craned her neck back, peering up at the floating stage high overhead. Tauran gave her a reassuring smile as they waited to be recognized.

After a few moments, Tauran heard a small voice in his head, indicating that the tribunal was ready to receive them. Before he could warn Aliisza of what was about to happen, magic coursed through them both, and they found themselves seated upon another bench, on the floating stage, directly before the tribunal.

Aliisza gasped at the sudden change in her surroundings and nearly lost her balance. As she recovered, she hissed in vexation and eyed the whole setting warily.

The three members of the tribunal were all solars, great humanoids that stood half again as tall as either Tauran or Aliisza. Their skin was silvery in color, and their eyes blazed with a topaz glow. Wings of white, similar to the astral deva's but far larger, lay folded against their backs. Their faces bespoke supreme authority tempered with wisdom and benevolence.

The solars turned and stared expectantly at Tauran.

The deva rose and approached them. "Noble tribunal, I seek your judgment over the creature known by many as Aliisza the alu, who comes here willingly today to accept your decision."

The solar on the left, the chief of proceedings, stood and looked down at Aliisza. Tauran saw that she seemed to shrink down the slightest bit. "Come forward, Aliisza," the solar demanded, his voice reverberating through the chamber like a rumble of thunder.

Aliisza eyed the creature with trepidation but rose to her feet and approached.

She stood next to Tauran, shoulder to shoulder, and pressed herself close to him. He could smell the rose oil on her skin. He could also smell the taint of her heritage, very faintly. He wondered how much of her consternation was real and how much of it was feigned, designed to guile him.

"Do you indeed come before this tribunal willingly, to be judged and sentenced?" the solar asked. Tauran could feel the timbre of the creature's voice vibrate in the stones beneath his feet. "You agree to be bound by the decisions of this court in all things, without coercion by any creature, mortal or immortal?"

Aliisza stood dumbly for a moment, and Tauran was just about to turn to her to see if she understood the question, when she blurted out, "Do I have a choice?"

A long silence followed as her words echoed into the deep recesses of the Great Hall. Then the chief of the tribunal spoke again.

"There is choice in everything, tainted one," the solar boomed. "You choose to place a blade at another's throat and threaten their life unless they do your bidding. Your victim chooses whether to appease you or die in defiance. With all of us, with every step we take, we make choices. What is your choice here today?"

Aliisza gave the solar a good, hard stare, and Tauran felt the tug of her effort to resist the compunction imposed on her. He suspected she was contemplating how she might strike the chief of the tribunal right then.

Finally, with a visible effort to relax, she said, "You say I have the right to choose, yet I cannot draw my blade and run you through. Nor can I run from this chamber and take flight, flee from this place that stinks with the same arrogance and rigidity that oozes from every follower of your blind god in the world beyond. You say I have a choice, but I cannot seem to change my mind now. What must I do to earn the freedom to die on my own terms, fighting my way clear of you and your condescension?"

Tauran gaped at Aliisza, surprised at her change of heart. He had sensed in her a true desire for mercy, a genuine need to ask forgiveness, even if she didn't understand it herself. But she had shifted away from that, he saw, had reverted to her more demonic nature, unrepentant and defiant even in the face of death.

The chief of the tribunal seemed to shine more brightly than before, as though righteous anger lent him radiance. Tauran knew that the solar was doing more, though. The creature was probing Aliisza, searching the depths of her emotions to find the core feeling hiding behind her outburst.

"That is not what is in your heart," the chief declared at last. "Your maternal instinct holds you back, pushes you to survive, to persevere in the face of inescapable doom. You speak in rage against the tribunal only because you are also conflicted by your feelings. And . . ." the solar paused, tilting its head to one side. "You are jealous of the attention we have given to your progeny. Ah, now I see why you fight with yourself."

Aliisza glared at her judge, but she kept her mouth shut. Tauran waited, wondering how the Court would proceed. The alu hadn't actually asked to be freed from her agreement. If she had, the Court almost certainly would have granted it—and immediately proceeded to destroy her, right then, within the Great Hall. She would wither and die, and the spirit of her child would become a petitioner, serving for eternity within the House of the Triad. But she had not asked for her release, merely put forth conjecture and asked hypothetical questions.

After the silence had grown almost interminable, the solar spoke again. "Do you wish to be free of your agreement? It is your choice to make, though you know the consequences of your decision."

Aliisza shook her head. "No, damn you. I cannot." Her voice was tight, breathy, and Tauran could see that a single tear ran down her cheek, but her eyes then hardened in some form of resolve. "For whatever reason, the human side of me has decided that I must protect my baby against such a fate." She drew in a long breath and at last said, "I freely and willingly submit to your judgment and sentencing. Spare me so that my child may be born and live."

Tauran wondered at her determination. He suspected that she still sought a means of outwitting him, of escaping her predicament. He knew her nature, her cleverness, and expected that she would fight him for quite some time before realizing she could not break free of her own oath. By then, of course, it would be too late. She did not know what was coming next, but he did. He dreaded her reaction when she learned.

The solar waited a moment, letting Aliisza's words echo through the chamber. Then he spoke one last declaration. "It is the decision of this court that your conscious mind shall be divorced from your body and imprisoned within a dimensional sanctuary. Your body will be placed in stasis while the offspring comes to term and is born. At that time, the child will be taken elsewhere to be raised and your body will return to the dust from whence it came. Your spirit will remain in the dimensional sanctuary for a period of one year, where you shall reflect upon your wicked ways in the hope that you find a conscience and a desire for forgiveness for your crimes. If, after one year has passed, you are found worthy of redemption, then your mind shall be set free and given a new form, one that is more suitable to your glorious nature. If not, then your consciousness will be cast into merciful oblivion as due punishment for your unrepentence. In no event shall you have any future contact with your child. So sayeth this court."

Aliisza made a strangled sound, and her eyes blazed in fury. That fury turned to horror as she realized what she had been sentenced to. Her terrified scream echoed through the chamber, making Tauran's ears ring.

CHAPTER EIGHT

Aliisza's chest ached. She couldn't breathe. The words of the celestial judges' decision sent shivers of horror through the alu, made her heart pound, made her gasp. It took her a moment to realize that the ear-splitting shriek was her own voice, wailing in dismay. They intended to deny her from ever seeing her child. The whole judgment had been one big trap.

Aliisza could not understand why such a condition would anguish her so, but the thought was pure anathema. She could not be parted from her body, from her child. It must not happen! The notion sent roiling panic through her, made her contemplate dropping to her knees and begging for mercy. That consideration stunned her. She named herself coward for it, but it didn't change a thing. She would do whatever was necessary to remain with her unborn.

Before the alu could draw breath and plead her case, the surroundings changed. She and Tauran were no longer standing in the Great Hall with its cavernous space and echoing sounds.

She suddenly felt very alone, disconnected from everything. At first, she thought she had closed her eyes, but she couldn't make them open. Yet, she could see. Everything around her was a gray void again, limitless, bereft of any distinguishing features. The alu could sense no up or down, as before.

But it was different. She was a part of the void, not just within it, but also distinct from it.

At least, for a moment.

Then the sense of existing, of being, faded.

When next Aliisza became aware, she was in a cool place, dim but not dark. She seemed to be floating on a bed of air, staring at nothing. She tried to focus on her surroundings, to gain some perspective on where she was, and in that flash of mental desire, she was lying in a room very much like the one she had been sequestered in when she and Tauran had first arrived at the Court.

Initially, Aliisza thought she was there again, for the place was familiar, yet some things seemed vague to her. Images at the corners of her eyes were indistinct, fuzzy, fading to nothing whenever she looked away. And it seemed objects were missing, things she couldn't quite remember but knew should be there.

After a moment more, Aliisza understood. She was creating the chamber, forming it from her memory. She was manifesting a reality, but her memories of the room were imperfect, incomplete, for she had not spent much time there. With that realization, the whole of the place began to waver, to shimmer and disappear.

"Easy," came a voice nearby, all around. It was Tauran. "Give it another moment."

Another moment for what? the half-fiend wondered.

Then she felt a sense of vertigo. The inexact, incomplete chamber spun. Somewhere, somehow, she sensed Tauran take her hand in his, and a surge of relief went through her, a feeling of stability, and all at once, they were standing together in the fully formed chamber.

Aliisza was in her natural form, dressed in black leather armor that molded to her curves in a most provocative way. Her sword hung on her right hip, the magical ring that protected her from physical blows was in its familiar place on the third finger of her left hand, and the ring that had belonged to Pharaun encircled the fourth finger of her right hand. Her other trinkets and the pouch of magical components for spells were there, too.

Tauran watched her intently, wearing that faintly wistful expression again.

Aliisza pulled her long sword and sliced through the celestial before he even reacted. She watched him flinch but was dismayed to see that the sword passed right through him without affecting him.

"Bastard!" she screamed.

The alu raised her hand, pointing at him. She uttered the words of a common spell, conjuring a trio of magical glowing darts that shot from the tip of her finger. The darts streaked directly at Tauran, but they vanished as they struck him. The angel didn't flinch.

"You can rot in the Abyss!" she screamed, furious at feeling so inept.

She spun away and ran toward the balcony. She charged through the opening and launched herself up in the air. Her wings spread wide, Aliisza took flight, soaring up into the heavens, which were filled with billowing puffy clouds glowing orange in the late afternoon sun. She pumped her wings rhythmically, gaining altitude, putting distance between herself and her tormentor as fast as she could.

As before, there was no ground, only an endless expanse of clouds. She kept the Court, resting atop its flattened mountain, behind her, setting a course directly away from it.

I did it, she thought. I slipped away before they could imprison me, before they could separate me from my child.

The alu wondered if she could escape the plane entirely. She had no idea how, and she wondered how long it would be before Tauran sent pursuit after her. She didn't care. She was free, at least for the moment, and she would never let them take her captive again.

She glanced over her shoulder and nearly stopped flying in dismay. The great structures of the Court were still there, no farther away than they had been. Somehow, she had failed to put distance between herself and the mountaintop.

She snarled and went into a dive, plummeting into the cloud cover, which stretched away in every direction as far as her eye could see, like an endless gossamer plain. Deeper and deeper she went.

Aliisza pulled up and hovered for a moment, listening.

There was no sound. She could see nothing except the gray glow of the cloud all around her. The coolness of the moisture chilled her skin, made her shiver. Slowly, she began to descend again, under control this time, swooping at a gradual rate.

The clouds did not end.

Frustrated, Aliisza began to climb. Almost immediately, she popped through the top of the billowing haze into open air. She had not traveled far at all.

No escape, the half-fiend realized in a panic. Trapped here forever. No!

Aliisza launched herself upward, folding and unfolding her wings for all she was worth, climbing higher and higher, soaring as far above the glistening stone of the Court as she could. Still she climbed, afraid to look down, knowing what she'd see as soon as she did.

The air grew thin and much colder, and the sky began to deepen. The first stars appeared overhead, and Aliisza chose one, began to fly toward it, still climbing, flying. Anything to get away from the accursed palace of Tyr.

When she looked down, the island was still there, though it had become somewhat smaller. But Aliisza knew she couldn't escape it. In despair, she cried out, screamed. Her voice spread out into the ethereal nothingness that seemed to surround the cruel imitation of the Court, diminishing quickly.

The alu felt utterly alone.

With a sob, she folded her wings upon her back and let herself plummet. She would rather die than remain trapped in such an insidious, horrible place.

◆ ◆ ◆ ◆ ◆ ◆ ◆ ◆ ◆

Myshik stood in a cool foyer. The half-dragon blinked, adjusting to the sudden shift in surroundings. His father, Roraurim, had explained to him the gift Uncle Nahaunglaroth had bestowed upon the cambion, but to witness it firsthand was stunning. Even standing within it, the warrior had difficulty accepting what he saw.

Slabs of polished onyx striated with deep red, almost purplish veins made up the floor. Columns of deep red stone rose to support a second-floor balcony. Torches burned at intervals upon the columns and the walls, set in black iron sconces and giving the chamber a warm, inviting glow. Several plush carpets woven in intricate patterns lay in various places upon the tiles. Tapestries and sculpted artwork adorned the walls and corners of the room. Several other doorways led deeper into the interior, and twin spiral staircases ascended to the balcony along either side of the rear wall.

Zasian stood in the center of the room, looking around

with a smile upon his face. The half-dragon could see why.

Two rows of servants, all beautiful human women with lustrous black hair and emerald green eyes, stood in lines facing the front entrance, smiling. Each had a unique appearance, and all wore gauzy dresses that revealed more than they hid.

"How is this place possible?" Myshik asked, his tone breathy with awe and excitement.

"Pocket dimension," the priest explained, strolling to a wall and studying a tapestry more closely. "Something of a magical mansion, actually," Zasian added. "All of this shapes and forms itself around the cambion's whims. Whatever he imagines comes to be. Quite the clever little sanctuary, don't you think?"

"Indeed," Myshik admitted. "Is it safe? Can we get back out again?"

Zasian shrugged. "Safe enough," he said. "Certainly more hospitable than out there, but if you fear being trapped, then by all means, step back through," he added, gesturing behind the half-dragon toward the entrance.

Myshik turned and stared back the way he had come. The shimmering curtain still rippled there like a pool of water, only vertical. As he watched, Vhok appeared, stepping through the wavering surface.

"Welcome to my humble home-away-from-home," Vhok said as he gestured at the doorway. The shimmer vanished, leaving a stone wall in its place. The cambion moved toward one of the staircases leading to the second floor. "It ought to ease some of the stresses of our journey considerably." He began to climb the stairs. As he did so, he issued a series of orders to the magical servants, sending dark-haired beauties scurrying to tend to various tasks. Vhok instructed some of them to begin preparing a hearty meal, while others were to serve the three of them as personal attendants.

Three of the women moved to accompany Myshik, who stood before the blank wall where the magical doorway had been, testing it. It was solid from edge to edge.

"We're quite safe in here," Vhok said from the balcony, casting a last look down at his two guests. "I've closed it to keep other things from wandering in. We'll open it in the morning."

Myshik nodded and turned to face the cambion.

"I need a good soak and an intense massage, and I imagine you'll find some tasks for your attendants, too," Vhok said with a lascivious smile. Then the cambion turned away, stepped through the double doors at the top of the stairs, and disappeared as the twin portals closed, his attendants in tow.

Myshik cast a glance at Zasian. "Where?" he asked. "Which rooms are which?"

The priest shrugged, still grinning, then turned to one of the maidens gathered close to him. "Which room is mine?" he asked the woman.

The attendant never stopped smiling, nor did she answer. She simply kept her gaze on the human, as though expecting something.

"Oh, wait," Zasian said, snapping his fingers. "I've got it." He looked directly at the attendant. "Show me to my chambers," he instructed. Immediately, the woman turned and led the way toward a door off the foyer, opening it and beckoning gracefully. Zasian nodded. "You have to frame everything in the form of a command. They're magical servants, can't speak. But they'll do anything you tell them. Enjoy!" he chortled, then vanished into his quarters.

Left alone with his trio of handmaidens, Myshik considered for a moment, then issued a command for them to show him his chambers. Once inside, he peered around. The room was decorated in a fashion similar to the foyer outside, with the same polished marble and granite. Tapestries and rugs covered most surfaces, and lamps gave off a warm glow. A magnificent bed sprawled against one wall, covered with fine-spun white linen, and a pool filled with steaming water occupied a corner. A writing desk stood nearby, a set of bookcases next to it.

Myshik glanced at the women who accompanied him. "Assume a form more pleasing to me," he instructed, and smiled as the servants shimmered and transformed before him into three gorgeous half-draconic humanoids.

❖ ❖ ❖ ❖ ❖ ❖ ❖ ❖ ❖

Myshik became conscious of an odd sound. A tiny bell tinkled somewhere in the chamber. The half-dragon had been dozing upon the bed of his guest quarters, having sent the trio of servants away. The bell invaded his dreams, startled him. He sat upright, feeling for a dagger he had slipped beneath one of the many pillows.

The draconic hobgoblin peered around the room, hunting the source of the sound. He spied the bell, hovering in midair above the writing desk. Myshik rose and approached it cautiously. The bell's ring was a sweet, delicate sound. The half-dragon reached out to grasp the handle.

The instant his hand made contact, the ringing stopped and the bell vanished. Kaanyr Vhok's disembodied head hovered in its place.

Myshik frowned and brandished the dagger. What is this sorcery?

"Oh, did I wake you?" the cambion asked, smiling. "I am truly sorry. Would you care to join us for dinner? It's about to be served."

Myshik lowered the dagger. "An odd way to send an invitation," he commented.

"Quite," the cambion replied. "But I love parlor tricks like that. So, are you ready to dine? It all smells delicious."

"I am," Myshik said. "Where?"

"Ah, not to worry, Blood of Morueme," Vhok said. "I will send a girl to fetch you."

Vhok's face vanished and Myshik sensed that he was no longer alone in the room. He turned to find one of the magical servants standing near the doorway. She waited, a faint smile on her face.

Myshik took a moment to refresh himself and dress, then commanded the servant to lead the way. When he emerged from his rooms and followed his escort to the dining room, the savory scents of roasted meats, seasoned vegetables, and fresh, hot bread hit him. His mouth began to water. The handmaiden guided him through the doorway beneath the balcony where the stairs met overhead. Beyond that portal, Myshik discovered a large, cloth-covered table surrounded by high-backed chairs. Zasian and Vhok had already set into the food, which was heaped high and steaming upon platters.

More food was laid out than a dozen people could finish, but that didn't stop the three travelers from trying. Myshik particularly enjoyed the braised pork loin with mustard sauce and the goose liver pâté smeared liberally on thick slabs of crusty bread. A handmaiden stood nearby and kept the three diners' mugs filled with dark ale.

After sampling the varied fare, the trio slumped in their chairs while the magical servants cleared the dishes away and brought a new onslaught of platters and bowls filled with every kind of dessert. Puddings and fresh fruit soaking in clotted cream mingled with delicacies made of spun sugar and hard sauces. Iced wine with fruit juice accompanied the treats.

When the three could eat no more, the platters were cleared. Vhok ordered a servant to remove the tablecloth, revealing dark, polished wood beneath. The cambion waved his hand over the surface of the table and uttered a phrase. The image of a large, detailed map formed there, glowing softly. Myshik gasped in delight, then he and Zasian leaned close to peer at the chart, which had been rendered in delicate lines.

Some of the features seemed familiar to the half-dragon. Mountains and lakes, flat plains and cities all appeared in abundance. Other things looked odd and out of place, or were missing altogether. Myshik saw what appeared to be geysers marked on the map, but he saw no forests. The half-dragon found the text indecipherable.

"We arrived here," Vhok said, pointing to a chain of mountains running along the left side of the drawing. "The City of Brass is here." The cambion slid his finger to a spot near the center. "Kurkle told us in the beginning it would take five days to get there if we remained on land the whole time. But that means going around this," and he pointed to what looked like a small sea inlet jutting down from the top of the map. "The Infernals. We can reduce our time by a day, possible a day and a half, if we gain passage across it, but the going is much more dangerous."

"What manner of boat can remain afloat without going up in flames and sinking in the fires?" Myshik asked, fascinated.

"The kind that is protected by the same magic as that in the ring I loaned you," Vhok replied, tapping the gem-studded jewelry on the half-dragon's hand. "Most of the trading vessels stay close to shore. Convincing one to head straight across may be difficult."

"Or expensive," Zasian said.

"But perhaps necessary," Vhok said, then turned to the priest. "Or not. Is there a reason to hurry?" he asked. "Should we consider the quicker route, though it may prove more deadly?"

Zasian frowned in thought. "Hard to say. Time flows differently in different places in the cosmos, and there is a certain element of vagueness to our plan that makes it difficult to determine how quickly Aliiszas will be in position. I could attempt some divinations tonight before retiring, if you like. Answers may be forthcoming on the wisest route to take based on our assumptions about what is happening in the House of the Triad. Though I cannot guarantee that the choice we divine eliminates unforeseeable complications."

Vhok nodded. "Yes, delve into it tonight and let us converse again at breakfast."

Afterward, the three spent a while in discussion of various topics of interest. Before long, the cambion suggested that they retire and gain sufficient rest, as he knew their travels the next day would be arduous. Myshik returned to his quarters accompanied by his three attendants and was soon asleep, thoroughly sated from his evening meal.

The next morning, the trio gathered at breakfast. The meal was just as sumptuous and extravagant as the previous evening. Myshik gorged himself as much for the delicious tastes as to make certain he would feel healthy and energized for the day's trek.

As they ate, Zasian revealed what he had learned the night before from his divinations. "It was a bit troubling," he said between mouthfuls of poached eggs bathed in a creamy cheese sauce. "The auguries I conducted hinted that time was of the essence, but it all felt somehow . . . wrong."

"What does that mean?" Vhok asked with a frown. He held a slice of hot bread slathered with fruit compote. He was about to dip it into a bowl of clotted cream, but his hand hovered over the dish, forgotten in his concern at Zasian's news.

"I don't know how to explain it," the priest replied. "It's almost as though the quicker we go, the further from our goal we'll be, but delaying only means diminished hope of success. I can't be any clearer than that. I don't really understand it myself."

The cambion's eyes blazed in anger, but Myshik sensed that Vhok's fury was directed at something distant, rather than at the human sharing his table. The half-dragon wondered what was behind the journey they undertook. Thus far, Vhok and the priest had been unwilling to enlighten him.

"I don't like how this is playing out. If she never reaches the gate or doesn't know what to do, we will be trapped in the City of Brass with no way to get home again."

"Not entirely true," Zasian countered. "There are other portals available, other ways of traveling between the planes. We might have to pay dearly, in either gold or service, to make use of one, but it is possible to find our way back by another route should our plan not come to fruition."

Vhok thought for a few moments longer. "What do you mean when you say 'the further away we'll be'? Aren't we going in the right direction?"

"Yes, yes," Zasian answered, "it's not so much a question of direction as one of . . . time. It's entirely possible that I've received two different possible answers, based on two different ways of completing the task. Divinations are notoriously vague and confusing, you know."

Vhok snorted. "You do not have to remind me of that, priest. I've attempted to divine more than my share of shrewd courses to take in my lifetime. I'm sometimes convinced the very act of learning a thing causes direr consequences than remaining ignorant and acting on judgment and intuition." The cambion sighed. "My gut tells me to hurry. Since we're no closer to an answer after your efforts, I'm inclined to listen to my gut. So we cross the Infernals."

Zasian nodded. "I expected such would be your decision. Based on your map, we will reach the shores of the Infernals after half a day of travel on foot. I might, however, find a more expedient means of getting there. I must spend a while in prayer, so I will tailor my divine inspirations to suit our journey and perhaps smooth the way before us."

At that, the priest withdrew to his chambers, leaving Myshik and Vhok alone. The cambion didn't seem in a mood for conversation, so the half-dragon finished his repast and returned to his quarters to gather his things. Vhok had instructed his servants to prepare food suitable for eating while traveling, so Myshik stuffed plenty of dried meat and waterskins into his pack.

Later, the three of them gathered in the foyer of the magical abode, and stepped through the shimmering curtain into the heat-blasted landscape of the elemental plane.

❖ ❖ ❖ ❖ ❖ ❖ ❖ ❖

Aliisza became aware.

She lay on a bed.

Her bed, within her quarters, within the Court.

It was night.

I don't want this bed, this room!

Slowly, she sat up, trying to remember what had happened to her.

There was falling, she remembered, a great plummet into the endless clouds. She let herself fall, never slowing her descent at all. It had gone on and on, growing darker as night seemed to settle and the air whistled past her. She sobbed for a long while, knowing she was destined to live out her year of captivity in that fashion, just as the celestial judges had ordained. She had agreed to it. She had been foolish, thinking that she had to choose life—any sort of life—over death, for the sake of her child. So that she could be its mother, she had thought.

Oh, how foolish she had been to let them trick her that way. But she had, indeed, let them.

Somewhere during that melancholy catharsis, she had slipped into some kind of a trance, a half-waking daze.

She didn't remember returning to her room, to her bed. She wondered how she wound up there.

A faint light, the glow of the moon, perhaps, shone through the window of the balcony. Aliisza arose from the bed, naked, and padded to the window. She peered out and saw the same horizon that had been there before. A sea of clouds stretched forever. The moon had indeed risen and shone down upon that eerie vista, casting a silvery glow everywhere. The alu listened, but the only sound she heard came from the fountain, gurgling as it trickled into the pool on the far side of the room.

Aliisza turned back and saw her clothing, her armor and weapons, laid carefully upon a chair. She dressed and donned her gear, then moved toward the door. She opened it a crack and peered into the courtyard. The soft glow of several lamps, set low on either side of the paths, bathed them in their honey-colored shine.

No one was there.

Am I to live here alone? she wondered. Is this what they intend? To drive me mad with isolation in this vast replica?

Anguish and fear began to well up in her again, but the alu grew angry with herself for such craven thoughts. She and Kaanyr had spent decades trapped beneath the cursed Hellgate Keep. What was a single year?

You didn't do it all alone, she reminded herself. You had companionship. You had Kaanyr.

Is that what they want me to realize? That I need others to make me happy? Is that how I'm supposed to find some measure of benevolence, some deeper understanding of my own wholesomeness?

She dismissed that foolish notion.

Don't let them win, she told herself. Outsmart them. Find a way.

Sighing and trying to regain her confidence, Aliisza pulled the door open and stepped out into the garden plaza. After one step, she stopped and gasped.

The soft glow of moonlight had a strange effect on the trees, gave them a haunting, celestial look. Each leaf seemed to glow with an inner silver light. A gentle breeze whispered through the branches, and Aliisza thought she could make out faint music in the tones. Numerous sets of chimes tinkled softly in the zephyrs, and the fountains gurgled serenely.

"It's quite placating at night, isn't it?" a voice said from behind her, in the shadows. Tauran.

Aliisza spun in place, suddenly on edge and angry again. "What are you doing here?" she snapped. "Come to torment me?" She spied him sitting upon one of the benches, previously concealed by a flowering hedge.

The celestial shook his head. "Not at all," he replied gently. "To comfort you, if I may."

Aliisza tossed her head in aggravated disbelief and turned away from him. "Don't patronize me," she sneered. "You came here to gloat over your trickery."

"I don't gloat," the angel said, and his voice held a bit of an edge to it. Something almost dangerous. "I leave that for your kind."

"*My* kind?" Aliisza said, incredulous. "And what, exactly, is *my* kind?"

"The self-serving, conniving, manipulative creatures who believe they are above the law and have little regard for anyone other than themselves," Tauran answered. "You think you should be allowed to do anything you want, no matter the cost, and you take pointed delight in watching the wretched squirm in your wake. *Your* kind."

Aliisza had to laugh at that. "Thus far, I've seen much of the same from you and yours," she said. When the angel began to bristle, she added, "Don't pretend you don't manipulate. Don't pretend you're not self-serving. You told me just enough of the situation to convince me to trust you, that you had my best interests at heart, when all you really wanted was my child. And you think you can make it all better by pretending foolish compassion and gentle sadness."

"You had every opportunity to turn me down," he retorted. "And my interests go far beyond myself. I succeeded in saving your unborn child's life, rescued it from your tainted influences."

"Ah, at last, your true, disapproving self comes to the fore," Aliisza crowed. "I wondered how long it would take, now that you have me trapped here." Then she gave the angel the most baleful stare she could muster. "I'll tell you this, though. I'd much rather be *my* kind than *your* kind," she said. "Arrogant, judgmental, and self-important, too afraid to think big and seize the moment. I may be everything you described, but at least I don't pretend otherwise. I know what I want, and I take what the world has to offer. I don't let any whining, sniveling, unworthy wretch stand in my way."

"And thus we see the foundation of our differences," Tauran said quietly, the edge of anger gone. "You care more about yourself than others, and I care more about others than myself. A crucial difference."

"How? Why?" Aliisza was honestly flummoxed. "What is there to possibly gain by caring more for something else than for yourself? How silly!" she said. The alu turned and began to stroll through the garden. She heard the angel rise from the bench and follow her. She laughed again. "And, by the way, a huge lie. By your account, you should care more about me than about yourself. If that were actually true, you wouldn't have brought me here and locked me in this . . . this *place*, knowing I didn't want to be here. How is that caring more for others than yourself?"

"It is precisely because I—and everyone here at the Court—care for your welfare that you are here."

"You mean the welfare of my baby, don't you?"

"That, too, and another part of the explanation."

Aliisza snorted in derision.

"If you don't wish to hear it, I shall leave you to your thoughts," Tauran said in response to her gesture, "but you asked."

"I'm beginning to regret it," Aliisza said. "Leave me alone. There is nothing you can do to comfort me. You and your tribunal consigned me to be here, knowing full well that it is a torture to me to be alone, with no creature contact."

"In the hopes that you would come to see the power and joy of making others happy, rather than just yourself."

Aliisza laughed again, but it was bitter. "I am a girl of carnal pleasures. I crave the delights of the senses. The touch, the smell of others nearby. They experience what I lust for and feel some joy and happiness, too."

"That is a false joy, short-lived, and such a tiny fraction of what is possible if you'd only open your heart to—"

"Enough!" Aliisza interrupted. She spun to face the celestial across a low-walled pool where a fountain with the statues of two human children at play bubbled in the cool night air. "Do not preach to me! I was sent here to contemplate. There was nothing in the judge's words about being tormented by the likes of *you!*"

Tauran spread his hands in acquiescence and remained silent, though he did not leave.

Aliisza could feel him watching her as she sat down upon the wall of the fountain, fighting to keep from doing the unthinkable. She would not cry in front of the angel. She could not let him see that.

To divert her feelings, she dropped a hand down to the surface of the water and trailed her fingers through it, making wave patterns and watching them mingle and vanish. From where she sat, the moon reflected off the water, though it was distorted and wavered incessantly. She thought about the child that had been growing inside her, thought about all the times in her recent past when she had been reluctant, afraid of harm, and at last understood why. She felt a sense of cold emptiness inside her because the child was gone. Or rather, *she* was gone from her child. She nearly gave in, then, nearly began to cry despite her struggle not to.

Tauran touched the surface of the water on the opposite side of the pool, and the moon faded from sight in its reflection. Instead, Aliisza saw a different kind of light radiating from within the pool, a warm, flickering light that she recognized as that of lamps. Despite the waves on the water, the image steadied and became clear.

The alu gasped. She saw herself in that image. Not her reflection, but a picture of her, lying still upon a bed, covered by a soft sheet. A figure, a creature with the facial features of a human woman, beautiful and serene, stood beside Aliisza's form, gazing down at her. Like Tauran, the woman had white feathery wings, and she wore the same style of white draping garments. She turned and walked out of the image, leaving Aliisza's body in full view.

"My body," Aliisza said, half to herself. "My corpse, my husk." She swallowed the thick lump she felt in her throat. "With my child inside. The child you took away from me, that I will never see," she snarled, and turned away.

"You asked before how I could explain the dichotomy of my benevolence. How I could care for you more than I care for myself, and yet do this unspeakable thing to you. There, in that image, lies your answer, Aliisza. All beings deserve my care, my compassion. Some accept it, embrace it, return it. Others do not. When those others force me to choose, I choose to defend the oppressed, the victims. That is the way of Tyr, his teachings."

"So, who will defend me from *your* oppression? Who will grant me relief from *my* victimization?"

"When you choose to deny others the respect and compassion they deserve, you fall outside of the circle. You are no longer on equal footing."

"No longer worthy, no longer eligible for your care and compassion," the alu spat with all the sarcasm she could muster. "It must feel good, being so perfect."

Tauran's sigh sounded tired, full of regrets. "I will not debate this with you any longer, Aliisza. You chose the path you have followed. Only you can find a route to a new path, through your actions and deeds. When you understand that, when you are ready to change, to show those around you the same consideration that you would want, then I will be here, ready to guide you. Until then, you will remain here and contemplate what it means."

Aliisza felt a pang of fear surge through her. She realized that, despite his arrogant superiority and obvious disdain for her, she did not want Tauran to leave her alone. "When will you return?" she asked, even though she really wanted to ask him to stay. She couldn't ask, though. She refused to appear that weak to the angel.

"Soon," he replied. "But you will not be alone, Aliisza. Others are coming. And you must face them," he said, and the alu heard a warning in those last words. It sent a shiver down her spine.

"What others?" she asked. "Face them how?"

"Those you have wronged in your life," the deva replied. "Those whom you've tread upon to get the things you crave. You must face them, confront what you've inflicted upon them, and decide for yourself what needs to be done."

Aliisza shivered. Suddenly, all the gentle shadows in the garden seemed much darker, more sinister. The chimes blowing in the breezes rang much harsher than before. For the first time in her life, Aliisza was terrified.

All of her personal demons were coming.

CHAPTER NINE

This way!" Zasian shouted, urging his companions to follow.

Vhok parried a club strike from a fiery centaur and jammed the blade of Burnblood into the creature's chest. The bandit bellowed and reared up in pain as the hole erupted with molten goo. The cambion had to fling himself backward to avoid his foe's flailing hooves. That desperate act nearly sent him over the side of the ravine behind him.

The centaur staggered away from Vhok, clutching at its wound, but two more took its place. The half-fiend spun, desperate to keep from being pinned against the edge of the drop-off. He ducked beneath a spear thrust and knocked the stone weapon aside with his scepter. The cambion feinted to his right, luring the pair of bandits to shift their weight that way. When they bought his bluff, he wheeled back to the left. The two centaurs, their black, stony bodies popping and crackling with the effort, struggled to keep up. Again, though, the cambion only feinted.

When he had the two opponents suitably off balance, Vhok made a half-hearted swipe with his sword at the legs of the creature to his left, forcing it to rear up to avoid the attack.

He followed through with another feint of escape to his right, causing the other centaur to sidestep.

That was what Vhok had been waiting for. As the gap between the two creatures widened, the cambion launched himself through it, tumbling past them to the other side.

Both bandits turned to try to prevent him from slipping past them. Though they flanked him, he was much faster and more nimble. He easily dodged their clumsy spear thrusts. One of them accidentally struck its companion. The injured centaur bucked and kicked at its counterpart, snarling some unintelligible curse in their native language.

Vhok landed on one knee, a few feet from Myshik. The half-dragon battled two more of the bandits. He swung his great dwarven war axe in huge arcs. He had already made contact at least once, for one of the centaurs limped, its foreleg dragging uselessly upon the ground. The pair of bandits kept a respectable distance from the whistling axe.

"More come," the blue-tinged draconic hobgoblin grumbled to Vhok as the cambion took up a position back to back with him. Vhok saw Myshik jerk his head in the direction of the newcomers.

Vhok glanced where his companion indicated. He saw that the blazing, smoking centaur he had initially wounded seemed to be guzzling some draught from a brass flask. The contents of the container must have been a magical healing substance, for Vhok could see the wound in the creature's chest diminishing.

Worse, the half-fiend could see another handful of centaurs in the distance. Their forms appeared as little more than hazy silhouettes in the drifting, acrid smoke that shrouded the landscape. It was obvious to Vhok that they were hurrying to join their embattled companions, crossing the spider-webbed maze of lava-filled ravines in great leaps.

The cambion swore softly and turned the other way, seeking Zasian. He saw the priest receding in the distance, striding upon the air itself. The human magically traversed a ravine, a gap easily twenty paces wide. Beside him, Kurkle moved in similar fashion, though the canomorph seemed much less certain of his newfound transport than the priest. The guide slunk step by step through the smoky air, peering about nervously.

Zasian paused halfway across a ravine and glanced back at his companions. When he caught Vhok's eye, he motioned for the half-fiend to hurry. Then he turned and continued, escaping the fight.

Vhok swore again. Sweat poured from his body, stinging his eyes and soaking his clothing and armor. The acrid stench of smoke and burning stone assaulted his nose and throat, making them sore and dry. His blade hung low, nearly touching the ground, for his strength had been sapped by the endless fighting. His arm felt leaden.

No, that's not quite right, Vhok thought. Lead would merely melt and puddle on the scorched ground here.

It had been a long, tiresome day, and the quartet of travelers had been journeying for only a short time. Upon returning to the fiery plane after their night's repose, Vhok and the others had found Kurkle impatient for the foursome to be on their way. The canomorph had urged them to make haste. He warned them that the bandits were gathering in force. The situation had grown beyond the mere inconvenience of a raiding party. For whatever reason, the tribal centaurs had taken a keen interest in the planar visitors and seemed intent on hunting them down.

"If we hurry and stay out of sight," Kurkle had said, "we can reach the Islands ahead and slip away. They won't follow us there."

Hoping the canomorph had a good sense for such things, the three visitors and their guide set off. Despite their best efforts, the bandits had stayed on their trail and continued to harass them. The group's progress had turned into a running battle.

Over the course of the morning, the land had begun to change. The rolling, open ground bisected by endless meandering ravines had flattened out. The ravines had steadily grown deeper, more sheer, and wider. Rivulets of liquid flame coursed through the bottoms of the trenches. As they progressed, the depth of the molten rock had increased. The land was gradually sloping downward, becoming isolated, flat-topped mesas of solid terrain surrounded by networks of wide lava channels.

No, Vhok thought, islands of land in a sea of lava. We have reached our destination. Now to see if the hound's prediction was accurate.

"We don't want to stay here," the half-fiend warned Myshik as the centaurs began to close warily. "Zasian and the guide are already moving out. I think we're at the Islands."

Myshik nodded in understanding. "Can you flee?" the half-hobgoblin asked, lunging forward and slicing at one of the four bandits. The centaur reared up and backward to evade the cut.

"I've still got a few tricks up my sleeve," Vhok said, gasping as he parried three different spear thrusts. In truth, much of his magic was already gone, exhausted during the running skirmish. But he had the means to escape the predicament he and Myshik were in. "The question," he puffed as he smacked a spear away with his scepter, "is whether *you* do."

"I do," Myshik replied, cleaving a spear in half as it strayed too close to him. "Help me get near the edge. The direction they went," he added. "Then I can take care of myself."

Vhok grunted his assent and drew a deep breath, prepared to pick up the tempo of the battle.

One of the centaurs nearest him snarled and reared up. It kicked at the cambion with its hooves. It held its spear aloft in both hands, ready to slam it down and run Vhok through. The cambion avoided the flailing forelegs and made a daring move. He dashed forward, beneath the rearing beast. He jabbed Burnblood up into the creature's underbelly just as it dropped down on all fours again. The centaur screamed in agony and teetered to the side as the half-fiend tumbled out of the way.

Vhok didn't waste time waiting to see how badly he had wounded the creature. He spun right, smacking his scepter against the flank of the next centaur, which had turned to evade an axe strike from Myshik. The blow echoed with the sound of steel on rock and sent sparks flying. The fiery beast howled something in its native tongue and stumbled away from Vhok.

Out of nowhere, the cambion took a spear to his shoulder. The glowing tip of the blade glanced off his armor, but the force of the strike was enough to twist his arm nearly out of its socket. The cambion grunted in pain and took a step away, closer to the cliff where he and Myshik would escape. His shoulder throbbed and he could barely lift his scepter.

The half-dragon, seeing Vhok's success, leaped forward, swinging his mighty weapon down hard across the gutted centaur's shoulder. The concussive boom of the blow staggered the bandit, driving it down. The blade bit so deeply into the creature's torso it nearly cleaved the beast in two. Myshik kept going. He yanked his blade free and dashed into the gap in the bandits' line, joining Vhok. The pair stood near the edge, then, and the centaurs could no longer come at them from all sides.

The cambion felt two arrows slam against him, one on his thigh and one in his gut, but both bounced away. A spell he had woven over himself earlier still held, deflecting the missiles, but the blows stung. He knew the spell wouldn't hold much longer. He spared a quick glance in the direction the arrows had come, and saw that the remainder of the bandits had arrived. He and Myshik faced nearly a dozen of the scorched, blazing creatures. The newcomers could not squeeze into the fight directly, so they held bows at the ready, waiting for opportune shots.

"Too many!" Vhok called to the draconic hobgoblin. "Time to go!"

Myshik nodded as he drove a centaur back with two broad swings of his axe. An arrow flew past his ear and made him flinch. "Get ready!" he shouted. "You'll know when!"

Vhok didn't know what the half-dragon had in mind, but he didn't doubt that Myshik was capable. The cambion parried another spear thrust and slipped his scepter into its loop on his belt. With his sword still out for defense, the half-fiend pulled a tiny bit of gauze from an inner pocket. The spell he intended to cast required a bit of smoke as well.

I wonder where I might find some, he thought wryly.

Myshik whipped his axe at his closest opponent once more, then jumped back to one side, right against the edge. His movement separated him from Vhok, allowing the centaurs to close in between them.

Vhok kept one eye on the half-dragon as he struggled to keep the press of centaurs away from himself. Whatever you're going to do, the cambion thought, do it!

The draconic hobgoblin drew in a deep breath just as two more bandits surged forward to surround him. The centaurs seemed to laugh with glee, though it was difficult for Vhok to be sure, given the creatures' strange, cracking language.

Regardless, it was all cut short as the Morueme scion unleashed death and destruction upon his foes in one sharp exhalation.

Blinding light and crackling energy erupted from the half-dragon. It shot out in a line, surging through several of the gathered bandits in front of Myshik and Vhok. The cambion flung a hand up and spun away, futilely trying to protect himself. The afterimage seared his vision for several heartbeats, making his eyes water.

Vhok cursed the fool half-hobgoblin at first, then realized that Myshik had most likely cleared the press of centaurs away from the two of them. Unable to see how close his foes were, Vhok trusted that he could cast his spell unmolested. He waved the gauze around himself and triggered the magic.

The cambion felt his body change. He became insubstantial, as light as a feather. His eyes no longer hurt, and though the effect was disorienting, he could "see" in every direction at once. He had become nothing but an amorphous puff of smoke, virtually invisible and immune to the attacks of the remaining bandits.

Vhok began to drift away, mentally commanding his new form to float in the direction Zasian and Kurkle had gone. He spied the priest and the guide waiting on the next island. The wind blew incessantly across the plane, buffeting him, but he compensated by drifting slightly against it, as though he swam upstream to cross a river.

Behind him, he could see several centaurs down, unmoving. A few staggered about, injured and clutching at their eyes. In their pain and blindness, they paid little heed to the draconic hobgoblin in their midst.

Myshik roared a primal challenge and waded in among the survivors. He cut a swath through the bandits with his axe, feeding on some berserk rage that lent him strength and resolve. As Vhok wafted farther away, he watched in amazement as the half-dragon sliced and hewed his enemies. Each axe blow delivered a resounding boom and sent centaurs staggering or flying back from the hobgoblin.

At last, Myshik had downed or driven all his enemies away. He gave a single shudder then, and his shoulders slumped. His axe dangled at his side and his breath came in deep, panting gasps.

Vhok realized that he had exhausted himself. Come on, Myshik, he willed. Get moving before more show up.

As if sensing his companion's mental summons, Myshik hefted his axe once more and turned in the direction that Vhok and the others had fled. He began to sprint toward them. As he built up speed, he unfurled his wings. Vhok had never seen Myshik fly and wondered if the vestigial appendages could hold him aloft.

At the very edge of the plateau, Myshik leaped into the air and soared over the flowing lava. He hurtled right toward Vhok, though the cambion knew the half-dragon could not see him in his smoky form. The draconic hobgoblin spread his wings and glided.

Vhok could see that it was not true flight, but the wings held the half-dragon aloft well enough to clear the gap. Myshik's momentum carried him across faster than Vhok could drift, and the draconic hobgoblin just cleared the lip of the next plateau before touching down. His momentum carried him forward a few steps, and he settled in a heap upon the ground.

A moment later, Vhok arrived and dismissed his magic. His body reformed to its fiendlike state and his feet settled to the broiling ground once more. He stepped closer to Zasian and Kurkle, who stared in the direction they had come.

Several centaurs had recovered, and still more had appeared. They faced the foursome and all could see that they had unlimbered their bows. The creatures formed a line and took aim at their quarry.

With a muttered word and a gesture, Zasian summoned a magical wall crafted of stone. He shaped it in a semicircle along the edge of the plateau. It was tall enough that none of them could see over the top.

Vhok heard the sound of arrows smacking against the opposite side. He shrugged and turned away, sliding down to rest. "Will they follow us?" he asked.

The canomorph made a strange barking sound, and the cambion realized it was a snort of derision. "They cannot," Kurkle said. "They are great leapers, but the Islands are too much for them. Sometimes, they use magic to foray out here, but they cannot come in force."

"Then we are safe," Myshik said, his voice weak with weariness. "They will trouble us no more."

Kurkle snorted again. "Nay, not safe," he said. "Other things lurk here. We must be wary. Watch the skies, the flow between islands."

Vhok eyed the territory with doubt. The sea of lava, dotted with mesas of solid land, stretched as far as he could make out in the hazy air. The molten rock sloshed and churned, hiccuping bubbles and gouts of liquid fire randomly. The whole horizon shimmered and wavered from the heat.

"How far does this go?" he asked.

"Not far," Kurkle replied. "A short trek, if we were on solid land. But we must find a way to cross. Your magic," he said, turning to Zasian. "Can you use it to let us walk upon the air, as we did before?"

The priest nodded. "You still can," he said, "for a bit longer. But it will vanish after a time, and I cannot bestow it upon the others," he said, gesturing at Vhok and Myshik. "The half-dragon cannot glide from island to island—some are too far apart. Vhok? What magic have you?"

The cambion shook his head. "Not much," he answered. "Too much went against the bandits, or to aid in escaping them. And I am bone tired, anyway. I say we stop for the day and resume our journey tomorrow. Zasian and I can plan new magic to help us cross this."

"It's not safe here," Kurkle argued. "We should press on."

"It's safe enough for my magical mansion," Vhok said. "You'll have to come with us, Kurkle."

The canomorph gave the cambion a doubtful look, but at last acquiesced with a nod.

"This wall of yours is handy, Zasian," Vhok remarked as he dug the miniature archway out of his belongings. "The centaurs can't see us disappear. If they do get over here, it will seem like we are long gone."

With that, he summoned the portal leading into his posh extradimensional abode and gestured for everyone to enter. The cambion was the last to pass through the doorway, and once he was gone, the shimmering passage winked out of existence.

❖ ❖ ❖ ❖ ❖ ❖ ❖ ❖

Though the mid-morning air was crisp and cold, the sun shining on Aliisza's face warmed her skin. She drew a deep breath and caught the scent of fragrant blossoms emerging from the flaky-barked branches of a felsul tree in the tiny garden. Spring had come to Sundabar.

Two young children, a boy and a girl, played in the garden. They dug in a bare patch of dirt with their hands. As the boy made a path, the girl moved a wooden block painted to look like a coach along it. Neither of them noticed the half-fiend in their midst.

The children kept their voices soft, near-whispers meant only for one another. Aliiszacould not make out what they said, but she caught an edge to their tones that hinted at apprehension. They played, as all children did, but they had dread in their hearts.

The door from the house opened, and the children's mother—no, their older sister—emerged, clothed in a simple dress, perhaps a bit threadbare, covered with an apron. Her shoulder-length ebony hair framed eyes of brilliant blue, eyes that expressed deep sorrow in all that the young woman beheld. She offered a smile as the two children glanced up at her, but the expression belied the look in her eyes.

"Remember," she said to the pair, "don't leave the garden. I'll be back near sundown." Her tone was light and upbeat, but Aliisza could hear a catch in her voice that told a different story. "When you get hungry, there's some bread and cheese in the cupboard. Don't eat it all—I don't get paid until the morrow, and that's all we have left."

The young woman moved to the garden gate, passing very near Aliisza. She never acknowledged the alu. She pulled on the latch of the gate and opened it. As she stepped into the narrow street beyond, she turned and gave the children one last smile, then pulled the gate shut after herself.

Aliisza saw the two children peer at the gate for some moments afterward. The boy sighed and turned back to his digging, but the girl, whom Aliisza could see was a few years older, rose to her feet and went to a bench beneath the felsul tree. She plopped herself down and hunched over, staring at the ground. Her eyes welled with tears. She drew her sleeve across her face, scrubbing them away.

"When I get bigger, I'm going to take Dada's sword and kill that man," the boy said, kneeling in the dirt. His eyes were watery, too. "I'll stab him right in the gut."

"No, you won't," the girl said, defiantly wiping her eyes. "Not even when I have to work for him, too."

Aliisza had enough. With a snort of disgust, she turned away. The little wretches weren't going to ruin *her* morning. She found herself standing outside the garden, near the gate. She could see the older sister making her way down the lane. The alu decided to follow. She didn't know why.

The young woman crossed the square, pushing her way through milling merchants hawking their wares and the goodwives who bought them. Her gait was slow, almost reluctant. She paused for a moment to stare at a barrel filled with old, withered apples, and even at Aliisza's distance, the alu could hear the girl's stomach rumble. Tearing her eyes away from the food, the girl entered an alley. She passed a handful of doorways, the back entrances of several shops, until she came to her destination. She stepped inside.

Aliisza followed her, compelled to see what sort of man she might work for that would raise the ire of a mere boy. To her surprise, she discovered that the building housed a tailor's shop. Bolts of fabric lined shelves along every wall, while spools of thread filled several wooden boxes atop work tables. A loom stood in one corner, a half-finished weave of fabric stretched across it. Two other doors led from the chamber, one toward the front of the building, most likely to the shop. The other door was on a side wall, behind a table bearing a pile of fabric scraps.

A squat man with greasy hair and an ocular clenched in one eye glanced up from where he had been sorting needles. He scowled. "You're late," he growled.

The girl lurched to a halt, dropped her head, and stared at the stone floor. "I'm very sorry, Master Velsin. I had the morning sickness again, and I just couldn't—"

"I don't care what ails you," he snarled, stomping around

the corner of the table. He grabbed her by one arm and jerked her to face him more directly. "You're to be here by seven bells, not a moment after. Next time you're late, don't bother coming at all."

The girl's mouth trembled as she stared at her employer. "Y-yes, Master Velsin," she breathed.

"Now get in there," the man snapped, flinging her arm free and jerking his thumb toward the side door. "Yrudis Gregan wants to see some new dresses."

The girl cast her eyes down to the floor again and mumbled, "Yes, sir." She moved woodenly, untying her apron as she approached the door.

Aliisza rolled her eyes, trying to feel uninterested in the girl's plight, but she understood what the young woman's illness meant and felt a pang of sympathy anyway. Despite her desire to leave the shop, to return to the street outside, she followed the girl.

The cramped chamber beyond was dim, lit only by a single oil lamp on a small table in the far corner. An obese man filled most of the rest of the room, his considerable bulk spilling over the sides of a single rickety wooden chair. He was dressed in plain clothing and wore an apron, though it was caked with flour and other smears. He sat with his arms folded across his chest, a severe look on his face.

"It's about time," he said, glaring at the girl. "I've been here since seven bells."

"Yes, Master Gregan," the girl said. "I'm sorry."

"Of course you are," the man replied. "Well, no more dilly-dallying. I want to see how they fit. Not going to buy my daughter such expensive dresses without knowing how they fit, you know." He gestured at a disheveled pile of fashionable dresses heaped in the corner. "Start with the blue one," he said.

"Y-yes, Master Gregan," she answered, picking up the dress atop the pile. She held it up, looking at it.

"You don't really think you deserve to put on dresses like that, do you?" the man asked, his tone demeaning. "They aren't for trollops like you. You must think you'd be very pretty in a dress like that. Maybe even prettier than my daughter?"

"N-no, Master Gregan," the young woman said forlornly. She began to unbutton her own dress, turning away as she slipped it over her head, leaving herself in only her small clothes.

"Stop that," Yrudis Gregan said sharply. He leaned forward, an eager, lascivious grin on his face. The chair creaked in complaint beneath his bulk. "Turn around so I can see you. No trollop is going to tell *me* she's prettier than my daughter. Turn around so I can see you!"

Aliisza found herself back outside the tailor's shop. She was breathing faster than normal, and there was a tightness in her chest she hadn't noticed before. She realized she was clenching her fists, and she relaxed them.

Angry? she thought. Am I angry? What do I care what happens to that girl? I didn't do that to her. It's not my problem. She turned to depart, prepared to dismiss all thoughts of the young girl from her mind forever, when she noticed a man standing in the alley, dressed in soldier's gear, watching the shop.

An air of both sadness and fury hung about him, both at the same time. He stared at the tailor's doorway, his eyes boring unseen holes through the walls to learn what was happening inside. Once, he almost took a step forward, as if he were going to march right in there and put a stop to it, but he didn't budge. He just stood there, fighting against himself.

Aliisza knew, without knowing *how* she knew, that he was the girl's father. His wife had died some years before, giving birth to the boy in the garden. He was their sole parent, taking care of the three of them ever since. She also knew that he was dead, a ghost like her, a figure no one could notice. He couldn't help his daughter.

He had died not too many nights before, ambushed and slaughtered along with the rest of his Sundabarian patrol, the victim of fiendish orcs under a gibbous moon in a narrow canyon.

❖ ❖ ❖ ❖ ❖ ❖ ❖ ❖

Myshik awoke, just as he intended to, in darkness. His chamber was silent save for the gurgle of a fountain. It was nearly dark in the room, lit only by the soft glow of some magical light emanating from nowhere in particular. The half-dragon stretched and sat up.

"Come to me," he commanded softly, and instantly, a figure stood before him, one of the servants Kaanyr Vhok had offered as part of the palatial accoutrements of his magical safehold.

The figure, a human woman dressed in diaphanous silks, smiled and waited, watching the draconic hobgoblin mutely.

Myshik arose from his bed and dressed quickly, donning his full armor and weaponry. He felt rested, refreshed. He was also giddy with anticipation. He checked over his gear once, twice, a third time, knowing he could make no mistakes and survive.

"Lead me," he commanded softly. "Show me the door to the canomorph's chamber."

Without a word, the servant turned and began to walk. She moved through Myshik's own door into the tapestried and carpeted hallway beyond. She moved silently, crossing the floor on dainty feet that seemed to barely touch the ground.

The draconic hobgoblin followed, trying to emulate her as best he could. He was not a deft being, and his boots thudded more loudly than he would have liked.

The beautiful servant paused in front of a door, not far from the half-dragon's own. She wordlessly pointed at it and stood still, watching him and smiling gently.

Myshik thought carefully about how to word his next instruction. If he did not explain it thoroughly and correctly, the consequences would be disastrous. Finally, he formulated his order. "Without disturbing Kaanyr Vhok in any way, enter his chambers, retrieve the sculpted archway that creates this place, and return with it to me."

As the servant vanished, Myshik slipped through the door and entered Kurkle's chambers. The half-hobgoblin was assaulted by overwhelming heat. He gasped as waves of it crashed against him, carrying the stench of burning stone. The ring upon the hobgoblin's finger repelled the brunt of the devastating swelter, but he broke out in a sweat immediately.

The room looked nothing like a guest room. It appeared more like a small hollow upon the blasted landscape of the Plane of Fire, a sheltered spot among low stone ridges made of scorched and glowing hot rock. The light was dim, as it had been in Myshik's room and in the hall outside, so his eyes had no trouble spying the figure curled up within the hollow.

Kurkle was sleeping in hound form, but his canine head rose up at Myshik's approach. The canomorph let out a low growl and leaped to his feet as the half-dragon rushed at him. He hefted the dwarven war axe high in the air and swung forward.

Kurkle tried to jump clear of the strike, but Myshik was

too quick and the canomorph too slowed by the daze of sleep. The axe bit deeply into Kurkle's flank. The impact reverberated with a rumbling boom and knocked the fiery creature aside.

Kurkle yelped in pain as he sprawled away. He tried to stagger upright, but his hind legs didn't work properly. With a keening whimper, the canomorph began to shift form, changing into a half-orc. As he transformed, his belongings appeared, and Kurkle fumbled in a pouch strapped to his hip.

Myshik strode forward again. He pulled his axe back for another blow, eager to strike before his foe extracted the object he sought. Kurkle yanked a flask free and tried to guzzle the contents and roll clear of the draconic hobgoblin at the same time, but even as a humanoid, his injured legs hindered him.

Myshik slammed the axe down hard, splitting the half-orc's skull.

Kurkle's eyes went wide and glazed over as the concussive thump caved most of his head in. The flask fell from his hand and tumbled to the scorching ground. Its contents leaked onto the searing rock, evaporating in thick wisps of greenish steam. His body flopped onto the stones, limp.

Myshik sighed and cleaned the blade of his axe on the dead guide's tunic. "Sorry, dog-man," he said softly as he stepped away. "Nothing personal. You were just in the wrong place at the wrong time." He moved to the door and paused, looking back. "But then again, I never liked being called 'drako.'" With that, the half-dragon slipped outside.

The servant had returned and waited patiently, the arch clutched in her hands. Myshik listened for a moment to see if her subterfuge had roused the cambion. He heard no cries of anger, no alarms. He feared that Vhok might have warded his room with magic to protect himself from just such an act.

Foolish, trusting fiend, Myshik thought as he took the

arch from the servant. My father and uncle do not enter into pacts with the likes of you.

The half-dragon proceeded into the dining room. As he expected, it was empty and dark. He studied the large table that dominated the chamber, wondering if his axe held within it the power to destroy the thing.

Only one means to find out, he decided.

Hoisting the axe, he raised it as high as his arms would stretch and called on all his strength. With one powerful downstroke, Myshik slashed the head of the axe against the surface of the magical table. With an ear-splitting crack, the thunderous weapon sundered the table, splitting it into two separate halves.

Myshik smiled in satisfaction. That ought to do it, he thought. Time to go.

The hobgoblin turned and hurried from the room. He strode toward the entrance of the palace. He approached the door, sealed shut with stone, and recalled how Vhok had opened it the previous morning. Myshik had made certain to pay careful attention so he would be able to mimic Vhok's gestures precisely. He blew through the arch and watched as the shimmering curtain appeared.

Behind him, the half-hobgoblin heard a muffled shout. The glow of a lantern brightened the hallway above and behind him, from the direction of Vhok's chambers.

"Hope you enjoy your new home, demon," Myshik muttered softly. He stepped through the portal. "You're going to be here a while," he added as he stepped into the heat and smoke of the tortured Plane of Fire. "In fact," he finished, "I sincerely hope forever." The half-dragon then held his lips to the arch and blew once more.

The magical doorway winked out.

CHAPTER TEN

"Damn that traitorous, blue-skinned bastard!" Kaanyr Vhok roared, holding a fragment of splintered wood. He stared at the ruined dining table. He wanted to wrap his fingers around the half-hobgoblin's neck, choke the life from him. He could feel his own neck bulging from anger. "Damn him and his cursed axe, too! Damn his whole clan to the foulest pits of the Nine Hells!" Vhok screamed, flinging the shard across the chamber. He turned and stalked out of the room.

Zasian, who had just neared the dining chamber, had to press himself against the wall of the corridor to avoid being overrun by the stalking cambion. As Vhok stormed past, the priest said, "Your fears were correct. Kurkle is dead."

Vhok did not acknowledge his companion's words. He already knew the ivory sculpture that would permit them egress from the mansion was gone. It only made sense that Myshik would have killed their guide and destroyed their map.

Leave no stone unturned in the act of betrayal, Vhok thought bitterly.

After the cambion passed, Zasian spun and followed, a frown on his face. "I am not sure how we can extricate ourselves from this space," he said. "Removing the focus from within the extradimensional pocket precludes us from—"

"I swear," Vhok interrupted, "when we *do* get out of here, I'm going to roast that hobgoblin on an open spit!" He reached the front door, nothing more than a stone wall without the arch. He pounded his fist against it. "And I'm going to go to that mountain, and I'm going to gut his father and his uncle," he added, beginning to pace. "Damn them," he spat again.

"Calm yourself, Vhok," Zasian said, taking a seat on the bottom step of one of the twin staircases. "One thing at a time. First, let's figure out a means of extricating ourselves, then we can worry about revenge."

"Blast!" the half-fiend snarled. "I trusted him. I trusted *all* of them! What kind of a fool am I?" His anger was so acute that he could see spots swimming in his vision. All he wanted was one chance to confront the draconic hobgoblin. One chance to impart due payment.

"Indeed," Zasian said. "But circumstances were chaotic and dire. The dwarves pressed the fight, and we had only moments to choose. And your sorceress unexpectedly succumbed to injuries beyond our ken to address. A plan is only good until the first bow shot is fired, then battle is a series of adjustments. You know full well that you cannot make any progress in any endeavor without adapting, and that you must trust that *some* things, or someone, will not behave as you anticipate."

"To the Nine Hells with *that*," Vhok spat, dismissing the priest's words with a wave of his hand. "Never again," he vowed. "No one ever gets Kaanyr Vhok backed into a corner this way again. I trust no one but myself."

"Including me?" Zasian asked quietly. "Are you going to condemn me now solely on the virtue that I am not you?"

Vhok stopped pacing and stared at the priest. "Have you

given me cause not to?" he asked, giving the human a baleful stare. "Or are you in league with Myshik? Clan Morueme?"

"Yes, of course I am," Zasian responded, a dangerous gleam in his eye. "I plotted to trap myself within this posh prison from the very start!"

Vhok smirked. "More clever ways of deflecting blame have been utilized before," he commented. He folded his arms across his chest and continued to stare at his counterpart. "What better way to throw me off than to appear as a fellow victim?"

Zasian threw his hands in the air. "Then your cause is already lost," he said, rising to his feet. "If you believe that, then you know that I have lied about everything, even the prediction of Aliisza's capture and confinement within the House of the Triad. And thus," he added, turning and ascending the stairs, "this entire journey has been one elaborate charade, a worthless endeavor that I put myself through for no good reason, when I could have easily sent you through the Everfire and left you helpless on this plane, with no guide and no hope of returning, and not bothered with all the rest of the hardship!"

Vhok watched as the priest reached the top of the staircase. His anger, though not abated, began to crystallize and focus on the true source of his woes. He knew it would have been much easier for Zasian to betray him earlier in the game, if that had been the Banite's intention from the start.

"You're right," he said, spreading his arms in acceptance. "I cannot explain why you would have willingly suffered through all this if you had intended to send me here and abandon me."

"I'm glad you're finally seeing sense," Zasian replied, leaning against the banister at the top of the stairs.

"Indeed," Vhok said. "But also understand the larger implications of this betrayal to me. Clan Morueme knows I am here, so they also know my army is leaderless, vulnerable. I am now forced to consider which course of action is more urgent—continuing with my quest, or returning to Sundabar to stave off a powerful enemy. An enemy, I should add," he said, giving Zasian a meaningful stare, "that might consider Sundabar itself ripe for the picking."

Zasian nodded. "The thought had crossed my mind. But I think your situation in the Silver Marches is secure for the moment. It will take the dragons tendays to organize and muster their forces for such an attack."

"There are other ways they could wreak havoc," Vhok countered.

Zasian shrugged. "Even if they attempted to take control of your Scourged Legion by subterfuge, it would require significant time to draw the whole army together and do anything with it." He shook his head. "No, I think we should keep moving forward. Success in this gives you the tools to thwart them more handily."

Vhok knew the priest was correct. He still worried about being away while the cursed dragons maneuvered.

"And Aliisza is waiting for you," the priest added. "If we don't press on, she's trapped there for good."

Vhok drew in a deep breath and sighed. "Of course," he said. "I knew from the start that nothing else would matter if I fell short in this quest. That still holds true. Reach the Lifespring, gain its power, and all the rest will fall into place."

"Very good," Zasian said. "Then let's work on getting ourselves out of here." He turned away from the railing and strode toward his room.

"Where are you going?" Vhok asked.

"To pray," the priest replied. "I think divine intervention will be necessary to get us out of here."

And what am I supposed to do in the meantime? Vhok

silently asked. He looked at the sealed doorway and pounded it once more with his fist.

❖ ❖ ❖ ❖ ❖ ❖ ❖ ❖

Aliisza could not bring herself to look down into the square below. She knew the hustle and bustle of the Sundabarians was not entirely real, but a conjuration from her own mind. Indeed, every aspect of the world around her—from the cobbled streets to the azure sky—was an illusion, part of the game her mind was playing with her. Such was the magical power of the strange prison in which the angels had incarcerated her.

The dead soldier she had witnessed, the plight of his orphaned family weighing heavily on his restless soul—this had been only the first of many tragic tales the alu had witnessed. There had been others, so many others. She had turned away from each of them, dismissing them all.

Theirs are their own burdens to bear, she had thought. You make of the world what you wish, and take what you can. If you are not strong enough to survive its hardships, then you do not deserve its rewards.

Eventually, it had all grown to be too much, and she had been forced to escape it. She had soared into the sky, had found a quiet spot atop the Master's Hall where she could observe from afar.

Only to rest, she had told herself. And see if this silly trick of the mind will tire itself and vanish.

Yet even from her high perch, Aliisza could somehow sense the haunted lives below, each one a tale of sorrow and misfortune wrought by her own destructive pleasures. She could feel where each ghost hovered, experience its own despair and anguish. Because they were, in part, manifestations of her mind, she found herself psychically linked to them.

Stop it! Aliisza screamed into the recesses of her consciousness. I don't want to see this anymore!

And just like that, it was gone. Sundabar vanished, replaced by the celestial courtyard. The folk of the city evaporated, and the alu found herself utterly alone once more.

It was nighttime again. The fragrance of the myriad blooms within the garden wafted past her on gentle breezes. Those same zephyrs stirred the wind chimes hanging in the silver-leaved trees, setting them to faint and gentle songs. The warmth of the sun faded from Aliisza's skin, replaced by the coolness of a hint of dew in the air.

The alu snorted. *This* isn't real either, she thought.

She understood that she could change her surroundings at will. She had learned that early on. But no matter how hard she tried, no matter what place she conjured from her past, the illusion left her solitary, bereft of companionship.

She had started with Hellgate Keep. Though she recalled every wall, every corridor within that blasted prison with perfect clarity, she could induce no other fiends to fill it. The place simply echoed with her own lonely footsteps. She did not really want to be surrounded by a horde of slavering, power-hungry demons, but somehow, the miles of passages and scores of chambers within its confines didn't seem right without them.

Then she had attempted to bring about a number of locales she associated with Kaanyr. She tried to conjure their sumptuous chambers in the halls of Ammarindar, the interior of the war tent they had used during the siege of Menzoberranzan, even just a simple cloistered room with her lover inside. Each time, the alu was able to recreate the environs perfectly. But no sign of the cambion ever appeared.

If she wanted people, she had to settle for the ones she had hurt.

Emotional blackmail, she often thought in disgust. That's

all this is. Well, Tauran, you can't make me feel sorry for pitiful wretches just by denying me any other contact!

Aliisza sighed and looked around the garden. She found herself wishing more and more frequently that the deva would return to her sanctuary. Despite all his faults and shortcomings, she craved him. In her illusory worlds, she didn't even enjoy the luxury of interaction. At least with Tauran, there had been genuine conversation.

The alu moved toward the pool. The angel had shown the half-fiend herself there, her physical body. She longed to see it again, to see the vessel that carried her child within. She longed to see the child itself.

The surface of the water showed only the night sky. The moon rippled within it, but nothing more.

No, Aliisza resolved. I will *not* sit here and ask. That's what they want. I can stand the solitude. It's just a matter of gutting it out. I won't give in to them. I won't!

With that, the alu turned and strode purposefully toward her quiet room. She wasn't yet ready to face the grieving martyrs again, but a little rest, a little unconscious oblivion, would do her wonders.

Tomorrow, she vowed. Tomorrow, I will laugh in their faces. Weaklings.

❖ ❖ ❖ ❖ ❖ ❖ ❖

"You know as well as I," Zasian said, "that divination magic is notorious for unreliability. We are fortunate that the augury was as clear as it was, frankly."

Vhok examined the scroll in his hand, doubtful. "I don't like this," he said. "We have no idea what will happen. You said yourself that the magic wasn't explicit enough to guarantee no mishaps."

Zasian shrugged. "Short of calling on an ally of Bane himself for aid, we have no alternative. I could summon a creature loyal to the Black Lord, one who could enter this place and assist us, but the price for such service would be steep. The risk might be as great or greater than this," he said as he gestured at the crumpled parchment in the cambion's hands. "Regardless, it will cost us valuable time. Do you wish to wait a full day and call on a planar ally to assist us?"

Vhok frowned. "You have nothing better? Nothing more certain than this?" Vhok asked, rattling the scroll.

"Do *you?*" Zasian asked. "If so, bring it forth and let us be gone at once. Otherwise"—he gave Vhok a glare—"do not question me about it again. I have told you the sum total of our options. You must pick between expediency and safety."

Vhok sighed. "Very well," he said. "I've always wanted to see what was on the other side of oblivion."

The priest snorted but said nothing further.

The half-fiend examined the scroll in his hands. It had lain forgotten in his belongings for some time, given to him by Lysalis. The fey'ri sorceress had intended it for an emergency, but none had ever come up when it had seemed necessary. Over time, it had settled to the bottom of a satchel he kept with him. Only Zasian's divination reminded him that he had it.

A single spell had been scribed upon the scroll, one that created a magical retreat, in much the same way the ivory arch did. It required the use of a length of rope, easily produced from the equipment Vhok and Zasian carried with them. Under normal circumstances, the cambion could cast the spell from the scroll and open an extradimensional space, then use the rope to climb into it.

But opening one extradimensional space within another was far from ordinary. All who dealt with forces arcane knew the dangers of combining pocket dimensions. The cambion had heard enough tales of wizards, in their foolishness, tearing great rents in the fabric of the planes by doing such things. He hardly felt eager to try it himself. Nonetheless, that was precisely what Zasian's augury had suggested.

Vhok and the priest faced one another in the entryway of the palatial retreat, before the sealed doorway. The rope rested on the floor between them. Once Vhok completed the arcane words written upon the parchment, the magic would be completed and the spell cast.

"Before you begin," Zasian said, "let me imbue us with a bit of divine protection."

"To provide succor against what?" Vhok asked. "Whatever's going to happen, do you think our paltry defenses will change the outcome? Save them for when they might do us real good."

"As you wish," the priest muttered, and motioned for Vhok to proceed.

Vhok took a deep breath to steady himself and scanned the page one more time before beginning. Then, slowly and clearly, he began to read aloud, uttering each word written in the obscure language of magic. As the syllables rolled off his tongue, their counterparts vanished from the page. The ink faded to nothing bit by bit.

When the cambion completed the final phrase, he felt the power of magic slide through him from the page. He sensed it channeling outward, into the rope before him. The rope began to stir, snaking one end of itself upright into the air. The line rose higher, until its end was just above the two observers' heads. A strange crackling sensation filled the air, and Vhok felt his ears pop.

Light and sound exploded all around the half-fiend. He felt his insides churn and tumble, threatening to burst outward and engulf his skin. He lost his sense of up and down and thought he was floating in a sea of swirling color. A wind howled and buffeted him, knocking him about. He could see nothing.

Vhok opened his mouth to call to Zasian, to scream. Something flowed into him and down his throat. His eyes ached, his muscles turned to jelly, and when he thought he couldn't stand it any longer, he felt himself launched elsewhere. His body sailed through the blinding nothingness toward a tiny pinprick of darkness. That miniscule hole expanded in an instant, became a black sphere of oblivion that sucked him toward it.

Vhok did not want to be swallowed by the great black thing. Death lay inside. He tried to swim away from it, tried to claw his way in a different direction, but his efforts were futile.

The blackness engulfed him.

The cambion hit something, hard, and felt himself stick to it. Another object slammed into him, just as hard, and it stuck to him just as tightly. It stole his breath from him. He was glued to something hard, while something else adhered to him. Together, they hung above a roiling sea of fog shaded orange and gray, while a sky filled with sloshing, lapping fire surrounded them overhead. He peered down at that strange fog in terror, afraid that the object to which he was affixed would release him to fall forever.

Vhok's ears popped again, and the whole universe turned upside down.

No, Vhok realized, it righted itself. It was upside down before.

He was lying on his back upon baked and smoldering stone, staring up at a smoky gray sky lit from distant and unseen fires. Around him, a sea of lava burped gouts of gas and jets of flame. The Elemental Plane of Fire.

Thank the fell ones, Vhok thought. I never thought I'd be so happy to be here.

The half-fiend tried to sit up, then realized a great dead weight still lay atop him. He feared at first that it was Zasian, hurt or killed during the expulsion. A quick look revealed that it was Kurkle's corpse.

Of course, Vhok realized. Everything got ejected.

"Vhok!" Zasian yelled from somewhere nearby. "Vhok, are you there?"

The cambion shoved the canomorph's body off himself and stood up. "Yes!" he called, and he spun around, trying to find his companion. He discovered that he was on the Islands. In fact, it was the same chunk of solid ground where the priest had erected the wall of stone and they had disappeared into the mansion. "Where are you?" he shouted.

"On the wrong side of the hell-cursed wall!" Zasian replied. "Help me! I can't hold on much longer!"

Vhok snatched up the rope lying at his feet—the same rope upon which he had channeled the magic of the scroll—and moved next to the semicircular barrier. With a thought, he levitated to the top of it and stepped onto the narrow top surface. He peered over the far side.

Zasian, half-submerged in the lava, held on to a small chunk of rough rock at the base of the wall. He peered upward at the half-fiend. He didn't seem terrified, though his eyes did convey a sense of nervousness.

"Need some help?" Vhok asked with a grin.

He knotted a loop in the rope and lowered it to his companion. When the loop reached Zasian, the priest took hold of it. He released his grip on the rock and settled lower into the lava, but he clung to the loop and hoisted himself up. Working together, the pair managed to haul him to the top of the wall. As he rose, liquid stone sloughed off his clothing and equipment, sizzling and darkening as it dripped back to the molten flow. Zasian clambered to the other side with Vhok's aid, and dropped to the ground. The cambion floated down to join the priest.

"Thanks," Zasian said as he caught his breath. "I couldn't do anything, or I'd slip off." He took a look around. "Amazing that we wound up here again," he said.

"What's that supposed to mean?" Vhok asked. He felt a sense of dread rising. His anxiety multiplied with the sense that time had escaped his grasp. Important events were afoot, and the cambion knew not whether he was ahead of them or behind them.

"I half expected us to wind up somewhere even more deadly than this," Zasian replied. "Perhaps a plane of oblivion, or one of extreme negative energy, like the kind that feeds the undead and keeps them animated. All things considered, we couldn't have asked for a better result."

"You suspected all that, and you still advised that we follow through? Are you mad?"

Zasian shrugged. "On the other hand, I did receive guidance in this matter from Bane himself, so I felt assured that we would survive the ordeal. Looks like I was right to trust him, wouldn't you say?"

Vhok grunted, unwilling to commit to an answer. The cambion instead looked around and changed the subject.

"So we freed ourselves," he observed. "Yet we have no guide and no map—only our imperfect memories of the route we wish to take and a vague sense of direction. Not very good odds."

"I like them better now than when we were trapped in that palace. I think we might have gained an advantage by escaping so quickly. The half-dragon, and by extension his clan, is not expecting us to return. At least not any time soon. It could even be the case that he is delivering the arch key to another who wishes to possess or control us."

The idea of a creature attempting to hold him prisoner infuriated Vhok. "I still intend to flay Myshik alive when I catch up to him," he said. "Clan Morueme does not understand what sort of trouble they've heaped upon themselves."

"As you wish," Zasian replied. "When we catch up to him, I'll hold him down for you. In the meantime," he said, standing, "let's be on our way." The priest began scraping lava, hardened to a tarry substance, from his clothing and skin. "Kurkle said this terrain didn't last long, but we should be wary of things lurking within it."

"I'm prepared for it today," Vhok said. He readied magic that would permit him to fly.

"A moment, my friend," Zasian said, holding up his hand. "Save your magic for later. I think I have just what we need." He chanted a few phrases in some unholy language Vhok did not recognize, then touched the cambion once upon the shoulder.

The half-fiend felt no difference in his condition.

The priest repeated the ritual and touched himself. "There," he said. "Observe." He took a step forward, as though he were ascending a staircase. He rose from the ground and stood above Vhok. He took another step and another, climbing a bit each time. "It's simple," he said. "Try it. Just imagine where you want to walk, and the air will hold you aloft."

Vhok gave his counterpart an appraising look and turned his attention on himself. He envisioned a pathway beneath his feet that sloped upward, then stepped forward onto it. His foot struck something invisible and solid right where he had conjured it in his mind. "Very creative," he said, "though not quite as fast as flying."

"True," Zasian replied as the two of them set out, rising high enough into the air to avoid the churning lava beneath them. "But unless you thought to invoke that spell twice, you'd either leave me behind or lose whatever benefit of speed you gained by waiting for me. Besides," the priest added, "we can do this far longer."

Vhok did not relish another day of walking, especially after the arduous experiences battling the bandits the previous day. But striding upon the air was smooth and easy, and without the need to observe the terrain beneath his feet, he could devote more time to studying their surroundings.

Islands stretched to the extent of the cambion's sight in every direction. From his higher vantage point, they reminded him more of bog lands than anything, though the solid ground was more barren. He wondered how deep the flow of molten rock was, and when he spotted some strange, large creature surfacing and submerging again, he knew the depth was considerable.

Later, a flock of flying creatures caught the half-fiend's attention. He could not get a good look at them, for they were distant and headed away from them, but they looked large and left a trail of smoke where they passed. He and Zasian opted to descend to a nearby patch of rocky island to wait for them to disappear. Neither wished to draw undue attention to themselves while exposed in the air. When the creatures were well out of sight, the pair continued on their way.

As they walked, both remained quiet, withdrawn into their own thoughts. Vhok brooded over the betrayal inflicted upon him, and fretted about developments beyond his ability to perceive or control. He did not often find himself so isolated and out of contact with his Scourged Legion, and he found the experience distasteful. He knew it was a necessary sacrifice in order to achieve the greater goal, but it rankled him.

The half-fiend's thoughts turned to Aliisza. Vhok wondered how she fared, whether she was even still alive. All that he worked for depended on her capture, and if anything went wrong, the entire scheme would be for naught. The notion of his plans crumbling down around him distressed him in many ways, but he also found himself worried for her well-being.

That and the baby she carried.

He wondered if he knew yet. He wondered what she thought of carrying his child in her womb. Was she happy? Did she bear any maternal instincts toward it? Vhok often doubted that a true fiend was capable of loving its offspring. He certainly felt little in the way of affection from his own mother.

Certainly not while I was slaying her, the cambion thought wryly.

But Aliisza was not a full fiend. She had her human side, as did he. Possibly, she would harbor some sense of protectiveness for her baby when it was born. He found himself hoping so. He truly would like to meet his child, perhaps raise it to serve him.

"Look," Zasian said, drawing Vhok out of his thoughts. He peered where the priest pointed and saw that the terrain changed ahead of them. The sea of lava with its islands of barren, blackened rock gave way to gently rising ground covered in things that looked like trees.

That cannot be, the half-fiend thought. *Nothing could grow here.*

"What are those?" he asked.

"I confess I have no idea," Zasian answered. "We'll find out shortly, though."

The pair continued their journey toward the rising ground. Before long, they set foot upon what Vhok could only consider to be the shore of the Islands. The ground was no different than anywhere else they had been within the plane thus far. It popped and crackled with radiant heat, and fissures crisscrossing its surface glowed with the light of deeper fire.

Vhok no longer paid attention to his footing. He was instead mesmerized by the treelike objects that spread before him. There were hundreds, a forest of them. Like trees, they sported a main trunk ascending from the ground. Numerous branches sprouted from the trunk at every conceivable angle, dividing into smaller and smaller branches until the smallest were no larger than the cambion's little finger.

Unlike any trees Vhok was familiar with, the things rising before him were formed of pure crystal.

They appeared in numerous colors, with white, pink, and purple predominating. They stood perfectly rigid, bending not the slightest bit as the acrid breezes blew through them.

Vhok approached the closest one and ran his hand along it. The razor-thin edge of the branch cut a perfect gash along his finger. The cambion jerked his hand back, swearing, as blood welled from the cut.

"That seems to bode ill for us," Zasian remarked. "I can't imagine that Kurkle intended to bring us this way. How did he expect to get us through this?"

"I don't know," Vhok replied, sucking on his finger. "Perhaps there is a trail to follow."

"Ah, yes," the priest said, nodding. "Good thought. Let's use what little we have left of our aerial paths to seek one out. I'll head this way," he offered, rising into the sky as he moved down the shoreline, "and you go that way."

Vhok moved back from the crystal trees and started off, using each step to climb higher into the sky as rapidly as he could. The cambion was soon puffing from the exertion, but he carried himself quite high above the world. He could see a good distance across the crystal forest, despite the haze and smoke. A dark line, unnaturally straight and cutting through the bizarre growth, caught his eye.

"There!" he called out, turning to look toward Zasian.

Three great flying things bore down on the priest, claws and beaks outstretched as though to rend him to bits.

CHAPTER ELEVEN

Vhok broke into a run, racing to aid Zasian. As he sprinted, he pulled Burnblood free with one hand and the magical wand with the other. He raised the spiraling shaft of wood and uttered the trigger word. The cambion felt arcane power erupt from the wand, but the four glowing darts that shot forth dissipated with a sizzling pop.

Damn, Vhok thought, increasing his speed. Too far away.

Zasian, surrounded by the three whirling, birdlike creatures, spun in place and made odd gesticulations. Vhok could see that the priest was drawing on his divine magic to defend himself. Sure enough, as the human finished his bizarre motions, the cambion saw all three of the creatures flinch and veer away. The priest took advantage of the lull to put some distance between himself and his adversaries by descending rapidly through the air.

The creatures appeared to be a crossbreed of bird and reptile. Like every beast they had encountered on the Plane of Fire, the trio seemed made of fiery stuff that smoked and glowed. As Vhok ran closer, he saw that their wings, too, guttered with inner flame, and the faster they flew, the brighter their glow became, like hot embers stoked by a breeze. The smoke he saw trailing from them came from those flaming wings.

Their lean bodies reminded Vhok of images he had seen of great-jawed beasts found in the hotter climes of Faerûn, particularly in the wetlands along the southern shores of the Sea of Fallen Stars. Huge snapping jaws lined with numerous rows of teeth looked powerful enough to crunch through bone and rend a man's leg off. Their rough, knobby-scaled skin appeared tough and impenetrable.

Whatever magic Zasian had invoked against the three flying monstrosities had only a temporary effect. The creatures wheeled about and began to close on the priest once more. One dived right at him, its mouth agape.

Though he continued to descend, Zasian pulled his weapon free and twirled the morningstar around. His descent was too slow to evade the flying beasts, as he glided rather than fell from them. As the creature closed in, the priest swung his enchanted weapon with both hands. The spiked head of the morningstar slammed against the underside of the snapping jaw, driving the assailant away. With a roar, it wheeled and retreated. The maneuver showered Zasian with sparks from its hissing wings.

The other two closed in for the kill.

Vhok wondered if he was near enough to employ the wand. He aimed it and discharged the magic once more. This time, the four missiles shot forward unerringly. They emitted shrill whistles as they zipped toward the nearest of the three beasts, turning in their path to follow the creature as it bobbed and weaved around in the sky. When the quartet of magical darts reached the beast, Vhok heard the rapid pop of each one penetrating that rough, scaly hide.

The bird-thing roared in pain, an animalistic howl. It

shuddered and flapped its wings awkwardly, tumbling for a moment in the sky. A heartbeat or two later, it regained its equilibrium and leveled off. Vhok had driven it away from Zasian, but the reprieve was only temporary for the priest. The monstrosity began to circle once more, angling its descent to intersect with its prey.

Vhok aimed the wand again and was on the verge of launching another volley of potent darts when his footing gave way beneath him. One moment he was dashing through the air, and the next he found himself tumbling forward as though he had misjudged a step. His instinct caused him to sprawl forward, to fall upon his hands and knees, but there was nothing to catch him. He plummeted to the ground.

Zasian's spell had expired.

In that first moment of realization, Vhok expected to drop like a rock, but as he recovered his wits, he understood that the spell was dwindling rather than vanishing instantly. He descended at a reasonable clip, just a little more rapidly than his levitation ability would allow. Still, the disappearance of the magic had thrown him off, and his fall was taking him out of the battle. As he recovered and attempted to stand upright, Vhok also realized that his movement had drawn him inland from the shore of the lava sea. He plummeted toward the crystal growths. If he fell into them, he would be cut to ribbons.

With a thought, the cambion invoked his levitation power and slowed his fall. Another moment of concentration arrested his descent completely. Stable once more, Vhok turned his attention toward Zasian, who still fell below him.

The priest staggered from the bite of one of the creatures. The beast had swooped in and clamped down on Zasian's arm and was dragging him through the air. Vhok saw his companion roll his head back in anguish. He struggled to grab hold of something within his black tunic.

The man's weight was significant and caused the bird-thing's flight to become erratic. At the same time, another of the three creatures latched onto Zasian's leg. Vhok heard the man's shout of pain. The priest was whipped around like a doll as the two creatures began to wrestle in the air over their disputed prize.

By the fell lords! Vhok inwardly cursed. He jerked the wand up and fired it again, mentally commanding two of the darts to strike each creature. The glowing missiles streaked toward their targets, but Vhok didn't waste time waiting to see how effective they would be. He slipped his hand inside his shirt and produced a small feather. Muttering an arcane phrase and spinning the feather between his thumb and forefinger, Vhok completed a spell that would permit him to fly. Immediately, he launched himself forward, preparing to use the wand again as he closed the distance to the battle.

The enchanted darts succeeded as Vhok had hoped. Both of the bird-things released their prey, and Zasian began to fall once more. Vhok could see that the priest's magic still slowed him, but he tumbled lifelessly, spinning as he fell. Worse, the creatures, in their thrashing struggle over their prize, had hauled him inland, over the forest of crystal trees. He was headed right toward them and would plunge into their razor-sharp depths at any moment.

Vhok shot forward, hoping he could reach Zasian in time. As he drew near, he saw that the priest was dazed, but not unconscious. Vhok considered grabbing the man and trying to rouse him, but he wasn't sure he could maintain his altitude if the burden was too great upon his magical flight. Then inspiration struck.

As Vhok surged closer, he pulled out a bit of gauze. Ample

smoke drifted in the air to make the spell work. Spouting the strange words of magic, he swooped past Zasian and tapped the priest lightly at the conclusion of the spell. The priest nearly vanished, transformed into a puff of vapor.

There, Vhok thought proudly, that should soften the—

The cambion grunted in pain as one of the three bird-beasts plowed into him from behind and bowled him over in midair. He felt jagged, scalding teeth sink into his shoulder as he was jerked to a sudden stop. The creature violently yanked its head back and forth. Vhok screamed in pain as he felt a large portion of his flesh being torn from his body. His arm went white hot and numb, and he dropped Burnblood into the crystalline lattice of mineral growth below.

As spots flashed in his vision, Vhok fumbled the wand up and forced himself to focus his gaze on the scorching-hot snout clamped on his shoulder. He breathed the trigger phrase once more and saw the magical darts leap from the tip into the scaly nose.

The pressure on his mangled shoulder eased immediately. The monstrosity screamed in Vhok's ear as it let go and dodged away. Swooning from the overwhelming pain, Vhok tried to right himself. He fumbled for control of his magical flight, but his mind was half-numb with agony, and he could hardly concentrate enough to orient himself, much less grasp the arcane power. With a groan, he braced for the inevitable, knowing he would die once he plunged into the crystal forest. The myriad edges of the latticework would rip him to shreds.

A high-pitched keening suddenly assaulted the cambion's ears. The penetrating tone was followed a heartbeat later by the sound of a thousand-thousand crystal goblets shattering upon a stone floor. In his uncontrolled drop, Vhok never saw from which direction any of it occurred. He simply knew he headed for it.

Vhok struck solid rock and bounced hard. The landing stole his breath from him. Combined with the pain he already endured, his vision faded. When he regained consciousness, he sensed healing magic flowing into his body, repairing his shoulder. He opened one eye and found Zasian leaning over him. Beyond the priest, the swirling smoke and ash of the orange-gray sky glowed unobstructed by any crystalline growth. Vhok had landed in a clearing.

Zasian sat back. "There," he said. "That ought to hold you for the moment. Your sword, good sir," he intoned, holding Burnblood out for Vhok to reclaim.

Vhok blinked and opened both eyes. "What the blazes happened?" he asked. He tried to sit up, and the sound of grinding glass crunched beneath him. He felt a multitude of tiny pinpricks gouge his skin. "Ow!" he muttered.

"Sorry," the priest replied, helping Vhok to his feet. "It was the best I could do on the fly. You're lucky I even thought of it in time." Zasian gingerly brushed Vhok's back clean of the shards of mineral while the half-fiend sheathed his prized weapon.

"Thought of what?" the cambion asked, peering around at the ground.

The surface was dusted with coarse powder, mostly white but with a smattering of purples and mauves sprinkled in. It looked as though a localized snowfall had come down within the clearing, which measured perhaps five paces across.

"Why, shattering them, of course," Zasian said. "It occurred to me that so much of this accursed place is made of rock, and not all of it superheated. I thought perhaps a spell designed to make such substances crack and crumble would come in handy. Turns out it did."

A shadow passed over the pair just then, and when Vhok glanced up, he spotted one of the creatures drawing up sharply after having flown past his landing point. It was circling around to dive at the two travelers.

"They are persistent," the priest said. "Kurkle warned us to watch the skies as well as the lava. I guess I should have heeded him better. Regardless," he added, "we need to get away from here." Zasian peered around. "I don't know if they'd try to follow us through this or not," he said, pointing to the crystals, "but maybe they won't and we can slip away."

The bird-creature swooped in close again, screeching in anger as it tried to find a way to attack its prey. The shards of crystal were enough of a deterrent to keep it at bay. It spun and wheeled away again.

Zasian muttered something unintelligible and waved his arms overhead. A thick mist sprang up around them, obscuring everything beyond a pace or two on every side. Vhok could barely make out the priest's form sitting next to him in the blinding white haze.

"That ought to slow them down for a bit," Zasian said.

"Too bad I cannot alter the two of us to a gaseous form again," Vhok lamented. "It would make moving through this odd forest much easier."

"Indeed," the priest agreed. "And that was quick thinking, by the way. Gave me time to gather my wits and work my own magic to return the favor." He put his finger to his lips and tapped it a couple of times. "I wonder," he said, more to himself than the cambion. "Yes," he said, apparently resolving whatever dilemma he had been pondering. "The decision, of course, is which direction to go?" he asked aloud, though he didn't seem to be asking Vhok.

"I spotted a path that way," the cambion said, pointing in the direction he had explored before the battle with the bird-creatures. "That seems the best choice."

"I concur," the priest said. "How far?"

"Not long, if we were on open ground," Vhok replied. "But much too far to try slinking through this mess."

"Leave that to me," Zasian said. "Let's give those nasty beasts some time to lose interest in us. If we remain out of sight in this mist, perhaps they will seek something more palatable and easier to catch."

The two travelers spent a few more moments waiting and listening. The screech of the flying beasts echoed through the crystalline forest a half-dozen more times. Each call grew a bit fainter, a bit farther away. At last, neither Vhok nor Zasian heard anything more of the creatures. A moment later, the mist dissipated.

"Shall we?" Zasian asked, rising to his feet. "I think a spiritual morningstar will serve us nicely," he added. He grasped hold of a necklace hidden within the folds of his outfit and spoke a few words.

A glowing, spiked weapon similar in design to the priest's real item sprang into view, hovering about shoulder high. Vhok gave it a cursory glance, recognizing the spell. Obeying Zasian's mental commands, the glowing morningstar moved to the edge of the newly made clearing and began pounding the branches of the closest crystal tree. Limbs of mineral vibrated and snapped, sending shards everywhere. Vhok flung up his arm to shield his eyes from the flying debris.

"Yes, I think we should stay well back," Zasian commented. "Let it do the dirty work."

The spiritual weapon continued, cutting a swath through the lattice just wide enough for cambion and priest to fit through. As it plowed deeper into the maze of bizarre protrusions, Vhok and the Banite followed it. After a time, Zasian began to get a feel and a rhythm for the fastest route, snapping only the thinnest branches off the ends of each growth. It wasn't as fast as walking, but they made steady progress.

Once, Vhok thought he heard the screech of one of the things that had attacked them, and Zasian held the magical weapon still while they searched the sky together. If it had come near, they could not see it, and at last they presumed that it had wandered away. The priest put the morningstar to work once more.

The spell ended before they reached the path Vhok remembered seeing, so Zasian summoned the spell a second time and they continued. Before long, the morningstar broke through to clear ground.

The path Vhok had seen was straight and wide. He saw no evidence of who or what might have made it, but it was clearly unnatural. Whatever had made the trail had done a thorough job, Vhok noted. No remnants of crystal lay scattered on the black and baking ground, no mineral dust indicated that any of the growth had been pulverized or crushed. No tracks remained that Vhok could see. It was impossible for him to discern how well traveled the path might be.

Shrugging, he started forward, with Zasian beside him. As they walked, they kept one eye on the sky, wary of being surprised again by the soaring, wheeling beasts. The bird-things did not return to trouble them again.

The land rose as they left the Islands behind. Flat shoreline became low foothills, which in turn became steeper mountains. Vhok could see the glow of magma trickling down from the higher elevations ahead of them. He hoped they would not face much steep climbing or fording of the molten rock. He suspected his wishes would be in vain.

The path began to wind more and more. It became a series of switchbacks that climbed the steeper slopes. In various places, Vhok and Zasian found narrow bridges crafted of black, igneous stone crossing deep gullies and ravines. Glowing magma coursed down those channels, and Vhok was thankful that some intelligent beings had constructed the road. He wondered how long it might be before they ran into the bridge builders, and whether they would receive a better reception than the centaur bandits had offered.

The forest of crystal remained all around them, and the individual growths grew higher and higher as they ascended the slopes of the mountains. Soon, the things were towering well over their heads, with trunks as thick as giants' waists. Vhok noted that the branches did not protrude from the main trunks until well overhead. Like a normal forest on Faerûn, the effect created a cathedral-like openness at ground level with a canopy of shelter overhead. The only difference, the cambion observed, was that fallen branches and decaying leaves were replaced by jagged shards of glassy stone and coarse powder that covered the land like snow. It might have been beautiful, but he dared not tread upon it.

After walking for a long time, Vhok broke the silence. "We need to find shelter soon," he said. "Nothing looks very inviting out here, though," he added. He could not hide the bitterness in his voice. He knew their rest would be far less comfortable without the luxury of his magical mansion. He was angry at himself for not planning a backup measure.

Yet another consequence for being too trusting, he lamented.

"That may be a problem," Zasian said. "Without enough rest, it may be difficult for either of us to rejuvenate our magic."

They plodded along, vainly seeking some sort of reprieve from the scorching ground and broiling atmosphere. Despite the magical protection of the rings both wore, the cambion felt his energy draining from him. Sweat soaked him through, his mouth was parched, and his nose and eyes stung from the acrid air. Everything smelled burned. He was sick of it.

Vhok realized that there was no day or night within the Plane of Fire. The sky remained that same roiling hue of orange mixed with gray and black, an endless stretch of smoky clouds churning overhead and reflecting the light of a million burning fires. He had no idea how long they had been traveling since extracting themselves from the dimensional mansion. He knew he was tired, though.

"We've got to halt," he announced at last. He stopped and propped himself against an outcropping of rock that jutted from a steep-sided slope running alongside the trail. "No more today," he added.

"There's no place to shelter us," Zasian argued. "Maybe the next bridge would suit us."

"Yes, an excellent idea," Vhok said, and he laughed, but he felt no mirth. "We can hide beneath it like trolls."

"You would prefer to just plop down here?" the priest demanded, his tone haughty. "Exposed? Visible? At the mercy of the endless, thrice-damned heat?" he shouted, visibly angry. He flung his pack down upon the ground, and when it began to smolder, he snatched it up again. "See?" he yelled, frantically patting the flames out on the scorched bundle. "There's no way we can set up a camp here! Everything will turn to ash in a matter of moments!"

Vhok sighed. He was too worn out to resent the priest's words. He knew Zasian was right, and he had only himself to blame. "I find it odd," he said at last, "that you do not point at me and shout blame, like so many of your kind. A follower of Bane who doesn't seize any opportunity to demean and accuse? How is it that you are so even-tempered?"

Zasian looked at Vhok with surprise. "What would be the point of that?" he asked. "I serve the Black Lord because I want to succeed. I've got better things to do than belittle quaking wretches afraid of their own shadows. Bane will judge me on my own merits, not on how much poorer I made another out to be."

"That sounds almost noble," Vhok said, a sly smile flashing across his face. "Are you sure that is what Bane requires of you?"

"It's true that many Banites seek every opportunity to tear down those around them in order to make themselves appear more powerful. I find that to be folly. They spend all their time circling the mountain, looking for others to push off, rather than making their way to the top of it."

The cambion grunted in appreciation of his counterpart's wisdom.

"That does not mean that I will not put an upstart underling in his place, if need be. I have little tolerance for those who merit punishment, but I see no sense in squashing genius. There is a difference between exerting one's authority and jealously trying to punish ambition."

"And so there's no sense of recrimination toward me?" Vhok asked. "No accusation of misdeeds on my part?"

"Why?" the priest asked in response. "Because you trusted that maggot of a half-dragon and his clan? I was there at the Everfire, too. Did I raise an objection? No. If I had thought your decision was folly, I would have told you."

"Would you now?" Vhok held some doubt that Zasian was being truthful with him.

"Just as I am telling you now that your growing frustration with our current predicament is folly," the priest said. "It does us no good to grow irate about it. We cannot stay here—we both know that. Our choices are simple. We either push on, or we give up and find a means to return to Sundabar."

Vhok sighed again. "I know," he said. "I'm just so damned tired. I—"

The cambion froze in the midst of his speech. He heard

a noise, from just beyond the bend in the trail. He reached for Burnblood and took a halting step forward, unsure if his weary mind had played tricks on him.

At almost the same instant, Zasian's eyes grew wide as he stared at something over Vhok's shoulder. He jerked upright and fumbled for something within his tunic.

The cambion spun around. He saw nothing. "What is it?" he asked, pulling his sword free. "What do you see?"

"There," the priest said, pointing with one hand while extracting a scroll with the other. As Vhok turned to look again at what seemed to be an empty trail, Zasian blurted out an unintelligible phrase in rapid, clipped tones. As he finished, a horde of dwarves, their hair and beards flickering flame, materialized out of nothingness.

❖ ❖ ❖ ❖ ❖ ❖ ❖

Dappled sunlight shone through the high boughs of the forest canopy overhead. Aliisza watched as a gray-haired woman tried to chop a log in half. Her arms quavered, and she had no real skill at the work. Her blows against the hardwood fell awkwardly or missed altogether. Once, she nearly took off her own toes.

Yet she persevered, righting the fallen log and hefting the axe again. Sweat beaded on her wrinkled brow and her breathing came in labored gasps. Finally, she succeeded in splitting the log, and sighed as the two halves fell away from her chopping block. The woman knelt down, clutching at her back, and collected the two pieces of wood. She hobbled to the front porch of her little cottage, a thatched-roof affair of coarse logs and mud chinking, and stacked the freshly split wood on the tiny pile she had started.

Aliisza watched her work for some time. It seemed to the

alu that the woman intended to chop all day, even though she made very little headway. Her diligence was made all the more pitiful because of the other figure standing there, also watching.

An elderly man, similar in age to the woman, waited motionless in the trees nearby. Tears ran down his face as he studied her efforts. He wore a Sundabarian military tunic, but beneath it, he was clothed in a simple woodsman's outfit, and the bow and quiver on his back marked him as a hunter.

He had died that night in the canyon, too.

Aliisza couldn't tear her eyes away from the scene. The man, a ghost, could only stare mutely and cry as his wife labored to survive. They had shared the cottage for many years, the alu knew, on the fringe of civilization. The man had kept them both safe, hunting food in the forest while the woman baked and cleaned. They were happy together. When the man had been called into service by the Stone Shields, he had stoically fulfilled his duty, even though he was well past the age of obligation. He had promised his quaking wife that he would be back soon, that she should go to live with her sister nearer to the city until he could return.

Of course, she had refused.

It was her home, she had insisted, and it was where she would wait for him to come back to her, when his obligation was completed.

She was still waiting.

No word had ever come back to her, no message that her husband had disappeared one night while on patrol. Though he was long overdue, she suspected nothing, only worried that the military had need of his services for longer than expected.

It wasn't too bad, she thought, except for the chores. She wasn't as strong as she once had been, and keeping up the property was more difficult. But she trusted that her man, her true love since both had been barely more than children, would come back to her.

Aliisza did not want to care. People die, she insisted. They grow old, or they are injured, or they are killed in battle. It is the way the world works. It is not my affair. Not my problem!

The alu turned away, weary from watching the ghost grieve for his forgotten wife. She didn't want to be there when he witnessed the old woman's death at the hands of a marauding band of tanarukks later that night. Aliisza knew the script by heart, even though she had not witnessed it. Somehow, it had embedded itself in her mind.

Enough! she silently screamed, and the vision faded. No more! she thought, thankful that the garden and fountains reappeared. Every time, she feared that they would not, that she would find herself stuck in a vision for eternity.

It was nighttime again, the moon high in the sky. Somehow, whenever she returned, it was night. She liked the night, the darkness. It pleased her, let her feel safe within its shadows. So no one can see me, she thought. So no one can examine these foolish thoughts I can't get rid of.

The wind chimes tinkled softly in the darkness and the leaves of the great tree glowed silver in the moonlight as Aliisza strolled toward one of the benches. She was halfway there before she realized another figure sat upon it.

"Tauran," she said, secretly thankful that he had come, but unwilling to admit it out loud. "Why are you here?"

"To see how you fare," the angel replied, rising. "Because I know you wanted it."

"Do you do everything I want?" she asked coyly, afraid to ask aloud the question truly in her mind. How much do you know? Can you see what your horrid visions are doing to me?

"Not quite," the deva replied. "As much as is necessary, for both our sakes."

Aliisza tossed her head. "What does that mean?"

"It means," the angel said, moving toward the pool, "that it's time for me to show you this." He dipped his fingers in the water and swirled them for a moment.

Before the half-fiend reached the edge of the fountain, he removed them. There, just as she expected, was an image, rather than a reflection of the night sky. She saw herself, her body, like before. It had grown bulkier, fat. Bloated.

Aliisza gasped. "W-why?" she stammered. "Why am I like that?"

"You are due to deliver soon," the angel said softly.

"No!" Aliisza cried. "That cannot be! I have not been here more than a tenday, perhaps two at most! No child could grow that fast! What is happening?"

Tauran smiled, one of those sad smiles that Aliisza had come to dread. It was a smile that meant, "I am about to tell you that your world will come crashing down once more."

"Time moves differently there, and here," he explained. "Where your body lies, time flows much faster. It has been the full term of your pregnancy there. Soon, your child will be born."

"And here?" she asked, fearful of the answer.

"Here," he answered, "time moves much more slowly. Though it seems as though you have been here a tenday or more, beyond this place, only a single day has passed. You have completed but one day of your year-long sentence, Aliisza."

"No!" Aliisza sobbed. "You bastard!"

CHAPTER TWELVE

Dwarves, Vhok thought in disgust. *Here, as far away from Faerûn as I can possibly be, there are damnable dwarves!*

The stout ones looked in many ways like their normal kin. Strong, sinewy arms and legs sprouted from thick, stumpy torsos. Though made of fire, their hair and beards were thick and bushy. Both their skin and clothing seemed fashioned of brass or bronze.

And most importantly, thought Vhok wryly, *they are all frowning.*

Those in the front rank brandished copper-colored war-hammers, while those in the back held short spears aloft. All of them were trying to approach the duo in a stealthy manner.

Invisible, the half-fiend realized. He grew angry that he and the priest had become careless, had stopped paying attention. *We are tired,* he thought. *Tired idiots.*

Vhok turned to Zasian to gauge the priest's intentions and spied another group of the flaming dwarves coming from the opposite direction. They, too, had been invisible a moment earlier, until Zasian's spell had revealed them. Between the two lines, they held both ends of the trail. They had planned their ambush well, for there was nowhere for the two travelers to run.

The two groups of fiery dwarves, realizing they had been exposed, slowed a bit and held their weapons higher. They eyed Vhok and Zasian warily but did not rush forward to attack, as the cambion expected. Instead, one from the first group stepped forward, a staff thrust toward the duo. "You will surrender to us, outlanders," he said in thickly accented Common. "Or you will perish by flame and weapon."

Zasian only stared. He seemed a bit bemused at the turn of events. He gave Vhok a glance. "Well?" he asked. "What do you want to do? Perish or surrender?"

Vhok realized the priest was barely preventing himself from bursting out in laughter. The cambion wasn't quite sure what was so amusing to the man. "I hardly think this is funny," he growled, low so the others couldn't hear him. "More gods-forsaken dwarves, and *we* had to stumble into the middle of them. I never want to see another dwarf in my life!"

"Surrender now, or we will slay you!" the leader of the creatures called, a bit louder and more forcefully.

"A moment, please, my friend," Zasian said, motioning to the dwarf for patience. "We are discussing your terms." He turned to Vhok and almost started laughing. "It's funny because I know how put out you are!" Zasian said quietly, still smirking. The priest chuckled for a moment, then managed to straighten his face. "In all seriousness, though, they have called for our surrender. Do you wish to fight our way out of this, or perhaps see if we can negotiate with them? We might convince them to guide us to the City of Brass."

Vhok grimaced. "I hardly think dwarves, hair afire or no, are interested in helping *us*," he said. "I'd as soon eat them alive as speak with them, and the feeling is mutual, I'm sure."

"Not necessarily," Zasian said. "These beings dwell far away from Sundabar and the Silver Marches. There's no reason to assume that they are aware of your animosity toward their kin or your reputation back home."

The leader of the dwarves, apparently impatient over the travelers' refusal to respond, barked orders at his squads of soldiers. The dwarves on both sides closed in on Vhok and Zasian. From a back rank, one even lofted a short spear into the air. The weapon struck the ground near Vhok's feet and wobbled there for a moment.

"I'll kill them all," Vhok hissed, reaching for Burnblood. "Every last one of them."

"No," Zasian admonished, taking hold of the cambion's arm. "Restrain yourself."

Vhok was on the verge of yanking his arm free, but the tone of the priest's voice gave him pause. He turned to glare at the man instead, to warn him against ever laying an unwelcome hand upon himself again.

"I told you I would speak plainly when I thought your actions were folly," Zasian said as the dwarves closed in. "Well, this is one such time. You do nothing to further your own cause by fighting them. They are intelligent—we can reason with them. Give it a chance before you become berserk with bloodlust against them."

Vhok clenched his teeth in fury, unwilling to acknowledge that the priest had a point. He only wanted to wreak havoc among the flame-haired nemeses and be done with them. But he knew that Zasian was right. Both of them were exhausted from travel and battle, and what they really needed were allies rather than enemies. Once more, he was being forced to trust where trust did not come naturally.

"All right," he said, yanking his arm out of Zasian's grasp. "We'll try it your way first." He released his blade, letting it slide back into its sheath, and held up his hands in supplication. "We agree to your terms," he called to the dwarves. "We have no wish to fight you." Then he turned and whispered fiercely to the priest, "But if this doesn't work out well for us, I will flay *you* along with Myshik!"

Zasian's stare was cold and indignant, but he didn't say anything.

The dwarf leader insisted that the pair drop all their weapons. It took several moments for the two prisoners to explain that their goods would burn to a crisp should they let them go.

"You have our word that we shall not lift a finger against you," Zasian said, "but we cannot allow our belongings to leave our possession. However," he added, reaching into his tunic, "we can offer you this as a show of good faith."

The nearest dwarf drew up in alarm when the priest began pulling something out, and the others raised their weapons higher, ready for trouble.

Seeing their concern, Zasian paused and smiled. "It is nothing to harm you, I promise. It is merely a token of our trustworthiness." He withdrew his hand slowly, letting them see that he held only a simple pouch.

Vhok recognized it as one of the numerous packets of gems they had brought with them to aid in smoothing negotiations once they reached the City of Brass. He wasn't sure he liked the idea of Zasian revealing how wealthy they were, but it was too late to object. If those dwarves were as greedy for the bright, shiny things as the dwarves back home, they might be softened up by such a gift.

On the other hand, the cambion thought, they might try to tear us limb from limb to see if we have more.

Zasian carefully opened the pouch and sprinkled a few amethysts into his palm. He held the gemstones out for the leader to see. The dwarf's bright, pupil-less yellow eyes burned brighter and he reached toward the stones with one hand. Very quickly, Zasian slipped the gems back into the small pouch and set the entire bag into the dwarf's palm.

"I would find something else to put those in," he suggested. "That bag is likely to turn to ash in a matter of moments."

The dwarf stared at the priest for several breaths, as if appraising him, then nodded and produced a small copper urn from within his belongings. He dropped the gems, pouch and all, into the urn and put it away.

"Your gift is most generous," he said, "though as our prisoners, everything you own belongs to us anyway. Do you have more?"

Zasian drew himself up and gave the dwarf leader a commanding stare. "We would prefer to think of ourselves as your guests," he said imperiously. "And consider carefully that you managed to get your hands on those without any sort of struggle. To obtain more, against our wishes, would be much more difficult. The loss of life would be tremendous, hardly worth the effort."

The dwarf's eyes grew wide again, though for a very different reason. He drew himself more upright, too. He was on the verge of challenging Zasian's threat. Then he appeared to think better of it.

"You will come with us," he announced. "We must take you before Lord Cripakolus, the azer clan chief. He will decide what must be done with you."

Vhok frowned. "We have traveled far and battled strange winged lizards in the sky. We are quite weary and must rest soon. Can this not wait?" He didn't relish the idea of being taken to some dwarven stronghold for questioning.

"No," the dwarf said. "But our camp is not far. Lord Cripakolus will want to meet you. We azer do not see such exotic travelers in our mountains very often. He will receive you as guests, not prisoners, if you give him more gems. As gifts, of course."

Vhok snorted in derision, but Zasian gave the cambion a warning look before nodding to the dwarf. "If your clan lord is willing to provide us with a guide to our destination, then we might be able to come to an arrangement that pleases him." Then, more softly, so that only Vhok could hear, he added, "What can it hurt? At the very least, they might be able to offer us more comfortable surroundings in which to rest. It can't be much worse than here."

Vhok still held reservations, but again, the priest's arguments made sense. And he had already agreed that they would follow it to some conclusion. He didn't see the point of changing his mind too quickly. He looked at the azer leader and motioned for them to proceed.

"Lead on," he said, glaring. "And pray that your clan lord accommodates us well."

The dwarf stared back at Vhok briefly, then turned and issued more orders to his soldiers. The troops took up positions as escorts, surrounding the two visitors. The fiery humanoids then began to lead their two charges up the trail, climbing the slopes of the mountain.

The path meandered just as it had before Vhok and Zasian had run into the dwarves. The trail switched back on itself multiple times, ascending the steep slope at a gradual rate. The land was solid, though it still popped, crackled, and spit jets of flame into the air almost constantly.

The smoky haze that was so prevalent at the lower elevations grew even more pronounced up the mountainside. Unlike the highest reaches of mountains on Abeir-Toril, the trees did not become more stunted and then disappear completely. Instead, the crystal-trees grew larger, creating a glassy canopy that almost completely blocked out the ember glow of the sky above.

It reminded Vhok of walking through an immense cathedral, not a comfortable sensation for the half-fiend.

The group crossed several of the narrow black bridges. Each had been crafted from blocks of glassy black stone. Each block appeared perfectly formed, rather than hewn. Vhok was certain the rock had been liquid at one time and had been poured into molds.

As they walked, Vhok whispered to his counterpart. "How did you know they were there?" he asked, inclining his head to indicate the dwarves. "How did you see them when they were still invisible?"

"Ah," the priest said, nodding in understanding. "My weapon. I can perceive invisible things with it at any time, even without concentrating to detect them. I keep the scroll handy to aid others without the benefit."

"If we had noted them sooner, we might not have wound up in their 'care,' " Vhok said.

"And we might also still be arguing about where to take refuge," Zasian shot back. "Think of the potential benefits rather than the consequences."

Vhok grunted. "I am trying," he said, "but old hatreds are difficult to overcome."

They continued for some time longer until at last they reached a valley, a broad flat shelf cut from the mountain near its top. Steep-sided ridges huddled on either side of it and provided protection. A great stone wall made of the same igneous rock bisected the valley, with a large gate set near the middle. A stream of fire leaked through a low gap at one place in the wall, then meandered the rest of the way out of the valley until it plunged over the side and became a tumultuous cascade skipping down the mountainside.

Vhok could see more of the flame-haired folk manning the walls. As the group approached, a heavy portcullis made of bronze—or some similar metal—rose, admitting them entrance. Just like on Faerûn, the clans of dwarves seemed to love mountain fortifications that were stout and forbidding.

Their escorts led them through the massive portal and into the enclosed space beyond, where a small village lined the main thoroughfare. Only a handful of buildings had been erected, constructed of stone and brassy metals. Vhok saw puddles of fire everywhere, and smoking vapors wafted across his field of vision. A handful of azer, gathering fire into large kettles or urns of brass, stopped and stared as the entourage passed. The cambion spied citizens of all ages, from the very elderly to the diminutive young. Vhok stared back at them all, trying to keep his distaste from showing on his face.

After passing through the small surface community, an advance outpost if the cambion read the situation right, Vhok and Zasian followed their escort into a great passage cut into the stone of the mountain. Twin valves of coppery metal could seal the great mouth of the cavern when needed, but they stood open, and numerous azer passed in and out under the watchful gazes of more soldiers, armed and dressed similarly to those who accompanied the travelers.

The interior of the large tunnel glowed the ember orange color of fire. Vhok observed that the stream that pierced the outer wall originated within the passage, flowing down from the ceiling and walls like thin syrup, then gathering into a pool upon the floor. From there, it wound its way through the village before disappearing over the side of the mountain.

The path was bisected by the great lava pool. A series of large stone blocks, several paces on a side, served as stepping stones. The top of each block sat perhaps the height of a man above the surface of the liquid fire, but Vhok still felt the great heat radiating from it. He realized for the dozenth time that he was parched and badly needed water. He wondered if it even existed on the plane.

Beyond the stepping stones, the path became solid again, rising higher into the mountain. Like many dwarf abodes, the central tunnel had been cut wide, ran straight, and bore many side passages. At one place, the route became a ledge within a gargantuan cavern where a lake of lava roiled and churned far below. The huge chamber featured stalactites jutting down from the ceiling. Unlike the familiar stone projections found in caverns in Faerûn, the ones Vhok observed were formed from molten rock that cooled as it dripped down from above. From time to time, great bubbles of superheated gases erupted from the lava, causing gouts of liquid rock to spew upward, adding to the bizarre geological formations.

At last, the duo's dubious honor guard led them into a palatial audience chamber.

The builders had adorned the entire place—floors, walls, columns, and ceiling—with brass sheeting, giving the place a coppery hue. Caldrons of fire lit the chamber, as did great flaming jets that roared up from the floor at regular intervals. Warriors dressed in brass suits of armor stood at attention along a walkway leading from the entrance to a steep-stepped dais on the far end, where a throne rose up to tower over all.

Numerous cages hung from heavy chains attached to the ceiling. Vhok could see bizarre creatures of fire imprisoned within them. Some, like the serpentine salamander with its humanoid torso and flaming, fan-shaped spikes, he recognized. Others, he did not. He spied three-legged lizards with their mouths atop their heads, tentacled horrors that hovered rather than sat, and a dozen other things besides. They paced restlessly or lolled without any interest in the goings on below them. Some sat and watched, their eyes white-hot coals with gazes that bored through observers.

"Lord Cripakolus," the escort leader announced in a clear, ringing voice, "Clan Lord of the Everash tribe, King of Smoke and Embers, I present to you two travelers found trespassing upon our mountain. They come bearing gifts. They, uh, have not been disarmed, your lordship, as they claimed their belongings would burn up should they leave their hands."

Vhok cast a glowering sidelong glace at the azer and rolled his eyes. He and Zasian approached the dais. When Zasian bowed deeply to the azer reclining upon the throne, Vhok did likewise. The cambion stole a quick glance around the room and noted with satisfaction that the other fire-dwarves looked on with approval. The pair stood upright again, and Vhok gave the priest a nod to take the lead.

"Greetings, Lord," Zasian began in an ingratiating tone. "We are but two lost travelers seeking safe passage through your territory. As your servant has so helpfully pointed out, we do come bearing gifts—gems, in fact. These we would be delighted to bestow upon you, if you would but consider aiding us in our quest."

Vhok watched Cripakolus's reaction. The azer lord sat upright and stared down at his two visitors with what Vhok could only interpret as greed.

He rubbed his hands together. "Gems, you say. I would see them," he said, folding his arms across his chest. "Produce them now."

Zasian nodded while Vhok bristled. "Very well, my lord," the priest said, still in his obsequious tone. "I have some right here." and he reached into his tunic.

"If he withdraws a weapon instead of gems," the azer lord said loudly, "slay him."

Zasian paused as the attending guards disengaged from

their posts and moved closer, warhammers ready. They left no doubt that they would carry out their leader's command instantly. Vhok reached for his blade, but kept his hand hovering over the pommel of Burnblood without actually drawing it.

Very slowly, the priest removed another small pouch of gems. He held it up so that all within the room could see, then he carefully drew the drawstring open. He tipped the little sack over and revealed a handful of rubies as they spilled into his palm.

Cripakolus made a noise of delight and leaned forward for a better look. "Excellent," he said. "You will hand them to my seneschal," he commanded, and a servant stepped forward from behind the throne.

Zasian slipped the rubies back into their satchel and held the container out. "As I told your fearless commander here when I gave a sack to him, you would do well to transfer them to a more sturdy container. That pouch will go up in flames in but a few breaths."

The soldier who had initially engaged them on the mountainside and who had accepted the first sack of gems gave a hiss of displeasure.

Vhok glanced over and saw him glowering at Zasian. It made the cambion want to laugh. Skimming off the top, eh? he thought.

"You will hand over those gems at once, Lakataki," Cripakolus commanded. "All gifts are my property until otherwise distributed."

"Yes, your lordship," the azer replied. Reluctantly, he produced the copper urn into which he had slipped the pouch of amethysts and handed it to the seneschal.

"Thank you for these fine gemstones," the azer clan lord said. "You are indeed generous."

Zasian bowed again, and Vhok mimicked him with only slight delay.

"Do you have more?" Cripakolus asked.

The priest gave a bemused smile. "Perhaps," he said, "but I think we will hold onto those for the moment. Consider them as bargaining funds," he said. "We have need of your assistance, for which we would be willing to pay well."

"Perhaps there will be no bargaining," the clan lord replied. "Perhaps I will take you into custody and confiscate all your belongings, including the remaining gems, as property of the clan."

Vhok stiffened and began to reach for his sword again.

Are we going to have to fight our way out of here? he wondered. He didn't like their chances, unless they could somehow enlist allies from the caged creatures overhead.

"You could do that," Zasian said carefully, "but such an act would almost certainly cost you much more than the gems are worth. We will not go down easily, if at all," the priest warned. "You do not want that fight, when cooperation and generosity bring so much more."

Cripakolus stroked his beard of flame for a few moments, lost in thought. All around the chamber, the tension grew. The azer lord's loyal warriors tensed, expecting the command to capture or slay the two visitors. Vhok mentally sorted through his remaining magical options, as he was sure Zasian was also doing. The cambion had very little left, and even if they did manage to win their way out of the audience chamber, they had the whole rest of the underground citadel to contend with. It didn't look good.

Damn you, Zasian, the half-fiend stewed. Why did I let you talk me into this?

Vhok was on the verge of levitating to get out of the impending fight when the azer clan chief spoke. "Very well," he said. "You are shrewd bargainers. I accept your gifts and offer you aid." Vhok sighed in relief, until he heard the fiery dwarf's next words. "As further compensation for our assistance, you will do something for us first."

Vhok drew in a deep, irate breath. "And what might that be?" he asked, making no effort to hide his displeasure.

We don't have time for this! he thought dismally.

"Some of our brethren work as slaves for our hated enemy, the efreet. You will go to the mines where they toil, kill all the efreet, and rescue the azer."

❖ ❖ ❖ ❖ ❖ ❖ ❖ ❖

The tavern girl leaned back and laughed. It was a merry sound, full of life and joy. The man upon whose lap she sat grinned from ear to ear, pleased that his joke had amused her so. Aliisza watched from a corner. She knew both of them, from her past. The alu felt the old jealousy rise up again, just as it had several years before. She turned and sought herself, the version of herself that had been in the tavern that night, disguised as a pretty young human woman.

There.

The half-fiend could see blazing green eyes, the sultry, pouting mouth. The memory of herself stared daggers at the tavern girl.

Aliisza remembered all too well.

The tavern girl, so pretty, so happy, was a favorite among the patrons. She always wore a smile, no matter how crowded or hectic the tavern might be. And she was renowned for her ability to work the knots out of a laborer's shoulders. Her fingers were strong, deft. They always knew right where to massage. They were her most prized gift.

Aliisza had hated the girl for her easy manner, her genuine

happiness, and the way she let her good mood spread to the customers. Most of all, though, Aliisza hated that the man was so enamored of the other girl.

The alu had been flirting with the fellow most of the evening, looking for a little companionship, maybe a roll in the hay in the stables. But he only had eyes for the sweet girl on his lap.

The tavern girl hopped up and proceeded to knead his muscles, pressing her fingers in all the right places. The man closed his eyes and sighed as the girl laughed and talked to everyone nearby. It made the memory of Aliisza sick with envy.

Remembering what she had done, Aliisza wanted to turn away. She had never felt any shame or guilt over her revenge—and she never would—but she also had never learned the tavern girl's fate after that night.

She watched as the girl excused herself and slipped into the back. She watched as the memory of Aliisza, still disguised, followed her. Behind the tavern, in the yard, the memory of Aliisza caught the girl just as she was returning from the jakes. The woman never knew what was coming. A quick kick to the gut, an elbow against the back of the head, and she was down, sprawled in the mud.

Aliisza watched, fascinated, as her old memory of herself bent down with a dagger and took the girl's thumbs. Such a little thing, not a terrible injury. But the little trollop could no longer carry a tray of mugs, would never rub a knot out of sore muscles again. The ghostly image of herself laughed as she did it. She mashed the girl's face into the mud to muffle her screams as the pain brought her back to consciousness. And Aliisza slipped away, returning to her true form and flying off, taking the thumbs with her so they couldn't be magically restored. She never turned back once, even as the girl lay sobbing and writhing in the mud.

But the real Aliisza remained. She watched as a cluster of patrons came out of the tavern to see what had befallen the girl. She stood in the shadows, not wanting to be seen, even though she knew the memories would never notice her. She stared as the man with whom the girl had flirted appeared. When he saw what had befallen the girl, Aliisza expected him to turn away in disgust.

Who would want a crippled girl? she remembered thinking at the time.

But he didn't turn away. Instead, he wrapped her ruined hands in bandages, and he gathered her up in his arms and carried her. She buried her head against his shoulder, crying softly. He took her through the yard and to the street, and accompanied by several others, went to the temple.

A priest of Ilmater met them at the door. He took one look at the girl and summoned them all inside. The priest, in his nightclothes, prepared a spell right then, in the sanctuary of the temple, before the altar dedicated to the maimed god. He laid his hands upon the young woman's wounds, pressed his flesh against hers, and prayed.

Aliisza knew then what would happen. The hands were healed. The woman regained her thumbs, as new and as whole as before. When the ritual was complete, when she had what she had lost, she knelt down and began to pray alongside the priest. The man who had brought her to the temple dug a pouch of coins from his tunic and placed it in the offering bowl.

The girl turned to him and smiled but shook her head. She would not let the man pay her debt for her. And Aliisza could feel it. She saw how it ended. She could sense the girl's holy aura grow, surround her. She became a priestess of the faith, and those hands, those soothing hands, became healing hands. She devoted herself to aiding others, gave herself to the service of Ilmater.

The thought that Aliisza had driven the girl to take on a new life of good works rankled her. She forced the image out of her mind. It faded, and she was in the garden again. The nighttime breezes, ever present, made the wind chimes dance.

The alu sighed. Even though she still loathed the woman, there was something . . . compelling . . . in her tale. She didn't know what it was, but watching her overcome Aliisza's retribution made the half-fiend feel weak, ineffectual. It was not a feeling she was accustomed to, nor did she much care for it. She grimaced and turned away from the garden.

"They married, you know," came Tauran's voice from somewhere behind her.

Somehow, Aliisza knew the angel would be there that night, though she hadn't seen him in several days. She turned and looked at him. He was sitting in the shadows, upon one of the benches. She held her breath, waiting to hear what else he had to share with her. She sensed that he had come for something more than a mere chat.

"The man you coveted married her. He loved her before what you did, but when he saw her selfless act afterward, watched as she turned to a life of healing, he fell in love with her even more deeply."

"Silly, the both of them," Aliisza said, dismissing the vision with a wave of her hand. "And I thought my penance was supposed to be all about how my crimes harmed the poor and innocent. That hardly seems to fit the bill," she scoffed.

"It was given as an example of how compassion and honest caring overcome acts of selfishness and pettiness. You think you invariably wreak havoc in the things you do, but when all is said and done, the goodness of the world endures. The people recover, share, support one another. It is the way of living things to aid each other."

"Again, quite silly," Aliisza said crossly. She wished he would get to the point. She feared he was going to leave her again.

"On the contrary," the angel said, "quite satisfying. People treat each other with respect because they feel better about themselves. In its own way, it's equally selfish—why do anything unless you benefit from it?—but the payback is tenfold, because all enjoy it equally."

"I think not," Aliisza said. "I think people do it because they are afraid. They fear that if they do not pay homage to others, someone will come along and dominate them, take control of them. And by cowering from that fear, they become beholden to it, as surely as if someone *did* come and master them. People act like weak, mewling things because they are afraid of true power. They are afraid that someone else will take it from them and use it in their stead. And they can't bear the thought of losing that, so they pretend they don't want it."

Tauran sighed. "Do you really believe that?" he asked, his voice faint, perhaps defeated. "Truly?"

Aliisza smiled. He finally understands, she thought. He cannot change me. "I believe it as surely as I believe you keep me here not because you want me to know love and compassion, but because you are afraid of what I will take from you when I am free."

"Then I guess there's no real reason to tell you that you have a son," the deva said.

Aliisza felt a shiver pass through her. A son? I have a son!

"Can I see him?" she asked, eager. "Would you show him to me?" She pointed at the fountain.

Tauran stared at her for a long time before speaking. "No," he said at last. "Not yet."

Aliisza felt anger flush her cheeks. "Why not?" she demanded. She crossed the open space to where he sat, intent on confronting him, though she knew she could not physically affect him in any way. Neither of them were truly there, in that garden of illusion. "Why won't you show me my son?" she asked, her voice much softer, more pleading than she had intended.

"Because," the angel replied, "he is nothing more than a weak, mewling thing, something for you to use as a stepping stone to true power."

Aliisza opened her mouth to retort, but she had no words. What he said was true. She couldn't both love her son and see him as a means to an end. The two could not be reconciled.

Tauran stood. "I think you finally understand," he said. "You're right—I cannot change you. I never meant to try. You, and only you, can change yourself."

"I don't want to change!" she whispered fiercely. "What you show me is nothing but pain and sorrow and loneliness! How can people want that? They never deal from a position of strength! They never have the ability to take what they want! How can that be better than being strong, independent, powerful? How can succumbing to silly romantic notions be preferable to steeling yourself against all those who would take from you?"

"I will come to you again," the angel replied, "when I sense that you know the answer to that question yourself."

"Don't go," she said. It was the first time she had asked him to stay. "Don't leave me here."

He smiled softly then and reached out to stroke her hair, her cheek. It wasn't an amorous touch, not filled with the heat of passion and arousal. It was gentle and kind, a touch of compassion and love. "Exactly," he said.

Watching the angel vanish was the hardest thing Aliisza had ever done.

CHAPTER THIRTEEN

"There," Lakataki said. The azer who had originally accosted Vhok and Zasian pointed down into the valley far below them. The cambion peered where the fire-dwarf indicated and spied the efreet's mine. A great wall of shiny brass, pierced by a gate and protected by towers at regular intervals, surrounded a pit dug into the slope of a mountain. The molten glow of magma shone from within that pit. The only feature that jutted up from the interior that the half-fiend could see was a spindly, peculiarly shaped tower. Everything else was hidden. The whole scene shimmered and wavered, distorted by the heat that permeated the plane.

"What do they mine?" Zasian asked, staring alongside Vhok. The priest seemed impressed with the sight.

"Liquid glass," Lakataki replied. "It spills out of the ground there, just bubbles up to the surface. They gather it and pour it into molds right there within the fortress, before it cools. It's the purest, clearest glass anywhere," he said, but his tone was more bitter than proud.

"And the efreet make their slaves work the mine," Vhok said. "Members of your clan are down there."

"Yes," the azer said. "But more importantly, it used to be

ours. The efreet came and stole it from us, captured or killed many and drove off the rest. We want it back."

"Where does the glass go after it is molded?" Zasian asked. He still stared raptly at the mine.

"Caravans take it to the City of Brass, where it is sold," Lakataki answered. "Merchants from every part of the multiverse bid for glass that pure."

"How many efreet are there?" Vhok asked. "How many should we expect to deal with?"

The azer sergeant shrugged. "Perhaps a dozen," he said. "Maybe twice that many live within the fortress, but half of them are usually away, raiding for more slaves to work the mine. Most of them are just cruel and greedy. There is one, though, the overseer. He is very clever. Hafiz al-Milhab. You must be wary of him. He is a giant even among his own kind."

"And how many slaves?"

"Perhaps a hundred, maybe more," Lakataki said. "Not all are azer. The efreet bring slaves of all types who are suitable to work the mine. Not all of them will thank you for their freedom, outlander," the fire-dwarf warned.

Vhok grunted in acknowledgment. That's going to be the *least* of our problems, the cambion thought.

"We will wait for you here," Lakataki said. "As Lord Cripakolus promised, if you free the slaves and return our mine to us, we will provide you with a guide to the City of Brass. Though why such sensible beings as yourselves would want to go there is beyond me," he muttered, half to himself.

With no reason to delay, Vhok and Zasian prepared to set out. The route down to the valley was steep and there was no trail from their vantage point, so Zasian performed his divine magic, granting both of them the ability to walk on air, as they had done the day before. Together, they descended. The pair kept their route close to the mountain, not wishing to have another unpleasant encounter with flying things that might mistake them for a meal.

The clan lord, Cripakolus, had been adamant. The two travelers were ordered to aid his clan in recapturing their prized mine and freeing the azer enslaved there. He had refused to even entertain the thought of releasing his two visitors, much less providing them a guide anywhere, until they had agreed. The duo were, in effect, his prisoners.

Of course, the azer lord had couched it in far different terms. He had told Vhok and Zasian that he could not in good conscience let honored guests roam the open plains beyond his mountain range while such dangers as efreeti slavers existed. The only way to ensure safe passage, he argued, was to eliminate the threat at its source.

Never mind that we're going to face them all at once, in their own territory, Vhok thought wryly.

After the half-fiend and priest agreed to the leader's terms, the azer held a great feast in their honor. It became apparent soon enough that none of the fire-dwarves expected the two to return from their rescue mission. The majority opinion among the azer was that the force of efreet was far too strong to be ousted by only two.

Vhok and Zasian had to provide their own food—nothing the azer consumed was of a temperature suitable for them—but they did sleep in relative comfort overnight. The shaman of the clan was able to create a chamber cool enough by enchanting a milky white sphere around it that kept out most of the heat.

After an equally festive breakfast with Cripakolus, the cambion and the priest were led outside, through a different cavern, to the back side of the mountains. There, Lakataki had taken them to the vantage point. From that point on, they would be on their own.

"Not very bright of them to just let us walk off," Zasian remarked as they worked their way down the mountain. Walking upon the air, even at the steep angle they chose, offered the decided advantage of being able to bypass the crystalline trees that peppered the slopes. "They didn't really dangle much incentive for us to return," he added.

"I see no reason to," Vhok said. "The foolish sergeant admitted that caravans travel to the City of Brass to sell the glass. I think we can figure out a way to go the same direction," he suggested, chuckling.

"It makes me wonder which of us had the more realistic expectation. Is Cripakolus that foolish, or did he bait us into departing, figuring he got two bags of gems out of the deal, if nothing else?"

"He really doesn't lose, I suppose," Vhok remarked. "Either we do as we say and he gets his mine back, or we try and fail and he gets rid of us without any trouble, or we just leave, and he gets rid of us without any trouble."

"I guess the real question is, should we pay a visit to the efreet when we get down there?" the priest said. "Do you think he'll be interested in finding out that a troop of azer is hiding in the mountains, spying on him?"

"It might convince him to find a way to get us to the City of Brass more quickly," Vhok said. "I wonder how hard it will be to get in to see him?"

"Perhaps we should try the back entrance," Zasian suggested with a smile.

When the two of them got close enough to the fortress that they feared being spotted, they paused. "This is probably close enough on foot," Vhok said. "To the top of the tower?" he offered.

"Seems as good a starting point as any," Zasian replied.

Vhok nodded and put new magic into use. With a word

and a touch, he transformed them both into vapor. They could no longer speak, but their destination was unobstructed and visible. Together, they continued on, traveling as gaseous clouds. They were virtually invisible among all the blowing smoke and ash that perpetually wafted through the plane. They closed the rest of the distance to the brass walls and maneuvered to one side, far from the main gate. Then they went up and over the wall.

The interior of the fortress seemed barren and utilitarian to Vhok. Other than the tower, there were two other buildings, long and low, against the two side walls of the place. They appeared to be either barracks or prison cells.

Probably both, the cambion mused.

By far the largest feature of the mine was the pit itself. Like a great, inverted ziggurat, the hole in the ground was terraced at regular intervals, growing smaller with each successive level down. Slaves worked at every level. They lined the terraces, struggling to maneuver huge copper basins into place beneath sluggish flows of white-hot material that oozed from the walls. Above them, cranes hoisted filled basins into the air and to the side, to be replaced with empty ones. Other slaves worked the substances into molds, using large hinged and counterweighted frames to tip the basins sideways. The liquid glass, cooling to a bluish color, seeped into the molds, hardening into clear, pristine objects. Vhok witnessed an endless cycle of harvesting.

Their transformation spell would expire soon, Vhok knew, so he pushed onward, rising easily with the heated air currents toward the top of the tower. He flowed into the domed and columned enclosure of a cupola there, where a lone efreeti served as a lookout.

The efreeti leaned against the banister and stared over the work being done in the pit below. The creature was thick-limbed like a giant, though his bony head, with its smallish horns, reminded the cambion more of a demon than anything. The efreeti's skin, brick red in color, seemed to shimmer and smoke from the heat he gave off. Vhok knew that such genies normally stood twice as tall as the half-fiend, but the one before him was no more than his own height. The efreeti had used magic to reduce himself, to compensate for the low ceiling within the tower, which had been built by dwarves.

The cupola was perhaps six paces wide, large enough for the cambion and the priest to slip inside and transform unnoticed by the genie. As Vhok restored himself to solid form, Zasian appeared beside him. The priest gave the half-fiend a gesture to hold, then fetched something from within his tunic. He nodded to the cambion to proceed.

Vhok crept up behind the efreeti and slipped Burnblood around his neck, at the same time sliding the creature's over-sized falchion from his sash and tossing it away. The genie tensed, but the half-demon pressed the blade tighter against the creature's throat. "Easy there," he said. "Don't ruin it all by dying. We just want to talk."

The genie held still a moment longer, then slowly relaxed. "I yield," he growled. His voice was a deep, crackling rumble, reminding Vhok of a burning blaze. "Do not slice up poor Amak."

"Excellent," the cambion said, spinning himself and his captive slowly away from the banister to face Zasian. The priest clutched his necklace in his hand and seemed prepared to invoke divine magic at the slightest hint of trouble. "My companion there," Vhok continued, "is ready to end your life with a word of power if he thinks you are not dealing justly with us. Do I make myself clear?"

The efreeti tried to nod and nicked himself on the

half-fiend's blade. "Undoubtedly clear," he said. "Amak will not turn on you."

Vhok smiled. "Good. We wish to speak with the overseer. A big, nasty genie named Hafiz?"

"Yes, yes," the efreeti said, trying to nod enthusiastically. "You must speak with Hafiz at once. He is the overseer here."

"Excellent. This is working out well, don't you think? Now, how should we go about finding Hafiz?"

"I will take you to him, yes, indeed," Amak said. "If you will just release me, I will show you the way at once."

"Now, if I let you go, I can trust that you won't give me any trouble, right?" Vhok said. "Otherwise, my companion here will be forced to disintegrate you or something equally unpleasant. You don't want that, do you?"

"Absolutely not," the efreeti said with all sincerity. "I promise, no nonsense."

"All right, then," Vhok said. He stepped back from the efreeti and removed his blade from the creature's throat.

Amak the efreeti half-turned and gave a glance at his tormentor. When he saw Vhok, he seemed to start the slightest bit, but he did not otherwise acknowledge the cambion. "This way," he said simply, and motioned toward an opening in the floor leading to a set of stairs. "I will take you to the overseer."

Vhok went down first, in order to keep Amak between himself and Zasian, who brought up the rear. They followed the staircase down, which wound around the hollow inside of the tower for several turns. The walls of the tower were pierced with narrow openings that permitted light to enter the vertical chamber, though it was dim. At the bottom of the stairs, Amak motioned that they should pass through a large door set into the wall. The door appeared made of thick brass set into an equally stout frame.

When Vhok pulled on the door, it wouldn't budge. He gave the efreeti an accusing look.

Amak frowned, seemingly puzzled. "Pull harder," he urged.

The cambion slipped his sword into its sheath and took hold of the handle with both hands. He gave the door a hard yank but it would not open. "All right," he said, turning to chastise the efreeti. "What's going o—"

The creature jerked a single fist forward and smacked it hard into Vhok's face. The cambion grunted in pain as he recoiled from the punch. His head bounced hard against the door, sending stabbing pain through his skull and sparks crackling through his vision.

Amak lashed out with his foot, driving the heel of it into Zasian's chest. The priest staggered backward, almost losing his balance. Rather than pursuing them, the efreeti faded from view.

"Zasian!" the half-fiend croaked, dizzy. He fumbled for his blade. "He's escaping!" Vhok shouted.

Burnblood didn't seem to want to work properly, and the cambion slid to the floor as his balance left him. Settling on his backside, Vhok cursed his complacency. He knew the magic the efreeti was employing all too well; he and Zasian had used it to gain access to the tower and surprise the creature. The efreeti was turning the tables on them.

Insubstantial, his physical body a roiling cloud of vapor, Amak settled to the floor like a puddle and slid underneath the door. Vhok reached for his wand as the gaseous figure slipped away bit by bit. The half-fiend leveled the magical device in the direction of their quarry and grunted the command word. Four sparks darted from the tip and crackled as they snapped into the misty form. The attack didn't have a noticeable effect, but Vhok knew that such magical darts could hurt even vaporous creatures.

He readied the wand to fire off more missiles, but the last of the efreeti's form slipped beneath the door and escaped.

"Damn it to the Nine Hells!" Vhok swore. He slumped against the wall and closed his eyes to try to get the chamber to stop spinning.

"Here," Zasian said, stepping over to the cambion. "A little healing. Sorry I wasn't faster," he added. He placed his hands upon Vhok's head and said a prayer.

Vhok felt the soothing magic flow into him and dissolve the pain pounding behind his eyes. When Zasian finished the ritual, Vhok waved the priest's apology away. "We both let down our guard. He'll pay," the half-fiend promised, rising to his feet. "But we've got to catch up to him, first."

Zasian grabbed the handle of the door and yanked hard. "Definitely locked," he said.

"Fortunately," the cambion said, "I have just the magic to solve this little problem." He muttered an arcane word, and the bolt in the lock clicked.

The Banite pulled on the handle and the door swung open easily. The duo braced themselves for an attack, but none came.

As Zasian swung the door wider, they could see a massive, smoke- and flame-filled warehouse beyond. The doorway led onto a rocky platform near the ceiling of a vast, open space. Vhok realized that the room before them was cut into the mountain, beneath the tower. Instead of brass construction, everything was glowing, popping stone. Fumaroles along the sides of the chamber vented hissing, foul-smelling gases. Jets of fire spewed from cracks and holes like the magical flames from a wizard's hands. The entire warehouse chamber shimmered from the undulating heat and rising smoke.

A caravan of great bronze-colored wagons filled most of the floor of the warehouse. Wide and flat, the wagons held stacked molds filled with still-cooling glass items. Vhok realized the efreet would not unpack the molds until the wagons reached their destination, in order to minimize breakage. Large beasts of burden, vaguely similar to blazing rothé, were hitched to the wagons. It appeared as though the caravan would be departing soon.

"There," Zasian said, pointing.

Vhok peered in the direction the priest indicated and spotted a wispy vapor moving against the updrafts in the room. It was headed toward a congregation of efreet who had gathered near a pair of huge bronze doors at the front of the chamber. They seemed to be in the midst of a jovial discussion. They loomed over the handful of manacled azer working at their feet, but one stood a head above the rest.

The cloud of wispy white swirled close and transformed. Vhok recognized Amak the moment he materialized. The efreeti bowed low to his imposing counterpart and began animatedly talking and pointing toward the door where Vhok and Zasian stood.

The larger efreeti, whom Vhok suspected was Hafiz the overseer, looked up and spotted the two interlopers. Anger contorted his expression. The cambion saw him reach for the massive falchion tucked into his sash as the others around him did the same. The overseer pointed and gave harsh commands, and the rest of the efreet spread out, moving toward the duo. A few remained behind, cracking whips at the azer to keep the slaves working.

On impulse, Vhok raised his arm and gave a friendly wave. Then he turned to Zasian. "Let's go meet him," he said. "Win him over. That's why we're here, right?"

The priest gave Vhok a bemused smile, mildly surprised at the suggestion. "All right," he said at last. "It just might work."

Vhok slipped Burnblood into its sheath and considered

how best to reach the floor of the warehouse. A narrow set of steep steps cut into the natural stone wall descended toward the ground level. The staircase and the wall next to it cooked the air with their heat and fire.

"Meet you at the bottom," the cambion said, and leaped over the end of the rocky platform. He channeled his innate magic, floating down to the floor at a casual pace. When he settled his feet on the ground, he strolled toward the efreet, who were stalking toward him menacingly.

Hafiz led the pack. Bare-chested, he looked fierce and angry. He had adorned himself with brass jewelry, necklaces and earrings, and a set of bracers on his thick, muscular wrists. The horns jutting from his furrowed, demonic forehead were slightly lighter in color than his deep red skin, as were the tusks protruding from his mouth. He did not look in a mood to parley, but Vhok maintained his air of calm and casual friendliness.

"Greetings, O exalted Hafiz!" he called out, waving again. "My companion and I"—and the cambion jerked a thumb over his shoulder toward Zasian, who had taken the stairs—"come before you today as weary travelers seeking your aid. I pray we can offer you some mutual benefit in exchange, hmm?"

Hafiz, taken aback slightly by Vhok's disarming smile and words, drew up a few paces from the cambion. He turned his falchion point down and leaned against the pommel as he studied the half-fiend. The other efreet fanned out to form a semicircle around Vhok. Zasian joined his companion and offered a bow before the overseer.

"Who sent you here?" Hafiz demanded, his voice even deeper and more rumbling than Amak's had been.

"No one," Vhok said. "Well, that's not entirely true. A foolish azer clan lord showed us where this magnificent mine was, and asked us to rid it of your presence, but we thought better of such nonsense and came instead to pay homage and negotiate some assistance."

At the mention of the azer, Hafiz bristled. A deep growl issued from him and his eyes glittered. The other efreet reacted similarly. "You are pawns of the azer?" the overseer said. "They think they can send two puny outlanders to slay us? That is rich!" The efreeti laughed, a thunderous, echoing sound. He leaned back, guffawing heartily.

Vhok maintained his smile, but he seethed at such disrespect. Puny, indeed, he thought.

When Hafiz regained his composure, Vhok continued. "Our thoughts exactly," he said. "Obviously, we offer you notice of their presence in the mountains overlooking this mine. If you wish to capture them, that is your concern. We, however, must reach the City of Brass as quickly as possible, and thought perhaps we might offer ourselves as guards for your next caravan heading to that august city."

Hafiz eyed the cambion with a smirk. "You wish to go to the City of Brass?" he said. "How excellent. I have just promised my brother a new shipment of exotic slaves for his amusement." To the other efreet gathered around, he said, "Seize them."

❖ ❖ ❖ ❖ ❖ ❖ ❖ ❖

Aliisza wanted to scream. *Just die already!* she thought. *Choke, or cut your own head off, or drown in your soup kettle. Whatever you do, get out of my head!*

But the old woman didn't react. She took another hack at the log, trying in vain to split it. Another feeble attempt, and the log skittered away again. Aliisza tried to turn her back on the scene. She could still feel it going on. The elderly man, standing in his soldier's uniform, bow slung across his back. She felt him watching the woman, the tears welling in his eyes.

She hated them both.

She felt his pain.

The alu forced the image to fade. Instead of the garden at night, though, she found herself inside the tailor's shop. The girl with the apron appeared in the back doorway. Master Velsin stared at her in anger and sent her to the private room, where she would spend the day half-naked in front of lascivious men who ogled her and pawed at her body and worse.

No! Not this again, Aliisza groaned. Enough!

The alu jerked her sword free and tried to slice the girl's head from her neck. The blade passed right through the image. The girl never reacted. She slowly, inexorably made her way into the dim room and began to disrobe. Aliisza tried to hack at the girl, the dresses, the lecherous Yrudis Gregan. The scene never changed, never wavered.

Aliisza flung her sword away and forced the image to fade.

She saw no garden, only the temple of Ilmater. A young woman, face beaming, prayed to her new god, thumbs pink and fresh. Aliisza summoned a magical ball of flame. She tried to blast the girl, the temple, scorch it and burn it to the ground.

No one reacted. The temple remained intact.

The alu yanked a dagger from her boot. She stared at the blade, feeling her heart pound. She would put it into her own eyes. They couldn't make her see the visions if she had no sight. Anything to make it stop. She held the pointed end up, stared at the very tip.

With a rush of resolve, she rammed the dagger into her own skull.

White light blazed, and pain. So much pain. She screamed,

yanked the dagger away. She clutched at her ruined eye, trying to hold the hot dampness in place. The pain made her dizzy. She sank down to her knees, sick to her stomach.

The other one, she told herself. Finish it.

Still clutching the dagger, she felt for the tip, placed it upon the closed lid of her remaining orb. The pain made her hand tremble. She didn't think she could do it.

Before she could think about it, she shoved the dagger home.

The world spun and went dark in a haze of pain.

Aliisza came to awareness. The sun warmed her face, but the air was cool. The alu heard the sound of two children playing. The streets of Sundabar bustled with life on the far side of the garden wall. Her eyes were closed, but she could see the brightness of daylight through the lids.

She brought a single hand up to her face. Afraid, she touched one eyelid. It was intact. She turned away from the sun and let her eyes flutter open.

She could see. The memory of the terrible pain remained with her.

Damn you, Tauran, she cried, thankful and angry all at once. I can't live this anymore. Please! Help me!

She hated herself for being so weak. It wasn't just the visions. She might have been able to watch them all day long if they were merely visions. It was the sorrow. She felt what her ghost tormentors felt. She knew their suffering. The anguish seeped into her, made her hurt. She couldn't block out the hurt.

The girl with the apron appeared, spoke to the children. Aliisza didn't even hear the words. The sadness radiating from their father, standing in the corner of the little garden, was drowning the alu. Numbly, she followed the young woman. She felt the girl's worry, felt her concern for her siblings.

And for her unborn baby.

There isn't enough food, the girl thought, and Aliisza could hear her. The rent is overdue. Sadil needs new shoes, and Kaiga, a cloak. How can I take care of this baby? Master Velsin will be angry that I'm late, but it was so hard to arise and dress. I need to eat, but the children need it more.

Stop it, Aliisza pleaded. Stop telling me this.

Oh, an apple, the girl thought, slowing by the barrel of fruit. Just one. I could take it—he wouldn't see.

Yes, Aliisza silently shouted. Take it! Eat it! Take care of your baby!

No, the girl thought. I shouldn't. It's not right.

Fool, Aliisza scolded. Serve yourself first. The merchant will not know the difference.

How could I raise my child to be truthful and honest if I cannot even follow that advice myself? the girl thought. No, she decided firmly.

That last thought hit Aliisza hard. How can I look my own child in the face, if I ever get to see him? she wondered. What would I tell him of myself? What could he care?

I'll beg Master Velsin for a few extra coppers, the girl mentally continued, ignoring Aliisza's revelation. Just a couple, to help with the food. I'll even . . .

The last thought from the girl came to Aliisza as an image, and it made her cringe. She was willing to debase and humiliate herself, let the cretin touch her, for the sake of her younger siblings and her unborn baby.

To the hells with that, Aliisza thought. Enough.

The alu raced ahead to the tailor. She entered the back room and found the man sitting at his work table, laying out fabric. The stink of his lecherousness roiled off him. She found him disgusting. She wanted to kill him.

You worm, she thought. You're too low to seek out the

willing pleasure of a harlot? You have to prey on this girl? What did she do to you?

To Aliisza's utter amazement, the man was looking at her. He seemed surprised to see her standing there.

"Who are you?" he asked. "What are you?"

Aliisza couldn't speak. It wasn't real. It wasn't happening. Was it?

"Coward," she said. "I ought to slide this blade through your gut right now, let you dangle upon it and bleed out. It would take several days, you know. And I've got time."

The man blanched. "I don't know you," he stammered, standing and backing away. "Tell me what you want. Coins? They're in the strongbox. T-take them. Please. But don't hurt me."

Delighted, Aliisza crossed the floor and stood directly opposite the man, facing him across his work table. "Never mind who I am," she said. "All you need to remember is that I exist, and I know where you live."

The man swallowed hard.

Aliisza picked up a needle from the work table. "The girl that works for you," she said casually, examining the tiny shaft of metal. "The one who's late?"

Master Velsin nodded vigorously. "Yes. Lizel," he said.

"Well, if you ever touch her again, or let any of your customers touch her, I'm going to come back here and tie you to this table and find all sorts of interesting places to put your needles. Are we clear?"

The man's eyes widened. "Y-yes!" he said. "C-clear!"

"You're going to pay her better, too," the alu said. "How much do you give her to work here?"

"Um," the man began, scrunching up his face in fear. "Three coppers a day."

Aliisza fumed. "She could make more than that selling

her body on the Silk Way!" she growled. "You *are* a wretch. I should make you pay her what *you* earn! No," she said, inspired. "I should drag you to the district and let you service the dandies. I hear some of them secretly worship Loviatar. They pay well for the privilege of using you in their worship rituals, but we'd let Lizel have the coin. Wouldn't that be fun? Yes, I like that," she finished, smiling.

The man whimpered. "I'll give her five silvers a day," he yammered, wringing his hands. "And no more of the other. I promise!"

"Good boy," Aliisza purred, walking around the work table to stroke his chest with her hand. Master Velsin quaked at the alu's touch. "And you're going to excuse her for being late, because she's with child, and she has to take care of her little brother and sister. And you're never going to dock her pay because of it, right?"

"Right," the man whispered. His eyes were nearly rolling back in his head from fright.

"Because, after all, I know where to find you, don't I?"

"Yes," he gasped. "I swear, it will be as you say. Now please, leave me be."

Aliisza chuckled and headed toward the door. She paused and turned back. She gave the trembling man one last baleful stare and said, "Yrudis Gregan had better be out of this shop before Lizel gets here." And with that, the alu walked out into the daylight.

It took her several moments to notice that the ghost of Lizel's father was no longer around.

CHAPTER FOURTEEN

Vhok sighed as he yanked Burnblood free. "You disappoint me," he said to Hafiz. "I thought you'd be much wiser and more reasonable than those silly azer."

On the cambion's left, Zasian went through the complex motions of a spell, and Vhok felt a surge of preternatural power course through his body. The priest then dived to the floor and rolled, disappearing beneath one of the wagons. Two efreet dashed after him.

The half-fiend tensed his muscles and felt strength surge into his limbs. He twirled and shifted his blade experimentally, and waited as the horde of efreet surrounding him closed the circle.

"You were the unwise one," Hafiz growled, stepping back and watching his minions work. "Did you really think we'd welcome strangers here? Spies from our enemies sent to learn our defenses before attacking us?"

The closest efreeti lunged at Vhok. The genie towered twice as tall as the cambion and the creature's slice arced down toward Vhok's head. The half-fiend parried the blow, throwing all of his newfound strength into the counterstrike. The clang of it rang through the great chamber. He felt satisfaction as his opponent's blade whipped back from his driving force.

Startled, the efreeti nearly lost his grip on his weapon, and spun to recover it. The reaction put him in a vulnerable position.

Vhok saw the opening and jumped inside his foe's reach. He raked his long sword across the efreeti's abdomen. The genie roared in pain, but Vhok didn't stay near to see the severity of the injury. He let his momentum carry him forward. He leaped high on the follow-through and landed atop the nearest wagon. He bounded across the large molds with their glass castings to the opposite side. There, the half-fiend paused and spun in place.

Two of the onrushing efreet closed the distance, and Vhok saw that their oversized blades were long enough to reach him despite the width of the wagon. Three others began to skirt the conveyance, determined to surround and capture him. Two of them vanished suddenly, disappearing from his sight.

"We told you we held no loyalty to the azer," Vhok said as he parried the first of several falchion strikes from his two opponents. "You didn't even wait long enough to see our goods to bargain with," he added, giving Hafiz a disparaging shake of his head as he knocked a second falchion away and jumped down on the far side of the wagon. He had no intention of letting invisible efreet sneak up on him and catch him unaware.

The hulking efreeti overseer sneered. "Whatever you think you have to offer, I can merely take from you anyway, once I have captured you," he called. "Unless you fight too long and hard and my warriors are forced to slay you instead," he added.

Vhok ignored the words of the great efreeti and ducked

beneath the wagon. He scrambled forward, toward Hafiz. When he reached the end of the transport, he darted between the beasts hitched to it. The creatures paid him no mind, but the licking, crackling flames radiating from their bodies scorched his skin and made him flinch.

Just as the cambion was about to run past the pairs of fiery rothé, a wall of searing flame burst across his path. The towering barrier rose from the floor directly in front of the creatures, causing them to rear up in alarm. Vhok skidded to a halt just before he plunged into the crackling curtain. He cringed from the heat, feeling his skin blistering in spite of the magical ring upon his finger.

Vhok spun around to dash back the way he had come. Two efreet waited for him there, one on each side of the wagon, between the back pair of rothé and the front of the vehicle. They thought him trapped, and they grinned malevolently as they leveled their falchions at him.

Rolling his eyes at their simple ploy, Vhok mentally thrust himself upward. He rose into the air, levitating beyond the reach of the licking, consuming flames and the gleaming curved blades the efreet wielded. He smiled as his foes' grins turned to expressions of consternation. They leaped at him, slashing at his feet as he ascended, but Vhok managed to block their strikes with his own blade.

The cambion turned in place as he rose, looking for Zasian. The priest had disappeared when the fight began, right after he had cast the strength magic upon Vhok. The half-fiend spied the pair of efreet who had gone off in pursuit of the Banite, moving slowly among the wagons as though searching.

He slipped away, Vhok thought. But did he leave altogether?

The cambion knew they had no reason to stay. Hafiz had

no interest in negotiating, and Vhok doubted anything he said or did was going to change the overseer's mind. Zasian must have come to that conclusion, too, and if the priest was smart, he'd already cleared out.

That's what I'd do, Vhok thought. So I will. He can take care of himself.

Vhok prepared to invoke the spell that would transform him into a gaseous cloud once more, but as he began the incantation, a sizzling beam of fire struck him in the back. The cambion cried out from searing pain and his spell was ruined. He nearly lost his balance and toppled over, but he righted himself and whirled around to see what had caused his injuries.

Below him, an efreeti pointed a finger at him, precisely in the direction of the blast that struck him. Nearby, the overseer had enlarged himself and stood more than twenty feet high. He strode forward, his massive falchion swishing through the air in great swaths. With such a huge blade, the gargantuan efreeti could reach Vhok where he hovered in the air.

Even as Vhok took note of the new threat, a second genie aimed a digit in the cambion's direction and let loose a scorching ray of fiery energy. Seeing it coming, Vhok was able to spin out of the way, and the beam shot harmlessly past him. But it crackled as it passed, and the half-fiend could smell his tunic smoldering.

Bastards, the cambion fumed. Have to find another way out, now.

The half-fiend fished in one of his inner pockets and yanked a wad of something sticky from it. He chanted arcane words and concentrated on rising into the air at the same time. When the spell took effect, Vhok vanished from sight. Immediately, he reversed his direction and began to descend. The mess of fiery beasts and barriers still burned below him.

I hope that confuses them, he thought.

The cambion watched Hafiz come closer, still peering toward the ceiling. The overseer paused, frowning, then Vhok saw him grin and stare right where the half-fiend dropped toward the floor. Hafiz swung his massive falchion at Vhok's body. The huge blade whooshed through the air in a tremendous arc, coming right toward him.

So much for stealth, Vhok lamented.

The half-fiend swung Burnblood around and used the long sword to try to deflect the impact of the great falchion. The force of the blow drove him sideways several feet. It knocked him off balance and sent a cold pain shooting up his arm. Vhok grunted involuntarily.

Hafiz reversed his swing and brought the blade around for another swipe at Vhok. The cambion didn't think he could take another strike like the previous one. In desperation, he looked below and saw that Hafiz's crushing cut had knocked him away from the licking flames. The cambion released his levitating magic and let himself fall, hoping he would drop enough to evade the overseer's attack.

The ploy worked.

Vhok tumbled to the floor in a heap, just a few feet to one side of the infernal barrier, as the falchion whistled over his head. The landing hurt and knocked the breath from him, but he struggled to his hands and knees and sought a safe haven. The next wagon in the long caravan had not yet been hooked to a team of rothé. Vhok scrambled toward it.

Another sizzling blast of heat, no thicker than a stiletto, slammed into the stone beside the half-fiend. Vhok jerked back and rolled sideways. He kept rolling as another scorching beam hit him in the shoulder. He clamped his teeth together to keep from grunting in pain. Another spin of his torso, and he was finally under the wagon, away from the magical attacks.

The cambion didn't waste time. He climbed to his knees and looked around, desperate for a way to exit the chaotic battle. The great doors, where the caravan would depart, remained shut. Vhok had no idea how difficult they would be to open, so he discounted that option.

Vhok remembered the door high atop the platform, where he and Zasian had entered. He shifted to the far side of the wagon and stole a glance that way.

A single efreeti stood upon the shelf of rock, blocking the exit. The door had been pulled shut, but it could be locked only from the near side, so Vhok guessed that he could incapacitate the guard and slip through. The only question was whether he could reach the platform unhindered. Hafiz was able to track him despite his invisibility.

Nothing left but to try, the half-fiend decided. Can't stay here and get slow-roasted.

Just as Vhok was readying himself for the dash to freedom, Hafiz's giant feet settled to the floor on either side of the wagon. Other efreet also began to gather, surrounding the wagon. The huge genie's fingers closed around the conveyance and it began to rise.

Vhok realized Hafiz's plan at once. Remove the cambion's cover, and the other efreet would swarm him. He considered slicing at the oversized digits in an effort to thwart the trick, but he knew that would sacrifice his magical invisibility. Though Hafiz had figured out how to spot him, the others had not, and Vhok felt compelled to maintain any advantage he could.

Instead, Vhok reached up and grasped the rear axle of the vehicle with his hands, then stretched his feet forward and hooked his booted toes over the other axle. As the wagon rose into the air, Vhok went with it, clinging to the underside. The efreet closed ranks around the spot where Vhok had been, their blades drawn. They sliced, jabbed, and poked at the empty space before them. It was clear to the cambion they attacked blindly, with no true idea if he was there or not.

Thank the abyssal ones for small favors, Vhok thought.

Hafiz hoisted the wagon waist-high and pivoted with a grunt of exertion. Vhok realized the size of the vehicle blocked the overseer's view of the place the other efreet attacked, and he had no way of knowing that Vhok was no longer there. The massive genie shifted his weight and tossed the wagon to one side with a thud. Vhok clung desperately to the axles with his magically enhanced strength as he bounced hard with the impact. The vehicle rolled a few paces from the gathered efreet, and Vhok traveled with it.

When the wagon glided to a stop, the half-fiend rolled out from beneath it on the far side. Vhok crouched behind the vehicle. Using it for cover, he turned toward the commotion. If the opportunity came, he would make a run for the stairs to the platform.

But by that point, Hafiz, as well as his minions, had realized their quarry was not where they thought. The others looked around uncertainly, but the overseer seemed to realize how the cambion had escaped his trap. The giant genie slowly turned his glare toward the wagon.

Vhok surveyed his escape route, wondering if he could slip past his large but ponderously slow foe. He was about to sprint across the open floor when the disembodied voice of Zasian suddenly echoed in his ears.

Vhok, I'm near the front of the caravan, by the azer slaves. Lead Hafiz to me and we'll finish him. Answer to confirm you understand.

The cambion stole a glance toward the front of the caravan line and spotted a handful of chained and manacled azer. The flame-covered dwarves loitered near a wall, unattended. Vhok could not see the priest, but he trusted that the man was there, hiding. It was the opposite direction from the high door and freedom, but if they could slay the overseer and turn the tide of battle, he was willing to take a chance.

In the time it took Zasian to deliver his message, Hafiz had taken two steps and was nearly at the wagon. He held his falchion high in one hand and reached for the vehicle with the other.

"I'm on my way," Vhok muttered softly. "You'd better be ready, because Hafiz is almost on me." Vhok did not wait for the Banite to respond. He leaped out of his hiding place and lunged forward, swinging Burnblood.

Hafiz followed the cambion's movement with his eyes, but his enlarged body was too slow to react. Vhok ran between the genie's legs. He swung his sword as hard as he could and drew a long gash across the inside of Hafiz's calf as he passed. Scalding hot blood the color of magma spewed out, burning Vhok, who became visible because of his attack. Ignoring the pain of the burning blood, the cambion kept going, racing toward the azer and their taskmaster.

With a roar, Hafiz turned and limped after him. The other efreet, who had been watching from behind the overseer uncertainly, could see their quarry once more. They chased after him, too.

Though Vhok was much quicker, the oversized genie's strides covered more ground. Vhok realized that the overseer intended to stomp on him, if he could.

The half-fiend ran faster.

Vhok saw that the azer watched the approaching half-fiend and his pursuers with trepidation. Manacled and chained together, they could not move fast, but they turned and fled the onrushing genies as best they could. Tripping and scrambling, they left a gap near the wall where Vhok and Zasian could make their stand.

The cambion could only hope it wouldn't be his last.

Vhok reached the front of the line of wagons and looked around, seeking the priest. Zasian was nowhere to be found. Suddenly fearing that the Banite had tricked him into being a decoy so he could escape, Vhok stole a quick glance over his shoulder.

Hafiz, bleeding profusely from the wound Vhok inflicted, had lost ground. He still bore down on the half-fiend, and he held his falchion high, but several paces separated the two of them. The other genies lagged even farther behind.

Vhok saw an opportunity. He ran once again in the direction of the wall. When he neared it, he leaped high in the air. As he hit the wall, he kicked with both legs. Using all his strength, he powered himself up and over and back in the direction he had come. At the same time, he spun around to face his pursuers.

Hafiz was startled by the half-fiend's sudden reversal of direction. He staggered to a stop as Vhok flashed toward his chest. The massive genie tried to move his falchion to defend himself, but he was too slow.

Vhok angled his sword at the efreeti's chest and plunged the blade home.

Blood spurted everywhere, coating Vhok in its blazing heat. For a moment, the cambion clung to his weapon, fighting the agonizing pain of being doused with the fiery blood of the genie. Then Hafiz, staggering and bellowing, grabbed at Vhok with his fist. Vhok felt the genie's crushing grip surround him. He let go of his blade to try to squirm free.

Hafiz stumbled down on one knee. His breath was rasping in his chest, and hot, glowing blood flowed freely down his torso. With a baleful glare, he held the cambion before himself.

"You worm," he growled, weakening fast. "I will dash your head against the floor!"

The overseer, swaying uncertainly, hoisted Vhok high overhead.

Vhok pushed against the powerful fingers that held him. "Any time now, Zasian," he called out. His words came only as a strained grunt. Though he could feel Hafiz's grip weakening, the power of that grasp was forcing the air from his lungs.

The efreeti wavered, then collapsed.

The oversized genie toppled to one side, his arm swinging downward. Vhok found himself rushing toward the hard stone floor, though no longer clenched tightly within the efreeti's grip. The cambion wriggled out of the overseer's fingers and went into a tumble as the massive hand hit the ground with a resounding thud.

The half-fiend rolled across the floor and came up on his feet, gasping for breath.

Hafiz lay motionless, molten blood spreading beneath him. His body returned to its normal size. The hilt of Vhok's blade, still protruding from the overseer's chest, became visible beneath the corpse.

The other efreet who had been pursuing Vhok, fully half a dozen, stood gathered around their leader, as still as their fallen overseer. They all shared expressions of shock and dismay.

Then, almost as one, they looked toward Vhok.

"You will die!" one of them said, and the cambion realized it was Amak. The sentry stepped forward and bent down to grasp Hafiz's falchion, which had also returned to its regular dimensions. He rose and stalked toward Vhok. "I will slay you myself," he snarled, and raised the weapon to attack.

Vhok reached for his scepter and discovered that it was

no longer strapped to his belt. Somewhere along the way, it had jostled loose. Scalded by igneous blood, his sword still jammed into Hafiz's chest, he stood before the enraged genie, weaponless.

The cambion backed away from the efreeti. "Now would be a really good time to show up, Zasian," the half-fiend muttered. He looked around for his companion, but the priest had vanished.

The other genies closed in, forming a semicircle around their prey.

❖ ❖ ❖ ❖ ❖ ❖ ❖ ❖

As Aliisza became conscious, she realized she was floating in a gray void. This is different, she thought.

Before, for several days, perhaps, she had lingered in the moonlit garden with the magical fountain. Before, she hadn't been certain whether she had slept or not. It had been hard for the alu to tell the difference between slumber and a mere absence of consciousness. All she could be certain of was that time had passed, and every time she became aware, she found herself in that oasis.

At least the visions had ceased.

Aliisza spent considerable time reflecting upon the significance of the switch. Did I change something? she wondered. Did Tauran? Was that what he was looking for? For me to act? To defend, or protect?

Whatever the cause, she had welcomed the respite of returning to the garden. The visions had worn on her, made her more than weary. Her emotions had become raw. She felt things she had never known before. She wasn't sure she liked that. A part of her still resisted the impulse to save, to protect. She didn't want that responsibility, that weakness. She felt exposure, vulnerability in such kindness and compassion.

She had mulled the implications of her imprisonment over and over. Each time, exhaustion had taken over before she could come to some conclusion. Eventually, she had vowed not to think about it any more, at least not for a while. She had wanted merely to be. As an escape from those tormenting visions, she had welcomed the solitude of the garden. Even as she had settled down to rest, there had been an expectation of something, anticipation of an event, an occurrence. She had known she was waiting for Tauran. But she had been in no hurry for it to happen.

That had been before.

The gray void startled her. A change. What did it mean?

In the next instant, she was within her quarters, lying upon her bed. She hadn't come there much during her captivity, preferring the sights, sounds, and sensations of the garden to her bedroom. She wondered why she had brought herself there instead.

Rising up in the bed, Aliisza realized she was naked. That hadn't happened in quite some time, either. She looked about. Her clothes, her weapons, all of it lay draped over or resting against a nearby chair.

Something felt different. It . . . perturbed her.

Deciding to explore, the alu slipped out of bed and hurriedly dressed. Then she headed into the garden. It felt strange, different from the place she had grown used to.

At first, she assumed that Tauran had arrived, was sitting in the deeper shadows, waiting for her to regain consciousness. She peered about, staring into the recesses of the garden where the moonlight did not reach. The wind blew softly and made the chimes tinkle. The leaves of the trees fluttered in those breezes, their silvery color flashing like strange fireflies swarming amongst the branches.

There was no sign of the angel.

What is it, then? Aliisza pondered, searching her own awareness. What is different?

When she finally figured it out, the realization hit her hard. She was real. She existed. It wasn't merely a dream state, some out-of-body consciousness she felt.

She was flesh and blood again.

The thought made her stumble, nearly fall. Uncertain if she could trust her suspicions, she tested. She tried to dismiss the garden. Nothing. She willed her surroundings to change to daytime, for the sun to shine and the moon to vanish. The sky didn't alter.

Everything felt different because it *was* different. Her mind was no longer creating the place; she actually stood in the middle of the real garden, no longer a prisoner within her own mind.

"It must feel strange, after all this time existing only as a spirit," Tauran said.

Aliisza whirled to find him standing at the periphery of the garden, smiling.

"What happened?" she asked. Her voice was barely above a whisper.

"You happened," the angel replied. "You acted. You rushed to her aid. You took a stand," he finished.

"I know," Aliisza answered, "but I didn't want to. I didn't want to feel that." Disorientation flowed through her. Her real body felt things again, things she had forgotten about. Aches, unsteady balance, an emptiness in the pit of her stomach. She had to make sense of it. "It's dangerous, caring for others. You leave yourself open to . . . to pain," she finished. The words sounded foolish in her ears.

"Yes," Tauran said, and his voice was gentle, consoling. "It is hard to care for others, to lend them aid, to offer them solace and guidance. Because you give something of yourself in the process. And you fear that it will come back to injure you if you let it." The angel walked to Aliisza, took her hands in his. "You wall up your feelings because of fear. Fear of that pain. Everything we do in life, we do out of fear. Fear of betrayal—fear of pain."

"Fear of death," the alu finished.

"Yes," the deva said, growing excited. "Exactly. You fear all those things, yet you believe you can overcome them, if only you never let anyone get close to you, never get close to anyone. You think you can control those fears by protecting yourself from them. But the truth is, we are all powerless. In the end, those fears materialize despite our efforts."

"Then why bother living at all?" Aliisza asked, desperate. She did not want to feel those emotions. They terrified her. "How does making myself vulnerable change anything? It only makes it worse!"

"Ah, it would seem to from the outside looking in," Tauran answered. "But you know differently now. Don't you?"

"No," Aliisza said, trying to mean it. But she didn't. "I don't want to care!" she protested, knowing her words were false.

She did care. She cared about Lizel, admired the girl's courage, determination even in the face of so much adversity. She envied the young woman's convictions. Most of all, she craved the bond that girl would have with her child. Aliisza wanted that. She wanted to love her son.

Aliisza wanted her son to love her in return.

"Ask anyone," Tauran said as the alu's thoughts came full circle. "Anyone who has ever loved and lost will tell you it's still worth it. Despite the pain, the vulnerability, the joy that comes with caring cannot be diminished. In truth, you cannot have one without the other."

"It's still selfish," Aliisza said, sagging to the ground at the deva's feet. It was too much. "You still pursue it to please yourself."

"Of course," Tauran replied, settling beside her. "I serve Tyr for the sense of satisfaction I feel. You wish for your son to love you because you want the good feelings it brings. No one who looks openly and honestly inside themselves could claim otherwise."

"Then how is that better than serving yourself?" the half-fiend demanded, tears welling up in her eyes. "How can you mark one as good and the other, evil? I see no difference."

"Yes, you do," the angel said. "You know you do."

Aliisza tried to shake her head, tried to tell her counterpart that it was all the same, but she knew otherwise. In goodness, there was boon for all.

And in that moment, in that instant when she finally grasped how wonderful kindness and compassion could be, how it built and reverberated among all living things instead of destroying them, she felt ashamed. Her entire life had been nothing more than an endless series of terrible acts, all designed to bring her satisfaction at the expense of others.

She leaned close to Tauran, reached out for him. The angel took her in his arms, hugged her close. She pressed herself against him and sobbed.

For a long time, they remained like that. Aliisza simply let the grief wash through her, scouring away all of her shame and guilt. The catharsis was profound, immediate. Somehow, the angel was drawing her taint from her, and she felt clean, new, alive for the first time. The energy Tauran gave off didn't pain her anymore. It fed her, nourished her body and spirit together.

At last, they drew apart. Tauran peered into Aliisza's eyes, as though searching for something there. She smiled at him, a grin that grew. She knew it showed her affection for the angel, her appreciation for all that he had done to bring her to that moment.

"I am whole," she said, and she reached up and caressed the deva's cheek.

He was so beautiful, she realized. Not just physically, though there was that. No, his inner strength, his convictions shone from within. She would have envied that if she didn't understand how he could share it with her. What she once would have wanted to wrest from him for her own use, she instead craved that he share with her. For in sharing it, it became even more bountiful, limitless.

"I have a surprise for you," the angel said, standing. He reached down and pulled Aliisza to her feet. "It's time."

The alu looked at her friend, confused. "Time for what?" she asked.

"To meet him," Tauran replied.

Aliisza's heart leaped into her throat. Her son! It was time to meet her child.

"N-no," she stammered, afraid. "I—I cannot."

"Why?" Tauran asked, genuinely puzzled. "You want to love him, and he you."

"Yes, but . . ." How could she explain it? she thought. How could she make sense of it herself? "I'm afraid," she said at last, raising her arms helplessly.

"Of what?"

"That he will not love me," she replied, and the tears welled up again. "That he will look upon his mother and know all the terrible things she has done, and he will turn away."

"That is possible," the deva said.

Aliisza looked at him, taken aback. His words surprised her. She had expected the angel to try to dismiss her fears, make her believe that all would be fine.

"You cannot predict, nor can you control, what is in another's heart," Tauran explained. "You can only give of yourself and see if something good comes in return."

"The risk . . ." Aliisza began, knowing it would always be there.

"Is worth the reward," the angel finished for her. "Without one, you cannot truly have the other."

Aliisza took a deep breath. "I know," she admitted. "But I am still afraid."

"Look how close you are, though," Tauran said. "Look what you've come through to achieve this. To turn away now would be tragic."

Aliisza thought through everything that had happened to her. Her struggle had been monumental, and through it all, the only thing that had ultimately mattered to her was to see her child born, and grow, and be happy. In a way, she had already sacrificed everything on his behalf. She knew then that it didn't matter what he thought of her. She had already given him everything she had.

"Take me to him," Aliisza said, mustering her conviction. "I want to see what he has become."

Tauran smiled and took her hand. "I don't need to," he said. "He's been here, with us, the whole time."

Aliisza felt a lump form in her throat. Here? All this time? He's watched me! Saw me laid open, bare, all of my failures! Oh, by the gods, no!

Tauran tugged at the half-fiend, gently pulled her along to the far side of the garden.

There, in the shadows, Aliisza could see a form. He was sitting on a bench, his face masked in darkness.

Her son.

He was larger than she expected, an adult. Much time had passed since his birth. Tauran had warned of it, but the impact didn't truly hit her until just then.

I've missed his childhood, she lamented. I wonder how much he will look like me, how much he will resemble Kaanyr. Thinking of the cambion made her pause a second time. Kaanyr. What will he think? What will he *do?*

As they approached, her son stood. He wore a simple white tunic and leggings, very similar to the clothing many of the inhabitants of the House donned. He was not as tall as Aliisza would have expected, given Kaanyr's stature. But he was graceful.

He stepped into the soft light of the moon, and Aliisza realized she didn't even know his name, but the thought that she ought to ask Tauran that question vanished the moment she saw his face.

Ghost white hair, shorn short, framed an aquiline face the color of a dusky evening sky.

The garnet eyes of Pharaun Mizzrym's progeny stared back at Aliisza.

CHAPTER FIFTEEN

Aliisza felt the world shudder around her. So many emotions, so many thoughts hit her all at once. A part of her mind thought it was a trick. Tauran had brought some imposter to her, some half-drow that could not possibly be her son, in order to trick her, to test her somehow. But peering at that face, with its slightly arched eyebrows and high, delicate cheekbones, she knew it was her son.

Hers and Pharaun's.

All that time, she had believed she carried Kaanyr Vhok's whelp within her. It was the only outcome she had considered, and when the error of her thinking made itself clear, she wanted to kick herself for her own foolish shortsightedness.

More emotion flooded through her. It began with a tingling, a feeling of something pressing against the back of her skull, at the base. Some dam that was on the verge of bursting hovered there.

And it was gone, and a torrent of memories hit her.

Aliisza staggered at the arrival of the onrushing visions. She watched them unfold inside her head as though she were there all over again.

She was standing in the passage of the Master's Hall,

facing Zasian Menz. She was disguised as Ansa, dressed only in a nightshirt, and he was reprimanding her for her prowling so late at night.

"You put me in a very difficult position, child," he said.

"Yes, sir," she replied. "I will be more careful."

"And now," the seneschal added, pulling a pendant from his shirt, "I must prepare you for your impending journey."

Aliisza started, unsure what the handsome man meant, but suddenly wary. "What journey?" she asked, prepared to edge away from whatever the man had been about to inflict upon her.

"Kaanyr Vhok needs you to do this," Zasian replied, twirling the pendant in his fingers. "A very long and arduous journey, a potentially deadly one."

Aliisza's mouth gaped. "Who is Kaanyr?" she asked, feigning ignorance. "I don't know what you're talking about."

"It's all right, Aliisza," the seneschal answered. "I'm helping him. We've entered a pact to take the city together. I know your task is to secretly discredit Helm Dwarf-friend, but Vhok needs you for something more important now. We're going to meet you at the other end of this journey. You will be our key, to unlock the portal that is hidden. Without you, we cannot hope to succeed."

And he had proceeded to tell her many things. He had known she was with child, and he explained that her condition was necessary to make her journey. Her pregnancy would be the bait that would draw Tyr's lackeys to her, would tease them into capturing her with the intention of sparing her. He admonished her that she would need to protect the baby, whatever the cost. He had gone so far as to place a magical spell, a *geas*, he had called it, upon her to force her to comply. He explained that it would act subtly, without her knowledge, because she would not know that it existed. She would not know her own role in the game, for the angels would ferret it out of her. She had to be ignorant, he explained. He had given her instructions to follow, a litany of tasks to complete once she remembered them.

And, before she could protest, before she could resist, Zasian Menz had made her forget it all.

She had gone through all the trials and tribulations without that knowledge, believing she had simply been caught and confronted, a quirk of unfortunate chance. She had spent her captivity fearful and ashamed that she had somehow failed her cambion lover.

But it came rushing back. Every last bit of it, including her anger and feelings of betrayal that Kaanyr would use her so, would endanger their child for some greater scheme of his. He had put her in that position himself.

Aliisza understood, too, that Zasian had set conditions for her to recall those forgotten memories. He had set the trigger to be her first glimpse of her own child.

All of that recollection, the whole of it, had been locked away in Aliisza's mind. Seeing her son had unleashed it. It had taken but an instant to regain, but the flood so overwhelmed her that she gasped and dropped to the ground, exhausted.

She tried to draw air. She needed to make sense of what she had just learned, to reconcile it with everything that had changed about herself during the tendays and months of solitude, of self reflection. She struggled to wrap her mind around it, but it was just too much.

And something more bombarded the alu.

Magic coursed into Aliisza's mind. Spells materialized, planted there by Zasian, powerful dweomers set to trigger once she had regained her lost memories. He had hidden them away, like the memories themselves, to keep the celestials from seeing them. She understood his intentions in the heartbeat it took for the arcane power to manifest.

In a second heartbeat, the magic activated.

Aliisza felt a rush. Something vanished from her, some veil that had been drawn over her mind. Magic, she saw. Powerful and blinding force, designed to make her view certain events a particular way. All of the agony she had experienced, all of the doubt and guilt that had consumed her during her visions became an artificial thing. The shame she had felt, the divine guidance that had led her to exhibit compassion and kindness lifted, separated from her. Aliisza saw it at last for what it was.

Trickery. Deception. Manipulation.

Tauran the holy celestial, Tauran the kind angel, Tauran of the uncompromising, idealistic convictions, had used magical coercion to change her point of view. The pain, the sorrow she had felt on Lizel's behalf was not her own. It had not come from the visions alone. Divine magic conjured by the lackeys of Tyr had created it, amplified it, and thrust it upon her.

And Zasian's spell had cast it off again.

She saw the world without guise once more. She understood her role within it, her part to play. She was a half-fiend, a powerful and cunning entity who showed no mercy, who tolerated no weakness. She knew what she wanted, and she claimed it for herself. That was how it had always been, and that was how it would remain forevermore. No one would control Aliisza through foolish, weepy emotions. Not Tauran, not Kaanyr, not ghosts from past lives.

Aliisza wanted to shout, wanted to jump up into the air and crow. A shout of triumph, to show she could not be chained. But she was still a prisoner, and there was more of Zasian's magic at hand.

A blinding flash of light struck her, knocked her consciousness from her body.

The disorientation of the seneschal's magic made Aliisza's

awareness spin. It felt as though she had left her body, was floating somewhere far beyond herself, like she had felt within the gray void. But it was different, much more frightening. And it lasted only an instant.

Then the alu discovered that she was staring at herself. She felt odd, not entirely right. Some sensations were missing, some new ones replaced them. As she stared, Aliisza watched her own body crumple to the ground. It looked as if she had fainted, but she was still awake.

Awake in another's body.

The half-fiend gasped, and her voice was different, more masculine. She swayed and stuck a hand out to the bench to steady herself. That hand was charcoal in color, with thicker fingers. Aliisza stared at it, realizing at last where she was.

She inhabited her son's form.

The half-fiend sank down, taking a seat on the bench, overwhelmed. She watched Tauran kneel down to check on her body, concern on his face. He leaned in close and listened to her breathing and sighed in relief.

"She fainted," he said, looking at Aliisza. "Your mother just wasn't expecting to see you as your father's son," he explained, kindness in his voice.

Aliisza didn't trust herself to answer. She swallowed hard and nodded.

"I guess you're a bit overwhelmed, too," the angel said. "You rest for a moment while I take her to her bed. Then we'll talk. You still have a lot to figure out, I suppose."

You don't know the half of it, Aliisza thought. She felt like glaring at the deva, but she instead gave him a weak, uncertain smile.

Tauran hoisted the alu's body onto his shoulder. Then he turned and trudged from the garden, through the portico toward the half-fiend's quarters.

Once he was out of sight, Aliisza drew a great, shuddering breath and tried to steady her nerves. Everything at last made some sense. Zasian had embedded latent magic within her that would cause her to shift bodies. She wondered what became of her son's consciousness.

Did we trade places? Does he now inhabit my form?

The alu felt a brief pang of regret, but it was short-lived. An opportunity lay before her, one that she was just beginning to recognize and understand. Zasian had locked so many secrets inside her that when they finally were released, it had been a flood. All of the memories, the magic, had come out in a rapid jumble, too fast to comprehend. They had slammed into the alu in only a few heartbeats, the moment she had seen her son's face. But with a few moments to herself, sitting on the bench, she was starting to grasp the seneschal's intentions. Zasian had thought everything through.

And he'd set it all up, she realized, so that Tauran wouldn't notice a thing. As far as the angel was concerned, Aliisza still resided in her own body, was still adjusting to her newfound sense of compassion and selflessness. Zasian had planned well. He had given the alu a means to escape, and to escape notice in the process.

Aliisza smiled to herself. She had an appointment to keep. Kaanyr was waiting on the far side of a portal, and she was the only one who could open it for him. She had to keep the deva from guessing the truth, would have to play it all carefully, but she would get to that doorway. She would unlock the ancient path. Nothing was going to stop her, so long as she kept her cool.

And there would be hell to pay. Everyone was accountable. Tauran, Kaanyr, Zasian. They all would answer to her wrath.

◆ ◆ ◆ ◆ ◆ ◆ ◆ ◆ ◆

With his back pressed against the stone wall, surrounded by furious efreet who towered twice as tall as himself, Vhok had but one place to go. He levitated. As his feet left the ground and he rose into the air, Amak recognized the trick. The genie snarled in rage and leaped forward to deliver a killing blow before Vhok could evade him.

The cambion doubted he could slip away in time.

At that moment, the wall beside the half-fiend distorted. An arm, clad in black and silver, jutted from the rock as though it had grown there. It elongated, became a torso and head, and the rest of Zasian appeared, stepping free of the wall. He held his arm out, pointed, and uttered a phrase of power.

The Banite emerged from the wall slightly to one side of Vhok and the genie. Amak had been so focused on reaching the cambion that he did not see the priest in time. The efreeti jerked and stumbled to a stop, understanding that the human was bringing magic to bear, but he could not retreat from Zasian's outstretched finger or swing the falchion to defend himself.

Zasian nimbly darted toward the efreeti and tapped him once on the hip with the tip of his finger. As the priest sprang away again, out of reach of the genie's blade, a crackling sheen of dark energy swarmed over Amak. The black force flowed like roiling tendrils across the genie's body.

Amak shuddered and seized up. He arched his back and his eyes rolled back in his head. A great, primal scream emanated from him. He dropped the falchion and fell to his knees. The black energy crackled and faded, then the genie pitched forward, facedown. His body twitched a time or two, but otherwise lay still.

The other efreet stared in shock and awe at the corpse of their companion.

Vhok floated down to the ground. He came to rest beside Zasian, who stood glaring at the genies with his arms folded across his chest. The cambion drew a deep breath and added his own baleful stare.

"I trust no one else wishes to continue the folly of this dispute," Vhok said.

The gathered efreet began to mumble among themselves. None stepped forward.

"Excellent," Vhok said with a smile. "Then let me reiterate that my associate and I merely wish to find a guide to the City of Brass. We have no interest in wresting your precious mine from you."

Negotiating a trip to the efreet's capital was surprisingly easy. Vhok and Zasian observed a brief power struggle among the remaining genies to determine who would assume control of the mine. That task was interrupted by a short-lived slave revolt, which Vhok and Zasian helpfully put down. When the dust settled, the new efreeti leader agreed to transport the two visitors to the City of Brass as quickly as possible.

Before long, the cambion and the priest were racing across the Infernals, the small sea of magma between themselves and their destination, upon a magical flying carpet. A single efreeti commanded the conveyance, sitting cross-legged at the front. Vhok and Zasian sat side by side behind their guide, keeping a careful watch all around. They did not care to have another unpleasant visit from the flying beasts.

A hot wind, stinking of sulfur, whipped the half-fiend's hair. Smoke drifted in great clouds across their path, and their guide did his best to avoid the worst of it. Below them, the ocean of lava frothed and churned, and Vhok understood the difficulties they would have faced trying to cross it in a boat. The ships that traveled upon the Infernals stuck close to shore because the sea was a tempest away from the coast. Keeping a craft afloat would have required something close to a miracle.

From time to time, the efreeti guide cast a fearful glance back at the pair. He seemed nervous about their intentions toward him. He regularly promised swift and accurate service and tried to assure his guests that nothing would interfere with them arriving at the City of Brass as fast as the carpet would allow.

Vhok was delighted with the turn of events. He and the Banite were speeding toward their destination, no longer trudging across broiling stone and free of assaults from native creatures. He congratulated himself on the decision to visit the mine, even though Hafiz had nearly delivered them into slavery or death.

After another period of travel, Vhok spotted it. Through the haze and smoke of the searing atmosphere, he spied the myriad spires of the City of Brass. They rose on the horizon like a multitude of fingers jutting up from the sea of lava, topped with minarets. As the travelers drew closer, the magnificent city came into view. From their distance, Vhok estimated that the city stretched forty miles or more across. The entire place rested within a great hemispherical bowl of magnificent size that floated upon the sea of fire. The city rose like some misshapen ziggurat from within that bowl, with the Grand Sultan's palace—the Charcoal Throne—near the center, at the highest point.

The guide steered the carpet closer and swooped lower, angling toward a place on the rim of the bowl. As Vhok peered ahead, he saw a huge gate there, an entrance to the city.

The half-fiend leaned forward and tapped the efreeti on the shoulder. "Why not just take us to the center of the city?"

he asked over the howling wind. "A nice inn, perhaps, some place that caters to travelers such as ourselves. No need to stop at the gate."

The genie cast a sour glance back at Vhok and adjusted his flight path. "It is forbidden," he explained. "All visitors must arrive by one of the gates around the city. To do otherwise is to break the Grand Sultan's laws."

Vhok rolled his eyes, but he shrugged and motioned for the efreeti to continue on his course. The cambion leaned over to Zasian. "I guess the Grand Sultan wants to make certain he gets his gate taxes," he said with a grimace.

The priest only nodded.

The efreeti slowed the carpet and guided it down as they neared a large open plaza before the gate. A broad set of steps descended from the edge of the plaza into the sea of fire. Vhok supposed it had been built so that creatures native to that element and others upon floating craft could arrive and depart easily. At the moment, no one was there.

The genie set the flying carpet down close to the gate. As the great rippling tapestry touched down, Vhok stood and stretched. Zasian rose beside him and stepped off the carpet. Once Vhok disembarked, the genie gave them a cursory salute. "Simply announce yourselves to the guards, and they will charge a small fee to pass through," the efreeti explained. "Welcome to the City of Brass," he added. "Enjoy your stay."

Before Vhok could respond and thank their guide, the efreeti had the carpet aloft and was speeding away.

The cambion chuckled. "I think he's happy to be rid of us," he said. "Maybe he thought you were going to slay him with a touch and steal his magical carpet."

Zasian shrugged. "I considered it," he said. "It was such a wondrous piece of magic," he added ruefully, watching the carpet and the genie grow tiny in the distance.

The pair turned and strolled toward the gate. The portal was massive, with a great set of brass doors barring passage. Within the large doors, a smaller pair was inset, and those stood open. A pair of efreet, bare-chested and red-skinned, flanked the smaller portal. They seemed completely disinterested in Vhok and Zasian.

When the two visitors reached the gate, the efreeti on the left gave them a sharp glance. "State your name and business!" he ordered.

"Kaanyr Vhok, Lord of the Scourged Legion, Ruler of Ammarindar and points beyond. I am just visiting. And my associate here . . ." he said, gesturing toward the priest.

"Zasian Menz, Seneschal of the Master's Hall in Sundabar in the service of Helm Dwarf-friend. Also visiting."

The efreeti eyed them for a moment. He brought a hand up and scratched his chin. "Very well," he said, as though reaching some monumental decision. "Ten pieces of gold apiece to enter."

Vhok coughed to hide his surprise. "Is that all?" he asked sarcastically. "A pittance, considering." He fetched a small garnet from the folds of his tunic and handed the efreeti the gem. "Will that cover us both?" he asked.

The genie studied the stone for a moment, then slipped it into a small brass box hanging from his belt. "Ought to do," he replied. Then he stepped aside, giving access to the door. "Welcome to the City of Brass," he said, and let the two visitors enter. "Enjoy your stay."

The passage through the gate was longer than Vhok expected. It was a narrow tunnel running through the massive doors, which appeared to the cambion to be made of solid brass. He could not imagine anything so heavy remaining upright.

On the far side of the passage, he was assaulted by a

cacophony of sights, sounds, and smells. The first thing he noticed was blessed coolness. The city did not radiate endless heat like the rest of the plane. Vhok wondered what sort of magic would be required to accomplish such a feat. He didn't ultimately care, though. He welcomed the change.

A broad thoroughfare led from the larger gate, and like any city, it was lined with buildings. Businesses of every conceivable nature filled those shops, and the patrons who visited them spilled out into the wide street. Vendors hawked their wares from wagons and carts, bartering with customers in a constant din that made Vhok's ears roar. It all looked so familiar to the cambion, and yet everything was completely different.

The assortment of life dazzled the half-fiend. Never had he seen such a variety of folk. Humans mingled with demons, devils, and efreet everywhere. Salamanders, their serpentine torsos snaking out behind them, moved freely among the others. The cambion even spotted a fire giant gliding through the morass of citizens, window shopping.

Slaves, many of them azer, moved through the street, too. Some accompanied their masters, often led by chains attached to collars, while others traveled independently, wearing only heavy brass bracelets to denote their status.

None of the legion gave Vhok or Zasian a second glance.

The smells of sweat and exotic food wafted to the half-fiend. He spied a street vendor doling out skewers of meat to any with coin. Some of the flesh had been charred beyond recognition, and some of it still burned as he sold it. But the merchant had enough human customers that he offered more palatable fare, too.

Vhok's stomach rumbled.

"Hey, you two," a voice called. "You need a guide, yes?"

Vhok glanced over to a young man, a human, standing

off to one side. He pointed and gestured to the two arrivals, nodding vigorously.

The cambion smirked. "You know your way around this maze?" he asked, filled with doubt. "You're more likely to lead us into some blind alley so your friends can try to strong-arm us out of a few coppers."

The young man looked wounded. "I would never presume to insult such powerful lords," he said earnestly. "I offer you comfortable travel to anywhere in the city," he said, producing a small bronze statue from his pocket.

Vhok peered closely at it and noted that it appeared to be a casting of a hippogriff. A horselike creature with the wings and head of a great eagle, the statue was posed so that the beast reared up on its hind legs. "How is that going to help us?" he asked, still suspicious.

In answer, the young man tossed the statue down and uttered some unintelligible word.

Immediately, the statue grew in size and bloomed to life. In the time required for Vhok and Zasian to step out of the way, the thing became an actual hippogriff, and a massive one.

Vhok saw that it sported a special saddle, along with a pair of wicker panniers hanging from either side. The hippogriff snorted once, then screeched loudly. It pawed the ground with talons rather than hooves.

"You see? I can get you anywhere you wish to go, and fast," the young man said, beaming.

Vhok looked at Zasian.

The priest shrugged. "Might as well," he said. "It will take us days to fight our way through the city otherwise."

Vhok considered the man's words and nodded. "All right," he said, turning to their would-be guide. "You get us to the Sultan's Palace without mishap, and I'll make it more than worth your while."

The boy's eyes widened. "The Charcoal Palace?" he said with a hint of awe. "Why do you wish to go there?"

"Why, to see it, of course," Vhok answered with a silly grin. "What visit to the City of Brass would be complete without seeing the fabled palace of the most powerful efreeti in the multiverse?"

The young man still seemed doubtful, but he nodded and climbed onto the back of the hippogriff. Settled in his saddle, he gestured for his two customers to board.

"You want to go to the palace right away?" Zasian asked quietly.

The cambion nodded. "Yes," he replied. "After our dealings with Hafiz the overseer, how do you rate our chances of success bargaining with the sultan?"

"I see your point," the priest said.

"Exactly. So I think we should consider other means of getting in."

The Banite gave the half-fiend an incredulous look. "You realize that you're plotting to break into the palace of the most powerful genie in the city, don't you? Perhaps the most powerful genie in the multiverse!"

Vhok patted Zasian on the shoulder and grinned. "We don't have to get back out, do we?" The priest rolled his eyes and shook his head. "So we only need to know where we're going, and stay ahead of the guards. We'll find an inn nearby after we've scouted a bit. We can rest tonight, cast an augury to make sure Aliisza is where she needs to be, and slip in tomorrow."

"As you wish," the priest said. He didn't sound at all convinced.

Vhok saw that the pannier had a hinged door in its side. He stepped closer to the conveyance and looked inside. Swinging the narrow door open, he stepped into the basket and latched the door. The rim of the pannier rose to just below his armpits.

Zasian walked around the hippogriff and boarded the opposite container. Once both travelers were safely in their baskets, the young man gave a sharp command to the hippogriff. The magical beast screeched and reared up slightly. The sudden shift threw Vhok off balance and nearly tilted him out of his seat within the basket.

"Hold on tight, Masters!" the boy cried. Then the hippogriff launched itself and its burden into the air, and they were off.

As smooth and delightful as the magical carpet ride had been, the journey within the pannier was equally unpleasant. The hippogriff's motion was sudden and jerky, and Vhok found it nearly impossible to maintain his balance. Their guide steered the beast haphazardly, shifting and climbing, rolling and diving incessantly. With each change in course, the cambion found himself crumpled in a heap at the bottom of his wicker basket. He finally managed to remain upright by bracing his knees to both sides and clinging to the rim with both hands.

Despite his discomfort, Vhok found the view of the great city to be splendid. The metropolis bustled with life and activity in every direction. Great thoroughfares zigged and zagged between massive palaces of marble, sandstone, and brass. Markets as large as some small communities back on Faerûn spread out between the edifices. The half-fiend was sure that tens of thousands of citizens roamed the market stalls, exchanging coins for all manner of goods.

Canals of flame coursed throughout the city, creating a network of glowing avenues between the solid routes. Small boats plied those fiery paths, poled along by navigators working hard to deliver cargo and passengers to their destinations.

The whole city teemed with life and trade.

At last, the trio drew near the Charcoal Palace. The building was immense, rising like some magical many-spired basalt mountain out of the city. A latticework of walkways, plazas, and shiny, brassy domes seemed to defy gravity. A great fountain of purple fire plumed in front of the main gates, where a dozen well-armed and armored efreet stood guard.

"How close can you fly without raising their ire?" Vhok shouted to their guide. "I'd like to get a better look."

The young man raised an eyebrow in wary surprise, but he nodded and guided the hippogriff closer. The trio circled the palace twice, not quite flying within the perimeter of the walls. Vhok spotted a female efreeti standing upon a balcony. She appeared to be watching them through a long brass tube. Her robes were colorful and gaudy, and he supposed she might be some vizier or advisor to the sultan.

On the third pass around the palace, Vhok leaned out as far as he dared to gaze into the inner sanctum of the sultan. He sought a particular locale within the palace, a great open courtyard.

He spied it.

The courtyard lay at the base of a large tower. It formed a semicircle around the spire, and a single causeway spanned it, leading from the door of the tower to a middling defensive wall beyond. That was their destination.

Vhok had seen enough, but needed a view from ground level. He leaned forward to shout instructions to the boy to set the hippogriff down near the purple fountain, but the words died in his throat as a crackling blast of blinding white energy engulfed them.

The hippogriff screamed in agony and lurched sideways in the sky. Vhok felt the pannier tip sideways and he began to fall out. He grabbed frantically at anything and his fingers locked onto the rim of the basket, but he felt no resistance, no gravity pulling against him. He looked up and saw that the entire saddle and pannier had broken free of the hippogriff. Zasian huddled inside the other basket, but the guide and his mount drifted free.

Vhok spun himself upright and reached across the baskets. "Grab on!" he shouted to the priest.

Zasian pulled himself hand over hand along the ruined saddle and panniers until he caught hold of the cambion's hands.

With a death-grip on the Banite, Vhok summoned the innate power within himself to slow his descent. As the cambion felt the two of them ease into a hover, the saddle and pannier tumbled away. A heartbeat later, the boy and his mount zoomed by, also falling from the sky. Neither of them flailed as they fell.

The half-fiend struggled to keep himself and Zasian aloft. With the priest's weight, the cambion could not find the power to rise, but he felt certain that their landing would be slowed enough to avoid deadly injury.

Unless they were attacked again before reaching the ground.

Vhok whipped his head about, searching for the source of their misfortune. He spotted a figure above and behind him, riding upon a most unusual conveyance. The mount was a huge black fly that hummed and buzzed as it circled, coming closer to the pair of hovering companions. Vhok squinted to get a better look at their attacker.

Myshik grinned and steered his magical mount closer. The half-dragon raised his dwarven axe to strike at them as he passed.

CHAPTER SIXTEEN

The hardest thing to adjust to inside her son's body, Aliisza realized, was being unable to fly whenever she wanted. Wings were as much a part of the alu as her eyes. Instinct made her want to leap into the air and soar with a thought. Remembering that she could not was more difficult than she imagined.

The transplanted half-fiend stood on the outskirts of a small village where Kael—she had finally learned her son's birth name—was staying while visiting the House of the Triad. The village rested on one of the myriad floating islands in the celestial plane, larger than most and covered with lush green forest.

Tauran had brought her there, still cloaked in Kael's flesh and blood, after he had tucked her own collapsed body into bed. He had seemed concerned about Aliisza's condition at the time, but she noticed that he tried not to reveal his worry to the young man. He assured Kael that his mother would be fine, that she only needed more rest. Rest, and time to adjust to everything that was new.

Aliisza had done her best to play along, though she spoke as little as possible. She possessed but one chance to slip away from the deva. If she revealed that it was her consciousness inside her son's body, Tauran would learn the truth about her, about Kaanyr's journey, all of it.

If he discovered the deception, the angel would certainly prevent the alu from completing her part in the gambit.

After transporting Aliisza to the village, Tauran had left. "To attend to your mother," he had explained. The alu was thankful for his quick departure, though she knew time was of the essence. Sooner or later, the angel would figure out her trick and come looking for her.

The others living within the small woodland community were all servants of Tyr who had journeyed to the House of the Triad for some reason or another. They had not died, Aliisza realized. They merely had business on the home plane of their deity and lived there while visiting.

Most of the residents were human, though she met one odd creature that named its kind leonal. That one exhibited traits of both a human and a lion, and Aliisza could sense its celestial nature. All of the folk living there seemed to accept Kael without reservation or prejudice. Though she suspected that her son had been among them for only a short time, they treated him as a life-long friend.

She slipped away the first chance she could, as much to put some distance between herself and all of that warmth and friendliness as to begin her tasks.

She hiked through the woods on the outskirts of the hamlet. She sought something quite ordinary, but she feared that she would be unable to find what she needed.

Who knows if mushrooms grow on this plane? she wondered. Did Zasian think this through?

She carried a small flask made of iron, with a stopper fitted into its opening. It was merely a beat-up container she had borrowed from an old woman who had spent much of her life as an herbalist. The sweet crone hadn't even asked Kael what he might need with it.

There, she thought, spotting some fungus. Perfect.

Quickly, Aliisza gathered the mushrooms, stuffing them into the flask. She crammed as many as would fit; she had no idea how many would be sufficient.

When she was done, she tucked the flask inside Kael's tunic and considered how best to begin her journey. Again, the urge to leap up and fly hit her. The sensation of being grounded aggravated her a heartbeat later, and she nearly cursed in exasperation.

Then inspiration hit.

She had no wings, but that did not mean she couldn't muster a means of flying. All she needed was a few bird feathers.

Aliisza spotted a nest in the lower branches of a strange, tangled tree ahead of her. She approached it and confirmed that it was occupied. She opted to disturb the birds only as a last resort, and instead scanned the ground beneath the nest. When the alu spotted the wing feather, she grinned in triumph. It did not take her long to locate three more.

Four ought to be enough, she thought. If not, then I guess I'll be stuck out there. Until Tauran hunts me down, at least.

With feathers in hand, Aliisza drew a breath and focused her mind. Pinching a feather between her thumb and forefinger, she swept it across both her shoulders, as though stroking the place where her own wings might have been. At the same time, she incanted a phrase of magical power, invoking the arcane forces she needed.

When the litany was finished, Aliisza felt the magic snap within her. She knew, without being able to explain why, that she could fly. She trotted forward a few steps and jumped into the air. Immediately, she soared up among the treetops and shot through a gap in the canopy.

The grace and deftness of the magical flight was superior to the alu's natural talent. She had occasionally used it, despite her own wings, to maneuver more adroitly when needed. The only drawback to the spell was its limited time. She did not have a moment to waste.

Sailing over the tree-covered island, the half-fiend surveyed the landmarks she could see in the early morning sun. She spied one of the great mountains jutting up from the lower layer of clouds, disappearing again in an overhead blanket of white. She wasn't certain which peak it was, but she knew the four of them huddled together, so that was her destination. She mentally urged herself forward.

The alu pondered her newly restored memories. She reviewed Zasian's instructions about her destination. She remembered thinking that the seneschal's words had sounded odd, his description nonsensical. But having spent so much time on the celestial plane, she better understood what the man had been trying to communicate. The explanation still struck her as bizarre.

As she flew, Aliisza watched for other denizens of the House. She did not want a confrontation with some angel wondering where Kael might be going. She knew that her chance of crossing paths with a local would increase as she drew closer to the floating islands, so she evaded them as much as possible, adjusting her course and altitude.

As the alu drew closer to the great peak, she saw that it was indeed the central mountain, Celestia. The divine crag seemed to have no beginning and no end, only endless slopes leading ever upward or downward into the cloak of clouds. The half-fiend followed the closest slope upward, ascending in earnest.

Within moments, she vanished into the thick haze of a cloud bank. As before, when she had yearned to escape the prison Tauran had ensnared her in, she continued to fly. Higher and higher she rose, but she no longer expected to reach the upper limit of the fog. She kept pushing the magic, struggling to attain greater elevation.

The air grew cold and dark. Moisture coated her skin—Kael's skin, she reminded herself. It made her clothing soggy and chilled. She ignored it and kept rising.

The wind picked up, buffeting her. The rumble of thunder, still distant, reached her ears. She climbed, fighting fatigue, knowing her flight would fail soon.

When the arcane power waned, Aliisza felt as if she were trapped in a swirling maelstrom. A storm lashed at her, tossing her about. Rain and wind pummeled her borrowed body, and arcs of lightning crackled all around her, blinding and deafening her. The magic gave out, but it didn't matter. She was no longer in control of her motion.

The storm itself held the alu aloft.

Aliisza gave in to the tempest. She allowed it to carry her wherever it willed. She didn't resist, didn't try to fight it. Those had been Zasian's instructions, but the act took more courage than she could ever remember drawing from herself. She was sure she would die, ripped apart by the storm or dashed against the slopes of the great mountain.

After a while, the tumbling and spinning completely disoriented the half-fiend. She had no idea which way was up or down. She couldn't even be certain she traveled in a single direction. For all she knew, the wind simply swirled her in circles, tossing her along in gusts like some rag doll trapped in a hurricane.

She closed her eyes to keep from screaming in terror.

When the rain and wind and crackling lightning suddenly

ceased, it startled Aliisza. One moment, the storm raged at its mightiest, and the next, she was skidding across a cool stone floor. The body she had borrowed tumbled to a stop in what felt like a shallow puddle of water. She flopped there, too exhausted to move.

For many moments, Aliisza lay where she halted, panting. Her heart thudded in her chest, and she could not muster the courage to open her eyes. The storm still roared, but it was distant, muffled. The smell of rain was strong and the air felt damp. At last, she worked up her nerve and took a peek.

The alu lay on the edge of a broad, still pool of water. A faint mist covered it, so that it blurred in the distance and Aliisza could not see the far side. A white marble floor veined with gold formed the edge of the pool, gently sloping down to the water like a sandy beach. It, too, faded into the wispy fog on either side of her.

Massive fluted stone columns made of the same stone rose from the water, rows and columns stretching into the mist. They held up nothing. No ceiling covered the pool—only a blanket of night sky filled with stars loomed overhead. The columns had no tops, nor were they jagged, broken things. They merely faded as they ascended, like ghosts shifting to some ethereal state.

No walls surrounded the space—the edges of the marble floor simply stopped, and the tops of great storm clouds stretched outward from there, rumbling with dull thunder and flickering with lightning. The light illuminating the place seemed to emanate from everywhere and nowhere. The water gleamed darkly and reflected the sky, and the mist hovering over it glowed with a pearlescent and heavenly essence.

The alu felt queasy in that place. The same sickness that had affected her in the presence of Tauran early in her stay washed over her again, even more acutely.

Slowly, with much trepidation, Aliisza sat up. She ached from her rough landing, but no part of her son's body seemed seriously injured. Gingerly, the alu rose to her feet. Standing ankle-deep in the water, she listened for signs that she was not alone. The half-fiend detected only the faint dripping of water from her own clothing, and the muted rumble of the furious storm beyond.

Drawing a deep breath to steady her nerves, Aliisza took one tentative step farther into the water. It was neither warm nor cold. It merely felt wet, like a tepid bath. She took another step, and another, each one carrying her away from the marble shore and into deeper depths. After five steps, the water had risen to her thighs. After ten, it reached her waist. Three more, and she kicked off, swimming instead of wading.

The alu paddled slowly, listening. The luminescent fog wafted all around her, but was not so thick that she couldn't still see the shore she had left. The water smelled clean and fresh, not foul at all, but it was utterly lightless and murky. The myriad pinpricks of diamond white in the night sky reflected in its surface, shimmering and bouncing as she disturbed it.

The half-fiend swam close to a column. The pillar was huge, the width of a cottage. She reached out and touched it, felt where it descended below the surface of the water. She dragged a toe against it, searching for a lower end, but it continued on. Taking a gulp of air, Aliisza dived downward. She kicked with her feet and ran her hand along the column. Down she thrust, pushing herself deeper and deeper, seeking the base of the column and bottom of the pool. She could find neither.

With a start, she realized how deeply she had swum, how completely dark the depths of the water were. She panicked and reversed her course. She dragged her arms through the water, using her son's powerful muscles to pull herself toward the surface. She could barely make out a glow there, could only just see the light of a few faint stars. Those tiny fragments of illumination in a pit of blackness were the only things that kept her sane just then.

When she broke the surface, she threw her head back and gasped for air. Relief washed over her. She trembled, wondering how a place of such holy goodness could be so frightening. Even then, the inky black water terrified her. She wanted nothing more than to be standing on the dry stone at the pool's edge.

I can't do this, she decided. To the Abyss with Kaanyr.

The alu began swimming back to the shore. A subtle, creeping fear tingled along her spine. A sensation that something was directly below her, coming for her, made her shiver.

She swam faster.

An explosion of water erupted somewhere behind the alu. Despite her terror, she spun around and looked back. A great serpentine thing burst from the depths of the pool. Its arrival sent a cascade everywhere, splashing Aliisza and drenching her eyes.

When she was able to see again, the creature hovered above her, peering down at her.

Its snakelike body glistened with moisture, and its scales, a deep purple hue, flickered with a faint, subtle light that coursed over its body. Broad leathery wings held it aloft, their regular flapping making waves upon the pool's surface.

But it was the head that froze Aliisza's attention. A long, sharp-angled snout flared from a broad, flat head. A series of ridges and horns angled back from the jaw line, cheeks, and forehead. Two glittering eyes, flickering with the crackling of lightning, stared at the alu with a keen intelligence, and the mouth, filled with teeth the size of daggers, opened in a feral grin.

A storm dragon.

The beast opened his mouth and spoke, the words like rumbling thunder. "Welcome to my temple, little one. Who gave you permission to swim in my waters?"

❖ ❖ ❖ ❖ ❖ ❖ ❖ ❖

Vhok released the magical energy holding both himself and Zasian aloft. The pair fell again, but the maneuver served to drop them out of reach of Myshik's axe. The half-dragon lunged at them, nearly tipping over as he tried to strike, but the blade whisked harmlessly over the cambion's head.

Myshik cursed the two of them as he struggled to right himself atop his hideous insect mount. The giant fly wobbled and banked from the unbalanced weight, carrying its rider away. Once the draconic hobgoblin managed to right himself, he guided the fly around in a circle.

He was coming for them again.

"Down there!" Zasian yelled. Vhok grabbed both of the priest's hands and locked his grip around the man's wrists. Zasian grasped Vhok in return. But the Banite was jerking his head in the direction of the semicircular courtyard within the palace as he dangled in the air. "Go that way!"

Vhok shook his head as he tried to gain control of his magical levitation. "I would, but I can't!" he called, shouting to be heard above the whistling air. "I go up or down, that's all!" He managed to arrest their fall again, slowing them to a less deadly pace. "And right now, with your extra weight, it's only down," he added, straining to hold on to the priest. "Can you save yourself?" he asked. "Any magic left for flying or whatnot?"

Zasian shook his head. "Nothing. We cast it all at the mine. But I might get Myshik with something before he cleaves us both in half."

Vhok watched the half-dragon approaching again. The draconic hobgoblin held his axe drawn back and was swooping in for another slice at them. "Do it," the cambion said. "Hurry, because I'm dropping us the moment you're done."

Zasian nodded and released one of Vhok's hands. The half-fiend moved his free hand to hold onto the priest's other arm with a double grip.

Zasian grabbed at his pendant and muttered something Vhok couldn't hear. He gestured toward the approaching half-dragon as he finished the spell.

A blinding column of fire roared downward from the heavens. Vhok flinched at the sight of it. It bored down right atop Myshik and engulfed the Clan Morueme whelp.

Vhok didn't wait to see Myshik's condition. The moment the casting was complete, he released his levitation magic and once more, the duo fell from the sky.

Something blue tumbled past Vhok as he and Zasian fell, but he didn't get a clear view of it, for at that moment, a second object slammed into the priest, sending them both spinning. The blow wrenched Vhok and Zasian apart. The cambion felt the priest's hand slip away.

Vhok flailed in the air, still falling. Then his mind cleared and he slowed himself with his magic. He watched as his companion, who had caught the brunt of the blow, arced sideways.

The priest fell against the side of a dome atop the sultan's palace. It was a glancing blow, and Zasian skidded for a bit before sliding down the curved, steep side. He spread his arms and legs, attempting to halt his advance, but his momentum was too great, and he slipped over the side of the onion-shaped top.

Supreme luck was with the priest. The drop dumped him near a railed balcony just below the dome, and Zasian grabbed hold of the banister with one hand as he tumbled past. He jerked to a sudden stop and hung there for a moment, sagging.

Vhok wondered if his counterpart had the strength to hoist himself up, but he had other things to worry about. Upright and floating once more, he scanned the air for any sign of Myshik. He spotted the half-dragon gliding through the air below. The draconic hobgoblin no longer rode his magical mount, nor did he have his axe. He was using his wings to control his fall, descending at an angle and steering himself to avoid the buildings in his path.

Myshik landed, rather roughly, in a street near the purple fountain of flame in front of the palace. Vhok saw several of the efreeti palace guards move to confront the half-hobgoblin. The cambion was certain they would attack Myshik, try to capture him, but instead, it appeared that they treated him deferentially. They helped him to his feet and escorted him through the gates and into the palace.

Terrific, Vhok thought. They're on *his* side. All the more reason to hurry, he decided.

The cambion turned his attention back to Zasian.

The priest had climbed onto the balcony, and he leaned against the wall, panting. No one had come to the doorway from within, but Vhok knew his companion had little time. Zasian stood upright and made a familiar motion. The half-fiend recognized the gesture as the workings of healing magic.

"What now?" Vhok shouted to the priest when the spell was finished.

Zasian looked at him and shrugged. "We have to get down into that courtyard," he said, pointing. Vhok could see that the semicircular enclosure was directly below the priest. But the cambion was nowhere near his destination. Were he to levitate down, he would place himself on the wrong side of a massive defensive wall.

The two of them were separated by only ten paces or so, but it might as well have been the world right then. Vhok had no magic left to reach his companion.

"Your rope!" Vhok said, inspired. "Hold it up!"

Zasian nodded, understanding Vhok's intentions. He pulled a coil of rope from his belongings and held it up.

Vhok mouthed a spell and pointed at the coil. He felt a magical connection take hold, and he could control the rope.

"Hold one end!" Vhok said, and when the priest grasped the tip of it, Vhok began to magically reel the other end toward himself.

The coil was more than enough to stretch between them, and as soon as Vhok took hold of his end, he and Zasian started pulling.

A thin beam of scorching heat slashed near Vhok. The ray had emanated from the ground below. A second one blasted past the cambion, and a third struck him. He jerked in pain and nearly lost his grip on his lifeline to Zasian.

The half-fiend peered down and saw numerous palace guards gathered around the base of the tower. The efreet stood in a clump, launching the fiery rays at will. Other guards swarmed the palace grounds, moving to join them.

Vhok saw a trio of efreet dematerialize, turning to puffs of ghostly vapor. The gaseous creatures ascended, heading toward the balcony where Zasian pulled on the rope.

Vhok redoubled his efforts.

The priest cried out, struck by a pair of molten beams. Vhok felt a second one strike him, too, and the searing pain was almost too much. He felt himself growing faint, and he had to fight to maintain his grip on the rope.

"Don't slow down!" Zasian shouted. "When you get here, just drop! No levitation! Otherwise, they'll pick us out of the sky!"

Vhok raised his eyebrows at the priest's suggestion, but he didn't stop pulling. Zasian swung one leg over the top of the railing as the cambion drew near. A scorching blast nicked the priest, and another hit the rope, severing it.

Vhok was still a good two paces from Zasian. They both gauged the distance and mutely agreed that it was enough. Simultaneously, they jumped toward each other. Vhok released his magic as he and the priest crashed together. They wrapped their arms around each other as they fell once more.

The efreet's magical rays continued to arc through the sky, but the blasts missed the rapidly descending duo. Vhok fought the urge to slow them down. He knew that the speed of their fall made it difficult for the palace guards to aim, but it went against every fiber of his being to willingly plummet to the flagstones of the courtyard.

The drop seemed to last forever, yet the ground rushed up at them at a terrifying rate. Just when Vhok didn't think he could hold off any longer, Zasian yelled.

"Now!" the priest barked. "Slow us down!"

Vhok willed the magic to take hold, but their momentum and the extra weight strained him to his limits. The cambion felt as if he were being crushed from below, but he managed to arrest most of their downward motion.

They hit the courtyard hard enough to send them sprawling.

Vhok felt the breath driven from his lungs, and he lay for a moment, struggling to regain it. White light marred his vision, and his left shoulder ached where he had landed on it. He would have stayed there longer, but the heat of a fiery ray hit the stones near his cheek, and he jumped up to look for cover.

The expansive courtyard lay well below the rest of the palace grounds. It was more of a natural rock garden than a courtyard, a veritable jungle of stone outcroppings, spindly trees, and tall grasses. The walls surrounding the garden rose thirty feet or more and curved inward near the top; climbing them was near impossible. Vhok was relieved to see that there was no evidence of the endless jets of fire and acrid, stinging smoke so prevalent elsewhere on the plane.

"Come on!" Zasian called. "This way!"

Vhok spotted the priest just ahead of him, charging toward an undercut beneath a large boulder. The efreet still fired their magical rays, and the cambion needed no encouragement to follow the human.

Vhok ducked into a shallow hiding place and crumpled down beside Zasian. Both of them gasped, in pain and out of breath.

"We can't tarry," the priest said, ducking his head out for a quick glimpse. "They're already coming over the wall."

"No time to see if she made it?" Vhok asked. "How can we pass through the portal unless we know?"

Zasian give the half-fiend a hard stare. "What other choice do we have?" he asked. "All we've fought for—all we've struggled against—has been to put us in this position. Do you fear to take the final step now?"

Vhok sucked in air. "No," he said after only a moment's hesitation. "She'll be there."

Zasian nodded. "Then let's go. It rests at the far end of this enclosure. If we can reach it, they won't follow." The priest risked another quick glance, ducked back in when a singeing blast smacked against the rock near his head, then said, "Now!"

Together, Vhok and his companion rushed from their shelter. The shouts of pursuing efreet followed them, but they did not slow down. Racing from cover to cover, the pair charged through the undergrowth, using the environment to shield them from their pursuers. Vhok felt the hot burning of a ray strike his back, and he nearly lost his footing as the searing pain overwhelmed him, but he managed to stay upright.

The shouts of the chase never wavered.

All at once, as the two of them raced around a jagged spire of rock, Zasian slowed. Vhok nearly collided with the priest, but he veered to one side just in time. The cambion stared where his companion did. At first, he couldn't see what Zasian had spotted, but then it became clear to him, and he gasped.

A gargantuan serpentine body lay unmoving, coiled around a great chunk of basalt as big as a house that thrust up from the floor of the courtyard only a few paces away. The creature's scales glimmered purple-blue in the orange light of the sky. Vhok could see no sign of a head. He assumed it would lie on the far side of the basalt.

A ray of scorching energy whizzed over Vhok's shoulder. The beam struck the massive flank of the resting serpent squarely. With a shudder, the beast began to uncoil. Its head rose into view, towering over the cambion and the priest.

The snake peered down at the two intruders in its lair. It hissed and opened its mouth, lunging forward to strike.

CHAPTER SEVENTEEN

Vhok swallowed his terror and held still. For the second time, he fought against his instincts. One part of his mind tried to make his body run, but he held his ground. Indeed, he took a step closer to the massive snake, more into the open.

Beside the cambion, Zasian seemed rooted to the spot. The priest muttered something under his breath, and Vhok saw that he held his pendant firmly in one hand.

The snake's head descended toward them, mouth gaping. The maw was large enough to engulf both humanoids.

"Get ready!" Zasian shouted. Vhok had no idea what the priest meant, but the great mouth closed the distance between them before he could ask. "Now!" Zasian screamed. "Jump into it!"

Refusing to dwell on the idiocy of leaping *into* a giant snake's mouth, Vhok vaulted forward. Together, the duo landed on the lower jaw, just clearing the fangs. The snake clamped its mouth down, engulfing the pair in darkness. Vhok felt tissue and muscle enclose him, smelled the stench of the creature's flesh and venom surrounding him.

The cambion wanted to scream. The sensation of being

trapped overwhelmed, terrified him. He flailed about, suddenly desperate to get out. He felt his arm strike Zasian, sensed the priest squirming just ahead of him. Saliva drenched the half-fiend. The snake's insides pushed against him, sliding him along. He was being swallowed whole.

Oh, by the fell fiends, he thought, frantic to be free again, what have I done? Nothing is worth *this!*

Vhok kept his eyes and mouth shut as he slid along. He couldn't see, couldn't breathe. The sting of acids irritated his exposed skin. The constant pressure of muscle squeezed him, crushed him. He could only wiggle, and just barely.

Please, Aliisza. Be there. Hurry.

Vhok could feel himself swaying, and he wondered if the snake was moving.

Something hard struck him in the head. Zasian's boot, he realized. The priest was trying to kick.

My blade, Vhok thought, past the point of panic. Got to reach Burnblood! Cut my way free!

But of course, his arms were immobile, pinned against his body.

He was going to die, digested within the snake.

◆ ◆ ◆ ◆ ◆ ◆ ◆ ◆

Aliisza quaked in the water, watching the storm dragon hover over her. She hadn't expected him to speak to her. That wasn't part of the plan. Zasian had never mentioned it.

She wondered what to do next. She wanted to flee.

Instinct overcame rational thought and she turned and began swimming away. She paddled furiously with Kael's strong muscles, pulling for all she was worth toward the shore. It was so tantalizingly close, and yet so far away.

The dragon zoomed past and drew up before her, blocking

her path. "Answer me, little creature, or I shall slay you. Who told you to come and splash around in my pool?"

Aliisza turned away, swimming in another direction. Like a fish fleeing a bird of prey, she wanted only to escape.

The dragon dived into the water behind her.

Aliisza realized it was worse than having the wyrm hovering over her, for she could not sense where the beast was until too late. She stifled a scream and turned to draw herself toward the edge. She kept reaching down with her toes, hoping to find the solid bottom in the shallows. At the same time, she was petrified of poking her foot down into the dragon's gaping mouth.

The creature surfaced beneath her. But he did not eat her. Instead, he thrust her upward with his snout, tossing her high into the air. She sailed away from the shoreline, out into the middle of the pool. She brushed past one column, then struck a second one. The blow drew a gasp of pain from her, and she felt a few of her ribs crack. The alu slid limply down the column and into the water.

The dragon swam to her, his head barely out of the water, only his eyes and the top of his snout visible. As he drew close, he rose a bit and spoke again.

"Are you going to answer me, puny thing? What brings you here, to my private sanctum? Tell me, or I will devour you."

Aliisza blinked and tried to gather her breath. She could barely muster the strength to stay afloat, but she turned and began to swim away. Every stroke sent shooting pains through her midsection. She quaked but did not look back.

The storm dragon sighed. "Very well," he said. "I warned you."

Aliisza screamed as the huge wyrm pounced on her.

The beast's jaws engulfed the alu and clamped closed around her, leaving her in utter darkness. The force of the strike gathered water into the creature's mouth along with her, and she slipped beneath the surface of it. She tried to flail about, to pull her head into air, but the dragon's tongue was drawing her down, toward its throat.

It was swallowing her alive.

No! Aliisza silently screamed. Let me out! Oh, please, Tauran, find me!

The alu tried to claw her way to the front of the dragon's mouth, but contracting muscle all around her forced her the other way. Flailing in panic, Aliisza inexorably slipped into the storm dragon's innards.

A sense of dread and finality crashed over her, and she began to black out.

No! she thought, remembering, fighting the hysteria that gripped her. She glided to a stop and smelled the horrible, burning odor of the dragon's digestive acids all around her. There is a way out!

Aliisza held her breath and kept her eyes clamped firmly shut as she fumbled for the flask she had tucked away. Frenzied horror left her shaking, nearly unable to work. When her hands closed on the container, she yanked it free.

Grasping the stopper, she opened the flask and dug the mushrooms out with her fingers. She scrabbled to get hold of the top one, but she had packed them in so tightly that she had difficulty catching hold.

Idiot! she cursed herself. Too many!

Finally, as her lungs were beginning to ache, the first few mushrooms slipped into her hand. A tiny spark of hope kept her going. She upended the flask and felt more of the fungus drop into her palm. She flung the mushrooms everywhere in that absolute, engulfing darkness.

Finished, Aliisza tossed the flask away and felt around, frantic to find her way out. Her lungs burned with the need to breathe. She couldn't hold on much longer.

The wyrm lurched and Aliisza pitched backward, falling. She bumped against something that did not feel like spongy stomach. It felt like . . . cloth. And a belt. Someone else was inside the dragon with her.

Kaanyr.

Or Zasian. Maybe both of them.

Do something! she wanted to scream. Spots began to swim before her blind eyes, and the blood pounding in her ears was growing deafening. Everything burned. Her skin was on fire. Perhaps she hadn't brought enough mushrooms.

She was going to die.

The dragon lurched and Aliisza heard a great gurgle all around her. Then, suddenly, she felt the stinging flesh of the creature's stomach press in on her, tighten around her.

She opened her mouth, no longer able to hold her breath, and sucked in a lungful of foul odor and searing liquid. She gagged and fought not to breathe again, but her body was no longer under her own control.

She shot forward, her body gliding through a tunnel like a snail being squirted from its shell. She rushed onward and in the next instant felt a blast of cool mist on her burned skin. She shuddered and sucked in welcome air as she hurtled through it. She hit water with a jolting splash and the burning acid washed free.

Aliisza sank beneath the water, vigorously scrubbing the acid from her face. She needed more air. She shoved against the water and surfaced.

Gulping pure, fresh air was the most joy the alu had experienced in a long time.

When she could breathe again, she opened her eyes. The dragon writhed before her, as though in agony. He shook and jerked, regurgitated. A form flew from his mouth, along with a spray of mushroom bits. The figure splashed into the water near Aliisza.

It was Kaanyr.

The dragon roared and spun away, still twitching. He dived into the water and vanished, and Aliisza felt the fear again of not knowing where he was. She wanted to swim to shore, but she had no idea where that might be. Instead, she began stroking through the water toward Kaanyr.

The cambion thrashed and coughed in the water. Aliisza drew up just out of his reach and watched him flail. She did not want him to grab her and drag her under in his panic. Finally, he grew calmer and began breathing normally.

He opened one eye and peered around. He spotted Aliisza and both eyes flew open wide.

"Who in the Nine Hells are *you*?" he demanded. "Where's Zasian? Where's Aliisza?"

Remembering her altered form, the alu smirked. "You're looking at her," she said, the unfamiliar and masculine tone still strange in her ears. "It's me, you wretch."

Kaanyr peered at Kael's face for a long time, wary. "Aliisza?" he asked. "Why do you look like a drow?"

The alu shook her head. She wasn't sure how to explain to Kaanyr that she had given birth to another lover's son. "Long story," she said. "I'll explain later. We have to get out of the water before that storm dragon returns."

"Where's Zasian?" Kaanyr asked again. "Did he make it out?"

"Oh, yes," a booming voice said, echoing through the mist. It was that of the storm dragon. "I did, indeed."

Aliisza spun in the water, looking for the creature. Kaanyr spotted it first. The great wyrm was floating behind the alu, with only his head above the surface. His glare sent a chill down the alu's spine.

"Thank you so much for the timely rescue, Aliisza," the dragon said. "You shaved it very close."

"Zasian?" Kaanyr asked. "Is that you? What happened?"

"No, it's a trick," Aliisza muttered. "I fooled it with the mushrooms, and it's trying to gain revenge."

"Yes, Vhok it's me. I am one with this beast for now. We made it through. Or rather, *I* made it through. You two merely helped. Thank you for all your assistance, but now our ways must part. I have things to do, and you two must remain here."

"I don't—" Kaanyr began, but Aliisza understood.

"Dive!" she screamed. "Get away from it!" She spun and tried to submerge, but with her broken ribs, she wasn't fast enough. Kaanyr was too confused to react at all.

A tingling struck Aliisza then, a wave of energy that overwhelmed her. Every nerve in her body seemed to overload with sensation, crackle with agony. The alu screamed and went rigid, then sank below the surface of the water.

As she slid downward, vanishing into the murky blackness, she lost consciousness.

◆ ◆ ◆ ◆ ◆ ◆ ◆ ◆

Aliisza opened her eyes, and stared up at Tauran's face. The angel stood over her, a worried look on his mien. The alu noticed that he was disheveled, his clothing torn, and a bloody gash crossed his chest. Beyond him, she saw the night sky, and she could hear the muted rumblings of thunder. She was still in the storm dragon's lair.

Kael stood beside the angel, staring down with his garnet eyes. Aliisza was in her own body, and it took a moment for the alu to understand. She gazed at her son, getting a closer look at his face for the very first time. His eyes showed an intelligence that reminded her of Pharaun.

They also revealed a deep sadness.

He knows what I did to him, Aliisza realized. Then another thought swept through her: Why am I not dead, drowned? Kaanyr!

The alu sat bolt upright. Her head pounded with the sudden motion.

"Easy," Tauran said, helping her. "You need some time. Switching between bodies can exhaust you."

"Kaanyr," she mumbled, feeling as weak as the angel suggested. "Where—?" She looked around and spotted the cambion lying near her. "Is he—?" she asked.

"He'll live," Tauran said, and she could hear the sternness in his voice.

Aliisza sighed and leaned back. She wondered what the point was. Surely after her betrayal, Tauran would deliver final justice to both of them.

"What happens now?" she asked, gazing wearily at the deva. "What are you going to do with us?" She drew a deep breath, steeling herself for his answer. "Why save us if you only intend to put us to death?" she whispered.

Tauran said nothing for a moment, but a faint grimace crossed his face.

Aliisza stared hard at him. "What? What happened?"

"Your third companion," the angel said. "The priest."

"Zasian," Aliisza answered, feeling rage suffuse her. "The Banite. He used us to come here. He betrayed us."

"Yes. Zasian. But not a servant of Bane." The angel looked away, and for the very first time, Aliisza saw real fear and doubt on his face. "Zasian serves Cyric," Tauran explained. He looked back at Aliisza and his gaze filled her with dread.

"I need your help," he pleaded.

LISA SMEDMAN

The New York Times best-selling author of *Extinction* follows up on the War of the Spider Queen with a new trilogy that brings the Chosen of Lolth out of the Demonweb Pits and on a bloody rampage across Faerûn.

THE LADY PENITENT

BOOK I
SACRIFICE OF THE WIDOW

Halisstra Melarn has been a priestess of Lolth, a repentant follower of Eilistraee, and a would-be killer of gods, but now she's been transformed into the monstrous Lady Penitent, and those she once called friends will feel the sting of her venom.

BOOK II
STORM OF THE DEAD

As the followers of Eilistraee fall one by one to Halisstra's wrath, Lolth turns her attention to the other gods.

September 2007

BOOK III
ASCENDANCY OF THE LAST

The dark elves of Faerûn must finally choose between a goddess that offers redemption and peace, or a goddess that demands sacrifice and blood. We know what a human would choose, but what about a drow?

June 2008

RICHARD LEE BYERS

The author of *Dissolution* and The Year of Rogue Dragons sets his
sights on the realm of Thay in a new trilogy that no
FORGOTTEN REALMS® fan can afford to miss.

THE HAUNTED LAND

BOOK I
UNCLEAN

Many powerful wizards hold Thay in their control, but when one of them
grows weary of being one of many, and goes to war, it will be at the head of
an army of undead.

BOOK II
UNDEAD

The dead walk in Thay, and as the rest of Faerûn looks on in stunned horror, the very
nature of this mysterious, dangerous realm begins to change.

March 2008

BOOK III
UNHOLY

Forces undreamed of even by Szass Tam have brought havoc and death to Thay, but
the lich's true intentions remain a mystery—a mystery that could spell doom for the
entire world.

Early 2009

Anthology
REALMS OF THE DEAD

A collection of new short stories by some of the Realms' most popular authors sheds
new light on the horrible nature of the undead of Faerûn. Prepare yourself for the
terror of the *Realms of the Dead*.

Early 2010

PAUL S. KEMP

"I would rank Kemp among WotC's most talented authors, past and present, such as R. A. Salvatore, Elaine Cunningham, and Troy Denning."
—Fantasy Hotlist

The *New York Times* best-selling author of *Resurrection* and The Erevis Cale Trilogy plunges ever deeper into the shadows that surround the FORGOTTEN REALMS® world in this Realms-shaking new trilogy.

THE TWILIGHT WAR

BOOK I
SHADOWBRED
It takes a shade to know a shade, but will take more than a shade to stand against the Twelve Princes of Shade Enclave. All of the realm of Sembia may not be enough.

BOOK II
SHADOWSTORM
Civil war rends Sembia, and the ancient archwizards of Shade offer to help. But with friends like these . . .

September 2007

BOOK III
SHADOWREALM
No longer content to stay within the bounds of their magnificent floating city, the Shadovar promise a new era, and a new empire, for the future of Faerûn.

May 2008

ANTHOLOGY
REALMS OF WAR
A collection of all new stories by your favorite FORGOTTEN REALMS authors digs deep into the bloody history of Faerûn.

January 2008

PHILIP ATHANS

The New York Times best-selling author of *Annihilation* and *Baldur's Gate* tells an epic tale of vision and heartbreak, of madness and ambition, that could change the map of Faerûn forever.

THE WATERCOURSE TRILOGY

BOOK I
WHISPER OF WAVES

The city-state of Innarlith sits on one edge of the Lake of Steam, just waiting for someone to drag it forward from obscurity. Will that someone be a Red Wizard of Thay, a street urchin who grew up to be the richest man in Innarlith, or a strange outsider who cares nothing for power but has grand ambitions all his own?

BOOK II
LIES OF LIGHT

A beautiful girl is haunted by spirits with dark intentions, an ambitious senator sells more than just his votes, and all the while construction proceeds on a canal that will alter the flow of trade in Faerûn.

BOOK III
SCREAM OF STONE

As the canal nears completion, scores will be settled, power will be bought and stolen, souls will be crushed and redeemed, and the power of one man's vision will be the only constant in a city-state gone mad.

"Once again it is Philip Athans moving the FORGOTTEN REALMS to new ground and new vibrancy."
—R.A. Salvatore

WELCOME TO THE

WORLD

Created by Keith Baker and developed by Bill Slavicsek and James Wyatt, EBERRON® is the latest setting designed for the DUNGEONS & DRAGONS® Roleplaying game, novels, comic books, and electronic games.

ANCIENT, WIDESPREAD MAGIC

Magic pervades the EBERRON world. Artificers create wonders of engineering and architecture. Wizards and sorcerers use their spells in war and peace. Magic also leaves its mark—the coveted dragonmark—on members of a gifted aristocracy. Some use their gifts to rule wisely and well, but too many rule with ruthless greed, seeking only to expand their own dominance.

INTRIGUE AND MYSTERY

A land ravaged by generations of war. Enemy nations that fought each other to a standstill over countless, bloody battlefields now turn to subtler methods of conflict. While nations scheme and merchants bicker, priceless secrets from the past lie buried and lost in the devastation, waiting to be tracked down by intrepid scholars and rediscovered by audacious adventurers.

SWASHBUCKLING ADVENTURE

The EBERRON setting is no place for the timid. Courage, strength, and quick thinking are needed to survive and prosper in this land of peril and high adventure.

MARGARET WEIS
&
TRACY HICKMAN

The co-creators of the DRAGONLANCE® world return to the
epic tale that introduced Krynn to a generation of fans!

THE LOST CHRONICLES

VOLUME ONE
DRAGONS OF THE DWARVEN DEPTHS

As Tanis and Flint bargain for refuge in Thorbardin, Raistlin
and Caramon go to Neraka to search for one of the spellbooks of
Fistandantilus. The refugees in Thorbardin are trapped when the
draconian army marches, and Flint undertakes a quest to find the
Hammer of Kharas to free them all, while Sturm becomes a key of a
different sort.

Now Available in Paperback!

VOLUME TWO
DRAGONS OF THE HIGHLORD SKIES

Dragon Highlord Ariakas assigns the recovery of the dragon orb taken to
Ice Wall to Kitiara Uth-Matar, who is rising up the ranks of both the dark
forces and of Ariakas's esteem. Finding the orb proves easy, but getting
it from Laurana proves more difficult. Difficult enough to attract the
attention of Lord Soth.

Now Available in Hardcover!

VOLUME THREE
DRAGONS OF THE HOURGLASS MAGE

The wizard Raistlin Majere takes the black robes and travels to the
capital city of the evil empire, Neraka, to serve the Queen of Darkness.

July 2008